Praise for *Roman Crazy*
BY NINA BOCCI AND ALICE CLAYTON

"A comedic and deliciously whimsical romp only this pair could deliver. Alice Clayton and Nina Bocci have struck gold."

> —*New York Times* and *USA Today* bestselling author Christina Lauren

"I went CRAZY over *Roman Crazy*—this is simply a perfect romance!"

> —*New York Times* bestselling author Jennifer Probst

"Remarkable, refreshing . . . Clayton and Bocci have written a tender love story . . . all nestled within a love letter to the beauty of Rome."

> —*RT Book Reviews* (four stars)

"There are books that make you laugh out loud, make you teary, make you hot and bothered, make you smile. And then there are books that make you want to crawl inside them and live within their pages. That's what *Roman Crazy* is."

> —*New York Times* bestselling author Emma Chase

"*Roman Crazy* is a laugh-out-loud romantic comedy about second chances, friendship, and the beauty of Rome. You won't simply read this novel, you'll devour it as Alice Clayton and Nina Bocci transport you to Italy and guide you on an unforgettable adventure."

> —*New York Times* and *USA Today* bestselling author Sylvain Reynard

BOOKS BY NINA BOCCI

Roman Crazy
by Nina Bocci and Alice Clayton

ON THE CORNER OF
LOVE
AND
HATE

NINA BOCCI

GALLERY BOOKS

NEW YORK   LONDON   TORONTO   SYDNEY   NEW DELHI

G

Gallery Books
An Imprint of Simon & Schuster, Inc.
1230 Avenue of the Americas
New York, NY 10020

First Gallery Books trade paperback edition August 2019

GALLERY BOOKS and colophon are registered trademarks of Simon & Schuster, Inc.

For information about special discounts for bulk purchases, please contact Simon & Schuster Special Sales at 1-866-506-1949 or business@simonandschuster.com.

The Simon & Schuster Speakers Bureau can bring authors to your live event. For more information or to book an event, contact the Simon & Schuster Speakers Bureau at 1-866-248-3049 or visit our website at www.simonspeakers.com.

Interior design by Michelle Marchese

Manufactured in the United States of America

10 9 8 7 6 5 4 3

Library of Congress Cataloging-in-Publication Data

Names: Bocci, Nina, author.
Title: On the corner of love and hate / Nina Bocci.
Description: First Gallery Books trade paperback edition. | New York : Gallery Books, 2019. | Series: The hopless romantics series ; 1
Identifiers: LCCN 2018034238| ISBN 9781982102036 (trade pbk.) | ISBN 9781982102050 (ebook)
Subjects: | GSAFD: Love stories.
Classification: LCC PS3603.L396 O5 2019 | DDC 813/.6—dc23
LC record available at https://lccn.loc.gov/2018034238

ISBN 978-1-9821-0203-6
ISBN 978-1-9821-0205-0 (ebook)

The vote is the emblem of your equality, women of America,
the guarantee of your liberty.

—Carrie Chapman Catt

1

Thud. Whoosh. Slap.

   Thud. Whoosh. Slap.

The trio of irksome sounds repeated another half-dozen times. My eyes darted upward, a silent prayer falling from my lips.

Dear God, please give me the strength not to shove that tennis ball somewhere that would require surgery. Amen.

My coworker casually leaned back in his chair, his long legs outstretched and crossed at the ankles on the shiny surface of the conference room table. Beneath his brown leather loafers sat a report.

His *unfinished-yet-due-tomorrow* report.

I marveled at his ability to multitask. It would have been more appropriate if he had been, say, working. Instead, he was tossing a ball against the conference room wall with one hand while texting with the other. Even though he didn't take his eyes off his phone screen, he caught the ball every single time. If I hadn't been so annoyed, I would have actually been impressed.

The clock ticked against the pale yellow wall above his head. With each passing tick, the ball struck with a *thwack* to its right.

"Cooper, could you please stop?" I finally said, rubbing my temples to ease the headache that was forming.

Thud. Whoosh. Slap.

"Cooper," I repeated, glancing up from my laptop. "Hello?"

Thud, whoosh, slap was the only response I got.

Sliding back my chair, I stood up and walked around the long maple conference table. It was only when I got close enough to see the scantily clad woman in his text window that I noticed the wireless earbuds that were blasting music into his ears. As the ball left his hand, I touched his shoulder.

Startled, he lost his grip on the ball, sending it sailing behind him. "What's up?" he sputtered, quickly pulling his earbuds out. I didn't miss his hand sliding his phone into his pocket. He looked every bit like a teenager caught red-handed by the principal.

"Are you kidding me?" I exclaimed. "You've had music on this entire time? I read nearly two pages of the brewery expansion proposal out loud to you twenty minutes ago!"

At least he had the decency to look remorseful. "I thought you were talking to yourself, so I"—he motioned to the black Beats—"figured I'd give you your privacy while I caught up on work."

My eyebrows must have reached my hairline, because with a mildly guilty expression he pulled his legs down from the table.

I snorted. "Yes, I start all sentences with, 'Cooper, what do you think about' when I'm talking to myself. Were you just smiling and nodding for my health?" Shifting in his seat, he straightened. I huffed.

The small laugh lines around his mouth became more pronounced, an indication that he was fighting back a smile. "Emmanuelle," he purred smoothly.

"Don't *Emmanuelle* me," I clapped back. "That tone may work on your fan club, but not me."

He held his arms up in a defensive position. "Okay, okay, I'm sorry. What did I miss?" He grabbed for the papers in my hand.

Holding them back against my chest, I scowled. "Hope Lake Brewing Company. Expansion. Asking for input before it goes to the town council for approval."

He whistled and rocked back in his chair. "Council is going

to reject anything that comes across their desk from them. They hate the 'vibe' the brew house brings, and the addition would make the council's heads explode."

I nodded. "Yep, which is why the guys asked *us* for help. To try and edit the proposal to appeal to them. It's also why I booked us the conference room for this meeting that you just Tindered your way through."

"That's not a word, and I wasn't—" he began, patting his pocket absently. Probably making sure the evidence was tucked away safely.

I held up my hand. "Save it. I don't care what or who you're doing. Just that you're not paying attention. Again."

When the owners of HLBC, Drew and Luke Griffin, first came to our department, Cooper and I had championed their proposal to build a brewing company, tasting room, and outdoor entertainment space just along the lakefront. It was one of the first projects Cooper and I had worked on together, and it was just what we'd needed in town back then—a fun, innovative business that catered to every age. Now, six years later, HLBC was one of Hope Lake's most popular spots, and the brothers were looking to expand their space to include rooms for private events and a small restaurant. Cooper and I were supposed to be discussing how to approach the town council about it.

Looked like I'd just been talking to myself instead. "I'm going back to my office, where I can work in peace," I said. Exasperated, I started gathering up my stuff.

After a few seconds of awkward silence, he cleared his throat. "You're right. I'm sorry. Let's go over it. Again."

I stacked my files, feeling my blood starting to boil. Having to repeat myself irked me, but I needed his input whether I liked it or not.

Glancing up, I noticed Cooper readying to say something else when our shared assistant, Nancy, hurried in with the main office calendar and a fistful of Sharpies clutched in her hand.

"I've been searching for you two everywhere," she said, looking wide-eyed at each of us in turn. The conference table, at least on my side, was covered in charts, graphs, and photos of the lakefront. On Cooper's side—well, there was a lot of polished maple visible.

"Did you discuss the project?" she asked hopefully, her face falling when I shook my head. "Okay, well, I guess you'll handle that, uh, later. I'm sure." She gave me a look. *I hope,* she mouthed, then cleared her throat and pulled out the head chair of the conference table and sat down with the main office calendar in front of her. "It's time for the afternoon rundown—are you ready?"

Cooper groaned. Not at Nancy but at the calendar she had opened. It had been on my desk this morning when I'd filled it with upcoming appointments and meetings. By the looks of it, Nancy had managed to fill almost every empty space that remained.

We kept it old school at our office. Instead of using Google calendar or iCal, we used a large paper desk calendar with a color-coded legend, labels, and tabs to keep our government office running like clockwork. It's not as though we hadn't tried to modernize, but some of the, *ahem,* older department staff were frosty toward change.

Nancy, Cooper, and I worked at the Hope Lake Community Development Office on the top floor of Borough Building. In a small town like Hope Lake, my department was sort of the home base for everything. From simple things such as parade permits to more detailed ventures—for example, helping to secure funding for business owners like HLBC—the CDO, as we tended to call it, had its hand in pretty much everything. It wasn't big, but what we lacked in size and staff we made up for in energy and results.

"The upcoming week is brutal," Nancy apologized, looking at Cooper, who, not surprisingly, was on his phone again. "Emma, I'm afraid you're a bit overscheduled." She tapped a Sharpie on the table.

I waved a dismissive hand. "It can't be any worse than that

week the staff came down with the flu." I had practically run the office that week even though I was heavily medicated myself.

"It's close." She held up two fingers barely an inch apart. "You're back-to-back Monday. There is a pocket of time during the event this weekend with the future Mr. Mayor here and his opponent."

Cooper perked up then. He knocked twice on the wooden table. "Don't jinx me."

Oh, sure, you're paying attention now.

"You're a shoo-in. People love you, Cooper. And with the mayor already behind you, how can you not be?" Nancy assured him.

Nancy wasn't blowing smoke. Cooper had decided to run for office this year, and his magnetic personality made him the perfect political candidate. He was brilliant, liked by the majority of the town, and had confidence to spare because *he* knew he was the best choice for the job. Even I could admit that, and we were often at odds.

"Emma, I know you wanted to have a sit-down with Drew and Luke from the brewing company about the proposed expansion before they go to the council, but I don't see how it's going to happen."

Nancy jotted a note onto the calendar. Over the years, we'd gotten our system down to a science: orange for me, blue for Cooper, hot pink for our department administrative assistant, green for Nancy, and red for the mayor, because red was my dad's favorite color. Blue, not surprisingly, was the color least visible on the entire calendar. It was sporadically used, even from my vantage point, which meant that Cooper had a light schedule this week.

Shocking.

I chewed the pen cap, irritated. Nancy continued reading off meeting after meeting throughout the week.

"These two on Thursday—I can probably sit in on them to give you a break, Emma," she offered.

Looking over Nancy's shoulder, I marveled at the Technicolor scheduling system. It might have been old-fashioned, but at least it *looked* good.

Shaking my head, I pointed at the partially torn yellow Post-it stuck on the edge of the frame. That was how my father added mayoral meetings to the calendar. Stickies. He was nothing if not professional. "No can do, my friend. You're going to be at a ribbon cutting with Mayor Dad."

She looked up, her lips a thin, flat line. "I am? He didn't tell me."

Sighing, she jotted the information down. "I wish he'd told me I was supposed to go, too!"

She took her calendar duties *very* seriously. I for one appreciated it, and I knew my father did, too, even if he did use his own odd system to add to it. It kept all of us in line.

Together, Nancy and I figured out the rest of the week, Cooper staying silent and, surprise surprise, on his phone. We looked over the days, pointing and crossing out, trying in vain to find somewhere to squeeze in a last sit-down. "It's not going to work," I lamented, sinking into the chair beside her.

"Well, *someone* from the department needs to at least show their face at the city events meeting," she urged, looking pointedly at Cooper. A notebook was now on his lap, his hand moving swiftly over the page. He didn't look up when she said his name or when she repeated it a few seconds later. He was too deeply invested in whatever he was doing.

At least he's off the phone.

Tearing the Post-it off the calendar and balling it up in her fist, Nancy lobbed it at him. "Cooper!" she shouted, snapping her fingers as if she were telling a dog to sit.

Fitting.

He smiled at her. "I'm listening."

"Uh-huh, we need you to take a meeting or two on Thursday so Emma can head down to the lake to meet Drew and Luke. Unless you'd rather take the HLBC meeting."

"Thursday?" he repeated, sliding his phone out from behind the notebook.

When did he take that out? He was stealthy like a teen texting in class.

With a shrug, he shook his head. "Sorry, I'm booked all day and I've got a campaign publicity debrief at noon. That's taking up most of the afternoon."

"Doesn't that just mean you and Henry are meeting at the diner to play on Facebook and Twitter together?" I scoffed, feeling the blood rushing to my face.

Henry was one of my and Cooper's oldest friends. As a teacher, he had limited time to meet up with Cooper, so I understood Cooper's reticence to reschedule, but—

Then it hit me. "Wait . . . why are you having mayoral meetings during work and school? How's Henry getting out of class to meet you?"

Setting his phone down, he stood and straightened his tie. "I'll have you know, I'm meeting him at the high school. I wish I could help, but alas—"

"You can't," I finished, sliding out of my chair to stand myself.

With Cooper running for mayor of Hope Lake, the brunt of his work at the CDO was taking a backseat. I noticed, the staff noticed, and the mayor noticed. If it had been anyone else, they probably would have been fired, but Cooper was Hope Lake's golden boy. Once he was elected, we could hire someone new to replace him. But until that happened, it fell to us to pick up his slack.

Cooper walked toward the door, leaving his phone—aka his most prized possession—on the conference table. Surely he would be back in for it the second he realized it wasn't attached to his hand.

"Wait, you can't leave!" Nancy called after him. "I need the theater proposal paperwork. You guys have that meeting with the council on Monday and the mayor wants the weekend to review the specs. Cooper, it *has* to be before end of day since you have the debate tomorrow! Everything is done, right? Please tell me it's done."

"It's handled," Cooper said smoothly over his shoulder, tapping his temple. "And it's not a debate. It's a photo op, remember? Pose, smile, shake hands. You know, the usual."

"Thank God. I don't have time today to do it if you didn't," she said, pretend wiping her brow.

Smiling broadly, he clapped his hands together. "Oh, come on, Nance. Have I ever left you hanging?"

Her silence spoke volumes. If she'd had the time, and the inclination, she could have created a depressing list of how often that had happened.

Looking uncomfortable at Nancy's lack of response, Cooper disappeared through the door, only to reappear two seconds later. "That would have been bad!" he said with a tight smile, jogging in to grab the iPhone.

"Cooper, are you sure you can't reschedule your Thursday plans with Henry until *after* work so Emma isn't pulled in nineteen directions?" Nancy said quickly. "It's just about the local sports participation in the Thanksgiving parade. They're looking for guidance with the floats and theming—it won't exactly take up all your brain space. The other is an initial meeting to see if the CDO can finally purchase the old bank." Nancy already had a blue Sharpie at the ready, clutched between her fingers. "Or if you wanted to switch with Emma, you could meet with Drew and Luke and Emma could handle the parade instead. You'd probably get some free beer out of it."

For a moment, he looked like he was going to agree. His jawline ticked anxiously, a habit he'd had since we were kids. It appeared whenever he struggled with a decision. Reluctantly, I admitted to myself that it was happening more often than not.

"I'm really sorry, I can't," he finally said. "You know how important these meetings are for the core of my campaign. I've got to run. I'm late."

I glanced at the clock. "It's barely four."

"I have a thing."

"You came in at ten because of a 'thing.'" I air-quoted it because although he said those *things* were for the mayoral campaign, I didn't believe him. Call it years of experience or just a gut feeling. "Cooper, I need you to focus. You're all over the place, and things are going to start falling through the cracks here. We can't afford any missteps. Not when we're under a microscope. The council is looking for any reason to put the screws in this department."

Cooper's opponent, Kirby Rogers, had been on the town council for the past few years. He had made it his mission to strip the CDO—funding, staff, all of it gone.

With nothing but a grimace, Cooper left, leaving no opening for discussion. I shook my head at his retreating form.

"Forget him, I'll figure it out," I said, glancing between the calendar with the work appointments and my nearly empty personal calendar. "I can pop over to the brewery and see Drew and Luke on my way home Tuesday or Friday night. They owe me dinner, anyway," I said with a weak laugh, an attempt at loosening the anxiety-ridden ball in my stomach. *How am I going to accomplish all of this?* "Just see when they're free." I tapped away on my phone. Making a note, I double-checked my iPhone's calendar as Nancy read off the rest of the upcoming schedule.

"Emma," she said with a heavy sigh, "I don't want you to overwork yourself."

"I'm fine. It's an adjustment we're going to have to get used to since we're going to be picking up all the Cooper slack," I insisted, knowing that she was always worried about me in a big-sisterly sort of way. "Promise," I said after seeing her frown.

Months ago, before he had decided to run for mayor and before he had become so distracted by the election, Cooper had been an asset. I longed for those days. He had a gift, an ability to coax the very best of ideas out of you, and he transformed them into solid plans that we then presented to Mayor Dad and the town council. His undivided input would have been valuable here.

That part of Cooper I respected and enjoyed working with. Pre-candidate Cooper. Except lately, so much had changed. I missed the focused Cooper. The guy who would pull together a presentation in just a few hours. The guy I could count on to bring the best ideas out of me when I thought I had hit a wall. Or even the guy who got his work done on time. I hated myself a little bit because I was missing that coworking partnership. We did make a good team when we weren't arguing.

"Not for anything, but you'd think he'd want to head over to Hope Lake Brewing Company to see the guys."

"His head was so buried in his phone, he probably didn't hear you mention them."

Nancy nodded. "What do you think? Is this going to get better or worse as the campaign progresses?" She packed up her Sharpies and hoisted the large calendar off the table, mindful not to drop any of the Post-its and papers tacked to it.

I slung my arm over her shoulder. "Worse. So much worse."

2

Dating is like shopping the clearance racks: you sift through a lot of pretty yet questionable items in the hope of lucking out and finding that one perfect outfit.

The same could be said about the men I'd been with lately.

I'd had my fair share of the ubermacho, the supersensitive, the would-be feminists, and the still-live-at-home-at-thirty-five.

But lately work had become my life, and I wanted to find something that would bring me a little more joy. There had to be more to life than getting a contract flawless on the first try or finding the perfect business to take over a vacant building. There was always a little hopeless romantic lying dormant inside me.

That's why now, even after a lousy day at work with a few more hours' worth of work to do when I got home, I was heading out to meet a potential candidate for Mr. Right. *A much better candidate to spend my time with,* I thought as I walked out the door, *than our current candidate for Mr. Mayor.* We'd met on a dating app. When I'd swiped right during lunch, he'd swiped right, too.

And they say that romance is dead.

I got to the restaurant twenty minutes early in the hope of finding a good seat and, if I were being honest, an exit strategy just in case it went south fast like the last one. I was nothing if not pragmatic. When he'd asked for a suggestion of where we should go for dinner, I'd chosen La Bella Notte because it was the quintessential date-night, getting-to-know-you spot in town. Not that we had a ton of options, but it was cozy and romantic. It wasn't just the best place for carb overload—which I always craved when stressed (lonely, sad, annoyed with Cooper, you get the picture)—but if the conversation went stale, I could use the restaurant's history and the CDO's relationship with it as a way to revive it.

The place, built along the water, had come together a few years ago. My department had helped Guido, the owner and grandson of the original owners, expand the restaurant, opening it up onto the waterfront with a massive multiseasonal wrap-around porch. In the dead of winter, you could watch the lake freeze over while the snow swirled around you like in a snow globe. In the summer, you could wave to kayakers and outdoor enthusiasts over your tiramisù. It was picturesque, rustic, and just about as traditional Italian as you could get in the mountains of Pennsylvania.

It also happened to be one of my favorite places in town, which was why it wasn't a place that I visited willy-nilly with these dates. But this guy had ticked off all the right boxes. No red flags in sight.

Single. Employed. Lived alone. Philanthropic. Handsome. Did I mention single? My listing it twice was warranted because you'd be surprised how many married piglets were just trying to get laid. He was a doctor in his early thirties and lived in Barreton, the next town over. We'd been texting for the past month trying to find a night to meet. We seemed similar, so busy that we'd rescheduled four times already.

I was looking forward to tonight, but at the same time, I was indifferent. I couldn't quite put my finger on what made me pause. Maybe it was thinking about the work I could be doing or the myriad other things that needed my attention.

But I needed this. *Me* time with a side of like-minded adult male. I texted him as much before I even left the office.

> **ME:** I'm looking forward to finally meeting you!
>
> **ME:** We've got a great table. Private. I called in a favor.
>
> **ME:** You know, so we're not disturbed ;)

ROBERT: [read at 5:07PM]

> **ME:** Oh, and wine.

ROBERT: [read at 5:27PM]

As I waited for Robert, my iPhone, which was clutched in my palm beneath the crisp white tablecloth, pinged softly. Laying it on the table, I rested my chin in my hand and scrolled through the few notifications that I'd received in the short time I'd been sitting there.

Five texts from my mother. *Skip*. She could wait until after my date since she was only looking for gossip or to needle me.

MOTHER: Is he handsome?

MOTHER: Is he really a doctor?

MOTHER: Don't forget to smile.

MOTHER: Make sure nothing is in your teeth!

MOTHER: Don't slouch!

I loved her dearly, but she was a bit insufferable when it came to my (lack of) love life. When you've been happily married to your childhood sweetheart forever, you wish that same thing for your children. I got that, but it wasn't like I wasn't valiantly trying.

I scrolled through my notifications. Facebook birthdays, CNN alerts, my favorite Etsy shop was having a sale, and surprisingly, three texts from work. This late on a Friday night, no one should have still been at the building, let alone working. Not even me.

As I scrolled through the texts, my mood soured like milk left in the hot sun. According to Nancy, the proposal that Cooper had promised he would handle was a mess.

From my view in the far dark corner of the crowded restaurant, I could tell he was able to handle one thing, however: a leggy, artificially top-heavy blonde who cackled at everything he said.

"I have to leave early for an important campaign meeting," he'd said.

When would I learn?

The urge to charge over and dump his "meeting's" shared appetizer into his lap was strong, but instead, I responded to Nancy. I let her know that I'd take care of what was needed. *Again*. There was a reason I carried my iPad with me everywhere I went. When emergencies happened, I fixed them. Even when I was supposed to be having a date night to distract me from work. Which Cooper had somehow still managed to interrupt.

Opening the Dropbox app on my iPad, I downloaded the forms and the press release Nancy had uploaded to the cloud and got to work. The documents Nancy had sent weren't just a mess—they were a train wreck. The task should have been simple. Cooper had written a hundred new business proposals in the past, yet he'd somehow managed to misspell his own name in the very first line of this one.

By the second page, I was fuming.

I checked the time. What would the good doctor date think if he walked in in ten minutes and I was hard at work and chewing on a bread stick? Hopefully that I was a go-getter, responsible, dedicated, and clearly not afraid of carbs.

A part of me thought about leaving the proposal as it was and letting Cooper finally take the fall for his mistakes. But I couldn't risk having the CDO or Mayor Dad looking foolish. So in between bread sticks and more wine, there were switching, inserting, scribbling on some napkins, and more proofing than I cared to admit. I could tell that he'd half-assed this on his way out the door. After I'd gone through a few pages, I checked the time. Hmmm. My date was officially late.

> **ME:** Me again. When you come in, the hostess will bring you back to where I'm sitting. I'm working, but it's just to pass the time. Looking forward to seeing you!

ROBERT: [read at 6:11PM]

I glanced down at the read receipt. It looked like there would be no response, but maybe he was stuck in traffic. It wasn't exactly unheard of to get stuck on the highway between Barreton and Hope Lake. And it would make sense that he wouldn't text back while driving. He was a doctor, so he was responsible. I reconciled the thought with another bread stick.

EMMA THOUGHT: Don't judge yourself, they're small bread sticks.

While I sat working at my table, I was surrounded by couples engrossed in each other. I tried to ignore the moony eyes across the flickering candlelight as I worked, but after a while I noticed that a bottle of wine had appeared. There was a small card beside it.

Stood up?

It was scribbled in Cooper's messy handwriting. I recognized it immediately, for as put together as he was—or had been, up until the campaign—he had the penmanship of a second grader. My stomach lurched. I didn't need any more snide remarks from

Cooper today. I glanced over to his table to find him watching me. He raised a wineglass, smirking as his eyes flickered toward the empty seat in front of me. My stomach sank, but I masked my disappointment and flipped him off instead. *A girl has to save face.*

Clutching the phone, I scrolled through the flirty texts with Robert from a few days ago, the more to-the-point ones from yesterday, the ignored ones from tonight. The realization hit me like a sinking boulder.

> **ME:** Looks like maybe something came up. Perhaps another night then.
>
> **ME:** Speak to you soon :)

ROBERT: [read at 6:40PM]

EMMA THOUGHT: You chose poorly.

Outwardly I was fine. Especially with the audience, I would show nothing but a brave face. I was a single gal about town having a great dinner on my own like anyone else would. On the inside, though, I struggled to accept that not only was my date not coming but that I also probably came off as a bit . . . *much*. It was one thing to be stood up. But it was wholly another to have your chauvinist, manwhore coworker slash childhood friend slash enemy bear witness to it.

Firing back a message to Nancy, I mentally flipped him off again and included a second middle finger for Blondie, just because. Clutching my iPad, I nestled into my seat and worked on finishing up Cooper's work, fully giving up the pretense of waiting for a date who clearly wasn't showing. I spread my work unashamed across the table, avoiding the bread crumbs strewn about the white tablecloth. I pulled the crust off the bread, dipping it into the oil on my plate.

As I was about to bite into the warm goodness, I heard a voice telling the hostess that he was late for a first date.

Could this be him after all?

Sitting up a bit straighter, I looked down at my blouse to brush off some imaginary crumbs and held my breath as he began walking toward my section.

Holy hell, he was handsome. Huzzah!

Though he didn't look a whole lot like the photo he had sent me, I wasn't so sure I did, either. My profile featured a favorite picture of late, when I had been having a particularly good hair day. It wasn't the norm for me to have my hair down with the unpredictable late-summer weather, but it just so happened that it hadn't succumbed to the humidity that day. Half of my dark waves were tied back from my face, secured by oversized tortoise-shell sunglasses. The red bell-sleeved top I wore accentuated my curves, and the matching lips were a confidence booster. I wore the same outfit tonight, but I'd switched out the fitted tan skirt for a pair of skinny jeans and flats.

The man coming toward me was dressed in neatly pressed gray slacks and a green V-neck sweater that brought out his eyes. His light brown hair was perfectly styled in that *yes, I just got out of bed wink wink* look.

Take that, Cooper, I thought smugly.

Taking another quick sip of wine, I smacked my lips together, praying that I still had some gloss left. Smoothing my hair, I stood to greet him, extending my hand warmly.

My eyes were trained on his handsome face and his broad, blinding white smile.

His eyes narrowed, his smile fell, and his brows furrowed confusedly. "Hi?"

"Hi!" I parroted, shifting my weight between my feet.

Do I hug him?

Pull out his chair?

Take my top off?

"So good of you to make it. Hope the traffic wasn't too bad?"

After all, you're very, very, very late.

I watched his eyes glance over my shoulder briefly before giving me a crooked grin. "Forgive me, but do I know you?" he asked, resting his hand on the empty seat before me.

Two things I found out too late: The smile wasn't for me. And neither was the hot date.

It was for the equally attractive man who stood up at the table beside me in greeting.

We formed the strangest triangle.

"Marcus, is everything okay?" he asked. Now there was not one but two magnificently attractive men looking at me quizzically along with my entire corner of the restaurant.

Please don't let Cooper be watching this.

I didn't dare look over to him. The thought of him watching, recording for posterity, or just plain laughing was too much for my already bruised ego to take.

Someone next to me snorted, earning a jab in the ribs from his date, who looked on with sympathy. I was pretty sure a woman snapped a photo that would surely end up on a dating fails website later.

EMMA THOUGHT: There isn't enough wine in the restaurant to make this suck less.

"Sorry, I thought you were someone else," I whispered, keeping my head down. My hope was that the two would sit down so that I could forget that the whole thing had happened.

With two more curious looks, they took their seats, and I drained my wine and willed my face to return to its normal shade of not-mortified. Once my heart calmed, my cheeks cooled, and my ego climbed its way back up from the pit of my stomach, I went back to work quietly, all while refusing to glance over at Cooper and his date. I knew they were staring. I could already hear him chuckling. She guffawed.

Do. Not. Look.

After a few seconds passed, everyone else seemed to have moved on, but I still hadn't quite recovered. In my periphery, I could see Cooper and his date leaning closer as their evening went on. I huffed a sigh. *Focus, Emma.* I sent another text off to Nancy.

With her reply blinking, I allowed myself thirty more seconds of misery, deciding I'd lose myself in manicotti or cannelloni and . . .

"*More* wine?" the server asked, popping up out of thin air. She had been lurking since I'd arrived. Even with the sun fading behind her, I could see her eye roll. It was clear she was trying to suppress her irritation that I was *still* here waiting and hadn't yet ordered. *Trust me, sister. This night isn't going the way either of us planned.*

I glanced at my watch. It hadn't been that long, had it? My shoulders slumped.

It *had* been that long.

The server cleared her throat.

"Yes, I'll have another glass." She raised an eyebrow. "You're right, just give me what's left of the bottle. Take this one back to the table that sent it," I instructed, but then thought better of it. "On second thought, I'll take that one home with me."

Cooper had plenty of money—the least he could do was buy me a bottle of wine after everything I'd done for him tonight.

Maybe I should order another and put it on his tab.

She was judging me. I could tell. Nearly every woman in the place had shot a sympathetic gaze my way over the course of the night, especially the ones within earshot of the embarrassing scene a few moments before.

"Maybe you should switch to water," she suggested gently, moving the thick leather book full of Italian wines out of my reach.

"I'm sure drinking will improve my mood."

I wondered what she was thinking, looking down on me as I sat there in the romantic restaurant working. What *I* would have been thinking if the roles had been reversed.

"Or maybe you should order, or—"

"Or," I responded, dashing her hope of filling this table with a higher-paying check. "Just another thirty minutes," I said. "Then I'll go." I wanted to choke myself with a bread stick.

Speaking of choking, Cooper's date had drawn the attention of the tables around them when she crawled into his lap to help feed him what was left of their shared dessert. Her dress was hiked up around her thighs as she straddled and spoon-fed him tiramisù.

They were one bite, slap, and tickle away from a live-action adult film. If I got up to leave now, I'd have to say something to him. "Thanks for screwing me over, jackass. Again."

Drinks, dinner, flirt, giggle, flirt, giggle, was that a slap? I inwardly gagged at whatever pseudoromantic BS he was spewing. His date was obviously falling for it, given the haughty titters that spilled from her perfect pink-painted lips. Her graceful neck was thrown back as she laughed just before running a long, red-painted nail down his chest.

The server spied me glaring and turned to check it out. All she could see was his back and his hand resting on her knee, his thumb rubbing circles slowly against skin.

"I can slip you out the kitchen door if your ex is here," she offered conspiratorially. Any trace of annoyance was gone. It had been replaced with a sense of solidarity that women get when one of their own is hurt.

As if! I thought indignantly. *I wouldn't be caught dead dating Cooper!*

Even in my head my argument sounded forced.

When you grow up being dear friends with a person, you have two choices when things go south. Either you continue to love the person he becomes while still considering him to be one of your dearest friends. Or you watch him turn into an unrecognizable adult who makes dreadful choices about life and love—or sex, as it were—and make the hard decision to excise him from your life as much as possible.

Or you have a third choice. My "choice." Which was a combination of the two with the added-on, exhausting factor of having to work with that former childhood friend daily. It wasn't an ideal situation, but in a small town where everyone knew everything, you don't have many options.

Dwelling on the situation was souring my mood further. The less I focused on Cooper and his date, I knew, the happier I'd be.

I looked up, smiling at the server. "It's okay, but thanks. If I can just hang here a bit longer?"

Nodding, she gave me a sympathetic smile and headed back into the main part of the restaurant, subtly bumping into Cooper's chair with her hip. When she reached the swinging doors that led to the kitchen, she turned and gave me two thumbs-up.

There was another laugh, but it was from Cooper this time. A lusty boom, deep and gravelly. I heard it often at work. Never *at* me or *with* me, just in my presence, and it always elicited the same reaction: annoyance, followed by a steady stream of self-loathing, because at one point in my life, I had wanted him.

That, above all else, was a hard pill to swallow.

3

---

pulled the white napkin from the table and twisted it in my lap. Taking a deep breath, I kept working, but the longer I stared, the more the words in front of me blurred. Maybe it was the iPad, my dry contacts, or the annoying glare from all the candles surrounding the happy couples around me. Or maybe all three.

I ignored the metal bucket of cold water that reminded me that drinking a bottle of wine doesn't necessarily help with focus.

What felt like only minutes later, I checked my watch, its tiny diamonds winking in the candlelight. It'd been more than two hours since I had arrived. With my work now completed, I dropped it into my bag. It was time to head home. But not before I ordered food.

Picking up the menu, I settled on carb overload to soak up some of the wine I'd consumed. Thank God it was a short, leisurely bike ride home. It was an old habit to bring my bicycle to the office and take it everywhere. In hindsight, it probably wasn't the smartest mode of transport for a date, but Hope Lake had only one Uber driver. And chances were he had a long line of people waiting for him on a Friday night.

Waving over to the server who'd conspired with me earlier, I ordered La Bella Notte's famous linguine fra diavolo to go. The spicy kick would knock the miserable mood from my body.

"Guido knows you're here, so he'll bring out your dinner. He wants to say hi," the server said with a squeeze to my shoulder.

"Thanks, tell him I'll be right back. I'm just running to the restroom, and I'll be out of your hair."

I made quick work in the bathroom, eager to get my to-go order and leave. As I exited the stall, Cooper's statuesque date appeared in the doorway. She was even more flawless up close.

She was considerably taller than I, at least five or six inches, plus heels, in a sleek dress that hit just above her knees. You could tell that she had bought it because it made her legs look a mile long. If I'd had those legs, I would have worn that dress daily, but I was just at five feet, and no amount of heel could change that.

With a deep breath, I started fixing my hair in the mirror, smothering the years of jealousy I had harbored over women like her. Not just Cooper's endless swinging door of beauty-queen conquests whom he paraded around town, but anyone who hadn't suffered through the ugly duckling phase as I had: The braces you wore just as you got your period. The big boobs that sprouted way too early. While my friends were buying pretty, delicate training bras, I shopped in the grown-up section with my equally top-heavy mother. Over the years, I had grown to love my look, but every now and then, even the most secure women turn back into their awkward fourteen-year-old selves. This woman had definitely never had an awkward phase.

She was kind, too, apparently, as she pointed out that I had a bobby pin jutting out behind my ear.

"Thank you," I muttered, turning on the faucet.

Feeling her eyes on me, I was determined to keep mine down. I focused on the running water, fighting the urge to look up and ask her questions. Or tell her to run for the hills. The height difference was even more apparent when I was actually standing next to her. It was like I was in that movie *Twins* with Arnold Schwarzenegger and Danny DeVito.

"I have to tell you," she started, moving in closer to the mirror to swipe on some shockingly pink gloss.

I was taken aback at how loud she was in such a small space. Looking over, I noticed that her eyes were glassy and she had smudged her lip gloss onto her chin.

"I'd kill for your skin tone. It's flawless," she slurred, swaying in her towering heels.

When she turned to me, her brown eyes flitted across my face, giving me the once-over. Her arms were crossed under her breasts in what appeared to be an effort to make them look bigger or higher. I realized that she was just as likely to have insecurities as the rest of us.

Don't rob me of my hate!

He's out with her while you're fixing his work!

Yep, there's that. Hold on to that.

Giving her a small smile, I mumbled another thank-you and dried my hands. Turning to leave, I started as she placed a hand on my shoulder.

Steadying herself, she sighed. "I'm serious, your skin is enviable. I always wished I had olive skin. And this hair! Who's your stylist? It can't be someone here. This town is too small for any talent."

"Wait, what?" I stuttered.

The comment rankled me. You don't get to diss my town, lady. I cleared my throat.

"The guy I'm here with, he has an—I don't know—some kind of government job or whatever. He's *loaded*." The last bit she whispered excitedly, and despite my hatred of Cooper, I wanted to bitch-slap her for wanting him only for his money.

"His family built this town, I guess," she rambled on. "I only half-listened while we were eating dinner, but his mother sounds pretty famous." With an obnoxious eyebrow waggle, she pranced out the door like she had just won the lottery.

Famous? His mother is the governor, for Christ's sake.

"Numbnut," I mumbled at the closing door.

I counted to twenty before heading out, needing to clear my head.

The little pep in my step faltered for a second upon seeing Cooper's table empty; neither he nor Blondzilla were anywhere in

sight. I shouldn't have felt disappointed, but there was still a nig-
gling feeling that reared its ugly head as I wondered where they
were off to. Out of sight wasn't always out of mind.

Back at my table, the server handed me my take-out bag,
which was heavier than usual. "Guido threw in a dessert on the
house. He apologizes for not stopping over like he wanted, but
there was a proposal." She put her hand to her heart, rolling her
eyes. "Plus, the eight o'clock reservations are trickling in, so he's
busy trying to get everyone seated."

I forced a smile. "Tell him I'll call him next week about the
upcoming events calendar."

"Oh! I almost forgot," she added, spinning back around. "He
said to make sure you see the addition!"

"Will do!" When I had made the reservation, Guido had insisted I sneak a peek at the progress on the outdoor seating addition before I left. With the craziness of the evening, I'd forgotten.

"Check it out, it's almost done and beautiful! Can't wait to see
it totally finished," she said, squeezing my shoulder once more
before departing.

Throwing too much cash into the billfold, I scribbled a
thank-you and collected my tote and takeout. Instead of aiming
for the front door, I headed toward the only quiet section in the
restaurant—the newest part of the patio, which was down a few
stairs and hadn't yet opened to the public.

The wooden porch was built over the choppy lake below. Once
completed, it would provide an even cozier waterfront dining experience. The architect had modeled it after the Italian grotto
restaurants that dotted the Amalfi Coast. Thick wooden planks
were laid diagonally, giving the space a larger, more spacious feel.
A curved wrought-iron banister lined the edges overlooking the
water below. The grotto restaurant was built into a cave, so the
builder had fashioned the roof into appearing as though it were
hewn from stone. Large gray chunks jutted out from above with
a simple lighting system, which gave it a romantic glow.

The new moon cut through the clouds, its light dancing over the water. The choppy waves broke against the rocky beach, sounding like music. It was peaceful until my phone pinged again.

Checking it, I saw that the text was a thank-you from Nancy for sending the updated proposal. She'd already sent it off to my dad to review. I swallowed the anger at Cooper for screwing up yet another task because his date was deemed more important.

If his head had been where it was supposed to be, he could have fixed his mistakes in twenty minutes. But he had been pre-occupied with campaigning for months now, and it showed more and more every day.

I tamped down my mounting irritation at having to pick up his slack, when suddenly I felt a hand on my back.

"Emmanuelle." The voice was deep, even, and assured. There was a hint of a teasing spark that seemed to always ignite every sense in me no matter how much I hated it.

Speak of the Devil.

"Why must you call me that?" I groaned, staying focused on the sounds of the water. I prayed it would work to calm me like the yoga app I'd downloaded. It didn't.

"It's your name," Cooper said, shrugging. It was as if I hadn't corrected him a thousand times over the past twenty years.

"No one calls me that."

"Except your mother," he corrected smugly.

Turning, I narrowed my eyes at him, hating that he knew that. "Only when I've done something to annoy her."

"Well, *I* prefer Emmanuelle," he shot back, his eyes reveling in my annoyance. I swear he fed off my exasperation.

Taking a step forward, he gave me a small smile that barely showed his perfect teeth.

My grin melted off my lips. I took a step back, then another, to escape the cologne bubble he enveloped me in. He was like an insect using his scent to attract a mate. With another step toward fresh air, I wedged myself between the exposed rock near the banister and the lethal lothario: the man who had driven me crazy for more than two decades.

A corner of his mouth tipped up. "You sure know how to make a man feel special. Or is it that you *like* the feeling of the rocks against your back? Should I move closer?"

At his words I flattened my lips, ignoring that my heart was thundering so loudly I could hear it in my ears.

He grinned predatorily and stepped closer.

I held up my hand. "Stop trying to butter me up with your shtick. I'm immune, especially when I'm pissed, and you know it. You deserve my wrath tonight for leaving me, and the mayor, with an essentially unacceptable proposal. I just spent the past two hours fixing all of your mistakes while you were off at your *appointment*." I made air quotes for emphasis. "You pushing my buttons by being a slick jackass isn't going to make me less riled up over the fact that you're too preoccupied to function."

EMMA THOUGHT: You lose all filters with wine.

His face was frozen in shock at my outburst. "You're right, Emma. I'm sorry." Two words I hated hearing from him. Not because I didn't want him to apologize but because I knew that even if he said it now, he'd do something in another day or two to drive me up the wall again.

Who was I kidding? It would be an hour or two, not days.

Taking a deep breath, I took the anger down a notch. "What are you doing out here, Cooper?" I was grateful my voice came out calm and steady, instead of something akin to Hulk Smash Emma.

He moved like he was going to step forward again, but instead he rocked back on his brown leather loafers. He slipped his hands into his pockets in an innocent schoolboy kind of way. If I hadn't known better, I would have thought he was sincerely apologetic.

"It's about to rain. I thought I would offer you a ride home."

An image flashed of me sitting quietly mortified in the backseat while his date's head was in his lap. *No, thank you.*

"Something tells me your date wouldn't appreciate you bringing another woman home."

He raised an eyebrow.

"I mean to my home, not *your* home," I corrected quickly. He smirked. The left side of his mouth curled up, revealing the dimple to end all dimples. It wasn't fair that a man like him had one. Dimples were meant for carefree, lovable people—not . . . *him*.

He leaned forward against the rail.

"Don't fall over," I snipped.

Without comment, he slid his hands out of his pockets, rested them on the smooth iron, and started tapping his fingers. He looked every bit like an advertisement. Similar to his lanky date, Cooper was tall, well over six feet and change, and years of excelling at every sport he played had kept him in admirable shape. Fit and toned but not bulky. A closetful of well-tailored clothes didn't hurt, either. He was always well put together. Tonight was no exception, with a pair of tan pants and a light blue dress shirt.

It was his deep blue eyes, though, that drew everyone in. His light brown hair *did* need a trim, I noted. It was starting to curl around his ears, and he desperately needed a shave. That was probably intentional. He knew that the scruffy look worked for him.

"I called for a car to take her back to Barreton tonight," he said casually, not explaining any further.

My lips twitched, but I pressed them together to stave off a sarcastic remark. "Oh, yeah? Why's that?"

"Let's just say *I* can't spend time with someone who's that arrogant."

"However do you spend time alone, then?"

He chuckled but kept his eyes on the water. "She made it clear she thought small towns are a joke. Even I can't . . . *entertain* someone who doesn't see the charm here."

There it is.

For all the fault that I found in Cooper's behavior, and no

matter how irked I was with him, he did love this town. Almost as much as I did.

Rolling my shoulders back, I focused on the hefty weight of my takeout. The smell of the spicy sauce met my nose, and my stomach rumbled audibly. Oh, boy, that was loud. I needed to get myself home.

Hangry Emma + Cooper = an unpleasant end to an already unpleasant evening.

I cleared my throat. "Thanks for the offer, but I checked the weather before I rode over. All clear."

I tried to sidestep him, but he countered, matching me like a well-built chess piece.

A pawn against a knight.

He inhaled, his broad chest puffing up under his too-perfect shirt. "Take a deep breath. It's in the air tonight."

It was tempting to be able to prove him wrong, but I couldn't run the risk of a deep inhale. Not when all I smelled was him— warm and inviting mixed with the spiciness of the sauce that drifted up from the bag. If someone were to bottle this up and sell it, they would be set for their next five lifetimes.

"I can't. All I smell is your aftershave and whatever cologne you've dumped on by the gallon. Honestly, how are your eyes not watering?"

He winked. "I think your mother bought me this for Christmas last year. She loves it."

Gag. "You're ridiculous."

He bowed, sweeping his arm before him regally. "My friend, after all these years, I'd have thought you would have accepted that by now."

"I accept nothing when it comes to you. That includes a weather report."

"Go on," he encouraged, taking another long inhale. "I love the way the air changes when there's an incoming storm. It's cleansing, yet sweet."

He winked just as the wind picked up through the trees, rustling the leaves through the skinny branches. This guy even had Mother Nature under his spell.

The urge to dig out my phone and pull up the weather app to prove I was right was strong.

"It's going to be a good one, too; I can feel it."

"I'm sure it's your arthritis. I hear it hits once you turn thirty," I clapped back, squeezing the bag handle.

He took a step closer and leaned forward.

"Hey, not thirty yet, and trust me, Emmanuelle, I can be on my knees all night. No problem."

I gulped and was suddenly struck with a vision of him on his knees. Those mesmerizing eyes peering up at me as he disappeared under someone's—

My eyes fluttered closed for a second because it was jarring being so close to him. In a lot of ways, Cooper was like the sun: you couldn't fly too close to it, or him, without getting burned.

I'd found that out the hard way.

When I opened my eyes, I found Cooper back by the railing. It was as if I'd imagined the whole exchange. Our conversations were always fraught with tension, and tonight was no exception. I just had too much wine clouding my judgment.

This was the Cooper who was the most dangerous. Not in a threatening way, but in the way that made me forget that I was mad at him. The guy who could charm anyone with his masterful bait-and-switch tactics.

EMMA THOUGHT: Wine is *really* good at making sure you let your guard down.

"See?" Cooper said. He was leaning over the wrought iron, his arm extended, his palm open and facing up to the dark sky.

Damn you, Mother Nature.

He caught a fat raindrop. With a smug grin, dimple deep and full of mischief, he waited for me to respond.

Son of a bitch.

"I guess I have to take that ride after all."

4

————

I n the restaurant's parking lot, I stood underneath the flapping canopy that led back into the indoor dining space. Early-September rain poured off the material, puddling around my feet. Cooper was pushing my bike into La Bella Notte's basement for safekeeping. Within minutes of my agreeing to take Cooper's ride, it had started pouring.

I really hated when he was right.

Cooper's once dry and perfectly pressed oxford shirt was now sticking to his every muscle as he jogged to his Range Rover to pull the door open for me. His tan dress pants were stuck to his thighs. I focused on sloshing as fast as I could through the lot versus looking at the muscles through his pants because the last thing I wanted was for Cooper to think that I was checking him out.

He might have been the single most irritating person in the world to me, but still, I could appreciate his appearance.

EMMA THOUGHT: Remember not to drink wine when Cooper is around, and make appointment with eye doctor.

In the car, as if it were no big deal, Cooper pulled off his dress shirt, balled it up, and tossed it into the backseat with a wet *thwap* against the leather. Thankfully, he wasn't shirtless, instead wearing a thin white T-shirt that looked a few sizes too small.

"Baby Gap have a sale?" I quipped, side-eyeing the way the sleeve gripped his biceps.

Seeing what I was focused on, he flexed.

I rolled my eyes. "If you kiss your biceps or invite me to the gun show, I'm going to push you out of the car."

Instead, he reached over into the passenger-side space, and my breath caught as his damp arm brushed mine. Out of the corner of my eye, I saw his lips turn up into a smirk as he opened the glove box.

"Sorry about getting you wet," he purred, his deep voice even more gravelly than usual.

"Oh, please. Does that ridiculous innuendo really work on women?" I asked, but I knew the answer. *Yes, yes, it does. Often and repeatedly. Even, sometimes, on me.*

I didn't like where this was going. I wanted my irritation back. So I forced myself to remember him screwing up the theater proposal.

"Here, in case you want to dry off a little." He offered me a small golf towel.

With that I felt stupid. I was being ridiculous and mean. "Thanks."

"No problem."

"Thanks."

"You said that already," he said, pushing the ignition button.

There was an odd crop of feelings that always danced along the surface of my interactions with Cooper. I couldn't quite explain them away, but I certainly wasn't about to examine them, either. Whatever they were, I had to remind myself that this was Cooper, someone I'd been annoyed by for years. And I was irked by his lack of work ethic. Again.

"Nancy texted about the mistakes in the theater proposal," I explained coolly, fueling the latent irritation I felt toward him. At the mention of our assistant's name, he winced. *Good.*

"Listen, I didn't mean for you to get involved. I had it handled."

I swung my head around with what I hoped was a look of sheer disbelief on my face. "We both know you didn't. Cooper,

I know you've got a ton of shit going on with running for mayor, but you've still got a job and a team counting on you. I can't keep fixing everything."

He was quiet as he pulled out of the lot. His jaw muscles were grinding. I wondered if it was because he was deep in thought or just trying not to snap at me for voicing my opinion. One of my biggest problems with Cooper was that no one ever criticized him, and when you did—whoa boy, he didn't take it well. The golden boy could usually do no wrong, but since he'd started the campaign for mayor, he'd found out that not everyone thought the sun rose and set on his ass. Present company included.

When he turned onto the main road back into the heart of town, he finally spoke. "Look, I *am* sorry. I should have told Nancy that I'd be back in the morning. The time just got away from me."

His nonchalant tone frustrated me. I wanted him to take something seriously for once. No more excuses.

"You could have canceled your date," I blurted out, immediately wishing that I could pull the words back into my mouth. "Or just not rushed out of the office. There is plenty of time to get everything done if you'd just budget your time better. You're all over the place. If you weren't distracted by these campaign meetings, speeches, and going door to door to plead for votes, you'd—"

"You're right. I get it. Emma, you're the responsible one. Always have been and I'm . . ." He trailed off, not finishing the thought.

He gripped the steering wheel tightly. "You've got an idea for everything, and you love nothing more than lording that over me. I'm sorry—I figured I'd get to work on it early tomorrow and handle it with enough time to get it to your dad, and then I'd make whatever necessary changes on Sunday. I don't know why Nancy bothered you tonight. I would have made sure we were ready for the council meeting on Monday."

"I don't have all the answers, Cooper, and she *bothered* me because she knew the paperwork was wrong and needed to be fixed before the mayor went into the town council meeting and used something strewn with errors. You haven't exactly been Mr. Available lately."

"You know I wouldn't let him look like a fool, Emmanuelle. Your father—your parents, for that matter—mean the world to me."

I knew that he respected my father. After all, he was the man who'd pushed Cooper into running to succeed him in the first place, but it still chapped me to know that the date with gold-digging Bimbo Barbie had taken precedence over finishing a simple task.

"You need to adjust your priorities. He thinks you can do this. If you respect him like you're insisting you do, act like it. You can't cavort around town if you want to win. And *if* you win, you certainly need to—"

"Okay, okay, I know. All right? You're not telling me anything that I don't already know. Your father just had this conversation with me yesterday."

I slapped my leg out of frustration. "Then why aren't you listening, Cooper? So much is riding on this. You have to take it se—"

"For fuck's sake, if you say *seriously,* I'm going to stop the car and make you walk home," he said through clenched teeth. He gripped the steering wheel with both hands, his nose flaring as he huffed.

I crossed my arms over my chest. The top button of my blouse had sprung open, and, like a homing beacon, Cooper's eyes drew downward to check it out.

"Stop the car, then," I said to force his eyes to look into mine. "I'd rather walk than be stuck with you."

He made no movement to pull over. "Don't be ridiculous. You can tolerate me for a few more minutes."

Squeezing my arms tighter together, I fought back the chill that danced down my spine and started to shiver. Noticing it, Cooper adjusted the vents toward me and put the heater on low.

"Thank you."

He gave me a single nod and trained his eyes back on the road, though his fingers didn't ease up on the wheel.

"I *am* sorry," he murmured.

"Noted. Everything is done now, and right. It's at least one less thing you need to worry about before tomorrow. But, Cooper, I'm done cleaning up your messes." I sneaked in the last dig and turned toward the window. At some point I would need to let him decide whether he would pass or fail.

Leaning against the cool glass, I watched the rain sluice down the windshield. The steady back-and-forth of the wipers lulled me into contentment. Some of the edginess I had been feeling started to melt away.

Clearing his throat, Cooper slowed the car. Perhaps it was because of the rain, but the air in the car shifted into a heavy silence.

"I'm nervous," he said, so softly that I barely heard him. I noticed that his hands had eased up on the wheel. His knuckles were no longer white and strained.

"Excuse me?" I asked, taken aback because "Cooper" and "nervous" were rarely synonymous. "What could you be nervous about?"

He shot me a rueful look. "Tomorrow."

"It's like you told Nancy, it's just a photo op with my dad, you, and Kirby. You've had your picture taken for years—this isn't any different."

"It's not just that. Finishing the theater proposal. That paperwork was my first time writing something that would potentially happen if I'm the next mayor. That added a lot of pressure."

My immediate reaction was to laugh, but seeing his face and the nervousness coloring his complexion, I was glad I resisted. He was being serious.

"Add in how much I love and respect your father, and, well, I blanked. I panicked, and I did what I do best—"

"I know." I cut him off. I didn't need to hear him say whatever came next. *Avoid. Take someone out. Find someone to release some . . . frustrations with.* "Pressure makes us realize how important everything is. But, Cooper, the CDO is still your job. You've got to balance everything better."

He was silent. I took a deep breath.

Supportive, Emma. Be supportive.

"Listen, it's good to be nervous. I felt the same way sending my first email to your mother back when she was just a state representative. Now that she's the governor? I triple-check the spelling and punctuation of everything, and then I still wonder if I missed something. As if Governor Clare Campbell cares if I missed a comma."

Cooper chuckled. "You could not punctuate the entire email and she would still think you're the smartest person in the office." For a moment I wasn't annoyed at Cooper.

"Had you asked, I would have helped you," I offered. His eyes swung my way in disbelief. "Okay, I would have given you shit, but I still would have helped." That was enough to coax a smile from him. It was brief, but it took some of the edge off.

A little nudge of guilt settled in my stomach. After squeaking by in the primary race in May, I hadn't thought about the stress Cooper was under. It didn't excuse his behavior, but it put some of his absentmindedness into perspective.

"Don't worry about tomorrow," I continued. "You'll be side by side with Enrico Peroni, your biggest supporter in Hope Lake."

He turned, grinning. "Besides your mother."

I bit back a smile. "Yes, besides my mother. Both of them will be there cheering you on."

He curled his lips together, biting nervously on the lower one. "I just don't want to disappoint them," he said honestly, and I knew immediately how that felt. As the daughter of the mayor and under the constant scrutiny of the town, I was always afraid of making mistakes.

"You know my father loves you, Cooper." His face lit up. "One mistake won't ruin that."

"Are *you* coming tomorrow?" he asked as he turned toward the town square.

Of course I'll be there, I wanted to say. *Why wouldn't I be there?*

Cooper knew all too well that I would have rearranged my schedule to attend.

I nodded. "Wouldn't miss it," I admitted finally, ending the awkward silence that had filled the car. "You know, I prepared a statement for my father. A bit of a preamble, then you both have your moment and then Dad will wrap it up."

That was all it was *supposed* to be, anyway. Kirby Rogers had become notorious for using any platform to spout his crazy rhetoric and harebrained ideas.

"That's good," he said, rubbing the back of his neck. "If I'm being honest, I'm glad he'll be there."

"I can appreciate that. He wants to show support for you. Plus he's discussing the achievements of his many terms as mayor and the growing vision for Hope Lake's tourism, as well as the financial goals associated with both. There may or may not be a plug in there about how the CDO is behind so much of Hope Lake's growth," I added with a smile. Even though my father had someone in his office to look over his speeches, I always tinkered with them, too. "He's basically *implying* why you're a better choice to follow his term by laying out the reasons why we need to continue forward with progress that mirrors his work. Everyone—well, almost everyone—is happy with how things have been going. Why not keep the momentum up, you know? Having the sentiment delivered by someone people love is just a bonus."

He let out a long exhale, clearly relieved. "That's good. Thank you. I'm sure it's perfect." I knew he meant it. Regardless of how much we argued and disagreed, one thing Cooper always did was give credit where it was due.

"And most important, I threw in why my father thought that you were the best person to be his successor."

"Emmanuelle, you didn't," he groaned, but I was sure I spied a small grin.

"I did," I said seriously. "But don't read too much into it. I did it just as much for me as I did for him. We need you to win. Kirby would strip everything we've accomplished for years and have Hope Lake go backward." I paused, shuddering at the thought: out-of-work residents, no new businesses, no events to bring the town together. Basically, no hope in Hope Lake. "You know what I mean."

He nodded and said no more.

After five more grueling minutes of stone-cold silence, we arrived at my building. At that point, the storm had turned into a downright deluge.

We sat awkwardly for a few more seconds while I debated how exactly I was going to get inside without being knee-deep in water.

"They really need to clean out the sewer grates," I blurted out, and mentally smacked my palm to my forehead.

Sewer grates? This is what you talk about sitting with a guy in a foggy-windowed car during a blustery rainstorm?

EMMA THOUGHT: For a hopeless romantic, you're awfully hopeless.

Cooper's mouth quirked up. The antique-style streetlamps that had just been installed along Main Street shone through the windshield, highlighting his sandy-colored five o'clock shadow and the dimple that threatened to make an appearance.

"I'll text the public works crew to let them know." Cooper turned slightly to me, studying my face and staring at the dark hair that I could feel was plastered to my forehead before his gaze dipped to my lips for the briefest of seconds.

He cleared his throat, reaching into the backseat for my take-out bag. "This smells so good."

"It's spicy enough that it gives you a lasting kick but you're not screaming for a gallon of milk. It's the best," I admitted, taking the bag from him. I needed distance, and I needed it fast. Friendly Cooper always brought back memories that I wasn't willing to remember.

"I won't tell your mother you said that."

"She'd never let me live it down."

"It'll be like the Chef Boyardee incident all over again."

I watched, rapt, as he bit his bottom lip. His teeth sunk into the plump lip. I swallowed. "The what?"

He shifted in the plush leather seat. "Wait, you remember that, right?"

It wasn't often that Cooper looked unsure of himself, and this was one of those times. It was as if he wished he hadn't said it.

"I remember. I didn't think you did."

When we were younger, my parents would always throw parties and invite friends and family over. Once in junior high, we'd had a pretty crowded cookout. Most of the kids were playing whiffle ball in the yard, swimming or playing volleyball while waiting for the food, but Cooper had disappeared. It wasn't uncommon for me to watch him from afar like a lovesick puppy. After all, I *was* a lovesick puppy, an awkward teenage girl with feelings I couldn't work out about someone who had been my best friend since, well, birth. I figured he was off flirting with someone.

I walked into the house, searching for a drink, but stopped short when I saw Cooper sitting at the counter charming my mother. Even as a teenager, he'd had her wrapped around his little finger. In typical Cooper fashion, he asked my mother for pasta, knowing that she would make it for him. It was her *thing*. If you were hungry, she'd pull everything out of the cabinets to make you something homemade. She loathed anything processed. Even with a veritable buffet of BBQ food outside, he had somehow suckered her into cooking for him. He had a half-eaten plate of pasta and meatballs sitting on the marble countertop and a smudge of sauce across his tanned cheek. Mumbling around a mouthful, he nearly killed my mother with ten little words: "Emma, you were right—these *are* better than Chef Boyardee."

The wooden spoon had clattered to the floor, spraying the white tile with red droplets of sauce. My mother's mouth had hung open as she processed his words. To be fair, it wasn't what he said but instead what he implied that caused me to be grounded

40

for a week. Because he'd revealed to her that at some point in my fourteen short years on Earth, I had eaten processed, full-of-preservatives "Italian" food.

From a can.

I wasn't sure what infuriated her more: that I had tried it or that he felt the need to affirm that her cooking was better. For two weeks after that, while she and my father enjoyed her amazing cooking, I had to eat Chef Boyardee.

I laughed, thinking of him bringing it up over his biweekly dinner with my parents. He was the son they had never had but always wanted. Plus there was the awkward notion they had where they both hoped we would throw away the years of aggressive competitiveness and profess our undying love for each other.

Not going to happen.

"Promise I'll never mention Chef Boyardee around your parents again," he said with a laugh.

"I still haven't forgiven you."

He smiled, glancing at my lips once more before clearing his throat.

"I'll add it to the long list of things you're mad at me for," he mumbled as the door shut behind me.

Anytime I was alone with him, which was why I actively avoided it, I was transported back to that eleven-year-old girl who realized that the belly flutters she got when he walked in weren't a lactose allergy but her first full-blown crush. At twenty-eight, those feelings didn't remain, but the reminder of what they felt like did. There was no time for that, though, and besides, I'd hated Cooper for years. That wasn't an easily disguisable feeling. It was very black and white.

Either you like someone or you don't, and I certainly didn't.

5

Spending the weekend holed up in my apartment working wasn't a new habit. It was how I'd gotten through high school, college, and now adult life. It didn't help that Nancy lived in the same building as I did and was also a workaholic. She usually didn't mind the late nights or early mornings.

What also didn't help was that she saw me getting out of Cooper's car with my top button still undone and Cooper in his tiny undershirt.

She was standing outside our building, clearly locked out, again, as she stood there shivering with Larry, her soaking wet, equally shivering Pomeranian. Her eyes widened as I walked over to let her inside, Cooper's car still rumbling out front. "I'm getting this story later," she hissed as I pulled out my keys.

"Get changed, we're working tonight," I mumbled, unlocking the front door to let us inside. "And for the love of all things holy, get a new front-door key! One of these days I won't be here to save you." Glancing back as I held the heavy glass door for Nancy and Larry, I spied Cooper leaning over the center console of his car.

He was waiting until we got inside. *That was unexpected.*

I waved him off before Nancy noticed. Of course, she already had. He shot me a grin over the console, beeped, and drove off.

She leveled me with a look. "What was that about?"

"What was *what* about?" I asked, hoping my voice stayed even as I closed the door behind me. Any little break or jump, and she'd pounce on it.

"Hmmm," she said, shaking out her soaking wet arms in the foyer. "There's a story there."

"There is *no* story."

"Oh, but there is, my friend. One that ends with Cooper driving you home. In the rain. So romantic." She waggled her eyebrows. "I see that you didn't bring your bike back with you. Does that mean you'll have to see him again? Maybe tomorrow when you're wearing nothing but a trench coat and heels?"

I paused on the step that led upstairs, then turned. "Seeing him again implies that we were together tonight. He just drove me home because of the weather. My bike is still at Notte's. I'll get it tomorrow. Alone." I purposely ignored the rest of her comment.

"*So* . . . no trench coat and heels?" she asked hopefully.

With a sigh I tossed up a silent prayer for the strength not to strangle her and her one-track mind. Aware that the apartment building corridor was not the most ideal place for this conversation, I stepped back down to her landing. Standing outside her apartment wasn't much better, but I was working with the cards I'd been dealt.

"You've seen us practically rip each other's faces off at work firsthand, and yet you're still barking up this tree," I whispered. "How on earth could you think something could be going on?"

She shrugged, waving her hand in the air. Water dripped off her sleeve and splattered against my shirt. "Sometimes the best sex is with the people you think you hate. I don't write this stuff, lady, it's just gospel."

Brushing the water off, I laughed. "But I don't *think* I hate him, I know I do. Also, I feel like that is completely untrue."

"Whatever, I read it on the internet, so it must be true." She laughed. "Throw me a bone. I have to live vicariously through *your* sex life until Javier gets home."

Her husband, Javier, was deployed on his second tour in the Middle East. After his deployment, she had adopted Larry from the town shelter, converted their too-big house on the lake into a B and B—with the help of me and the CDO, of course—and hired a local family to manage it. Moving into my building and becoming my neighbor was her way of fighting the loneliness.

"You've got to stop with this notion, Nance. It's never going to happen," I said, turning around again to slosh up the stairs to my fifth-floor apartment. "Oh, and when you come up, bring the pooch. I picked him up a new toy."

"Whatever you say, boss." I heard her snicker as she unlocked her door.

One hike up to the fifth floor and a hot shower later, I was marginally warmer in my apartment but still wired from the night's events. Nancy and Larry arrived as I walked into the living room, towel-drying my hair.

"All right, lay it on me: what's so important that you're dragging us up here on a perfectly miserable Friday night? I was bingeing *Elementary* before his highness had to go potty and you showed up," Nancy whined, pretending to warm her hands over the electric fire that I'd turned on as soon as I'd walked through the front door.

Larry waddled over and plopped down on his dog bed by the hearth. Nancy had brought the bed up the week after she'd moved into the building. Once she realized that she had taken a job with an unapologetic workaholic, she figured it would help us both to have Larry keep us company while we worked. Larry, as usual, ignored us, curled up, and was snoring within seconds.

I paced in a small circle, rubbing the towel over my hair as I thought about how to launch into explaining why I ruined her night. Rolling up the towel, I tossed it into the laundry basket in the small hall closet. From my spot in the kitchen doorway, I watched Nancy as she settled into her favorite seat by the window.

I held up the take-out container of pasta to my nose and moaned. I was starving. "Want to split this?"

Shaking her head, she said, "Had some delish General Tso's earlier. If you're going to make me work, I can't sit here. I'll fall asleep." She stood, mumbling about how comfy the chair was before moving to sit on the love seat. She pulled her long legs beneath her. Opening her laptop, she lobbed, "And wait, I thought you were at dinner. Isn't that dinner?" She motioned to my takeout.

Popping the bowl into the microwave, I turned. "It's a long story, and yes, I'm sorry, we're working. I have a few ideas for that Jackson deal I mentioned the other day."

"I'll forgive you if you tell me one thing." *Here we go.*

I sighed. "I'm going to regret this. Go ahead."

She tapped her pencil against her temple, smiling. "Why was Cooper not wearing a shirt?"

I laughed. She was ridiculously persistent. "You're like Larry with a bone."

She groaned. "Oh, come on, give me something. He's so buttoned up all the time. Yet you two show up here, and he's smiling, relaxed . . . and shirtless. Which is a sight to behold. Thank you for that."

"Oh, my God, he was *not* shirtless. Don't say that out loud. Could you imagine if people thought something happened between us?" I demanded, my voice rising. "And for your information, he had to take off his dress shirt because it was soaking from the rain. Which is a *perfectly* reasonable explanation."

"Oh, relax. I'm just teasing. I have to be honest, though, I don't know what the big deal would be if you two were an item."

"Nancy," I warned.

That was territory that no one besides my mother was allowed to venture into. And the only reason my mom did was that she refused to take a hint.

"Okay, okay, no shirtless Cooper," she said with a resigned sigh.

"Shirtless Cooper is why we're working tonight," I explained, padding to the refrigerator. "You can binge-watch *Elementary* all day tomorrow." I smiled guiltily. "Wine?"

She nodded. "I'm curious about this whole Jackson business, especially now that I know a shirtless Cooper factors into it. You were vague the other day at the office. Gimme the skinny."

I kept busy in the kitchen while the microwave ticked behind me. I straightened my towels, rearranged a couple glasses, poured a glass of wine for Nancy and myself. Mindless tasks to keep my fingers busy while my brain went a mile a minute through the Jackson history.

"Well, what *do* you know?" I asked, opening the microwave door to stir my pasta.

"Not much. I know it was before I started, and it ended poorly," she said.

"That's putting it mildly. It was Hope Lake's version of a sex scandal."

"Was it really that bad?" she asked, leaning forward eagerly. "I know it was a while ago. I wasn't here when it happened, so finding info has been a challenge."

"Six years ago," I began, then paused. Had it really been that long? "Wow. I know it sounds cliché, but it feels like it just happened. No one really talks about it, thankfully. But people still remember it."

I walked over with the wineglasses, settling myself into the chair across from Nancy. Staring into the deep red liquid, I launched into the fiasco that had sent Cooper and me down the hate-filled path we were on.

"You can't repeat this," I said as I took a sip.

She motioned crossing her heart. "Promise."

"Cooper and I used to be really close. You knew that, right?"

She nodded. "What does that have to do with the Jackson deal?"

"I'm getting to it. In order to explain the Jackson deal, I have to go through my past with Cooper, and I know I've been vague with you about it."

"Go on," Nancy said. Sipping my glass of wine, I grimaced at the burn it left in my throat. There was the public story that was out there about the Jackson deal, and then there was the *story*. One that painted Cooper with a very unfavorable brush.

"As kids, there were four of us who were inseparable, especially after my friend Charlotte left town around second grade. That was right when Cooper's mom started with the state government and traveling all over the state.

"It was me, Cooper, Henry, and Nick. Always the four of us."

Even though we hadn't always felt tied to Hope Lake, we'd all come back as adults.

As with many childhood friendships, over the years our relationships had morphed into an interesting dynamic among the four of us.

"As we got older, Henry and Nick always seemed to—well, I think they thought there was something between Cooper and me, so they tended to try and leave us alone while they did their own thing. They're a bit like yin and yang, those two. And as far as Cooper and I went, it was the same thing. Between my dad as the mayor and his mother firing up the ladder in Pennsylvania politics, we were like two peas in a pod. We both had to go to a lot of political parties and schmoozing events for our parents. As we were usually the only kids there, we helped each other get through them.

"We were thick as thieves . . ."

Until we weren't.

"I guess with any friendship, there's ups and downs. We all went through a patch where we lost touch in college." I paused, not ready to disclose why I had started avoiding Cooper in college. "That was the hardest for me."

"Oh, honey, that's sad," Nancy consoled me, taking my hand.

I shrugged. "It happens. In hindsight it was sort of like a long-distance relationship. I think we assumed we'd come out of four years of being away from Hope Lake still being the best of friends. This place was sort of the glue that held us together. But when you get to college and experience that freedom and a whole new life, calling your buddies from home takes a backseat. When one of your buddies is a girl—well, let's say I wasn't even in the same car."

Nancy squeezed my hand. "What do you mean?"

"I was taking eighteen credits at Penn. Add in some housing drama, and I wasn't exactly great company. Cooper, on the other hand, fit in at Drexel like a glove. Philadelphia suited him, you know? Big city, lots of parties—"

"Lots of women," she interjected, rolling her eyes.

I huffed, "Yeah, that, too."

"Anyway, when I came back home, it was *awkward,* to say the least. I was trying to find a footing back here. Being away from each other for years didn't help an already fraught situation. Cooper stayed in Philly for months after graduation, and I didn't hear from him at all. I was—"

"—forgotten," she finished for me.

I nodded. "Then I started working at the CDO for Mary Nora." I paused at Nancy's sharp intake of breath.

"That woman is infamous," she gasped. "Javier introduced me to her once. She was friends with his grandmother. One time was enough for me to never want to meet her again. Thank God she was long gone by the time I joined the department."

I nodded, and poured myself more wine. "Yeah, she was . . . difficult."

"You're being kind, Emma. That woman was obviously a nightmare. So rude and arrogant."

"She's the reason that Cooper and I have the positions that we do. Did you know that? I worked so hard for her. Sixty hours and more a week, but nothing was ever good enough. She would call me at all hours, weekends, holidays. It didn't matter. Then, when she left, she convinced the town council to divide her position as the CDO coordinator into two and created positions for both

Cooper and me. I was gutted. She was an enigma. You'd have thought that as a successful woman she would have championed a fellow woman—especially an eager, hardworking one just starting out. Nope."

Nancy shook her head. "I've only heard stories, and nothing has been kind."

With a shrug I stood and stretched my arms over my head. "I did learn a lot from her. I think she's the reason I have a steel backbone now. Anyway, she was totally against all of my ideas. I tried and failed dozens of times to bring in some younger ventures. It wasn't until Cooper showed up and got a job there that she was willing to listen."

"That must have pissed you off royally."

"You have no idea."

The state of our already fractured friendship had been compounded by his moseying into the CDO and being welcomed with open arms by a woman who had shown me nothing but disdain since I had arrived.

"So what, he shows up suggesting the Jackson company and she immediately falls in love with it?"

"Not exactly. See, Jackson Outdoor Extreme, aka JOE, had been the first of its kind. It was going to be a hybrid of a sportsman shop, sort of a cross between the X Games and Rent-A-Center. Cooper went to Colorado one spring break, and they had a location there. He found out that they wanted to build a location in an already established outdoor enthusiast area. Cities with ski resorts, kayaking, hunting, fishing—anything that involved the outdoors and had a lot of people as either permanent residents or visitors. Hope Lake didn't exactly fit that description. We weren't big enough."

"So how did he get her to take a chance on approaching them?"

I frowned. "He did the work. He created the proposal, and he presented it to her and then the council and my dad." I remember offering to help, but he refused. He wanted to prove himself.

"Twenty-two-year-old Cooper sounds like a go-getter."

Unlike twenty-eight-year-old Cooper.

"He was cockier than he is now, if you could believe it. He was more inclined to use his mother's political positions to his advantage. It's how he coaxed the Jacksons to come here in the first place. They were originally looking at the Poconos."

"Logical choice," she admitted.

"Absolutely logical, but Cooper wasn't deterred. He was hell-bent on them coming here. It was a tough sell since we're so small, but Cooper convinced them that a newer location with no real competition was a benefit."

"Genius move."

"Cooper took the lead on the project, but he and Mr. Jackson never saw eye to eye on anything. The closer they got to signing the contract, the more heated the negotiations became. Cooper was unwilling to incorporate Mr. Jackson's thoughts and concerns into the contract, and Mr. Jackson was equally unwilling to see what he was suggesting. Then Haley Jackson appeared, and it all went to hell."

"She's what? The daughter?"

I took a deep breath and shook my head.

"Oh, boy, need more wine?" Nancy stood to grab the bottle off the counter and gave me a generous pour.

Taking a sip, I felt every stitch of anger I'd felt then rush back. "She was Mr. Jackson's new wife. Something like forty years his junior." Nancy's face pinched up. I chuckled. "Exactly. The long and short of it is that Cooper was Cooper and he got caught in a compromising position with the wife. Not just caught but immortalized on film. Someone had taken photos of them down at the site where they were hoping to build the complex. Needless to say, the family saw them and pulled out of the deal before we ever could finalize it."

"Why the hell would he do that? If the deal meant so much to him, why risk it all?"

"That is the multimillion-dollar question. I think—and this is just a hunch because we never talked about it—he honestly didn't know she was Jackson's wife when he met her. From what I could gather, he met her at a nearby bar and he was trying to show off by walking the site with her and telling her about his big plans. By the time he found out who she was, it was too late. The sad thing was that he did work really hard on that project, only to have it fail epically because he wasn't thinking with the right body part. Still, even knowing that it was a mistake, it was basically the final nail in the friendship coffin for us."

"What do you mean?" Nancy asked.

I shrugged. "We didn't talk much when he got back from Philly, but we weren't *not* talking, either. Does that make sense? The friendship had already been strained to the point of breaking. Add in the stress from working together under the circumstances that we had, and Cooper and Emma didn't really stand a chance at being what it used to be. And once the Jackson deal blew up, I couldn't look at him the same. It was like the Cooper I thought I knew never actually existed. All that hard work and potential for Hope Lake down the drain, and for what? A lay?"

"Why try and nab them again, though? Isn't it risky? You think you can get them back?" Nancy asked, standing.

I rubbed my hands over my tired eyes. "They actually approached me this time. They still haven't found their perfect East Coast location, and Hope Lake is at a different place now. Plus I'll be the one in charge this time, not Cooper. And we both know I wouldn't let sex get in the way of something so important."

AFTER HOURS OF WORKING on new sketches of the area that would hopefully house the Jackson business, I was too bleary-eyed to continue without reinforcements.

"Nancy, did you put on more coffee?" I asked, squinting at my watch. It was just before two. "Nancy, you alive?"

Looking up from my laptop, I could see she was slumped over the kitchen counter. "Great, I've killed Nancy."

Her head popped up. "What? I'm awake!"

She swiped at a drool puddle with her sleeve before toppling off her stool onto the tile floor. "I'm good!" She hopped up and opened the refrigerator door to pull out the cereal box that she had put in there after her midnight snack. If I had to guess, the milk was spoiling away in my cupboard.

"Go home, Ms. Drew, I'll finish."

"Are you sure?" she asked quickly, packing up her bags and collecting Larry before I could answer. She smoothed her red hair back into a clip and mumbled a delirious good-bye.

I yawn-laughed as she headed out the door. "Yeah, I got this. See you tomorrow."

After she left, I quickly crossed the chilly hardwood floor into my bedroom. Pulling a quilt from my closet, I snuggled up on my wide-seat leather chair. I had won the simple patterned blanket at church bingo a few years back, and it was the perfect antidote for whenever I was feeling a bit off-kilter. Pulling the soft quilt up around me, I tucked it under my chin and tried to shut my brain off. I felt both feverish and freezing, which meant I was definitely going to be downing vitamin C in the morning.

EMMA THOUGHT: Take better care of yourself. Quit the work and head to bed.

Which I would. After I checked Facebook.

Scrolling through my feed, I caught up on the local and national news, messaged my friend Charlotte, and sent my daily Happy Birthday messages to everyone celebrating. Just as I was about to shut down for the night, I spied Cooper's name toward the bottom of my screen.

Someone I didn't recognize had tagged him in a photo posted just a few minutes before. I glanced at the time—it was almost 2:30. Nothing good showed up on Facebook at that time in the morning.

Before scrolling down, I steeled myself for what was to come. Did I want to see what he was up to? No, of course not, but if he was dumb enough to get tagged on Facebook, that meant I wasn't the only one who would see it. Voters waking up and perusing social media with their early-morning coffee would be seeing it, too. Which meant it would likely lead to trouble.

Cooper had a love/hate relationship with how social life had become. Spending time in the public eye, I'm sure, had disillusioned him about the idea of social media documenting his every move, despite the benefits of it. He refused to have a personal Facebook or Instagram account. Everything was done using the campaign page. Having Mayor Dad as a government figure certainly made me overly cautious of what got posted where, but it was how I kept in touch with old friends and classmates.

His mother, Governor Clare Campbell, had been smoothing over Cooper's antics for years. Probably even more important, and more stressful for Cooper, was that Governor Campbell's ancestor had founded Hope Lake in the 1700s. They had a legacy and reputation to protect. All of this meant that Cooper *should* have toed the line when it came to public—or shouldn't-be-so-public—behavior.

Yet he didn't.

Thankfully there was no sex tape. *Yet.*

But there had been plenty of drunken behavior, a myriad of women, and appallingly poor decisions made by the only child of Governor Clare and Sebastian Endicott, Esquire. At one point in time, you couldn't turn a page in the *Hope Lake Journal* without seeing Cooper's face plastered across the Entertainment section. But as he got older, he toned the antics down. *A bit.* With the election heating up, I'd been hopeful that any residual bad-boy Cooper behavior would be shown the door.

But now this shows up. Whatever it was, I had a feeling it was going to be bad. *Son of a bitch.*

I shouldn't care. But that was the crux of my dilemma in dealing with Cooper. If he lost the election because of his antics, everything would change.

If Kirby won because Cooper couldn't keep li'l Cooper in his pants, well, let's just say that I couldn't be trusted with scissors, or anything else sharp, around him.

With a nervous swallow, I scrolled down to look at the post. Within a half a second, I was sorry that I didn't have the will-power to just shut it down and go to sleep. The photo had been taken at a bar in Barreton, one that I recognized easily.

The first photo was innocent enough. Cooper had his arm slung around a guy at the bar, clinking glasses. He looked relaxed, happy, and very, very drunk. I rolled my eyes.

At some point, we all did it—got out of the confines of Hope Lake for a night or two and let loose—but Cooper really should have known better. Everything always found its way back into the Hope Lake gossip circles.

I clicked through to the next photo, and there it was—the damning photo I was afraid of.

I knew it was him immediately. He was dressed in the same outfit as the first picture, but his hair was now really mussed. He was in a lip-lock with a gorgeous woman. Her long blond hair was pulled up and topped with a plastic crown.

And a BRIDE TO BE sash was dangling at her side.

6

On Saturday morning, I woke with a crick in my neck and my dead phone clutched in my hand.

Of all mornings for this to happen.

Jumping up from the warmth of my queen-size bed, I lifted the shade just enough to see that the town had come alive without me. Rumbling up the sidewalk was a road crew vehicle, the back filled with thick split branches. Must have been quite the storm that I slept through.

Plugging in my phone, I cursed the dead battery symbol that appeared. Sliding à la Tom Cruise in *Risky Business*–style into my kitchen, where the only battery-powered clock hung, I took one look and felt my heart freeze.

"Holy shit!"

It was 8:48, which meant I had less than fifteen minutes to throw on clothes and some makeup and get across the street to the Borough Building for the nine o'clock press junket.

Thank goodness I had a clean, pressed pair of capris at the ready. After the fastest shower of all time, I threw on my mustard pants and a blue-and-white-striped shirt, not knowing how cold it was outside. I didn't have time to run out to check or throw on the news. The priority was getting across the street, and I'd be doing it without knowing if Cooper had seen, or cared about, my message that I had sent him after seeing the Facebook post.

> **ME:** Hey, the campaign page
> is tagged on Facebook.
> You + woman with an
> engagement ring = lost election.

And no response last night or this morning. No surprise there.

Bursting out the front door of my apartment building, I shivered. The air hadn't warmed up after last night's wild rainstorm. I must have really been out of it, because I had apparently slept through a tree partially coming down next door and hitting the power lines.

Well, at least that explained the power outage.

"Good morning, Emma."

Matt and Nate from the road department were in front of my building with lawn bags and rakes, pulling out the fallen leaves from the sewer grates.

"Cooper mentioned these were pretty backed up. We'll take care of it right away. Let us know next time you're ankle-deep in water," Matt said, smiling.

"Thank you," I muttered, equally annoyed and grateful that Cooper had managed to follow through on his promise from last night *before* he went and stuck his tongue down an almost-married-woman's throat.

Speak of the Devil, I paused at the sight of Cooper across the street. My breath did the opposite of what I thought it would upon seeing that he was there, looking cavalier with his aviators on and dressed in a sharp navy suit: it quickened instead of calmed. The longer I stood watching him, the more enraged I got. The problem was, I couldn't place the root of the anger, just that I was feeling it and he was the recipient.

He was pacing in circles around the hearty trunk of my favorite tree in Hope Lake: a colossal weeping willow that generations of children had climbed, broken limbs in on the way down, and kissed each other beneath its drooping branches.

I took a calming breath and stared up at the oldest and probably my favorite building in town: Borough Building. It always reminded me of the building in *Back to the Future* that got electrocuted to send Michael J. Fox back to his own time. It filled me with a sense of contentment.

As I stepped onto the curb, calmer than I had been just a minute before, Cooper came toward me, sliding his sunglasses up to rest on top of his head. He looked ragged—and more than from just a sleepless night. Thinking back to his companion, I squeezed the strap of my bag. The urge to swing it over my head and hit him with it was strong.

"Where the hell have you been?" he asked, his breath tinged with coffee. As I got closer to him, I could see that his eyes were bloodshot.

"Funny, I was going to ask you the same question. Where's the bride-to-be? Sleeping the bender off at your house?" I quipped, trying to sound nonchalant, but the statement hung between us, heavy and telling. He looked like I'd slapped him with the accusation, which made me feel like I'd been stung by it myself.

Seeing that a crowd was gathering, he steered us behind the tree. Once, when we were in elementary school and the best of friends, we'd gotten married behind this tree during a field trip. The memory brought a brief smile to my face, but I quickly tamped it down. This was not the time for a walk down memory lane.

"I've been ringing your doorbell, calling, and banging on your door for almost an hour!" Cooper said through gritted teeth.

Oh, now you want to talk. When it's convenient for you.

Rolling my shoulders back, I inhaled, the cool air filling my lungs. "First of all, get over yourself, Cooper. I tried to warn you last night that there was photographic evidence of your run as what, a male escort? Stripper? I hope they paid you well."

The thought of him doing Lord knows what the night before had my blood pressure spiking. "I shouldn't even have bothered trying to help you. It's evident that you have jack shit for self-control."

"Will you hold on a second? Christ, it was just a bachelorette dare. I wasn't . . . they picked me! It's not like I *went* looking for trouble. The picture was never supposed to go up online!" he said, looking over his shoulder to be sure no one was paying attention. "Once I saw your message, I got them to take it down!"

"Uh-huh, sure, Cooper. You made a 'mistake,'" I said, using air quotes. "Is it the same mistake like Angie Carmichael? Or maybe something akin to Megan Dunleavy? Or, oh, wait, I know—what about Rachel Baker? Should I go on? Or are we done here? What *kind* of mistake was this one?"

With each name I tossed out, there had to be another twelve that I could have thrown back in his face. Normally Cooper was unapologetic for his callous romantic decisions, which was—believe it or not—something that I had a mild respect for. He was what he was, and if you didn't like it, he didn't have time for you. But now, with the election looming and votes in the air, he needed to at least *act* like a man who didn't sleep with every woman who crossed his path.

"I don't recognize those names. Should I?" he asked sincerely, and if there hadn't been a crowd of people milling about the lawn, I'd have knocked his head into the tree trunk.

"You're kidding," I said in disbelief. "What about the UPS driver last month? The new waitress at the country club at your mom's Fourth of July party? What about the substitute teacher that Henry was thinking of asking out?"

His look of bewilderment spoke volumes.

"You're disgusting. I don't want to see you screw up like you did with Haley Jackson and take this town down with you."

He didn't respond except for his face paling.

This time when I walked away, he let me go.

KIRBY ROGERS REMINDED ME of how movies in the seventies depicted used-car salesmen: swarmy, cocky, and dressed in a suit that was too big, as if he were trying to fill the loose fabric with fake confidence. Plus he had a ridiculous comb-over that you could probably spot from space. He carried himself like he owned the world, and people reacted to it. Whether positively or not, Kirby made an impression.

"Emma, you look so *good*," he said, extending his hand.

Mindful of the cameras around me, I gave him my most genuine-looking fake smile. When I clasped his hand, he tried using the momentum to pull me in for a hug, but I sidestepped him just in time. His wife padded up behind him, wearing an expression on her face that was cold as ice. "Ms. Peroni."

"Mrs. Rogers," I said just as coolly.

I didn't understand where her dislike for me stemmed from, but did it really matter? They knew I was in Cooper's corner— albeit grudgingly—but you didn't hate someone just because of her political affiliations, did you?

Apparently so.

We turned together when someone tapped the microphone. Cooper was standing off to the side to take some questions from the press, and I couldn't miss the way Mrs. Rogers checked him out when her husband wasn't paying attention.

Cooper laughed at something that one of the female reporters said as she touched his shoulder. Kirby noticed. Turning to his wife, he loudly whispered, "I'll never understand why Enrico is putting all of his eggs in that guy's basket. Especially when there's a giant hole in it." At that a handful of nearby onlookers chuckled.

I rolled my eyes. This was going to be a long morning.

The press had gathered on the front lawn, cameras and micro-phones at the ready. It wasn't just the *Hope Lake Journal* covering the shoot. The *Barreton Leader* and *Mount Hazel Gazette* from neighboring towns had sent someone to cover it as well, because Cooper was a big draw. Photographers from around the state were in town to capture the first side-by-side photo of Cooper and his opponent to run in their own papers. More than half of Pennsyl-vania's cities had probably never heard of Hope Lake before today, but they would now. The governor's son starting his own (potentially) historic political career? That made for quite the story.

One of the male reporters tapped his recorder to get started. I inched forward just to catch a little of what he was saying.

"Good morning, this is Hudson Louis from 6ABC in Philadelphia. We're here today in Hope Lake, a blip of a town in the northern tier of the state. Although you might know it for its outdoor tourism, what you might not know is that it's also the birthplace of the Honorable Governor Clare Eugenia Campbell. This is, quite literally, the town that Campbell built. Governor Campbell's family has resided here for generations, and today her only child, Cooper Campbell-Endicott, is following in the footsteps of his family's political dynasty."

Another journalist was just starting up. The logo on his mic broadcasted that he was from a radio station out of Erie. "On some level, a Campbell has run for public office since first arriving in the country," he said. "Now, some three hundred years later, a new generation of Campbells . . ."

Each journalist, whether from radio, television, or newspaper, had a similar spiel. Given the sheer number of counties they represented, it was obvious that this press conference was a big deal—yet Cooper had spent the night before with a bride-to-be dangling from his arm. Either he didn't understand the magnitude of the situation, or he was too wrapped up in himself to care.

I was wagering it was the latter.

Cooper and Kirby were taking their places on the front steps of Borough Building. It was male posturing at its purest form. Cooper had a few inches on Kirby, and Kirby knew it. Adjusting his back, he would puff out his chest just before a photo was taken. Cooper, on the other hand, looked at ease. It was more *GQ* than *Washington Post,* but it worked. The press was eating it up, and Kirby, well, he was steaming.

"Kirby, can you tell us anything about what your plans are for the coming months? How do you plan on coming out ahead of Cooper?"

Like a shark, Kirby bared his teeth before he launched into his attack. "There's more to politics and governing than being a showman," he said with a sneer, sliding a glance over at Cooper, who appeared unaffected. Instead, he looked like he was one autograph away from signing cleavage. There was a stark contrast between the people surrounding each candidate. Cooper was swarmed by women, both press and fans alike. Kirby had a much smaller, conservative crowd whose opinion used to hold a great deal of weight around town.

That alone should have made Cooper nervous—that was a crowd whose votes held huge sway. The lack of attention on their end didn't sit well with me.

"Isn't anyone going to ask Cooper anything?" Nancy asked from beside me. It was so noisy, I hadn't heard her approach.

I shook my head. "Doesn't look like they're asking him anything of substance."

"Unless it's his phone number," she mumbled.

As if the reporter heard her comment, the gentleman from Barreton lobbed out a zinger. "Cooper, how's the singles scene here in Hope Lake? Is there anyone left in town that you haven't dated?"

Cooper, thankfully, didn't miss a beat.

I, on the other hand, felt my face burn. *Me!* I should have shouted. *Nancy!* I could have said. There had to be more women he hadn't charmed out of their pants.

I hoped.

"While I appreciate the interest in my social life, no matter how boring it is, I'd rather we focus on the matters at hand," Cooper started smoothly, carrying on about his idea for a rail biking system to take over the abandoned railroad tracks.

"That's worrisome, don't you think?" I asked, lowering my voice. We were surrounded by the crowd: Cooper and Kirby supporters alike. The idea of the wrong person eavesdropping made the hair on my arms stand up.

"What is?"

"That they kept focusing on his social life."

Nancy shrugged, pointing to where the *Journal* crew was looking bored and chatting among themselves. "If anyone asks Cooper anything of substance, I'd have thought they would."

Finally Cooper had another question thrown his way.

"Mr. Endicott, what does your mother think about your efforts to become mayor of her hometown?" the reporter from Philly asked, holding up the recording device toward Cooper.

Cooper flashed a smile, and a couple of the women full-on swooned. One even began fanning herself. *Good Lord.*

"Hope Lake means so much to my family, especially my mother, whose relative Montgomery Campbell founded it in the late 1700s. We have always had roots here, and I hope it continues on for many generations. My mother couldn't be prouder of my decision to run. I'm grateful to the residents of Hope Lake for many things, but having the platform to continue Enrico's work and vision is at the top of that list," Cooper said, smoothing a hand through his hair. As he continued singing his own praises, I watched as he pulled out every trick from his playbook.

Touching the buttons on his shirt to draw attention to his chest—*check.*

Shifting his hips to draw attention to his southern assets—*check, check.*

Rubbing his thumb over his bottom lip to make you think about kissing—*what?*

I sputtered and coughed unexpectedly, causing Nancy to slap me on the back. "Don't die on me. Not here," she teased.

"I'm fine. Stop slapping me!" I laughed, but she got in one last strong pat on my back. "They're eating this up now."

"Look at Kirby's face. He's so red, his head looks like it's about to explode off of his shoulders."

I nodded. "They're all focused on Cooper now. Kirby can't get a word in edgewise."

"Agreed. He looks livid," Nancy whispered, and pulled her phone from her purse to take a photo. "For posterity," she explained when I glanced over.

"You're a trip. The dial's definitely swung to Cooper's side for now, but he should be walking around, shaking hands and chatting voters up. Not letting his fan club fawn all over him. This isn't the time to pick up women." I paused. "I can't believe those words just came out of my mouth."

"Believe it," Mrs. Rogers said, sliding out from where she'd been eavesdropping behind me. I froze. She'd been lurking—that was never good.

"My husband will breathe new life into this town. Restore its values and put the focus back on Hope Lake, not on a beauty contest for the better-looking mayoral candidate. The last thing we need here is someone like Cooper Endicott running the show." When she turned, the crowd swallowed her up.

"Yeah, definitely not good, Nancy."

THE HULLABALOO with Cooper and Kirby lasted only about twenty minutes. By the time my father stepped up to the microphone, people were growing tired of the scene. Mayor Dad acted as a bit of a closer—a way to get the focus back to where he wanted, and that meant on Cooper.

He was dressed casually, passing up his usual suit for his favorite green Hope Lake Country Club polo shirt and tan slacks. His mayor belly, as my mother called it, bumped the podium, earning a giggle that reverberated through the crowd. In his left hand he carried his notes, which I'd copied onto index cards in large print for him the night before.

"Welcome, my friends. Welcome. I'm proud to once again stand here today as your mayor." He paused, pushing his glasses up his nose. I knew that tactic—he was getting emotional and needed to stall for time. He'd served as mayor for more than twenty-five years, and although he was looking forward to retirement, that didn't mean he wouldn't miss the job.

He cleared his throat. "One of these two gentlemen will replace me as your mayor in a few short months, and while I'm sad for this journey to be ending, I'm eager to see what adventures lie ahead and, more important, what achievements and progress await Hope Lake in the future." That was my line. I smiled at the cheers it received from the onlookers. "This is one of my last public engagements as the mayor of Hope Lake. That brings up a lot of feelings. Many of you will be sad to see me go; some of you, I know, will be applauding. But I hope more than anything that most of you will reflect upon my time as your mayor with fondness." He paused abruptly, but this time it wasn't because he was getting overly sentimental.

Kirby had scoffed so loudly that nearly every head had turned in his direction—except my father's. Over the years he had learned not to address people who drew attention to themselves. "Ignoring them frustrates them more," he would say.

"Clearly not everyone will bid me a fond farewell," he joked, earning him a few chuckles from the crowd. "That being said, I hope that those of you who believe Hope Lake is moving forward in the right direction will turn out to vote. Whether for or against me, you know how much I have encouraged everyone to exercise their right." He patted his stomach. "Even I can use a little more motivation by way of the exercise." More chuckles, and a few people were even wiping tears.

Whether you liked him or not, my father had devoted the better part of his life to public service. It was a sometimes thankless job in which he had gotten his fair, and unfair, share of grief, but he had always done it with a smile. Whoever won the election would have big shoes to fill.

He continued on for a few more minutes, barely glancing down at the rest of the cards I had prepared. Then he delivered the pièce de résistance that I was very happy I'd added at the last minute: "Just remember, always vote for principle. Although you may vote alone, you may cherish the sweetest reflection that your vote is never lost. John Quincy Adams said that, and I hope that come November, you'll reflect back on your vote as being one based on your beliefs, values, and principles."

That, my friends, is how you throw shade without anyone being the wiser.

With a small wave and a smile, he stepped away from the podium and disappeared into Borough Building, where I knew my mom was waiting.

The crowd was dispersing. Nancy begged off to run into the office before heading back home. Kirby and his wife had slipped off after the scoffing incident, and Cooper—well, he was being Cooper, casually leaning against my favorite tree while he chatted up the reporter from Philly.

With a couple of hours ahead of me, I took a deep breath and relaxed as much as I could. I was thrilled to see that my phone was alive thanks to the portable charger I'd brought. Checking it, I found it blinking with messages. If there was ever a case to reinstall a landline at my apartment, my mother would be it.

Mom cell, Mom cell, parents' house phone, Mom cell, Dad cell. *Ah, trying to mix it up to see if I was ignoring just her or the both of them.* If I didn't call her back soon, she would be calling Nancy to track me down. Or worse, "popping in" to cheer me up after I'd been stood up. I'd sent her a quick text last night to let her know so she wouldn't hound me. But usually when she "popped in" she brought lunch with her, so maybe it wasn't such a bad idea, considering I hadn't eaten yet.

I sent her a text instead of calling. That was me chickening out from having to explain, in the greatest of detail, why last night's no-show wouldn't keep me from looking for Mr. Right. If I was a hopeless romantic princess in a fairy tale, my mother was the true-love-cures-all fairy godmother.

Except she was bedazzled in animal print, not primary colors.

ME: Mother.

MOTHER: Oh, thank you Jesus. My
baby is alive! 🏛

ME: Mother, you're being dramatic.
You knew I was at the press event. I'll
bring a bottle of wine for dinner.

MOTHER: Yum! 😊 Don't judge, I didn't
see you with my own eyes. 👁

ME: Not AS dinner, FOR dinner. Red or
white, what's on the menu. And I know
you saw me. I felt your eyes on me.

MOTHER: Mannaggia, don't say that.
You might have the malocchio! We'll
get rid of it later. 🙏

MOTHER: White. I've got a hankering
for shrimp kabobs and don't laugh, I
was just lighting the holy candles to
pray that you were OK! You know I
have a couple in your father's office.

MOTHER: Cooper looked good, spoke
well too. I watched him from the
window. 😍 You know, behind him. 😉

Good Lord. She really was insufferable. That meant my father wouldn't be joining us, because he wasn't a fan of anything from the ocean. He must have kept his standing man date with his crew at the country club for their usual first-Saturday-of-the-month golf outing. Mom and I had a monthly dinner date, while Dad had beer, chitchat, and a friendly golf tournament with his buddies.

She called it our girl time. I called it the one thing that kept my dad from going insane.

> **ME:** No candles needed. I'm fine. Stop staring at Cooper's butt.

MOTHER: YES! Girl's Night 😉 PS it's a nice butt. 🍑

Is there a limit on how many emojis your mother can use in one text conversation? The answer is no, but there should be.

I would need lots of wine for dinner. And dessert.

> **ME:** Goodie

I wasn't exactly eager to sit through an awkward dinner while she dissected my carefully constructed dating profile before insisting that I should just let her set me up with a nice boy from town or church or . . . the *where* didn't matter to her as long as he was nice and respectful and his whole world revolved around me. Tall order, but that's what overprotective mothers like mine do.

Broken heart? She called the boy's mother.

Girls being catty at school? You guessed it, a phone call to make amends.

This was definitely not something that she could fix with a call.

Her friends all had daughters who had either married and then moved or moved and then married, as well as a few who, like me, hadn't moved or married and instead had chosen to focus on career. Her grandmotherly fertility clock wasn't just ticking, it was looking like the atomic clock counting down to the apocalypse if she didn't get a grandbaby to spoil soon.

The woes of being an only child. It required being the center of her attention, even when I didn't want to.

7

After the photo shoot, I decided not to waste the day by stewing over Cooper's potential troubles or his stupidity from his night in Barreton.

Back in my apartment, I pulled on yoga pants, sneakers, and a denim shirt and threw my hair into a high pony that swished with each step I took. The weather was improving along with my mood. Whenever I had the option to walk or bike around town, I would take it, especially in unpredictable weather. But with my bike still at Notte's, I would be hoofing it to get my usual Saturday errands done. Though lugging my dry cleaning down the stairs had me debating taking my car, the beautiful day won me over.

I had started going through my to-do list on my now thankfully fully charged phone when it buzzed with a text from Cooper.

JACKASS: Going to get your bike for you

> **ME:** No need. Will grab it later, thanks anyway.

JACKASS: Already on the way to drop it off at your apartment

ME: Not home

JACKASS: . . .

I found few things more annoying than five minutes of the elusive three dots, especially when waiting for a time-sensitive response. This sort of flub was how novice texters like my parents acted, not nearly-thirty-year-old men who knew the ins and outs of an iPhone.

He's probably preoccupied.

Either way, I had to admit that the gesture was oddly kind of him. Also, one hundred percent out of character.

He must need something.

So instead of a call, I sent a follow-up text to thank him and tell him to just leave it in the office. Short and to the point—I had errands to run. I headed into the main part of town to drop off my dry cleaning first.

Anytime I walked from my apartment into town, I marveled at how long it took to go such a short distance. Though it may have been only a few blocks, it took substantially longer than it should have, considering I would stop to chat with the owners at China Garden, Treasures Antiques Store, or just people on the street before actually getting to my destination. Instead of a ten-minute walk to the dry cleaners, it stretched to nearly thirty. When you were the mayor's daughter, *everyone* wanted to say hi. And you had to say hi to everyone.

As I navigated the litter strewn across the sidewalk, I realized that I really *had* slept through a crazy storm. Bins were upturned, branches were hanging from their trees by a thread, and a couple tables and chairs outside the café were tipped over. I stopped to pick up a plastic bottle that had blown out of a recycling container outside the dry cleaner's. Lining up, I readied my stance to practice my foul shot when I heard another *ding.* From a bike bell.

My bike bell.

"You're going to flatten my tires." I scowled, taking the shot with the bottle in lieu of turning. I missed, sending the empty plastic clunking to the ground to rest in the well-manicured lawn in front of the shop. Turning, I found Cooper coming toward me with my bike.

Correction, *on* my bike.

"How did you know I was riding it?" He dismounted gracefully, walking the last few steps toward me. His hands were on the handlebars, his knuckles white with strain, but why? It was an adult tricycle, and he looked ridiculous pushing it. I wished I'd seen him when he was still riding it.

"How did you know I was here?" I countered.

He shrugged. "It's Saturday. When you said you weren't home, I figured you were out running errands."

I didn't know how to process the fact that Cooper, who screwed up his own schedule on a weekly basis, knew mine.

"Did you ride that all the way from the restaurant?"

He nodded.

"All the way through town?" I was fighting back a grin. Thinking about what people had seen cracked me up. Cooper was over six feet tall, and though he wasn't supermuscular in the traditional sense, he wasn't skinny as a rail, either. The sight must have been ridiculous.

"I'm secure enough in my masculinity to ride an orange bike," he boasted, puffing out his chest a bit.

"Orange tricycle. With a white basket," I corrected. "And a dainty bell." I was mocked mercilessly by our mutual friend Nick, who thought a grown woman riding a tricycle was ridiculous, but he didn't see the practicality of it. Hope Lake wasn't a huge town by any stretch, at least not the populated part, and I wasn't a "serious cyclist." I didn't care for the miles of rocky-terrain trails that lined our mountainside or the river tracks that the town had smoothed out the last few years. I just enjoyed riding slowly and enjoying the town's scenery on wide, paved roads and sidewalks. Plus it was cute, and I looked adorable riding it.

Cooper grinned. "I have to tell you, the basket comes in handy for buzzing around town. I see why you're so fond of it."

"You know, the bike shop in Barreton has a green one just like it. If you win the election, I'll buy it for you. That could be your mayoral hook. My father has his notoriously goofy golf cart with the wonky wheels that he rides around town in. You can have your equally dorky tricycle."

He grinned. "So you're admitting it's dorky."

I huffed protectively. "With you on it, yes."

Cooper leaned on the handlebars.

My eyes fell to the sidewalk beside him, then to the trees and the leaves that would soon fall. They made for a great place to look so as not to focus on Cooper trying to be charming. *That doesn't work on me,* I reminded myself.

I focused on the basket that sat just behind his long legs. It was hooked between the back tires, just below the seat. It was wide, padded in an orange-and-white gingham print, and filled with the spoils from Cooper's busy ride over.

"How did you get all this in the short amount of time since you left the event?" I marveled. It appeared as though he'd hit every store on the way over. "And how are you getting it home? I don't have a sidecar to stick you in," I joked.

"Funny. I'm waiting for—"

Just then a loud silver pickup truck rolled up to the curb, rubbing its tires against it.

"Ugh," I groaned, stepping back as the window slid down to reveal a perpetually tanned, canary-grinning man. One of our best friends, just in time for his and Cooper's weekend lunch date.

Cooper isn't the only one who knows schedules.

"Morning, sunshine." Nick Arthur, resident pain in my ass, grinned. Every town had a guy like him: a charming, affable goofball whom the majority of people found irresistible. Like Cooper, he was handed everything on a silver platter. Unlike Cooper, it wasn't because of money, lineage, or the fact that his family was absurdly influential. Nick was just an endearingly agreeable guy, who just so happened to have teased me for years.

He had been doing it since we were kids. Was he really a pain in my ass? No, not at all, but it was our shtick. Bickering and teasing made us *us*. Nick and I argued like siblings. Cooper and I argued like . . . well, not siblings.

Out of the corner of my eye, I could see Cooper shake his head but smile at the bike before setting it beside him. He waved to us, holding up a finger to signal that we should give him a second before heading toward the café. He was smiling at a pair of women who were seated at a table in the fenced-off area near Viola's Sweet Shop. I didn't recognize them, but judging by the bags around their feet, they must have been shopping.

They looked like they were mother and daughter. Both beautiful, blond, and slender. The one I assumed was the mother was tittering over something Cooper had said. Probably something about them being sisters. I'd heard that comment before.

Having witnessed Cooper being an unrepentant ladies' man over the years, I would have assumed that his supply of cheesy one-liners and pickup lines would have aged right along with him, but alas, it appeared that the same old routine he'd been working on since high school still worked. Still watching them, I saw the mother wave her daughter inside to pay the bill. The moment she left the table, the mother was typing her number into Cooper's phone.

Turning away from the show of shameless flirting, I asked Nick, "Free next week? I need to speak with you about some work." Moving the conversation to business was always safe around Nick. "I have some ideas."

"There's a surprise." Nick chuckled, slapping his hand over the Arthur Landscape Architecture logo on his truck's door. He slid a knowing look toward Cooper, who was nodding a slick good-bye to the woman. "There's never been an idea that you haven't had, Emma."

"Not true, I just haven't yet found a way to keep you both from driving me insane. Where's Henry?"

Henry rounded out their trifecta for weekly lunch. As the quiet and generally most responsible one, he also happened to be my favorite of the three.

"It's detention Saturday," Nick explained, tipping his head back in the direction of the high school where Henry taught English.

"You know, for someone who never served detention as a student, he spends an awful lot of time there as an adult. Maybe he doesn't want to hang out with you guys. Ever think of that?"

"He *is* too wholesome for us," Cooper admitted casually, coming up from behind me with his hands in his pockets.

"Got her number already? New record," I said, grabbing the trike and rearranging the handlebar basket. As I pulled it toward me, I accidentally on purpose ran it over Cooper's foot. "Oops. Hope your new lady friend doesn't mind a man with a limp."

Rolling his ankle, he winced. "I'm sure in some way I deserved that," he mumbled.

"Nick, you didn't recognize that woman?" Cooper asked.

Nick looked around us toward where the mother and daughter were packing up their belongings. He shook his head, shrugging. "Should I?"

"You of all people should. She's the restoration expert we met last year, remember? The woman from Mount Hazel?" At hearing his explanation, I bit back the remark I'd had at the ready. *Restoration expert?*

"Oh, yeah," Nick said, waving a belated hello in her direction as she craned her neck to get a final glimpse of Cooper. "You wanted her to do something at the library, right?"

I was growing more embarrassed by the second. It wasn't like it was a far stretch to assume Cooper was trying to pick the woman up. *But still.* I hated when people jumped to conclusions about me. It was hardly fair for me to paint Cooper's actions with the same brush.

I waited for him to transfer his packages and bags into Nick's truck as they continued chatting about the work she could potentially do around town.

Nick pulled out his cell phone while he was waiting for Cooper to finish. "Okay, Emma, what day works for you to meet up?"

Opening my calendar app, I checked my schedule. "I'm free Wednesday from twelve fifteen to twelve thirty-five. Come by the office, and we'll get lunch and make a plan."

He nodded. "You and your plans, Emma. Also, how can you eat and talk in that amount of time? When do you digest? When do you have snacks or secondsies?"

"We're not Hobbits. Clearly you've been hanging around with Henry too much," I teased.

Cooper was nearly done unloading when Nick shouted, "Aw, for me? You shouldn't have!" He held out his hands toward Cooper over my shoulder, causing me to turn around to see what the fuss was about.

I followed his line of sight to a red box of chocolates that Cooper appeared to be trying to hide behind his dry cleaning. The plastic wrap surrounding the box crinkled as he laid it gently on the shady part of the truck's backseat.

Cooper narrowed his eyes at Nick and gave him the tiniest of head shakes. "Oh, they're for Emma?" Nick shouted, smiling at me. It was the last thing I expected or needed. Nick had enough ideas about Cooper and me. An innocent box of chocolates as a peace offering would only have him jumping to the wrong conclusions.

"They're not for you. I'm sorry. I can get you a box, though?" Cooper offered lamely, and I imagined the ground opening up to swallow me whole.

Speaking of jumping to conclusions.

This marked my cue to leave. No matter what I said, did, or thought, nothing about Cooper Campbell-Endicott would change. Not even his running for mayor.

Tamping down my reawakened annoyance, I moved my bike

against the parking meter outside the dry cleaner's. "You've over-stayed your welcome on my Saturday. Later, boys!" I shouted, disappearing with my bag into the shop and leaving them behind.

ONE BY ONE I checked off the items on my list, even managing to stop into Viola's Sweet Shop for an ice cream.

As I rode along the newly lined bike lane, my sense of pride surged, and I couldn't help but smile as I passed each new addition to the town. If you looked at Hope Lake like it was a ship, Borough Building and my end of town was its masthead. The bustling business section of town was its starboard side, and the stern was my parents' end of town.

The center of town was simply a square with a brick-paved pedestrian plaza surrounding a three-tiered fountain. In it, you could access all of Hope Lake's small shops and cafés. The other two points led toward the river, the mountains, or the lakeside. When the town's founders had built the town two hundred and fifty years before, they'd had the foresight to use nature as a guide. This time of year, just after the crazy summer rush, a few dozen people still milled about, but it was nothing like how busy it would be in the thick of July. The time when tourists flooded the town in search of the cozy, kitschy shops and the outdoor excursions that Hope Lake had become known for. A summer destination was what we hoped to become and what we were slowly getting to be.

The CDO had been instrumental in making this happen, what with the great number of improvements we'd helped make to the town. How many small pieces had I had a hand in helping to create? The new bike lane had been completed last fall, just in time to allow the Girl Scouts to organize a bike race for charity. The new antique-style lampposts lit up the town square and gave it that old-town feel that tourists loved, and the clock tower—which had been broken for a good thirty years—now ticked away thanks to a federal grant we had secured for cityscape improvements. Hiring local had helped us complete everything under budget and on schedule: another feat we were proud of.

Those were the achievements made possible by having someone like Mayor Dad in charge. With both him and the town council on board, we had been able to secure more grant money for all of the improvements we'd made. Still, though, there was plenty of work left to be done. Some buildings were still empty and falling into disrepair.

That was another reason I was so nervous about the prospect of Kirby beating Cooper. Kirby and Cooper had very different opinions on what this town needed to do to thrive.

Cooper had a vision that was thankfully similar to my father's: building up the tourism offerings in Hope Lake and finding new businesses, especially locally owned shops, that would support the efforts to change the demographics of the population. Bringing in younger people, preferably our age with new families, was the ultimate goal. Without them, Hope Lake would melt into an aging population and a town full of retirees.

Kirby, on the other hand, had made it known that putting money into local and family-owned businesses wasn't a priority for him. Instead, he wanted to bring in megastores and big chains, the polar opposite of what we'd been trying to do for years. Half the reason the town had started attracting summer tourists was the emphasis we'd placed on local businesses. Why would we want to risk a formula that was clearly working? You couldn't ignore how polarizing Kirby's vision was when compared with that of Mayor Dad and his chosen successor. Because of that, Cooper should have been a slam dunk.

Yet he hadn't had that strong a showing in the primary. Granted, no one had run against him, but that didn't mean hordes of people were coming out of the woodwork to vote for him, either. That was worrisome.

On my way home, I took the road that led toward the school campus, where all of the public schools were lumped together on one huge parcel of land. From the outside, you could tell they were old. The elementary and middle school buildings had been built sometime in the late 1800s and the high school in 1909. I had hoped to use the free time before dinner to just sit and people watch, but I spied Kirby coming out of the elementary school. It wasn't odd per se—he did have two kids at the school—but why was he there on a Saturday?

That was when I saw his wife, approaching him with a stack of bright blue papers. Flyers, maybe? A woman appeared at the front door.

"Yeah, that's not great," I said aloud, tucking my bike behind the massive oak tree near the large brick Hope Lake Elementary School sign.

Kirby stood on the steps, prattling on with the teacher while his wife made trip after trip to the car. *What a gentleman.* Finally, on the last run, she pulled out what looked like a basket tied with a bright red bow.

Kirby handed everything over to the teacher, and then she and Kirby shook hands with her and made their way back to the car. From my vantage point, I couldn't tell what was in the basket, but I had an unsettling feeling that it wasn't good.

Kirby had always maintained that Cooper was out of touch with the everyday folks of Hope Lake, while he was proud to be one of them. He needed to be sure that every demographic saw him as the definitive best choice. If that meant Kirby was courting the teachers, Cooper was even more screwed than I'd thought.

8

Riding home from my errands, I got caught in a surprise rainstorm. I really needed to get better at the weather-forecasting thing. Soaking wet and trudging up the steps to my apartment with my bags after a long day of errands was the last thing I wanted to do on a Saturday night. Scratch that; having an early-bird dinner with my mother was the last thing I wanted to do on a Saturday night.

I loved my mother, but she could be a bit overbearing sometimes. Consciously I knew that she wanted what was best for me, but her vision of my best life and what I wanted out of life were drastically different. If it had been up to her, I'd have followed her path to happiness: married right out of college and started on the family plan immediately. And she still hoped I'd get to that path sooner rather than later.

Though she tended to be a bit overbearing on the love-life front, it could have been worse. She could have not cared at all. I kept the notion in the back of my mind that she just wanted me to have what she thought would make me happiest. Even if her advice *did* come with a lot of emojis.

On the way up to my apartment, the oranges from my stop at the grocery store broke free from my paper tote just as I got to the landing. I'd forgotten the cold medicine, but I had gotten the vitamin C. Too bad they were now bouncing one by one down the stairs. Why had I needed to have the top floor, again?

As the apartment door swung open, though, I got my answer.

When I'd first looked at this apartment building, I'd considered the unit facing the expansive Campbell woods. They were named after Montgomery Campbell, Cooper's great-great-great- . . . something or other grandfather, who had founded the town. A vast region of still unsettled, and thankfully protected, town-owned territory that stretched as far as the eye could see.

But then I had seen this apartment. The view out of the three angled bay windows in the living room made me smile no matter the weather, and the windows' wide white molding framed the town like a Norman Rockwell painting. I was elevated enough to see over the gracious oak, sycamore, and maple trees lining the streets below, and beyond them I got the full view of Hope Lake with all its colorful buildings. On a clear day, you could see out to the mountain where my parents' house sat hidden among the trees. When the sun set, it bathed the entire town in a warm orangey hue. Sometimes I would zone out staring at it. It brought me a sense of peace, especially after a long day at work.

I sighed. *Time to get ready for my wild Saturday night.*

My mom texted while I was in the shower, again while I was getting dressed, and once more as I was heading out the door. She would call only if there was an emergency, so I ignored her. That was the beauty of personalized text tones: I knew when to toss my phone into my bag and pretend it wasn't permanently tethered to my body like most of society and when I needed to answer right away.

Since dinner was just me and my mom, there wasn't any need to dress up, but if I didn't at least look presentable, she would *tsk-tsk* and proclaim that this was why I didn't have a man in my life yet. So I left the house wearing ripped black skinny jeans that my mother hated, a fitted white sweater with buttons on the shoulder, and my trusty red flats.

Thankfully, by the time I reached the parking lot out back, it had stopped raining.

I loved my car, but there wasn't much need for me to have one here. With the exception of getting up the mountain to my folks' place, I didn't travel many places where it was necessary to drive. I could work on the bus that took me into New York City or Philadelphia, and my bike got me around town. Getting to the top of the mountain where my parents lived, though—that was the one thing I needed my little old Jetta for.

My parents' house sat in a large clearing on Carey Mountain, sort of like a lighthouse on a cliffside. Although the drive out there didn't take too long, their house was the only one up there. Lampposts were sporadically dotted along the dirt road, so the only consistent light guiding you up the hill besides your headlights was the fading sun.

As I wound my way up the skinny road to my parents' house, I noticed that the number of downed trees was more substantial than I'd realized. Even with the damage, though, it was still breathtakingly beautiful out here near the small pond on their property in the early evening. Neither of my parents ever went near it, because it smelled bad and had a muddy bottom. But they loved the peacefulness they got from being away from nearly everyone.

I turned off the exit ramp and onto the gravel road that ribboned up to my parents' fieldstone house, causing a deer and a pair of grouse to scurry back into the woods as I rolled by. Just as I set foot onto the weathered wraparound porch, one of the heavy oak front doors swung open.

"Why are you here? I thought you were golfing!" I exclaimed, immediately suspecting the worst as my dad reached out to pull me into a hug. Nothing—except for the direst of circumstances—would cause my dad to miss his favorite night of the month.

"Hi, sweetheart. It's nice to see you," he said sweetly. Too sweetly. As he came forward onto the porch instead of pulling me into the house like he usually did, his broad frame blocked the doorway so I couldn't enter. "How was your day?" he added quickly, leaning his arm against the frame.

He was acting strange, and it wasn't just the couple of beers he'd likely had at the country club talking. I tried ducking underneath his arm to get inside the foyer, but he blocked me again.

"Is it Mom? Is she okay? Wait . . . is she *naked*? Am I early and interrupting *things*?"

I mock gagged, earning a hearty laugh.

"No, no. We just got here. I have a wonderful surprise." Nothing in his tone made me think it was actually a *good* surprise.

"Did you get me the dog I always wanted?" I asked sarcastically. "Mom wanted one, too, you know."

"I wouldn't worry about your mother. She couldn't be happier right now," he explained, stepping out of my way so I could head inside.

And there was Cooper standing in my parents' foyer, being smothered in one of my mother's bone-crushing hugs.

"Oh, look, you did bring a dog home," I groaned, stepping back onto the porch.

I could make a run for it. They haven't seen me yet.

I noticed a pair of car keys clutched in Cooper's hand as my mother squeezed him again. Maybe he was on his way out. Thank God.

"What is he doing here?" I whispered.

"Now, now, is that any way to talk about our future mayor?" my father asked, smiling broadly.

"You said it, not me," Cooper said, pointing upward and earning another moony smile from my mother. Even she wasn't immune to his charm when he laid it on.

Dad turned to me, his eyes slightly unfocused. "The rain washed the tournament out. The back nine was all water hazards, so I came home to surprise you." He squeezed my cheek affectionately as though I were still ten years old. He was trying to make me feel better about Cooper being there, so I decided to behave instead of making things awkward for him.

"Cooper and I saw each other at the clubhouse while I was having my postgolf beer," my father continued.

"But you didn't golf," I reminded him, laughing when he shrugged.

"Cooper stopped in with Nick, and we got to talking. I invited him over to discuss a few things. It's not really right if we talk at my office, so we're squeezing in meetings wherever and whenever we can."

"And we're so happy he's here," my mother interrupted, patting Cooper's hand like she would that of a well-behaved toddler. "And running for mayor—I couldn't think of a better replacement for my honey."

My father smiled at his ridiculous wife. She was practically beaming at Cooper. There must have been wine during dinner prep. She was still wearing her rainbow waist apron over a pair of zebra-print capris, which were paired with a plunging-neckline top. Her hair, though, was oddly understated for a change. She must not have realized she was having company other than her only child. Her long dark hair, so much like mine, was pulled up in a twist, showing off her massive golden hoop earrings.

"Mother."

"Oh, don't 'mother' me, that makes me sound old," she huffed, still patting Cooper's hand. *Jesus.* If she kept this up, we'd need to surgically remove her from him. "I'm trying to talk Cooper into staying for dinner. Wouldn't that be nice?" She said this pointedly, while at the same time wrapping her arm around his like a persistent octopus. She leveled me with her gaze, daring me to say something other than the expected *Of course you should stay, Cooper.*

Judging by the cat-eating-the-canary grin that he was sporting, he was waiting for it, too. Not willing to give either the satisfaction, I deadpanned, "Sounds fun."

My father closed the door behind me, snickering as I tossed

my purse and umbrella into the small overstuffed closet next to the stairs. "Seriously? You couldn't have warned me?" I whispered to him as my mother continued to fuss over Cooper.

He looked tired and still a little bit drunk. "We had two or three beers while discussing things. Cooper had to drive me home," he snorted.

"You still could have warned me," I said, resting my head on his shoulder. Sometimes you just needed your dad to lean on while you worked through complicated emotions like hate mixed with irritation mixed with confusion.

"It slipped my mind, Em. Your mom was supposed to tell you."

"Way to throw her under the bus." I laughed and dug out my phone from my back pocket. Upon seeing her texts, my stomach sank.

Damn it. I shouldn't have ignored her.

MOTHER: Em, Wonderful news! Cooper is staying for dinner. 😍

MOTHER: You don't mind, right?

MOTHER: Dad is a bit sauced. It's hysterical. I'm watching him try and take off his shoes. It's been ten minutes and he can't figure out the laces! They're already untied. 😂

MOTHER: Speaking of sauced, we're having pasta since your father is here. No shrimp ☹️

MOTHER: Cooper brought me chocolates! He knows how much I love my sweets.

MOTHER: Cooper should always wear blue, it brings out the color in his eyes. I still think you two would . . .

I didn't bother to finish reading because I knew where it was going. If I had encouraged her crazy notions about me and Cooper, the same ones that she'd been entertaining for years, we'd have been married with babies by now.

So I wouldn't tell her that I secretly agreed with her: he *should* always wear blue. And wait . . . the chocolates had been for her? *Damn conclusions.*

Taking another look at my dad still smiling, leaning on the door frame, and my mother hugging Cooper for the millionth time that evening, I sighed, defeated. "Let's get this over with." And with that I headed off into the kitchen.

DINNER WITH COOPER is actually enjoyable.

No matter how many times I repeated it or pinched myself, I didn't quite believe that I was actually thinking it. It hadn't started that way. Before my parents had brought out the meal, it had been slightly awkward because they had left us alone in the dining room while they "finished plating."

All that meant was that my mom had cleavage showing and my dad was a little more toasted than I realized. It doesn't matter what age you or your parents are—hearing them giggling and flirting was still enough to make me want to crawl under the table.

Cooper had sat quietly as we waited, working furiously on his iPhone. I'd watched him work. He looked stressed. More than I'd seen him look in ages. His skin was a bit purple beneath his eyes, his hair wasn't done up like it usually was—styled within an inch of its life. And . . . was his shirt wrinkled? What was going on?

"Cooper, are you all right?" I asked when the silence from his side was too much to bear. Usually it was easy to ignore each other versus bickering, but that was at work. At my parents' house, it was awkward.

"The meeting for Monday morning was changed to eight fifteen. In case you didn't see it," he said, keeping his head down.

"Thanks, I got Nancy's email."

A few seconds of silence passed as he kept typing. His fingers were flying so fast over the keys, I wasn't sure he'd even heard me. "Cooper, are you okay?"

"Huh?" He looked up from his phone, startled. "Oh, sorry. Yeah. Just trying to remember if I called someone earlier. I didn't check it off the list." He turned his phone to show me a detailed checklist full of reminders. Most of which weren't cleared.

He looked positively ragged. "You still have all of that stuff to do?" I asked, shocked to see a list of at least a dozen items. When I had given Cooper a hard time last night about forgetting everything, I'd assumed it was because he was preoccupied with his date. But it looked like that wasn't the only thing occupying his mind. "I hadn't realized how much you had on your plate."

Nodding, he glanced at his watch. "Yep, and not much time to do it." He paused, running his eyes over his checklist again. "Am I supposed to do anything for the theater project this weekend? It's on my list, but I thought I saw the theater paperwork signed today when I ran into the office."

I wanted to say, *No, I told you at least twice that I did it on Friday night because the council meeting is first thing Monday morning and you weren't going to meet the deadline,* but after seeing how exhausted he looked, I decided to give him a break. "Nope, already handled. You've got a lot to focus on here, Cooper."

He smothered a yawn. "Yeah. I mean, I think I can juggle everything, though."

Good Lord, he couldn't have been more wrong. Was that really how he wanted to measure his success nowadays? Not awful at campaigning + so-so at work = a win?

"Cooper?" I began, but when his eyes met mine, I paused. I was going to suggest he take a break—maybe some vacation time from the CDO just so he could focus—but that was me butting in where I probably wasn't wanted. So I decided to change the subject.

"You should make sure you get all your messages in before my dad comes out," I teased. My dad was notorious for how much he hated "tech at the table." I slid my own phone back into my pocket.

Cooper smiled. "I remember." He shut off his phone's ringer and slipped it into his pants pocket.

Once the four of us were seated, my attitude toward Cooper defrosted further. Having my parents present meant that the two of us were forced to be on our best behavior. Add in Cooper being too exhausted to be his normal annoying self, and we weren't as aggressively antagonistic with each other.

My parents' opinion of Cooper had grown over the years—even as so many people had cut him off because of his teenage antics. Since returning to Hope Lake after college, he had fallen back into his groove with them.

"Cooper, how is your mother? She hasn't been back here in ages," my mother said. "I have to call her, catch up."

When we were kids, with his mother so busy with work, my parents had been sort of adoptive parents for him. He would come home with us after church for milk and pastries that we would pick up from town. Afterward, Cooper would spend time helping my father figure out his technology when his computer or phone was on the fritz. When that was done, he would play cards with my mother before the nanny or someone else from the house staff would pick him up. So out of respect for my parents, I tended to curb the judgment I usually lobbed at him whenever we were in their presence.

"She's good. Always busy. She's in Pittsburgh? No, wait, Philadelphia? I can't remember." He laughed and took a sip of water. "I'll tell her you asked about her. I know she misses you both."

The dinner was *almost* fun because my parents were master storytellers. They looked forward to any time they got to regale interested listeners with their crazy stories. One of my father's favorite things was to engage people in discussion, banter, arguments—anything that allowed him to share his ideas with someone else.

That was why my dad had devoted his life to small-town government all these years. Sophia Peroni, too, was no slouch. She was on every town event staff and service organization and still volunteered for the Hope Lake Elementary School PTA even though I was twenty-eight years old and had long since graduated. I believe it was an immigrant trait that I respected so much. Their parents had come to town with almost nothing, and it was their way of giving back to the town that had welcomed them.

"Emma, what are you thinking so hard about?" my mother asked, smiling.

"Nothing specific, just thoughts," I lied, tamping down the thoughts about my running for public office like my father. While those ventures weren't in my future, as I preferred to work behind the scenes, my dad was grooming Cooper to follow in his footsteps.

Whereas I was happy writing grant applications, chairing safety commissions, and doing whatever else I could do to help the wizard behind the green curtain, so to speak.

I zoned out listening to their conversation. My mother was prattling on about how Cooper was the best choice. That he had always yearned for the brass ring and that this campaign would be the golden circle for him.

"Emma?" my mom shouted, startling me and causing my fork to splatter sauce across my white top.

"Shit!" I dipped my napkin in the water glass and rubbed, but the sauce was all over me. "Sorry, what did you say?"

"Honey, are you okay? You were staring at Cooper and not saying anything. Even when we said your name," my father said, his lips twitching as he fought back a smile. It was when I looked at Cooper that I realized what he'd said.

You were staring at Cooper.

"Sorry, sorry. I was zoned out thinking about . . . stuff," I lied, trying to eat quickly since everyone else was nearly done. Just how long had I been sitting and staring?

Judging by Cooper's grin, it had been a while. The dimple was front and center.

"Carry on. I'll catch up," I mumbled around a mouthful of pasta.

"Cooper, have you thought any more about what we discussed with your dating life?" my father asked brusquely. He didn't get angry or irked with Cooper often, but this subject seemed to be the straw that always broke the camel's back.

Cooper sighed, picking up his napkin and blotting his lips. Placing it on the table next to his plate, he folded his hands in a move that showed his annoyance all too well. Gone were the easy posture and quirky smile. He was rigid and stern, neither of which was a good look.

"I'm still considering it."

"What's 'it'?" I asked, looking from my father to Cooper and back again. "Is there something going on that I don't know about?"

"It," my father began, "is how Cooper's *extracurricular* activities are affecting his campaign."

An unsettling feeling began building in my stomach. "Oh," I said, feeling the heat in my face rise. I hoped that it wasn't noticeable, but judging by the knowing grin on my mother's face, it was.

Cooper cleared his throat. "Enrico feels that some of the time I spend outside of work alienates voters, since they might see me as, you know—"

"A playboy? A lothario? An unrepentant Casanova?"

Cooper waved me off. "Yeah, yeah, okay, I get it."

"Exactly why he needs a wife," my father announced.

I turned my head to him. "Hold up there, Mr. 1950s Mentality. He doesn't *need* a wife." I surprised myself with the comment. I backtracked. "I mean, he just needs someone who's not quite as . . . disposable."

"Like a friend?" Cooper suggested, earning approving nods from my parents.

I shrugged. "I suppose."

Cooper crossed his arms over his chest. "I'm considering my options."

"As a third party uninvolved in the campaign, and as a voter, I think you should do more than consider it."

"I know why your father thinks this is a good idea, but why do you?" Cooper asked, shifting uncomfortably in his seat.

I sighed and mirrored his position. Arms crossed, back rigid, all business. "The last few press events have had questions from journalists regarding your private life, and it's only going to get worse the closer we get to the election. Giving them a nonstory, like, say, you having a steady girlfriend, might be what you need to get a decent margin over Kirby. He's going to exploit the fact that he's got the wife and two point five kiddos, blah, blah. Might as well beat him to the punch by *also* being 'a model citizen.'" I added the air quotes for emphasis. It seemed ridiculous that you needed to have a family to be the right person for the job, but that was life. "Control the narrative around what seems to make you an easy target for scrutiny. Think about what happened in the bar in Barreton. If that photo had stayed online, Cooper, it would have been appallingly bad."

My father blew out an irritated breath. "Do I even want to know?"

Cooper shook his head. "You don't, and I already explained that to you, Emma. It was a dare. I didn't seek her out or anything."

Holding up my hand, I waved him off and kept going. "*I* believe you, but do you think my opinion is the only one that matters? Do you think Kirby or his crack team of investigators care about things like the truth? If they had the photo, they would have used it to prove that you're flighty, flaky, and incapable of settling down. They could've spun it to their advantage."

I looked over to Mayor Dad, whose face was turning an unpleasant shade of purple. "Dad, don't worry about it. Cooper took care of it." In reality, *Cooper* should have worried about it.

"What I'm getting from both of you," Cooper interrupted, "is that I need someone to make me appear to be what? Off the market?"

I rolled my eyes. "You're not a house, Cooper. Having a girl-friend—"

"—or a wife!" my mother chimed in.

"Mother. Back on topic. Having a girlfriend makes you appear settled down. Able to be counted on because you've got someone you depend on and vice versa. People tend to see political men as reliable when they're attached to someone. Why do you think all the presidents have been married?"

"Not all!" Cooper exclaimed.

"What?"

"I said, not all. James Buchanan wasn't married."

"Okay, that's one president who wasn't married, a thousand apologies," I said, laughing when his eyes went wide. "I can and will apologize when I'm wrong, Cooper."

"He was also the only one from Pennsylvania."

"It's like you want me to argue with you."

"Now, now, you two. You sound like an old married couple," my mother interrupted, standing and going around to Cooper's seat. She placed her hands on his shoulders, unable to keep the smile from her face. "Not that anyone asked my opinion, but, Cooper, I agree with Enrico and my Emma. You need to save face here."

I knew it would happen before it did. She pinched his cheek like she had done when he was a little boy who had scraped his knee while running through her garden. "I love you like my own, but you're only making things worse by not settling down or at least *appearing* to be settling down."

Cooper looked properly chastised, his cheeks pinking in the dim lighting of the dining room. It was one thing for my father to suggest it, or even me, but for Sophia Peroni to tell you to quit being a Casanova—I guess that was the ticket to getting him to agree.

"It needs to be someone familiar," he finally said quietly. He looked across the table to me.

I nodded. "Sure, that would help. A shorthand, you could say."

Cooper's face grew redder. It wasn't very warm in the room and my mom hadn't continued pinching his cheek. I leaned forward, focusing on his face and trying to get a read on what was going through his head, because his eyes were twinkling and the dimple was deepening. I was about to speak when he uttered the words I'd never thought would leave Cooper's lips.

"Are you interested?"

9

was having a stroke.

There wasn't the smell of burning toast, though. Wasn't that the first sign? Something burning? Oh, wait—that was my face. And there was sweat. Great, now I was sweating, but why?

EMMA THOUGHT: Maybe I need to get my hearing checked. I must be hearing things.

My head felt like it was going to sizzle and pop right off my shoulders in all its red-faced glory, then roll over to my shocked parents and confused Cooper with my stunned expression immortalized forevermore because what the hell had just happened?

"I'm sorry. *What* did you say?"

Cooper's face, unlike mine, wasn't turning red but paling. Fast. Prior to my reaction it had been full of light and hope with that damnable dimple showing, and now . . . well, now he looked like someone had kicked his puppy and I was the kicker.

I didn't like it.

But I also had no idea what was going on.

"Judging by the fact that you look like you ate something bad and it's about to come shooting out *Exorcist*-style," Cooper said slowly, "I don't know if I'll be repeating the question."

Though I heard his words, I still didn't quite grasp what he'd just asked.

"I'm sorry," I finally said. "I guess I'm a cross between shocked and stupefied, considering our less-than-amicable history. I'm surprised you'd even suggest this."

"Emma," my father gently warned.

"No, no, Enrico. She's right. I just thought—never mind. It was a bad idea. Sorry I asked."

"I'm sorry—I'm not trying to be rude. I'm just genuinely in a state of confusion."

Cooper held up his hand as if to show it was no big deal. I could tell he was bothered by my reaction, but what did that matter? This was insane.

Right?

EMMA THOUGHT: Right.

"Anyway, where were we?" Cooper asked, rolling his shoulders back as if to shake the whole thing off. "I'll think about it more and we can move on, okay? Okay." He grabbed a forkful of now-cold pasta and started chewing aggressively.

That was another thing about Cooper that would forever drive me bananas. Once he was done discussing a topic, that was it. No one else could chime in.

There was a sense of awkwardness that hung over the table like a cloud, even as my parents launched into telling us where they planned on going after the election was over and the new mayor was sworn in.

With the wife-or-girlfriend subject essentially dropped for now, my father turned to pull up some wrapped posters that were leaning against the table at his feet. I'd been so lost in thought that I'd missed my mother and Cooper clearing the table and his helping her bring out dessert and coffee and place them on the sideboard. My father hauled up the signage to the table.

"Emma, do you have any thoughts on these?" he asked, holding up two sign mock-ups.

The first one was a run-of-the-mill political yard sign. ENDI-COTT FOR MAYOR was printed in red, with white and blue stars and stripes in the background. It was fine, but if I had been an average townsperson, I would have just driven past it without giving it a second look.

"Boring." I stood, walking over to take the poster from my father. "It's something you'd see anywhere in America for any government position, from school board to county clerk. Same for the other one," I said, pointing to the one held just behind the first. It was similar, just a few color changes. "Meh. You don't want *meh* for anything."

"Tell us how you really feel, Em," my father said, chuckling.

I smiled, setting it down on the now-cleared dining room table. "Hey, you asked."

Cooper grabbed it, eyes narrowing to examine it critically. Jotting a few notes on the back of it, he nodded. "Great point. You were right, Enrico. Emmanuelle," he said softly, turning toward me with a smile, "you've got an eye for this."

My eyes slid to my father, who was beaming proudly. He slapped his leg. "I told you! My girl knows her stuff. My last re-election campaign, she designed everything."

"It's not like we needed to try that hard, Dad. You were a shoo-in in the past—how many elections?"

"Don't sell yourself short, Emma," my mother said, shooting a glance toward Cooper. "You're a natural for this type of work. Between your organizational prowess, your out-of-the-box ideas, and your priceless connections all around town, you're a natural. Just like your father."

Inside, I was doing a little shimmy at the praise. Though I'd never had the drive to want to run for office myself, I did enjoy the preparation that went into a successful campaign.

"I have another, you mind?" Cooper asked in a hopeful tone. I could tell he was nervous by the way he was smiling. It was crooked, unsure.

I hadn't planned on involving myself in Cooper's campaign. Hell, this was supposed to have been my night with my mother. Not whatever the hell this was. He had my father coaching him. I'd do my civic duty and call it a day after voting.

"Last one. I have a ton of work to do tonight," I explained, ignoring my mother's pout.

At that Cooper smiled, a powerful, flirtatious tool that would make anyone's insides turn to jelly. Especially someone like me, who wasn't used to having the full extent of it used against her. Good grief.

"Last one it is," he said cheerfully, but I didn't believe him for a second. There were piles still leaning against different surfaces in the room.

"Mm-hmm." I rolled my eyes, turning my chair to face him. "Let's get this over with."

He brushed his hair out of his eyes.

My mother, of course, melted. "How could anyone even consider voting against you, Cooper? You're so handsome."

Cooper, in a rare and unexpected reaction, blushed.

"Thank you, Mrs. Peroni, but I don't think that this"—he said, motioning to his face—"is what people are voting for."

"You're not aware of your fan base," I mumbled.

Clearing my throat to break up the Cooper-does-all-things-right love fest, I signaled to my dad to get the show on the road. He turned the poster toward me, and this time, my reaction was instantaneous.

"This. Is. Perfect."

"Really?" Cooper said, sitting up straighter. His complexion brightened, making him look like a peacock preening for attention. "That was my design."

That made sense—he knew how to market himself to people.

"But—" I began.

"Of course there's a but." Cooper sighed, grabbing a Sharpie to make a note for the graphic designer on the back. "Hit me."

"Tempting, but I'd rather not touch you and contract something."

"*Emma,*" my dad admonished.

Cooper pulled a face, scrunching up his nose, but then he looked at me out of the corner of his eye and winked, making me smile. He nearly beamed. For a brief second, it was reminiscent of how we had been as kids: inseparable.

Shaking my head to bring myself back to reality, I examined the poster. This sign had the same dimensions as the first one, but it had an edge to it that made it stand out. It was what it said: ONWARD, printed in a large white font against a bold green background.

"The font for 'onward' needs to be a smidge larger, with a cleaner edge, so it stands out from a distance. I would also revise the background color—maybe go a shade darker on the green, so it's closer to the town's signature color. No one usually uses green as a background, though, so you're already ahead of the game."

Standing up from the table, my mother grabbed the largest sign and started to unwrap it. "Oh, you're so good at this! Just one more?"

"I said last one—okay, *fine,*" I conceded, mainly because she was already turning it toward me.

The outer wrap said *Billboard*. "The people of Hope Lake already see you every day—do they really need to see you on their commute to work, too?" I quipped. But with just one look, I felt my heart stop. People might actually get into an accident seeing that much Cooper from the road.

I'd never seen this photo before, but I would have remembered it if I had. Whoever had taken it deserved an award. Cooper looked political, powerful, and really damn hot: a striking combination. His usually tousled hair was styled just enough so that he looked polished but not plastic. The suit he wore was tailored to his body in such a way that it made you wonder what was beneath it. And his crisp white shirt and a tie in the same shade of green as the font reading CHOOSE ENDICOTT FOR HOPE LAKE. The image drew you in and made you not want to look away.

For once I didn't have a mouthy quip or a snarky jab to toss: Cooper had nailed it.

"Thoughts?" Cooper asked, biting his thumbnail. He crossed his arms over his chest protectively.

"Good, fine, perfect. No changes," I rattled off quickly, feeling the heat creeping into my cheeks. I simultaneously wanted to set fire to the poster and make a thousand copies to paper the town with. "It'll stand out against Rogers's new signage."

His face fell, and the thumbnail was again being worried between his teeth. "You've seen it?" Cooper asked nervously.

"Not exactly, but they'll be out soon."

"How do you know?" my father asked, stacking everything neatly and double-checking that all the posters were perfectly lined up. I got my overly orderly quirks from him.

"I saw the Rogerses at the elementary school this afternoon delivering flyers and a sign."

"Why didn't you say something earlier?" Cooper asked. "Did you see the posters? Did they look good?" He sounded annoyed. That was how I preferred him: curt and straightforward. Not muddying the waters with flirtatious smiles and pretending we were still friends. Thankfully, his tone cleared my head like a splash of cold water. We worked best when we were professional and indifferent and without my years of hang-ups clogging things up.

"For someone with zero political experience, he's coming off like he knows what he's doing," I explained, glancing over to my father for backup. "And I'm saying something now."

"Prior to running for town council, that is," my father added, rubbing a large hand over his tired face. "Kirby is considering his unopposed town-council victory as his politico boot camp."

"Listen, a win is an ego boost for anyone. But that doesn't mean he's qualified for mayor," Cooper interjected.

I swallowed a snide retort. Luckily, my father was on the same page.

"Cooper," he warned, "people could say the same thing about you and your lack of experience. Like Emma said, we need to focus the narrative on what we want and why you're qualified—not why Rogers isn't. We can't let him steer this ship."

"Yeah, well, he's somehow managed to rile up a portion of the town by making unfounded accusations about the CDO being mismanaged and funds going missing or slandering the public works guys for being 'on the take'—who says stuff like that? There hasn't been a group that he hasn't yet insulted. Why shouldn't we play just as dirty?"

"He's nudged a small but loud group to champion his cause," my mother interjected. "I hear the ladies at lunch chatting about it. There's something he's tapping into that's worrying me."

"On top of that," my father interrupted, "your charm used to work well, but now Kirby seems to have found a way to exploit it."

"I'm surprised he's not putting *that* on a yard sign," Cooper groaned, letting his head fall into his hands.

"They're too clean for that, Cooper," I chimed in. "But they're still going to be aggressive. After all, he's trying to fill the position that Mayor Dad has held for more than twenty years with little to no scandal. He's going to come at you full force."

"Damn, we're so behind," Cooper said, typing furiously into his cell phone and chewing the inside of his cheek. Another nervous habit.

"Not really. If we can solidify all changes, you can email yours to the printer tonight."

"*We?*" my mother offered, doing an awful job fighting back a smile.

"You, them, whoever. Don't listen to me, I'm not steering this ship." I waved my hand.

"Maybe you should be," Cooper said bluntly. "Why don't you run the campaign?"

"You're high." I laughed awkwardly, looking at my parents. They weren't laughing.

"This is ridiculous," I said incredulously. "First the fake dating, and now this?"

I stared at the top of his head, waiting for a punch line. Was this night a joke that everyone was in on except for me?

"Emma, I wouldn't suggest this unless I absolutely had to," Cooper said, not looking up at me.

"You can't possibly be serious."

I turned to my dad, expecting to see a teasing smile, but his expression was dead serious.

"Dad?"

"He's right, Emma," he said slowly. "It's not a half-bad idea."

Damn.

"You're both crazy to even think that I'd—"

Judging by the way they were talking with their eyes, they'd already discussed the possibility. I could tell by the way my dad took a deep breath, preparing to make the shift from conciliatory parent to mayor giving a speech: an ass-kissing politico speech meant to influence constituents, not appease angry daughters.

"Your instincts are always spot-on, Emma," he began. "You know the ins and outs of a campaign—hell, my last win was thanks to all the work you did. Besides, it'll look *slightly* less like favoritism if Cooper's old friend was leading the charge instead of his mentor, who just so happens to be the current mayor. Think of the optics." He clapped me on the shoulder like he would any constituent.

"Except"—I looked at Cooper—"we're not really friends, right? We haven't been for a long time." I could feel the old hurt bubble up. There were warring emotions in play, and I needed to get this over with.

"We work together," I added quietly. "That's the extent of our relationship. I know you," I said pointedly at my father, "don't understand *those* optics, but those are the facts. There is no

Cooper and Emma anymore. That's been gone and buried a long time, Dad. Muddying the waters with . . . with this . . . would be terrible for all of us."

Way to suck the air from the room, Emma. But it was true. Why pretend that we were something we weren't? Fake friendship or not, someone would end up getting hurt, and that person would likely be me.

My parents' expressions were a mixture of sympathy and disappointment. I understood why. My father saw so much of himself in Cooper and wanted us to rekindle our friendship, which I didn't get. At all. My father was kind and upstanding and had been in love with my mother—and *only* my mother—since he was fifteen years old. Cooper hadn't loved anything for that long. Except maybe the town, which was the only reason I had even considered supporting him for mayor in the first place. I could separate the principles of the candidate versus the lack of morals of the man. But that didn't mean I wanted to be involved directly in helping him win.

Cooper's eyes were focused back on the phone in his lap. I was about to snap at him for not paying attention when he mumbled, "The governor thought you would be the perfect choice."

"Excuse me?" I gasped, stunned. I lurched forward. "You spoke to your *mother* about this?"

It was one thing for my dad to entertain this wild idea. But for Cooper to speak to Governor Campbell about it . . . I was at a loss.

How could I say no now?

"We're just going to step into the kitchen while you two work this out," my father said, pulling my mom's hand.

"Peacefully, calmly, and without breaking Nonna's china, please," Mom added.

I put my hand up. "Oh, no. You guys are a part of this, too, in case you forgot who else agreed to this."

They both winced but sat back down. The angrier I got, the higher my voice went, and I didn't want to sound like a screeching crazy woman. I felt a familiar twisty, sick feeling building in my stomach when I looked at Cooper. Even though he looked distraught, I stood my ground.

"Explain," I barked, folding my arms over my heaving chest.

He shifted in his seat, keeping his head down. "We spoke today about strategies and how we can keep a slight lead against Rogers. She stressed that one vote can make or break a campaign, so I need to maintain a solid, consistent message to garner consistent support. She'll attend as many meet-and-greets or speeches as she can, if we think it'll help. I said it would but that I didn't have them set up yet. She asked when you were starting your campaign strategy."

"Why would she ask that?"

"I may have led her to believe that you were already on board."

"Why the hell would you do that?" I stood up abruptly from my chair and started pacing around the room, trying to calm down.

"I thought that you would agree!" he shouted. I was so angry at him that I started shaking.

"But you never even *asked* me! You know how much I respect your mother. Do you even realize the position you've put me in? How it will look for me if I say no now?" *Not to you, to her*, I wanted to add but kept it to myself.

"Then don't say no," he said hopefully. *As if it were that easy.*

"You know I can't do this, Cooper. You should never have brought me into this without asking."

My parents remained silent, hands clasped on the table, worried expressions on their faces. Cooper and I fighting was something they'd grown accustomed to. This—well, this was a different set of feelings altogether.

Cooper's hopeful smile was gone, replaced with a genuine look of desperation. "I *need* your help. We both know this lead won't last. Kirby's coming after me."

I closed my eyes and took a deep breath. My ears were ringing, my throat was itchy, and damn it, my heart wanted to give in because I *knew* that I would be a great addition to the team. But thankfully, my brain won. Taking a deep breath, I decided to stand my ground. I had to put me first. And that meant associating with Cooper Endicott only when necessary.

"You don't need me. Your name recognition alone will get you a win—just keep your nose clean and your antics off the web. As far as Rogers goes, you, my dad, and the governor will work that out. Play to your strengths. I'm sorry. I can't help you with the election."

10

_____

Bright and early Monday morning, my mood had improved slightly. I wouldn't say that I was happy, but I wasn't a walking ulcer anymore. There was only a fifty-fifty chance that I would tear someone's head off if they looked at me sideways. That was probably the best anyone was going to get today.

Fact was, I'd felt awful the past two nights, tossing and turning over whether or not to text Cooper at three in the morning. I had been harsh—deservedly so, because I hated that he'd talked me up to his mother without asking—but I could have gone a little easier on him than I had. Especially after seeing him struggle so much over the laundry list of things he still had to do and how hurt he'd been when I'd said no to helping him. I'd thought about it all through church. Sitting in the pew yesterday morning, I'd festered over whether I'd done the right thing by shutting him, and his campaign manager idea, down.

But the more I reflected on things throughout the day, the more I felt at peace with my decision about staying out of the election.

The urge to reconsider that gesture, however, flared up when I began checking my email over coffee at my kitchen counter.

From: campbell.clare@pa.state.gov
To: peronirigatoni@gmail.com
Subject: Thank you

Dear Emma,

I hope this finds you well. I understand that my son has spoken to you about his campaign. I have to tell you that when I heard you were going to help him, I was thrilled. He needs someone like you—a take-charge kind of woman who champions the work that he'll be able to do as mayor—to keep him focused on what has to be done and not get sidetracked by minutiae. You're going to make an incredible team, Emma. Be his equal partner. On and off the political circuit.

You know the old saying "Behind every great man is a great woman." This is only the beginning for him, and with you in his corner leading the way, I can't imagine how far you'll both go. We both know he'll push your buttons, but I know that you'll push right back. Without making an excuse for his behavior, know that he's coming from a good place. A place deep in his heart that knows that you're the best choice for him on this election. Even if he's not willing to admit it.

If I can share some wisdom to be kept between us: look back on how Cooper was reported on before he won the primary. The articles then were aggressive but fact-based, while today's reporting climate seems to be accusatory, debasing, and, most important, containing blatant untruths. There's a story there. Ferret it out, and I believe this mountainous uphill battle may become paved with sand instead of tacks.

From a mother first and a governor second, I thank you for what you're doing both for my son and for Hope Lake. You know how much the town means to me and to my family, just as it means so much to you and yours. I'm eager to see what you have up your sleeve as we push on in this election. My cell is below if you need me for anything.

All the best,
Clare

It had come through to my personal email address, not work, which meant that Cooper had given her my address. It had come through at four in the morning. I smiled—her hours were just as ridiculous as mine. I couldn't imagine the stress she was under on a daily basis, and now she was worrying about her only child running for local government on top of everything else.

What annoyed me, yet again, was that Cooper had had two days to come clean and tell his mother the truth. Why hadn't he told her that I had said no?

Because he's trying to get you to say yes and is shamelessly using his mother to get you to agree.

Smart plan. He knew that I respected his mother tremendously and would be hard-pressed to tell her no.

I spent the better part of an hour dissecting what all of it meant. I narrowed it down to two possibilities:

1. There is no underlying jackassery on Cooper's part, and she wrote me this email out of the goodness of her heart.
2. Cooper is employing his degree in jackassery and really wants me to help, so he's using his mother's influence and his knowledge of how much I respect her to get what he wants.

EMMA THOUGHT: This is smart on Cooper's part, and you would do the same thing.

Damn it.

ON MY WAY into Borough Building, I struggled to carry my three new projection mock-ups and a half-eaten banana for breakfast because in all my errand running over the weekend, I'd forgotten to buy milk for my Cheerios. Turned out, the delirious and exhausted Nancy *had* put the gallon of milk in the cabinet Friday night, and we had both forgotten to move it.

All in a typical Monday morning.

Speaking of Nancy, she was waiting for me with coffee when the elevator door opened on my otherwise empty floor.

She started pulling the charts from my arms, dropped them to the floor in piles, and handed me the cup that she'd put on the counter. "You're a lifesaver," I sighed gratefully.

"Remember this when you're shopping for my Hanukkah gifts in a few months," she teased, pushing me toward the receptionist's desk.

"Noted," I said as I made my way to my office.

She lingered in the doorway.

"Something up?" I asked, and took a sip of the coffee.

"We, uh, had a visitor before you got here," she replied, pulling out a file folder from under her arm. "This was taped to the front door."

I eyed the folder suspiciously. Nancy wasn't the nervous type, but something was making her edgy. The front of the folder was stamped PROOF, and I could see the telltale font of the *Hope Lake Journal,* our local newspaper, poking out from the top.

I swallowed thickly. The governor's message about the current reporting echoed through my mind.

"Did you open it yet?"

She shook her head. "But this was stuck to the front, addressed to your dad."

AS A COURTESY TO ENRICO

It was typed on the editor in chief's letterhead. A hundred scenarios presented themselves to my mind. Did it have something to do with my father? Had the paper decided to drag Mayor Dad through the mud for supporting Cooper? Maybe it was something unrelated to the campaign—but why would they deliver it as a mock-up and not just run it?

Then a feeling of dread settled in the pit of my stomach. What if it was about Cooper?

"Open it and see," Nancy said quickly. "The suspense is killing me."

As I opened the folder, the headline screamed out at me.

NEW DIRECTION FOR HOPE LAKE
ROGERS VOWS TO END FRIVOLOUS SPENDING
AND STRIP DEPARTMENTS OF OVERLAP

My blood boiled as I scanned the article. Certain words jumped out at me: Fraud. Scam. Backhanded deals. With each line, my blood pressure climbed.

"Who the hell wrote this? This is full of lies!" I shouted, grabbing a pen from the desk to underline the blatant fabrications. "We did *not* spend tax dollars on the fountain project—that was a grant that Cooper got! We busted our asses to get that money! How are they allowing this to be printed? If Rogers is behind this, it implicates the council as *also* being complicit in shady dealings, because this is *beyond* shady! Who was the editor on this? When is it running? Has anyone tried to call Peter yet?" Peter was the editor in chief of the paper, and he'd always stood by printing only the facts. At least he had until now.

Nancy stood with clenched fists, her eyes wide. "I wish I could say I can't believe they're printing this, but it's going to sell a ton of papers, so that's probably why they're running it. I'll make sure I get ahold of Peter this morning to ask him about it!"

"It's irresponsible of Peter to do this. As editor in chief, he shouldn't be publishing anything without seeing this information sourced. Had he come to my father with this, we could have provided a dozen documents showing him it's bull. Good Lord, what happened to legitimate journalism? I could say that the sky was pink with polka dots every Tuesday and that the giant spaghetti monster in the sky told me so, but that wouldn't make it true!"

Nancy grabbed the article from me, scanning it. She huffed a sigh, pointing to the last paragraph. "The freelancer claims to have sources confirming everything." She turned to me. "Did your father and Peter have a falling-out? He's always been so fair to him. Even if they disagreed in the past, he's never run anything potentially harmful against him and certainly never patently false. I'm not sure why he's letting this go to print."

I took the article back from Nancy and read it carefully, seeking out the buzzwords I knew would be in there. Sure enough, not only was it strewn with falsehoods about how my department and others within Borough Building were indiscriminately spending tax dollars, but they were also slandering my father and his years of scandal-free public service by claiming that he had received kickbacks and possibly skimmed money off his projects. They even managed to call into question his ownership of the land surrounding my family's house and where Cooper was getting his campaign money from. According to the article, the tax money claim was a part of an embezzlement scandal that went as high up as the governor.

"Has my father seen this yet? Has Cooper? Has the governor?" I asked, fumbling for my phone to call Mayor Dad. My father and Peter, like many people in Hope Lake, had gone through school together and knew each other well. They'd had some run-ins over the years about the direction of the paper, but never like this. "Shit. Straight to voice mail."

"Your dad walked in with Cooper this morning. Sun wasn't even up yet. I was outside with Larry when I saw them heading in," Nancy explained.

"I wonder if Peter sent Cooper a copy, too," I thought aloud, wondering if they were meeting to try to work up a plan of defense. "Attack ads are one thing, but being on the receiving end of an onslaught of bullshit and having to defend yourself against slander is something that no one wants to do." Especially when you were already balanced on a tenuous and fraying tightrope to begin with.

"Why is Cooper even doing this to himself? It might have been fun for him to run in the beginning, but now it just seems like he's being pummeled with a constant deluge of malicious gossip. You couldn't pay me enough to deal with that," Nancy said, fanning herself with the folder.

"The *lead-up* to the primary was fun for Cooper," I clarified, remembering the excitement surrounding his announcement. People had been thrilled that another Campbell was entering the political field, especially locally. "I think the buildup and excitement were what he thought would continue." I sent off a quick message to Cooper and my dad asking where they were. "Not all of this mudslinging."

"Hell, *I* hoped it would continue, and I wasn't even running. It looked like a blast. It's got to be hard, though, having so many love you and then turn on a dime. I thought he was moving beyond being plain old Cooper, Governor Campbell's only child and the legacy of Hope Lake, to become Cooper the politician, a relatable yet politically savvy guy."

"Maybe that's what he needs to go back to," I said, thinking about the differences between the primary and now. "More public events; volunteering; showing the town that he cares and that he wants to be involved in supporting it firsthand. If he only does positive things, the paper will have no choice but to print it."

Nancy nodded but looked skeptical. "Kirby is out for blood, though, and it looks like he's found an ally," she said. "I can't help but think this is only the tip of the iceberg."

"You're right, but there are ways around the paper: Facebook, social media, all the viral crap the kids do nowadays. Why not fight fire with fire?"

I thought about the damage the bachelorette photo could have caused had it stayed online and been leaked to the public. For now, Kirby—who so far seemed the opposite of social media savvy—was grasping at straws as far as Cooper's social life went. There were rumors, of course, but nothing concrete. Conjecture was fine until there was proof to back it up. Thankfully, Kirby hadn't been in town when the Jackson scandal had hit. Now that the election was in full

swing, I was hoping that wouldn't be dragged back up from the sew-
ers. Especially not with the Jackson family considering us again.

"What are you thinking?" Nancy asked.

I sighed. "I'm thinking of how bad this could get. There are
people out there who can make this into a total circus instead of
a political race. Cooper's an easy target. Hell, he's never hidden
the man he is. It's just a matter of when and what people find out.

"I'll be back," I Schwarzeneggered.

I took the emergency stairwell instead of waiting for the elevator, bouncing down the stairs with my phone and the proof. By
the time I got to the landing on the first floor, the wheels in my
head had started turning.

Walking a bit more calmly now that I had a plan, I stepped
into my father's deserted hallway but stopped dead when I saw
who had just stepped out of my father's office.

I hadn't seen Whitney Andrews in years, but I would have recognized her anywhere. She hadn't changed at all. Her long blond
hair was still blown out in perfect waves. She was still as well put
together as ever, every bit the high-powered attorney in her fitted
black suit and Louboutin heels.

Whitney had been my first college roommate, best friend, and
part of the reason that my friendship with Cooper had imploded
so many years ago. I didn't know what she was doing there, but if
I had to guess, given the early hour, she'd stayed in town last night
after a drive over from Philadelphia.

With Cooper, most likely.

*Is she here because of the conversation we had at my parents'
about his love life?* I wondered. Cooper and Whitney had a long
shared history. They'd met during my first family weekend in college, when Cooper, Henry, and Nick had joined my parents for
the festivities. Whitney and Cooper had hit it off and ended up
dating for a few months.

And he'd never told me.

Had I not walked in on them one night, I'd likely never have known. So after freshman year, I had requested a new roommate. Seeing them together wasn't exactly enhancing my college experience. It seemed silly, maybe, but I wanted no part of their relationship, whatever it was or wasn't.

Why is she here?

Why do I care?

Straining to listen to the low murmurs still coming from my father's office, I waited until Whitney disappeared down the hallway and into the corridor near the elevator before I tiptoed toward the door.

The large oak door was ajar, a thin stream of light falling onto the patterned carpet outside. "Cooper, son," my father was saying, his voice taking on the tone he'd used with me only a few times in my life. He saved it for when I had done something monumentally stupid, which, thankfully, wasn't often.

In Cooper's case, he used it a lot.

"You need to make changes. Look at this article! I feel like this is only the beginning. I know you know this, but you don't seem to actually *get* it. Every little thing you do will be used against you. Anything that even *remotely* seems like it could be detrimental has to be nixed. Your friend Whitney is right. I'm glad you've brought her in to help."

Cooper mumbled something that I couldn't make out. I heard a laptop close and a chair scoot back over the floor. I moved from the carpet runner to the sliver of hardwood right in front of my father's office, so my footsteps would announce my arrival. I heard my father clear his throat just before I walked in. They were both staring wide-eyed at the door. *Maybe they expect Whitney to reappear.*

They visibly relaxed upon seeing me, the air leaving them in a *whoosh*.

"Emma, good morning. What are you doing down here? And so early," my father said, pulling me into a hug. "Go easy on him," he whispered, too low for Cooper to hear.

"Am I interrupting?" I gave my father a sidelong glance, trying to read his expression. It was closed off, like shutters were drawn over his emotions. There was no way for me to glean anything from his silence. Had I not overheard the bits of their conversation, I would have had no idea what I'd just walked into.

"We were just finishing up," Cooper explained, walking behind me to close the door. "I've got another meeting to run to in a few minutes."

"Yeah, I bet," I mumbled.

"What?" he asked, his eyebrows furrowing.

Maybe he sensed the shift into argument territory, but my father changed the subject. "You got one, too?" he asked, gesturing to the folder in my hand. He walked around the desk to hold up his own proof.

"Has Peter said anything about this, Dad?"

Shaking his head, he took a seat behind the desk. "No, and I've called *and* emailed. I'm about to walk down the street and knock on his front door."

Cooper looked to my father nervously before clearing his throat. "If these headlines keep running—"

"—they'll do irreparable damage," I finished, stepping around him to stand by the window.

The breeze ruffled the thin drapes. This room held so many memories for me, from my childhood through getting a job here right out of college.

Turning to look at Cooper, I thought about his taking up residence in this office someday. Would he be able to hold himself to the standard that my father had for all these years? My father had been the mayor for the better part of my life—could Cooper be the mayor for that long? Did he have twenty-six years of scandal-free governing ahead of him? Could he command respect and treat everyone fairly—do everything necessary to ensure that Hope Lake continued to thrive and blossom to its full potential?

The answer to that wasn't exactly black and white, but I did believe that he was far better suited for the job than the alternative.

I couldn't imagine someone like Kirby sitting in this office. He was shallow and malignant and, from what I'd witnessed the other day at the press conference, willfully ignorant. And this office meant a lot to me. I'd practically grown up in here. I'd colored pictures on the floor when I was in preschool, I'd pretended to be the mayor during "take your child to work day," and the desk, unbeknown to anyone except my father, still had a collection of crayon drawings beneath it from when Cooper and I were seven. One year we'd ditched the babysitter who was watching us while our parents attended a small holiday party upstairs and drawn a picture of ourselves holding hands on the underside of the desk.

No matter how much Cooper infuriated me, I couldn't let Kirby win this office. I was going to go through with my plan.

I turned, looking at them both sitting in pained silence.

Cooper looked like he'd been through the wringer. Whether it was just this newspaper article, the campaign in general, or some other force that was causing him to look stricken, I didn't know. I was trying not to care, but I kept thinking back to the article that would run tomorrow. The newspaper proof was rolled in my hand. I hated that it carried so much power.

Tossing the paper onto the desk, I said, "I've got some things to work out. Cooper, enjoy your *meeting,* then come find me before you leave for the day. We have to talk." With that I shut the door behind me as I headed back to my office.

Deep down, I knew what I had to do—I just needed to work up the gumption to do it. On the way back up to my office, I pulled out my phone.

I typed a response to the governor, telling her that I would help however I could.

Then I started a list of requirements that I would take to Cooper. If I was going to do this—be his campaign manager—he would need to toe the line. I had conditions, and if they were not met, there was no point in my even entertaining the idea.

I just hoped I wouldn't regret it.

11

My day had gone from bad to worse. Just a few minutes after leaving Mayor Dad's office, I found an email waiting in my inbox stating that the town council had rejected the theater proposal. The one I'd spent my entire Friday night working on. And their reason was bogus: budgetary concerns. The decision had Kirby written all over it, and it only reinforced my choice to help Cooper.

Just after lunch, Nancy popped into my office, carrying another cup of coffee for each of us.

"Hey, how goes it?" I asked.

She smiled dreamily. "Got to talk to Javier about three in the morning. I'm exhausted but so damn happy."

That explained the tired yet lovesick eyes. One of the things that I needed to get better at was making sure that I wasn't monopolizing her time, especially on the weekends. Just because I was a crazy workaholic didn't mean that I had to turn Nancy into one, too.

"Why is it so quiet?" I asked, scoping out the empty office.

"Cooper treated everyone downstairs to ice cream after lunch—he asked if you and I wanted to come, but you were on the phone. He brought you back an Emma Special—it's in the freezer," she explained, and I didn't miss the faint smile. "It seems he's already listening to your advice. We've got the place to ourselves for at least a little while—something that's *way* better than ice cream."

I haven't given him any advice yet. Why the thoughtfulness?

"Why didn't you go? Larry loves Viola's," I teased, expecting to hear his little nails clicking across the hardwood. Since adopting him, Nancy let Larry spend a few days a week with her in the office, since otherwise he'd be too lonely by himself all day: just one of the perks of working for an organization that cared about *all* of Hope Lake's citizens, including its four-legged ones.

"He's snoring away under my desk. We had an early-morning vet appointment after the call with Javier. He's still recovering."

"I was wondering why he didn't follow you in here."

"I think he's embarrassed about his cone of shame. He's barely tolerating me today."

"Cone?" I began, but the reason dawned on me. "He was fixed today. Poor baby. I'll get him some treats later and drop them off."

"Before I forget, how do you feel about this?" she asked, unrolling one of the sheets that she'd brought to my desk earlier to reveal some color sketches. Whenever I worked on a big project, I needed someone else to doctor them up because my rudimentary drawings weren't going to win us any contracts. Nancy, on the other hand, had an eye for detail and was always ready to take on more responsibility and help out the team.

EMMA THOUGHT: Nancy could be Cooper's replacement. YES!

"Excellent. I know that being an assistant is boring, but I have some ideas to get you more involved. I'm cautiously optimistic, but if this new plan works out—"

She squeezed my shoulder. "I appreciate whatever it is: trust me."

WHEN EVERYONE HAD CLOCKED OUT for the day, I called Cooper to ask him to come to my office. I felt a bit like a principal calling up a misbehaving student. I suppose, in a lot of ways, that was accurate. He asked if he should bring my father, but I insisted that this matter was best discussed just between us. If Cooper wasn't amenable to my suggestions, there was no reason to involve Mayor Dad.

Within a few minutes he was in my office, seated by the window across from my desk and staring out at the town below. "You really did get the best office in this building," he remarked, placing a hand on the oak window trim. It didn't sound like jealousy, more like reverence: something I wasn't used to hearing from Cooper. From my office at the back corner of the building, you could see miles of trees that lined up as an infinity pool would. The gorgeous view certainly helped when you were a workaholic and always in your office.

He turned to me, crossing his arms over his chest in a protective way. His light green shirt was unbuttoned at the collar and looked sharp against his gray dress pants. He would have looked business casual, since he was without the jacket, and relaxed if it hadn't been for the tense position of his arms. His light brown hair was mussed in that just-so fashion that always made him look like he'd rolled out of bed after a night of fun.

If he were going to be mayor, he would have to work on keeping his appearance a little more accessible. *More everyday man,* I noted. Cooper, for his part, was just sitting there and waiting. I didn't know if he was waiting for a response to his comment or just for me to start.

Clearing my throat, I pulled out the piece of paper that I'd worked on all morning. It was strewn with notes, some crossed out, some drawn over to make them stand out. They were important points that I just *had* to remember.

"I've been thinking about our conversation from the other day," I began, sliding my chair out and getting up from my desk to pace. I padded across the carpet without my heels on. The squishy feeling of the carpet helped me think. I glanced down at my hot-pink toenails against the navy rug, pausing to shore up my thoughts. "You asked me for help the other day," I said simply.

He nodded, and I watched his lip twitch. "I did . . ."

Clutching the note in my hand, I glanced at it to make sure I was staying on track for this conversation.

"I've been thinking. I wouldn't forgive myself if I thought I could make a difference in your campaign and didn't try. If I say yes to this wild idea of yours to help you, Cooper—as your campaign manager, by the way, *not* as your fake girlfriend—I'm in charge." I rolled my shoulders back, injecting some confidence into my spine. *This is like any other negotiation,* I told myself. It didn't matter that the person on the other end of that negotiation was Cooper or that my helping him could cloud our already strained working relationship. I couldn't lose sight of the bigger picture.

He straightened and smiled. "You're in charge. Done."

"But no one can know it."

"What do you mean?" he asked, looking confused. His brows furrowed and his nose scrunched up as he worked out what I was saying. "You'd be the campaign manager, right? Everyone would know that you're in charge. It wouldn't exactly be something we could hide."

"Yes and no. I'll be calling the shots, but as far as anyone on the outside would know, I'm not involved at all. We need people's focus to remain on you: your goals, your platform, and whatever else we want them to pay attention to. I don't want their focus to be on me. They'd skew my position as your campaign manager as giving you an unfair advantage somehow and come after me, you, and my father, and that's not something that I'm willing to let happen. It's bad enough that someone is putting this bullshit in the paper. I have a distinct feeling that this isn't a onetime deal. They'll continue digging, and when they can't find anything, they'll make stuff up. And I'm not going to risk my father's twenty-six-year-long scandal-free career ending with him being slandered because they think he's been pulling strings somehow." I paused to let him take that all in.

"Think about it: if we go public with me as your campaign manager, it could be read as Mayor Peroni trying to further his agenda without necessarily being the mayor. He'd just be the Stromboli to your Pinocchio."

Cooper nodded imperceptibly, and stood. "I can honestly say I have no idea what that means, but okay, I see your point—no one will know. What are the rules and regulations I have to follow, Captain?" he asked lightly, pausing in his circling to try to lighten the mood.

This is off to a roaring start.

I leveled him with a look that said, *Sarcasm is not welcomed here.* "Again, I'm in charge. Not you, not my dad, not my mother, not Governor Campbell or anyone from her team: me. We'll confer with our families for important decisions to get their opinions, but not on everything, every day. If that's what they wanted, they should have volunteered to do this themselves—and I'm the one running this campaign now."

"Okay, so you're in charge. That's easy enough—what else?" he said quickly, so much so I wondered if he was afraid I'd change my mind if he didn't immediately agree.

"You say that now. I haven't even told you what I expect you to do."

Cooper waved his arm for me to continue, smartly keeping his sly remarks to himself.

"You need to take a leave of absence from the CDO."

The words hung in the air. Cooper, at least before the campaign, loved his job. Almost as much as I loved mine, but something had to give. He wasn't focused on anything here anymore, and it was showing. If he was serious about running for mayor— and winning—he would need to give something up.

He looked uneasy, as if I had just ripped the rug out from under him. I suppose technically I had. "You mean—"

"I mean, you need to take a bit of a sabbatical for this. Just until the election is over. It's not that long. If you win, you'll have to leave anyway. Plus, really, it will help me in the long run to be able to keep you one hundred percent focused on campaign work, not on campaign work and CDO work on top of it."

He scratched his chin thoughtfully. "That doesn't make sense. Why wouldn't you just keep me on because I'm here to help you? One less person means more work for everyone."

I laughed softly, shaking my head. "Cooper, when was the last time you were in the office for a full day?"

He stayed silent, but I could tell by the puzzled expression on his face that he couldn't come up with the answer.

"August first," I answered myself, pulling out a stack of papers and file folders. "This is everything that you're supposed to be helping me with but, because of the campaign, you haven't. Emails go unanswered, phone calls are transferred to me to work out because you're pulled in too many directions—unfortunately, the job that pays you has been what's suffering. I've been cleaning up as much as I can, but if I'm going to help you win this thing, I need to hire someone who'll be able to actually help me here. Not dump everything onto me at the last second. I need me time, too."

"You want me to quit? What if I don't win? Then I'll be unemployed!" he exclaimed, raking his hands through his hair. I could tell that convincing him might take a little bit of my own political savvy.

"Not quit," I explained calmly. "Take a leave of absence. That way, I can get the help I need in the interim and you can get the time you need to focus on the campaign. Besides, you don't *need* to work, Cooper. You're not exactly living paycheck to paycheck."

It was one of the perks of being a member of Hope Lake's legacy family: Cooper had access to *years* of family money.

"I know that, but I like to work," he explained. "I like knowing that I'm a part of something that will outlast me."

"Nancy deserves a promotion, and if you step aside to let her have it, we can hire a new support person to help us out—just someone temporary until after the election. Nancy already knows this department inside and out; it's a natural next move for her. Besides, you can spin it like you're creating jobs and you're not even the mayor yet."

A laugh bubbled up. "You're brilliant sometimes. You know that, right?" he offered.

"Let me finish my thought before you sing my praises. Let's get back to the ground rules."

He nodded, pretending to get ready to jot down the list.

"We'll only tell people we trust implicitly about me running the campaign: Nick, Henry, obviously our parents, but no one else. That means we need to be careful with meeting each other, especially since you won't be working in the office anymore. Agreed?"

"Agreed," Cooper said, relief flooding his face. "This could be good for strategy, too. If people don't know you're working with me, they might gossip in front of you. Maybe we'll learn a thing or two about what people are expecting from the campaign, figure out how to get their votes and cast some doubt about Kirby." Though he was right, it didn't sit well with me.

"I'm not a fan of overt duplicity," I began, uncomfortable about the idea of using my coworkers to influence the campaign. "Even though you're not running against someone who plays fair, I think us being shady isn't the right play here, either. For now we start with the facts, and right now, people think you're not serious enough to do this. It's not just your personal antics—which have to stop, Cooper, or I walk—but also the fact that you haven't exactly been forthcoming about what your goals or plans are. There's no substance. No platform. The constituents want meat and potatoes, not fluff and baloney."

Cooper was nodding at my every word. He looked like a bobblehead doll.

"Are you listening or just agreeing to get me to shut up?"

His eyes widened. "I'm listening. I promise I'm taking this seriously. What else?"

"You need that girlfriend."

Famous last words.

12

Two weeks later, I was still getting used to my new routine at the office. Here by seven, meetings beginning at eight sharp. With everything now going through me and no longer divided between myself and Cooper, I was at the office even longer than usual. Sometimes I didn't leave until after eight. Then afterward, no matter how tired I was, I went home to continue working on Cooper's life, campaign, and everything in between. It wasn't bad per se, just different and a bit exhausting. Nothing I couldn't handle once I got used to it.

"Knock, knock," Cooper said from my doorway. I looked up from answering an email to see him leaning against the doorjamb. His navy tie was loosened, and the top button of his shirt was undone. He looked a bit weary—red-faced and sweaty, probably from all of the walking he had done this afternoon. The fall heat wave we were having wasn't helping the situation.

"I need a break," he groaned, taking a handkerchief from his pocket and blotting his forehead. He closed the door, leaning against it. "This is exhausting. You didn't include time for lunch"—he checked his watch—"or dinner. Did you realize that when you made me this hellish schedule?"

"Oh, poor Cooper," I mimicked his whining tone. "It was

just—what today?" I thought back to the campaign calendar I'd created. "Senior center, church council meeting, road crew updates with the mayor, and the Boy and Girl Scout meeting, right?"

"You say it like it wasn't exhausting," he groused, frowning and clearly expecting sympathy.

"It's working, isn't it?"

"Speaking of working, I miss being here. No one seems to miss me," he said with a sigh.

Oh, but they were. The office wasn't the same without him. At least not for me. I couldn't quite place the feeling, but without him the place felt *off*. It was quiet without the throwing of the tennis ball, and I strangely missed seeing his hurricane of a desk now that Nancy was sitting there. Not to mention that his showing up here today had people talking and *casually* walking by my office on their way out the door to sneak a peek at him.

"What are you doing here?" I checked the small pocket calendar that I kept in my purse at all times. His activities weren't in my phone or anywhere in my laptop or on the work calendar. I kept them hidden away where no one could see them. Just in case. It was likely overkill, but I wasn't taking any chances that someone would tie me to the campaign. "You're supposed to be heading to senior bingo at St. Pete's Parish Center right now, remember?"

"Do you have anything to eat in here?"

"No, and please answer the question. I'm very busy."

He pushed off from the door, coming to lean in front of me with his arms stretched out on my desk. "I wanted to talk to you about the bingo. Well, a lot of stuff that you've got me doing, actually. Especially with the seniors." At that he smirked, rolling his lips together as he tried to fight back a smile.

Oh, no. I knew that look. This was either very good or very, very bad.

"Cooper, you promised to take this seriously. You being the bingo caller is a great way for you to be involved in a community event that hosts a lot of influential voters. They're expecting you tonight. To listen to them about what they'd like to see done. Hear their gripes. Assess their needs. This is the ideal time for you to bring up your thoughts about their monthly activities and how you would be able to help them achieve their goals if you're mayor. Talk about the proposal for building the outdoor theater in the park. That's something they'd love to have here."

Not to mention the fact that the senior ladies' group was very talkative around town. "If you brought any of this up, they'd disseminate it for you in a natural way. Keep them on your side."

"We need them to love you."

Cooper threw his head back and laughed, deep and raspy. I watched his Adam's apple bounce as he chuckled. "Oh, they love me, all right. They also think I'm ten years old."

It was my turn to curl my lips together. Mrs. Mancini, the leader of the seniors' group, was a card. Widowed for many years, she prided herself on being a little off the wall. "They're eccentric," I told him.

"They made me peanut butter and jelly this morning at the center."

"So?"

"They cut the crust off."

"And?"

"They gave me goldfish crackers."

"You don't like goldfish crackers?"

"Ask me what my drink was."

Playing along, I asked, "Cooper, honey. What did the nice senior citizens give you to drink?"

"Funny. They gave me a big glass of milk. Whole milk! I don't even know the last time I drank milk!" he said, exasperated.

"I'm waiting to hear what the problem is? You're still hungry, is that it? You said I didn't give you time to be fed. I don't see a problem with them feeding you. It's not gourmet enough? Snob."

He threw his hands up in the air. "Yes, I *am* starving, but that's not the point. They'll be at the church hall later and are bringing me macaroni and cheese for dinner."

"There you go, problem solved."

He continued, ignoring me. "They wanted me to play cards. One of them asked me if I was a Boy Scout. What does that have to do with anything? I thought I was supposed to be answering constituent questions and discussing my ideas. Are you sure we're going in the right direction?"

He'd hit the nail on the head. It was a part of my plan: to reintroduce him to the town as Cooper Campbell-Endicott, the mayoral candidate who cared about Hope Lake's citizens—not just Cooper, Governor Campbell's only son, or Cooper Endicott, codirector of the CDO. Or Coop, the guy who'd romanced half the town's available female population and left a trail of broken hearts behind. That was the version we needed to make people forget or at least convince them that he'd changed. Or simply grown up.

"I wanted you to start with the seniors because they're influential. Going to bingo tonight will kill two birds with one stone. You saw some seniors this morning at the center, and you'll get the rest tonight at the church hall. They talk, all day long. You can hear what they're kvetching about. Use that to focus on what they care about. You're showing people that you're in tune with the community *and* that you're actually interested in their day-to-day lives, which they appreciate and will talk about. That's what we want."

"It just feels like it's a waste of time. Why can't I just ask them what they want?" he asked, rolling his eyes. "I basically ate with them, and now I'm going to call a few bingo games. How does that help me win the election?"

I held up the campaign calendar. "It's not a waste. It's not overt but covert. Trust me."

"I do," he said, still sounding unconvinced. "I guess I don't see the point if they're just going to treat me like a kid."

"I understand that plight, probably more than you realize. They still see both of us as children of powerful political parents. While that's not necessarily a bad thing, some people can't quite separate the fact that we grew up." I was happy to see him nodding his head.

"But it works in your favor. Just after you left the center, Mrs. Mancini called my mother. You're going to be seeing a lot of her. She's volunteered to be on the campaign committee. Same goes for the elder Dr. Bishop and a few other seniors you met with today. That's what I'd hoped for, Cooper. These visits work, whether you agree with them or not."

"Really?" he said, but he didn't sound convinced. "Mancini's probably volunteering just to keep trying to fix me up with someone. I could barely get a word in edgewise today without her shouting 'What about my granddaughter?' from her seat."

"Oh, yeah?" I paused. *Well, you do need a girlfriend . . .*

"I see the wheels turning," he said, interrupting my thoughts. "She's a runner, like me, tall, also like me, loves the outdoors, card games, and dancing."

"Like you," I finished.

"Yes, sounds perfect, right?"

I schooled my features, plastering on a bright smile. "Yes, actually."

"She's a sophomore. *In high school.*"

"Oh," I breathed. "Yeah, not good."

"No! But she's nothing if not persistent. I'm starting to see why Enrico has been hammering me about finding someone serious."

I stood, slipping my feet into my shoes. Walking around the desk, I leaned against it to be next to Cooper.

"I wanted to talk to you about that, actually," I said.

He straightened to his full height, towering over me. Good thing I wasn't intimidated by his size. Staying in my position, I looked out toward the door. This topic had been tough enough to discuss the first time. For me to bring it up again was surely going to be awkward.

"Talk about what? I've been doing everything you've said. I've followed every direction," he sputtered, coming across defensively.

"Fixing you up," I blurted out, forcing my eyes to stay forward.

"That's the one part of my campaign plan we still need to put into action. While people's opinions are starting to come around, you're still seen as a playboy, and that's never good, Cooper. I just over-heard two women gossiping at the pizza place the other day be-cause they saw you on the news. And it wasn't about your campaign plans—frankly, it was the opposite of what we need them to think when they first see you. It can't be 'I hope he's great in the sack.'"

I hazarded a glance up at him. He had turned and was fo-cused on the wall behind my desk now. A credenza was against it, filled with photos, a similar setup to what my father had in his office two floors down. The photos might have been different, but the intent was the same: to share our best moments with anyone who came into the office.

One was a double frame of my parents and me. On one side was a photo from when I had graduated valedictorian from Hope Lake High; on the other was one from my magna cum laude graduation from the University of Pennsylvania. A silver filigree frame had one of me, Nick, Henry, and Cooper from the nature preserve before we'd left for college. We'd been taking turns sail-ing off a tire swing and landing in the still chilly lake below. Many of the other photos that lined the credenza were of the four of us: different scenes throughout our lives, when things had been simpler and less complicated among us.

But my favorite was from the first summer the four of us had been back home permanently, when we had planned the annual Fourth of July festival. It seemed like just yesterday, but when I did the math, I realized it had been just over six years before. It was actually the only photo on the table that was of just Cooper and me. We were lounging on a blanket in the middle of the park as fireworks exploded in the darkening sky. His arms were out-stretched behind him, and I was leaning on his shoulder as we faced away from the camera.

"Who took this?" he asked, walking over to it and holding up the dark frame.

I smiled, remembering finding it on my desk one morning so many years ago. "Your dad. He gave it to me the day you started working here."

"Really? I've never noticed it before," he said wistfully, setting it back down. "I thought someone took a photo, but you—"

"Said that it was the flash from the fireworks," I said, smiling at his expression of wonder.

"It came with a message, too," I explained, remembering the card attached to the frame.

"What did it say?" When he turned, he had an odd expression on his face.

"'Always remember the good times,'" I said, smiling at the memory. It was a simple enough saying, yet it was something I often forgot.

Especially when it came to Cooper.

"What were we talking about?" I asked, trying to bring the conversation back to less nostalgic topics. Walking down memory lane with Cooper never did me any good.

"I believe you mentioned fixing me up."

How could I forget?

"What are you thinking? Match? Winks? Whatever the apps are that find me the love of my life in thirty questions or less?" he said sarcastically, sliding his annoyed gaze over to me.

I turned, adjusting the hem of my lavender blouse, which had rolled up over my skirt waistband. His eyes followed my hands as they smoothed it. "No, I don't think an app is what we need here."

"So then what?"

"This may sound like it's coming out of left field," I said, going back around to sit at my desk. Looking up at him, I could see the worry in his eyes, wondering what the hell I was going to suggest. "I'm thinking that the best option is to dive into your little black book."

It was as if every sound in the building had stopped simultaneously. The buzzing of the fluorescent lights, the copier running down the hall, the *click-clack* of shoe heels in the hallway. Nothing. It was complete silence except for the slight fish noise Cooper was making, his mouth opening and closing like a trout's.

"You're kidding," he said finally, sinking into the leather seat in front of my desk. He looked stunned, and I suppose that's exactly what he was. When I thought about it, I sat much like he was, trying to work out if it was the right move. Nothing else seemed feasible in the time that we needed it to.

"Hear me out," I began, pulling out my notebook of thoughts. The word *familiar* was circled, traced over, and had lines shooting out of the top of it, reminding me that it was the key here.

"You've dated. A lot."

He shifted in his seat, as if he was uncomfortable with the line of questioning. Which was funny because Cooper was never shy about his conquests. In fact, Cooper wasn't shy about anything. Usually.

"I've dated, yes."

"A lot," I repeated, more for my own reminder than his. That was the part of his life that we needed to address to get the conservative voters on board.

"Your point?"

"We can't have you prancing around with someone new. The voters will see right through that. You need someone you're familiar with and, more important, who's familiar with you. Your quirks, your habits, your . . . likes and dislikes. Preferably someone you still keep in touch with from the past. Someone who lasted longer than five minutes."

His chest puffed out, and he winked. There was a flash of the toothy smile. "*I* last longer than five minutes."

I bit the inside of my cheek and closed my eyes. For the briefest of seconds, I let my mind consider a snappy retort before I lassoed it back into a safe space. "This is the opposite of how this conversation has to go. Cut the shit, Cooper. Focus."

He shook his head as if to clear it. "Okay, undivided attention."

"Let's forget for a minute that I'm a woman and that your natural default seems to be to flirt. Voters aren't going to be charmed by your blatantly suggestive behavior. Maybe a handful will, but that's not what we're going for. This has got to stop. You're not going to win anyone over by acting like a horndog all the damn time."

He was taken aback, looking shell-shocked at my aggressive tone. "I'm sorry," he said. "You're right, it's not appropriate."

"I'm not asking you to be a monk. I'm just asking you to think before you say something that is questionable. If you said the same thing you just said to me to anyone else, it would land you in a heap of trouble. Not to mention the fact that it would be splashed across the newspaper and social media."

"You're right. I apologize." He ran a hand through his already mussed hair. "I didn't really consider—I'm sorry."

We lapsed into an uncomfortable silence while I decided if I believed him. I sighed. "Accepted. Now we need to get back to the topic at hand: diving into your black book. We need to go through the list of possible girlfriends together. Narrow it down to the right person for the job."

His mood shifted, his nose flaring in annoyance. "No."

"Cooper," I chided, trying to impress upon him the gravity of the idea.

"No."

"I'm serious."

"No, Emma. You're not getting that kind of information. I'll find someone—as you pointed out—who's suitable."

"You said you needed my help, Cooper. This is me helping you." My voice pitch rose. I wasn't in the mood to rehash the arrangement.

"I did ask you for help!" he shouted, throwing his hands in the air. "You were horrified by the thought, remember?"

My heart jumped. Once, then twice, remembering his hopeful face that night at dinner when he'd suggested that I pose as his girlfriend. "I wasn't . . . it's just not . . . you didn't let me explain. It just wouldn't look right for the same reason people can't know that I'm running the campaign."

"You're the boss of the election. *This* isn't the campaign. This is you poking around in my personal life and relationships. A territory that you've made clear you find repugnant. These are the lives of women I've been involved with, and I . . . I can't go there with you. That is nonnegotiable. I'll do anything else you want, but I'm not going through my past with you."

I nodded and remained quiet until I calmed down, my eyes trained on the crumpled paper on my desk.

I hated that I felt like I'd overstepped. Obviously Cooper was stressed. *Maybe I shouldn't push the issue?*

But then I remembered that it wasn't just me who thought it was a good idea. Virtually everyone thought Cooper needed to appear more stable in the love department. I needed to stick to my guns. But before I could tell him as much, he spoke.

"Do you need anything more from me?" he asked, standing tall and walking to the door. Clearly he was finished with this conversation even though I wasn't.

"Remember, you're meeting with the campaign staff tonight."

"Where?"

"Mrs. Mancini's, after your last event today. I know you're swamped, but she offered to host. We need to discuss the upcoming debate at Hope Lake High. Especially making sure that you're prepared for more off-the-wall questions."

"I'll be there."

And with that he was gone.

13

First of all, I'd like to thank you all for coming," I greeted the group, handing out packets holding campaign information. It was every bit of knowledge and then some that I could put into a folder. "I realize we don't have a ton of time, but I think this is broken down into enough bite-size pieces that among all of us, we can really make a huge impact on the election."

When we had been deciding which trustworthy people we could approach to ask for help with Cooper's campaign, a number of residents had come to mind. We hadn't wanted the group to become unwieldy, so we'd pared it back to a half-dozen people I could trust not to spill the beans about my running the show: Nick and Henry, because they were as trustworthy as they came; my mother, because there was no way she wasn't going to be included in something involving Cooper. My mother, because she couldn't be left out of anything, and Mrs. Mancini's next-door neighbor and equally hilarious senior citizen, the elder Dr. Bishop. And Mrs. Mancini herself, of course. If it was just those people, my, and now my mother's, involvement would be kept out of the public eye. I trusted that no one would share that information with anyone outside of the group.

We were having the meeting at Mrs. Mancini's house because it was out of the way and she'd offered. Plus she was a hard woman to say no to.

Mrs. Mancini, surprising no one, was a huge fan of hosting. Her house was on the opposite end of town from my parents'. Whereas they were on the mountainside, she was on the lakeside, nestled into the woods beside it with only one other house nearby. Dr. Bishop, our former town physician, lived next door and was graciously helping us, even though she was well on into her eighties. A staunch political maven who had helped campaign for everyone from U.S. presidential candidates to my mom for the PTA, she'd provided me with a number of helpful ideas when I'd met with her the week before. Her son, the current Dr. Bishop, was here, too, partially helping us and partially keeping his eighty-eight-year-old mother out of trouble. If she hadn't been here, she'd have been on QVC buying food dehydrators or power tools. Her house could double as an appliance store.

"Okay, everyone, let's call this meeting to order! If you take a look at your individual tasks, you'll see that the tasks are broken up by type and by week. Not everyone will be active each week, but every task will be. Cooper, it's imperative that you follow yours to the letter. We've only got six weeks before election day."

He raised his hand. "Yes, Cooper?" I asked, shuffling pages around in my file.

"Thank you, Miss Peroni," he addressed me formally. When he'd walked in, it was apparent that he was still miffed by our black book conversation earlier. "Why are there photos of me from the Easter egg hunt in here for distribution?" he asked, holding one up as if it were evidence in a trial.

I curled my lips in to smother a laugh. It was one of my favorite days from last year. My father was supposed to be in the bunny suit for the Lions Club's annual Easter egg hunt, but he hadn't been feeling well. Since the younger Dr. Bishop hadn't thought it was wise for an ill sixty-year-old to be sweating in a heavy fur-lined bunny suit all day, Cooper had offered to fill in.

Everything that could go wrong did. The bunny head had fallen off just as a toddler was about to sit on his lap. The sight of Cooper had made her explode with tears, howling and crying until her mother had come running over. Of course, at some point in his life, Cooper had dated and jilted the mother, so that had earned him a slap in the face.

Add in the fact that he sat in melting chocolate so his pristine white bunny suit had a big chocolate ass. Overall, it had made the bunny portion of the day a categorical failure—yet it had humanized him in a way that the whole of Hope Lake appreciated.

"It makes you relatable," I explained, holding the photo up for everyone to see. "People think you're just Cooper Endicott, great-great-great-—you know how many greats it is—grandson of Montgomery Campbell and the heir to the Campbell legacy. You grew up in the biggest house on the hill. Your mother is the governor. Not to mention the fact that you dress . . . well, like that," I said, waving at his outfit. "People think you're out of touch. Something like this shows just how much you care about the town and the people who live here. Prior to running for mayor, you were always volunteering, yet no one knew it. I'm not saying we EDtv you and document everything you've ever done or are doing, but we need to construct a carefully crafted message showing people that the Cooper they know—the one who grew up here, the one who moved back here after college, the one who's dedicated his life to public service and the betterment of the town—is the one who's running. Not this caricature that Kirby is painting of you."

"Wait," Cooper said, holding up his hand again. "What's wrong with the way I dress?"

I shook my head and shrugged. "Nothing at all. But you're in a very expensive suit all the time. It probably costs what I pay in rent. If I'm noticing that, someone like Kirby is going to notice it as well and use it against you. He'll say that it shows you're out of sync with everyone else because you're a Campbell and that you can't relate to Hope Lake's citizens or their needs because of that. He'll flip the narrative against you. Instead of the Campbell name being a selling point, it'll be a liability as long as he's writing the copy."

"You're always so buttoned up, Cooper," Mrs. Mancini added. "Loosen up a little. You need to come down a couple pegs to the rest of us." She motioned for him to loosen the tie.

Cooper laughed, holding up his hands in mock surrender. "Okay, okay, I'll loosen up."

As if to prove a point, he tossed his bespoke jacket to the side and untucked his oxford shirt. In doing so, he showed off his toned, muscular stomach, making Mrs. Mancini blush. The elder Dr. Bishop whistled, her dentures popping out briefly.

"Hey, now, come on," Cooper called out, getting red in the face. "We're supposed to be changing the narrative, remember?" He shook out his arms and unbuttoned the cuffs of his sleeves before rolling them up.

Inexplicably, my mouth dried up. I had never paid attention to his forearms before, what with their ropy muscles and dusting of light brown hair. "Um, wh-where were we?" I stammered, trying to look away without it being obvious.

Judging by the way Mrs. Mancini was grinning, I assumed that I hadn't been successful.

BEFORE COOPER LEFT FOR THE NIGHT, I pulled him into Mrs. Mancini's small sewing room. I tugged the pocket doors shut and laid out the goals for the debate at the high school on Wednesday. Hopefully it would be a way for him to engage the teachers, the students, and the students' parents all at once.

"You've got the talking points memorized, I hope?" I asked, holding up the sheet with the bullet points of Cooper's key ideas listed. "We don't know what Kirby said to the teachers, but we can't worry about that. We just need for you to make him look like an unqualified A-hole and focus on getting your message across loud and clear."

"A-hole?" he said, laughing. "Did you really just call him an A-hole?"

"If the shoe fits. I'm not saying to call him that while you're onstage, but you've got a big brain. Make it work. Relay the message. You can do this."

"That was the nicest thing you've ever said to me."

My face warmed, and an odd sensation filled my chest. "Remind me to burst your bubble tomorrow with something bitchy. Keep the eyes on the prize, Mr. Campbell-Endicott."

"Yep," he said, looking not at the paper but at me. My face, my eyes, the flush on my cheeks.

"Are you blushing?" he asked, taking a slow step forward.

His eyes lit up. The right side of his mouth quirked up just before his tongue popped out, wetting his lower lip. Another step.

Then another.

Holding up my hand, I stopped him before he took his flirtation any further. "How many times do I have to tell you? Ease up on that swagger, sir. I—I'm not one of your ladies that gets jelly-kneed and swoony over you."

"You look awfully swooned to me," he whispered, and started to reach for my hand.

I cleared my throat and sidestepped him to walk to the center of the room. There was a tightness in my chest and a flutter in my stomach that wouldn't calm.

"I'm serious. Cooper, you've got to stick to the topics and commit this to memory. No going off book, we agreed to this," I said. His staring was making me anxious and fluttery, and I didn't like the way it made me feel. Or think.

"Everything is always by your rules," he huffed.

"What's that supposed to mean?"

"Do this, do that. Don't flirt. Keep it in your pants."

"You're not supposed to flirt with everyone and anyone. Not now, and certainly not with me."

He stepped forward again, but this time, the lightness and flirty eyes were missing. "You dictate what you want me to say. I agreed to it. Isn't that enough for you? I've done everything you've asked and then some! Forgive me for trying to make a joke."

I drew back, tucking the papers into the folder. "You asked me for help. I didn't seek this out. Are you having second thoughts? Is it too hard for you to focus on one thing?" I punctuated each phrase with a jab to his hard biceps, which flexed with each one.

He turned and paced around the small office angrily. "I thought that since we've known each other forever, you'd have—"

"Have what?" I couldn't imagine where this was going. We were all over the place and needed to get the train back on the tracks.

When he faced me again he looked . . . hurt? Perhaps troubled was a more fitting description, what with the dark shadows beneath his tired, slightly bloodshot eyes. Normally he had a light about him. It was something that I believed drew people in—it was part of why he was so well liked.

"I needed your help," Cooper said slowly. "But I thought you would have been different about it. Everything I do is wrong or just not up to the Emma Peroni Gold Standard. You're a lot to live up to. I had thoughts about how to do things, too, but I put them aside because I thought you'd at least ask my opinion. Instead it's been 'Do this' and 'Do that' like I'm your dancing monkey. It's like I have no say in my own campaign anymore."

"Cooper," I breathed, feeling an emotion I couldn't place. *Guilt? Sympathy?*

He held up his hand. "Let me finish, please. I know the past few years have been rough, but I guess I hoped this would have mended some fences. Instead it seems like it's making the distance between us greater. I'd hoped our working together would have helped."

His words delivered a kick to my gut. My mouth opened and closed a few times as I tried to find the right words. Hurting his feelings had never been my intention. At one point in our lives, I had liked everything about him. That wasn't something that I focused on often. It was just easier that way.

Without looking up, I fidgeted with my hands. "There are many things about you that I wish other people would see and focus on. You have to trust me that right now, people are focused on the bad. That's what Kirby is banking on: people's inability to see past your history to look at all the good you've done and will do when you win."

Cooper chuckled, but there was no humor in it at all. It was dark, grumpy. "You missed your calling in politics, Emmanuelle. That was the best nonanswer I've ever heard. I'll see you tomorrow."

"Cooper, I—" I began, but he waved me off, opening and closing the doors and leaving me to wonder why my opinion of him mattered so much to him.

14

The next day, Kirby visited the senior center. Mrs. Mancini reported that he was a grandstander and that his cocky, smarmy attitude would turn people off everywhere—and not just the seniors. He'd bragged about his ideas for *putting seniors to work,* as he called it. Apparently when he'd been asked to be the bingo caller, he'd scoffed at the idea and said he didn't have time. To make matters worse, he had promised that he was going to help the seniors move some furniture around the senior center and then left before following through. His appearance had left an awful impression, which I'm not ashamed to say made me feel great.

My mother always said that the way to win an election was to go straight to the people. Yes, commercials, ads, shirts, and other swag were great, but having Cooper speaking directly to the townspeople was going to be key. They included not only its senior citizens but its young people as well.

Sophia Peroni had always been a big advocate for young voters and making them feel like their votes were really making a difference. I remembered being knee-high, standing in the voting booth with her and being allowed to push first the buttons and then the touch screens as voting modernized.

It was with that reasoning that I wanted Cooper to engage a

young crop of newly registered voters, and doing so in a debate with Kirby was sure to be an exciting way to draw them into the fun (hectic, stressful) world of politics.

As the senior class adviser at Hope Lake High, Henry had made it an extra-credit project for the upcoming graduating class to sit and listen to a friendly mayoral debate between the candidates, so strong attendance was guaranteed. We had invited the parents to attend as well, and as a result the room was packed. At the last minute, I'd decided to livestream the event on Facebook so that those who couldn't squeeze into the auditorium could still watch it. Henry had graciously volunteered to film it himself.

Debates, on the whole, made me nervous. They were unpredictable, especially when they didn't have a moderator to wrangle the speakers back onto a subject. Mudslinging was always possible, too, especially with someone like Kirby involved.

Just before the debate began, Cooper and I were tucked away stage left, quietly searching for something to pass the time until the announcer indicated it was his turn to cross the stage.

When Cooper had first shown up at the school, I considered it a small victory to see that he wasn't wearing a suit or a dress shirt and tie but a pair of khaki pants and a pea-green sweater, something that made him appear relaxed and relatable. I was counting on Kirby arriving in his usual too-big suit and sideshow persona. The attendees would see right through that schtick. My hope was that the young adults of Hope Lake would take to Cooper and potentially influence their parents if they were on the fence.

Now that we were standing together backstage, I could tell he was nervous. The familiar jaw tic was back, and he kept peering around the side of the curtain to gauge the mood of the room. "You got this, Cooper," I said gently, brushing a piece of fuzz from his shoulder. "Be yourself. The kids will react to that, since you have about the same maturity level as they do."

"Hardy har har," he mumbled.

"I'm sorry," I said, smiling. "Look, you've got this. Just keep it focused on the kids. That's who we need to come back to Hope Lake. Like we did."

He nodded. "Kids, focus, redirect, nothing that will get me into trouble with parents." He blurted out the last bit, but it wasn't the usual smart-aleck comment—it was a genuine slip.

"Cooper, I'm not telling you to be a saint, just be you. They'll like you if you're genuine. If Kirby tries baiting you into addressing something about your personal life, don't engage. Just redirect like we talked about. Keep it on topic. He's weak on his policies, so make sure to take advantage of those slips."

"A saint. I've never been accused of being one of those," he said, laughing at my bewildered expression.

"That's not what I meant. I just—"

"I know what you meant."

I cleared my throat, feeling a pang of discomfort. I didn't want to think about a celibate Cooper. I had kept him in that category for so long that changing it now blurred my opinion of him.

"He's here," I said as Kirby walked onto the stage.

"Thank you, Emma," Cooper said quietly, squeezing my hand. "Seriously, thanks. For everything." He leaned down to me, and I held my breath as he kissed my cheek. It was unexpected, and what was more confusing was that it wasn't quick but . . . lingering.

"Wh-what was that for?" I asked bewilderedly, reaching up to touch the warm spot.

Cooper looked as confused as I was. "I—I don't know," he whispered before turning toward the curtains that led onto the stage, where Kirby stood at his podium.

Behind him, I crossed myself quickly and took a deep breath, praying that my stomach would stop flipping once Cooper went out onstage. *It's the nerves,* I rationalized. *It's only your nerves.*

Please, please, let this kick ass. Let him kick Kirby's ass.

Cooper walked onto the stage confidently, waving to the clapping crowd. They hadn't clapped for Kirby—a good sign.

From my vantage point, hidden behind the curtains at the side of the auditorium, I watched as Cooper stretched his hand out to Kirby. Who ignored it. I could tell the audience was eating up the drama between them already.

A few mothers elbowed their daughters and mock-fanned themselves as Cooper approached his podium. The students who weren't there with a parent chatted among themselves, saying things like "I'll vote for the hottie mayor." Something told me my dad would have laughed at that.

Cooper shook hands with Harrison Mercer, Henry's father and the school's principal, and the flashes went off. Admittedly, they were both very attractive, and it was clear that the student body thought so. Harrison pulled him into a hug before Cooper took his place at the podium. He didn't approach Kirby at all, which gave me the pettiest morsel of glee.

Harrison held a mic. Tapping it once, he spoke clearly. "Since there isn't a moderator today at the request of the candidates, they will each take turns addressing the audience and will then have a few minutes to respond. We'll go back and forth for one hour. Cooper, you're up first."

"Simple question first," Cooper addressed the audience. The clapping stopped abruptly. "How long have you lived in Hope Lake? If it's all your life or the majority of your life, raise your hand."

Still keeping one eye on Cooper, I pulled up the livestream on my iPhone so I could keep track of outside viewership throughout Cooper's talk. From my hiding place in stage left, I could see that about three-quarters of the room raised their hands.

"Wonderful, okay. For those of you who raised your hand, do you think that you'd like to continue living here after you graduate from school? If so, keep them raised, or lower them if you can't wait to get the hell out of here."

My stomach pitched when about half of the students lowered their hands. I shouldn't have been surprised; at one time I think most of us felt that way. Most of the rest of the raised hands were parents'.

"Understandable. I was like that, too, but I came back after college. My three best friends did, and then the majority of my classmates," Cooper continued, coming from behind the podium to walk the length of the stage.

Kirby was stewing. He didn't look like he was paying attention, and I hoped that meant he would falter on his response to Cooper's points.

Cooper looked natural. He was engaging the audience by making eye contact with as many people as he could, motioning with his hands, smiling at everyone. The feedback on the video feed was also coming in strong. Lots of hearts (figures), likes (thank God), a few wows (of course), and thankfully no angry faces. Yet. Those we'd have to deal with later, I was sure, but for now it seemed like all Cooper was getting was support.

"For those of you who want to leave, can I ask what would make you come back after school?"

Whispers erupted throughout the audience. Heads turned to their friends to get their reactions. Maybe they were deciding how to answer or how to avoid answering. Many of the parents looked forlorn.

"Yes, you," Cooper said, pointing to a young man a few rows from the stage, who had bravely raised his hand to be the first to answer Cooper's question. "What would make you come back after college?"

The student stood up, and I recognized him from the hardware store in town. His parents had owned it since his grandfather had passed away a few years ago. "Sorry, Mom, I don't want to run the store," he said honestly, looking to his mother for support. His mother took his hand and nodded knowingly. He turned to face Cooper. "I guess if I could get a different job around here, or even in Barreton, I'd come home. I just don't want to have to take over the family business. I'd like to be an accountant, but I don't think that's something that can be done around here."

Cooper nodded, looking sympathetic as the student sat back down. "Okay, thank you for sharing. I get it. I really do. By the way, I could use a good accountant, so see me after this." He laughed with the audience. "In all seriousness, though, this is something that, as mayor, is one of my top priorities. Mayor Peroni and the town council have done an incredible service to the town by bringing back jobs to the area with new businesses, and I want to capitalize on that momentum and keep everything going in the right direction. Who's to say that we couldn't have a kick-ass—er, I mean kick-butt—accounting firm here?" The kids laughed as Cooper sheepishly ran his fingers through his hair. He'd managed to correct himself quickly, but I didn't mind—his slip humanized him.

"Anyway, I want to build jobs right here, in Hope Lake. And that includes accounting firms. Maybe businesses in Philly will send you their work in a couple years once I've had a few years in office. My team at the CDO has been earmarking new ventures every day, and we plan to bring in more each and every year with the full support of the mayor's office. Progress is a one-way street. We can only move forward. And I plan to dedicate myself to that cause."

Cooper continued on like that for another half hour, answering more questions and hitting all of the talking points that we'd discussed. He was poised and articulate, and the audience was eating it up because he kept the conversation focused on their worries and needs. They didn't waver in their support. There were cheers and applause as he went over his plans, the loudest cheer erupting after he explained his plans for the town's two hundred fiftieth–anniversary celebration next year.

"Imagine our Sestercentennial next summer! It's going to be incredible, what with the ideas I and the CDO have come up with. All in time, all in time," he called out when they asked for specifics. "But, my God, we need to think of a better name for that. I'll talk to Emma Peroni about that. She's the genius behind everything."

He shot a glance to where I was hidden behind the curtains. The word *genius* ignited a burning sense of pride inside me. I could feel my face erupt into a blush. My lips flattened from trying in vain not to smile at either him on-screen or the live/in-person version. Both of whom had just dropped my name into a ring I was so desperately trying to keep it out of.

As Cooper walked back to his podium, finished with his first talking point, Kirby came out from behind his. Unlike Cooper, he didn't look comfortable at all. Instead, he was stiff, unrelenting, and awkward.

"You, the one who wants to leave," he called out to the young man Cooper had spoken to. "What if instead of your small family-owned store, you could manage something like an Ace Hardware or a Lowe's? A big, beautiful box store like the ones in Barreton? No college needed, no loans accrued, just a chance at bossing a huge team of people around instead of your family. That sounds better than a little hardware store, right?"

A silence had fallen over the crowd the second Kirby started talking. I wasn't sure everyone was even breathing. It was eerie and awkward. "Right? Anyone? Think about it. Big-box stores with hundreds of jobs, benefits, and cheap—well, cheap whatever they're selling. It's the future. That's what Hope Lake needs. More jobs, more opportunities that come from something like a national chain."

He continued on like that for a couple minutes, insisting that this was the right vision for the town. No one muttered, whispered, or spoke a word. There were a lot of sideways glances, head shaking, and elbows being knocked into neighbors as if to say, *Get a load of this guy.*

If I hadn't disliked him as much as I did, I would have felt bad for him.

He finished to no applause. Any one of his talking points could have been what had turned the audience off. But what was odd was that he didn't seem to care that no one was in agreement with his narrow-mindedness. He marched back to the podium and gave a big wave to the silent crowd.

The debate roared on. Cooper would deliver a solid, no-nonsense opinion, and Kirby would follow up with something priggish and clumsy.

When the time was up, Harrison strolled back onto the stage. "Thank you, gentlemen, for that . . . enlightening chat. Ladies and gentlemen, students and parents, I hope you all have gotten a better impression of who you'd like to lead Hope Lake. Our candidates will now have an opportunity to make a closing statement," he concluded, but only Cooper remained onstage. Kirby had walked off just as Harrison was stepping onto it.

When he heard that, Kirby rushed back to his place, taking the opportunity to speak before Cooper.

"We all know what we need to move forward. Progress for the sake of progress doesn't help anyone!" he exclaimed, waving his finger toward the crowd condescendingly.

Before he finished, someone in the audience shouted, "You're ripping off Harry Potter!"

The crowd laughed, and again, if I hadn't hated him so much, I'd have felt terrible for him. "Umbridge was right," Rogers mumbled into the mic before storming off the stage.

Not missing a beat, Cooper took to the mic again. "Thank you, everyone! I look forward to serving this great town for years to come. I hope I can count on your support. But even if you don't choose to vote for me, know that I will still support you if elected. And with that I have one thing left to say—I know there's a game this weekend—Crusaders Forever!"

The crowd roared as he bounded offstage, heading right for me. As he slipped behind the curtains, he was beaming. His blue eyes were lit up with an energy I hadn't seen in ages. He looked magnetic, bursting with pent-up joy. His hands shot up as he bounced in his loafers.

"Hey, get back out there," I mock chastised him, pushing him toward the drapery opening, but he was an immovable object. "They want an encore. You're not supposed to be drawing attention to the fact that I'm here!"

His big body didn't budge. I wasn't even sure he'd heard me because he just prattled on like I hadn't said a word.

"That was great, right? I mean, this is a great turnout and he was just . . . I mean, what was that? What the hell was he thinking?" he rambled quickly. "Hopefully they'll all vote. Holy shit, this is such a rush." He peered out from behind the curtains at the crowd, who were still cheering. The smile on his face was infectious, and as much as I didn't want to, I smiled up at him.

"You were so right, Emma. This was perfect. Thank you."

"You'll have to go to the game this weekend. I'm sure you still have a sweatshirt from high school."

With a quick wink, he grabbed our jackets off the hooks. "I may even have my old jersey."

He helped me into my coat, and after he pulled on his own jacket, he leaned down. I took it as though he intended to kiss my cheek again, but anticipating it this time, I panicked, freezing like a deer caught in headlights. Thinking I didn't want him to do it again, I went to move so he would miss, and instead I turned the wrong way just as he moved the final inch.

Cooper's lips touched mine, and we both froze.

EMMA THOUGHT: Girl, you turned the wrong damn way.

I was shocked, and my hands flew to his arms.

Push him back! my brain shouted. *PUSH!*

But my hands didn't push. They slid up the biceps that flexed beneath my touch.

For a second, then two and then three until I lost count, we were glued to the spot, too stunned to move, our eyes wide, trying desperately to figure out what the hell had just happened.

Was happening.

EMMA THOUGHT: Yeah, I got nuthin'.

When he finally moved, it wasn't away from me but closer, pushing his lips *just* a bit more firmly against mine. My fingers curled around his arms as his eyes fluttered closed.

We could hear Principal Mercer take the stage and address the still clapping audience. As the audience roared again, I finally pulled away, breathing heavily and feeling a bit light-headed.

"How about that, folks? Cooper Endicott!" Harrison shouted to another round of applause.

Why didn't I just back up? Why did I turn my head? Why are my face warm and my lips tingly and my heart thundering so loudly? There were a hundred more whys, and none of them had an answer.

Cooper's eyes were slow to open, his breath shuddering.

I could see that he was in shock, too. *Nothing to worry about here, folks.* An innocent and friendly thank-you that had gone a bit awry. With hopeful eyes, I looked up at him and waited for an *I'm sorry* or even a quip about *Was it good for you?*

But there was nothing but Cooper staring at me like he wanted to do it again.

And the biggest unanswered question of all was: Why did I have this overwhelming urge to let him?

15

For the first time in my years working at the CDO, I had no choice but to work from home. The day after the high school *incident,* I was lounging in yoga pants and a purifying mask, sporting a very pink and infected left eye. When I'd woken up that morning, I couldn't open it. I figured it was leftover mascara that I hadn't quite gotten rid of, but I popped by Dr. Bishop's office before work just in case. Turned out, spending three hours in a hotbed of germs—aka a school—wreaked havoc with your immune system.

Dr. Bishop had said it wouldn't last long but had recommended that I not leave the house as I was highly contagious. *Goody.*

I was video chatting with Nancy around lunchtime, waiting patiently for my prescription to be delivered from the pharmacy, when the doorbell finally dinged.

Thank God, I thought. I hung up with her, promising to check back in once my eye was a little less goopy.

"Coming!" I shouted, pulling on my plastic gloves to retrieve cash from my wallet. I didn't want to be responsible for spreading conjunctivitis around town. Typhoid Emma was not a nickname I wanted.

"Just leave it on the mat. Here's the total plus tip. Thanks for getting here so fast!" I exclaimed, slipping cash under the door.

I counted to twenty before opening it a crack. The last thing I wanted was anyone seeing me in my condition.

"Emmanuelle," Cooper said smoothly, holding up a small white prescription bag. His smile was toothy and full of mischief to match the twinkle in his eyes.

My smile dropped like a stone in a bucket. I swung the door closed again, slamming it in his face.

Then the strangest thing happened. I felt tingly. It wasn't my itchy eye but my lips. And the vision of Cooper being attached to those lips. Remembering what happened back in the high school auditorium sent goose bumps up both arms.

Not. Good.

He knocked again, and I could hear him shuffling around on the other side of the door. "That wasn't very nice!" he called, and I heard him opening the paper bag. "What's sulfacetamide? Sounds serious. Do you have an STD?" he asked, and I wondered what the hell my neighbors were thinking.

Whipping the door open, I took advantage of having startled him and grabbed the bag from his hand. Just as I was closing the door again, he pushed his foot between it and the jamb, effectively stopping me from shutting him out. "I brought you that. You could at least say thank you."

I just wanted to put my damn drops in so I would stop wanting to pull my eyeball from my head. "Thank you. I'm not trying to be rude, I just have a lot going on right now," I said sheepishly. That was the understatement of the year. "Now please leave so I can be miserable in peace."

I heard him sigh heavily. "Emmanuelle, I just want to chat. Not be a pain in the ass." He sounded disappointed but understanding.

Did my pleading work? Will he leave?

I couldn't imagine how crazy I looked with my hair pulled back into thick plaits, a bright green avocado mask on, sporting an oozy pink eye.

When I opened the door the rest of the way to check if the coast was clear, Cooper was still standing there, looking as serious as ever.

Damn it.

I watched as his eyes flitted across my face, documenting the mess of things going on. I felt self-conscious. Not a feeling I enjoyed, especially around Cooper.

"Good to see you're alive. Anyway, I have something else," he said, bending to pick up a plain white plastic bag with a paper one stuffed inside it.

"Listen, I know you're used to getting what you want, but I'm miserable, my eye is itchy, and I really just want to curl up, eat some cup o' noodles, and watch bad TV. Besides, you shouldn't be here."

He looked momentarily hurt, his brow furrowed. "Why not?"

I was exasperated on top of everything else. "Let's see: First of all, I'm highly contagious—I don't think running for mayor with gunk streaming out of your eyes would be a good look for you. Second of all, my helping you is a secret, and I don't need you raising any flags by showing up here with my prescription and whatever *that* is," I said, pointing to the other bag he held. "What is this, anyway?" I asked, raising the bag and shaking it.

"I was coming to bring you this when the delivery boy from Shea's Pharmacy pulled up. I saved him the trouble of walking up that indecent number of stairs. Honestly, you need to get that elevator fixed. And, Emmanuelle, you're being dramatic. Why couldn't I just pop in as a favor to an old friend?"

If it had been Nick or Henry, that would have been fine, but this was Cooper.

"How do I explain this nicely?" I began, simultaneously ripping open the prescription bag for the drops. "If I showed up at your place, no one would bat an eyelash."

"Why not? I'm sure people would notice you," he murmured, looking at me.

"Oh, I'm sure they'd *notice,* but I doubt they'd notice *me.* I would just be another woman using the revolving door to your bedroom. I wouldn't want my neighbors to get the same idea about me. I have a reputation as a *highly* classy lady."

Cooper rolled his eyes. "I have feelings, you know." With that, he slid around me to walk into the apartment.

"I didn't invite you in," I mumbled into the hallway. My nosy neighbor, who was leaving and had witnessed the whole exchange, shot me a withering glare. I smiled awkwardly at her and took ten seconds to calm my breathing before turning to face Cooper.

"Forgive me, may I come in?" he mocked. "I come bearing a peace offering. Even though you just insulted me, and yourself, in the process."

I pulled up short. "How did I insult myself?"

"You compared my bedroom activities to a revolving door, therefore highlighting your own prudish sensibilities."

"I am *not* a prude!" I scoffed indignantly, crossing my arms over my chest.

He set the take-out bag down on the coffee table and leveled me with a scathing look. "Oh, I know you're not. It's just too easy to rile you up, Emmanuelle."

With those words, the tingle in my lips was back. I decided to ignore it.

"*Emma,*" I insisted, putting my hand on the door handle. "I'm very busy."

"Clearly," he said with a laugh, waving a dismissive hand at my appearance.

I snapped my gloves off. "Listen, I've had a day already and it's barely past noon, so unless that's the salty goodness of cup o' noodles that I'm craving, I'm not interested. Now, if you'll excuse me."

As I opened the door to let him out, he pulled something from the bag on the table. He turned it to show me the logo stamped to the brown paper. My eyes widened.

Turning, I gasped. "Oh, my God—it *is* Pho 75!"

The restaurant was by the University of Pennsylvania. Prior to going to college, I had never had Vietnamese food. After one taste of Pho 75, though, I'd had no idea how I'd managed eighteen years without it.

I'd basically survived on it in college.

Sick? Run to get pho.

Hungover? Run to get pho.

Stressed? Run to get pho.

"You went to Philly?" I asked disbelievingly. The trip was nearly two hours each way.

He nodded, smiling shyly. "It's a peace offering. A fresh start, if you will."

"Plying me with delicious soup is a great way to let water flow under the bridge," I teased, enjoying the way his ears pinked up.

"Sort of," he said, looking down at his shoes.

"I'll put away the voodoo doll," I said, taking the bag into the kitchen. "For now."

Inside the bag was a myriad of containers, and the aroma was a delightful reminder of how much I missed this food. Would it have been in poor taste to shove my head into the bag and slurp the broth straight from the plastic take-out container? Probably, but I was suddenly so hungry I was seriously considering it. Flank and skirt steak, chicken, melt-in-your-mouth brisket, and then longans and dried fruit for dessert. There was more than enough for two people.

"I assume some of this is for you?" I asked, ignoring the fact that my palms had gotten sweaty.

"I was hoping to stay. Eat. Talk about . . . things. You know, I loved Pho 75, too. It was a little farther from Drexel, but I went often," he said, walking into the kitchen.

Swallowing a sudden bubble of nerves that popped up at the prospect of being alone together, I blurted out, "I'm going to go wash this mask off my face and—uh—medicate."

"This is in no way how I thought this conversation was going to go," he said with a smile.

I laughed awkwardly, turning toward the hallway. "What? You don't usually have conversations about contagions and conjunctivitis over lunch?"

Even after closing the bathroom door, I could hear his laughter.

By the time I emerged with a clean, face mask–free face, jeans, a T-shirt, and a makeshift eye patch thanks to an old pair of glasses and a sock, Cooper had already assembled everything into pots to reheat.

"I didn't think you could cook," I said, impressed that he'd managed not to burn my apartment down in the few minutes I'd been gone.

He shrugged, focused on stirring the pot. "I'm a pro at this part. It's better than using a microwave, in my opinion."

We worked in amiable silence for a few minutes, stirring and shifting pots around before ladling the pho into bowls he'd arranged on the counter. "You rummaged through my cabinets, I see."

"I wasn't snooping. Just looking for plates and stuff."

Glancing around at the setup, I teased, "No chopsticks?"

He laughed lightly, stepping forward. "I wasn't going to press my luck by giving you a weapon."

Leaning casually against the countertop, he watched me, a curious look on his face. I'd never noticed it before, but it was a small kitchen. He seemed even taller than usual in the compact space.

I cleared my throat. "Mind setting the table?"

Doing as I asked, he deposited the bowls on the small table and began arranging them as we had been taught in home economics many years before.

"Mrs. Smith would be thrilled that you remember how to properly set a table," I teased.

He stepped back, admiring his handiwork. "That was by far my worst class."

"Oh, please," I scoffed.

I moved back and forth between the small table and the kitchen, handing off more dishes and utensils before going back for the rest.

"Mrs. Smith loved you. You got straight A's through all four years of high school with her."

He took the tray from me and kept arranging. "She did love me, but I was still terrible at home ec. I think the only reason I passed was because her daughter was my partner every semester, and we only received group grades. It would have looked terrible if she'd failed her own child."

I pulled out two sets of chopsticks that I'd gotten as part of a Secret Santa gift from the office a few years back and had never used.

I handed them to him. "Here. I think you're safe today."

His hand lingered on mine for a second as I passed him the utensils. "These look new," he said, regarding his set as he pulled it from the cloth sleeve. "I thought you would have used them by now."

"Used what? These?" I questioned, wondering why he'd be interested.

"Yeah, these. I figured by now you'd have used them quite a bit."

I watched as he deftly twirled the shiny off-white stick between his fingers like a thin baton.

"How did you know about these? They were from the Christmas exchange years ago."

Then it hit me. "*You* bought these?" I asked, stunned that Cooper, king of the last-minute gift cards, had bought me a thoughtful present. I remembered the gift wrap they had come in. They had been interestingly wrapped, with way too much tape and a bow that didn't match. Now that I thought about it, that part made sense.

"I can't believe these were from you," I whispered, shocked.

He nodded, setting them down on top of each place setting. He even folded the napkins into decorative fans. Walking around me, he pulled out my chair, encouraging me to sit.

"You, me, Henry, and Nick had taken those cooking classes

before we left for college, and you kept talking about owning a nice set of chopsticks, so—" He cleared his throat.

I vaguely remembered the conversation, but I was stunned. Cooper had not only remembered what I'd said but gone out of his way to purchase something meaningful.

"Anyway, I just wanted to tell you that I should never have doubted you."

"Excuse me?" I asked, unfolding the napkin fan over my lap, still amazed at discovering a layer of Cooper that I hadn't known existed.

It was hard enough to read him on a daily basis. Being one eye down thanks to the conjunctivitis made it even harder to get any insight into what was going through that head of his.

"I just meant—" He paused and took a sip of water. "Can I be honest?"

I nodded. "I would prefer it."

He pushed around the pho in his bowl for a few seconds, as if lost in thought about where to begin. He skewered a piece of chicken with his chopsticks, pushing it into his mouth. Around it, he covered his chewing with his hand and mumbled, "When you first agreed to do this—you know, to help with the campaign—I questioned your motives. I thought given our—" He paused again, searching for the right word, so I helped him out.

"Strained friendship? Complicated history? Usual bouts of animosity?"

He nodded, scooping up more noodles and veggies.

"Yes, all of that. I wasn't sure you would have been willing to overlook it in order to help me win. Our past has been . . . not the best."

I thought about that for a moment. Laying the chopsticks on the bowl, I looked up and folded my hands under my chin. "You know, I can separate my feelings for a person from my feelings about the job he would do, right? Cooper, I do believe you're the far better choice."

He looked relieved, a small smile tipping up his lips. "Thank you. I know I'm a pain in the ass, but—"

"Wait, what? Hold on, let me grab my phone to record this," I joked. I pretended to push the record button on an imaginary phone. "Repeat that exactly as you said it. I'm going to use it as my ringtone."

"Yeah, yeah, you know what I mean."

We sat in silence, both of us focused on eating. There was so much to talk about, but just sitting and relaxing was nice for a change. I had forgotten, or ignored, how nice it was to just *be* with Cooper without being engrossed in an argument.

"About what happened yesterday," he began finally, staring at his nearly empty bowl.

"Yes?" I choked out. We were now entering uncharted territory.

Would he apologize? Make a joke? Both? What did I want him to say?

"I hope you know that I took your comments the other day seriously, and I don't want you to think that I was throwing it all back in your face by kissing you."

That is not what I expected.

"What do you mean?"

Shifting in his seat, he folded his hands on the table, looking forlorn. "I didn't mean to do it. I want you to know that I'm sorry if I made you uncomfortable."

I could see that he was beating himself up about it. Knowing Cooper, he probably thought that I was going to berate him.

"Looking back on it, I was so pumped up and excited from the speech that I got—I don't know. I got carried away, and I'm sorry."

"Cooper, it's okay. I'm not mad. I mean, I wasn't mad that it happened. It was an accident."

I said the word, but I was having a hard time believing that was what it actually had been. For me, at least.

His breath left him in a *whoosh*. "Oh, thank God. I thought you were going to quit on me."

I frowned. "One kiss isn't going to change my mind about helping, Cooper."

He looked relieved, smiling for the briefest of seconds before his eyes flickered down to my lips. "I'm glad. Total accident."

"Accidents happen. It's why they're called accidents." I laughed, but it sounded awkward and shrill. *Why?* I should have felt relieved, not . . . whatever this was that was happening in my stomach.

Not butterflies. Nope.

And even if they were, Cooper had just apologized for kissing me. So there was nothing more to discuss.

It was high time to derail this conversation. "Have you thought any more about the point we discussed the other day? Finding someone to, you know—" I asked.

Cooper sighed, looking down to stare at his soup. After a few seconds, he slowly nodded. I didn't expect it or the feelings of disappointment that blossomed from his simple affirmative head dip. Clearly I was coming down with something other than pinkeye.

"I reached out to someone after we talked the other day," he said quietly.

Something set my teeth on edge. Then my mouth let loose the one question I had promised myself I wouldn't ask after our conversation about my not overstepping his limits. "Do I know her?"

He swallowed a gulp of water, and after a few seconds he nodded, offering nothing else.

Do I ask? Do I want to know? Do I need to know?

No.

No (*Yes*).

No (*YES*).

It was like I knew the answer before he even said it. "Whitney."

My stomach lurched and dipped.

It suddenly all made sense. Why had she been in Borough Building that early morning a couple weeks ago? He had been considering her all along. Silly me.

Quietly I sat staring down at my lap. There was an unsettling feeling in my chest. When it moved down to my stomach, it rolled. If I were being honest—if he had given me free rein with his black book—I would probably have chosen her, too. Her parents were wealthy, her family had a political legacy like the Campbells', she was stunning . . .

She was perfect for this. For *him*.

But that didn't mean I had to like it.

"I saw her, you know, in my dad's office the other day," I said, biting the inside of my cheek.

"We see each other a few times a year. She moved back to Barreton a few months ago. She stopped in to say hi. She's come up to town a couple times since. It makes sense."

They *saw* each other. It didn't take a genius to figure out what that meant.

"Good, good." I coughed. "She's perfect for what you need."

He bristled. "She's not a couch that I'm buying."

I scoffed. "You know what I mean. She's the perfect Jackie to your JFK."

I laughed, but it sounded manic instead of jovial, as I'd intended. "She should come to an event soon. Or whatever." I stood quickly, and my chair toppled back, clattering to the floor. "I'll grab that later," I blurted out, picking up my dishes and walking hurriedly to the kitchen. "I'm done. You done?"

After a few minutes, Cooper joined me in the kitchen. I had already packed the extras into two containers for him to take home.

"You should keep these. After all, I got it for you," he said, looking concerned.

"It's okay, I have dinner with my parents tomorrow."

I don't.

"And a date the night after."

Lies, lies, all lies.

"It'll just go to waste," I explained, pushing the containers at

him. He placed his hands over mine. Did he feel their clammi-
ness? Why is *clammy* such an awful word?

EMMA THOUGHT: Why are you having a meltdown? Why are
you unable to function normally around Cooper all of a sudden?

"Oh, you need a bag. I'll get it," I said quickly.

Cooper wouldn't let go of my hands. "I get the feeling that
you're trying to get rid of me all of a sudden."

I huffed, trying to blow it off, but he couldn't be more right.
The unsettled feeling in my stomach was growing.

"Is this going to be weird?" he asked, running his fingers
through his hair. "I know you and Whitney haven't talked in a
while." He leaned against the counter.

In a while = ages.

"Not weird at all. No weirdness."

"Something tells me that's not true. Are you still mad about
everything?"

Was I?

"I don't know," I said honestly. "We never talked about it.
About her and you and you guys as a couple. After you started
dating her in college we just stopped talking, and—"

"And what?"

"It hurt. A lot. Losing a friend like that."

He frowned, reaching out for a second before pulling back.
"I'm sorry you stopped being friends with her on account of me."

"What?"

"What do you mean, *what*?" he said, stepping back.

"Cooper, I wasn't upset about Whitney. I knew her for a few
months. I knew you my whole life, and you suddenly ignored me
because you were dating her. Do you know how awful that was?"

Feeling foolish, I turned to grab a bag from under my sink.
I stacked the containers inside and tied it in a knot, annoyed
that my hands were trembling slightly. Last time I'd spoken with
Whitney had been at graduation, and we hadn't exactly been kind
to each other. I knew that when I saw her again, with Cooper,

someone would be swallowing her pride and having to put her big-girl pants on.

"Emma, it wasn't like that, but I *am* sorry. I don't know what to say other than that I'm sorry you felt that way."

"You never got it!" I exclaimed, standing at the counter and staring at the wall.

"Got what?"

I shook my head, grateful that he couldn't see my face and the tears welling in my eyes. "The three of you left me. For years. Starting college was hard enough, and I had no one to turn to because you guys—everyone went their separate ways. Just when I thought I'd at least have you there. You left me again."

"For Whitney," he finished, touching my shoulder.

There was a comfort there that I hadn't expected to feel. Cooper's hand shook slightly just before he squeezed. "I'm sorry, Emma. It's not what you think . . . I never realized . . ." He was having a hard time stringing sentences together. "I was a stupid kid who did stupid things."

Wiping away a tear that had escaped, I nodded. "It's fine," I choked out. Those feelings from years ago had surged back so suddenly, I couldn't quite get ahold of them. The nervousness, sadness, loneliness—all of it from being solo in a new city with none of my friends there for support. "I'll be right back," I said, scurrying out of the kitchen.

I leaned against the hallway wall, taking a few deep breaths to compose myself. Neither one of us was the same person as we had been back in college. It wasn't fair for me to hold those feelings over his head—feelings that he had no idea I'd had.

When I returned, I expected Cooper to be in the same spot, but he wasn't. He was about to turn on the faucet and squeeze soap into the sink.

"Leave it, I can do the dishes later," I insisted, trying to bump him out of the way.

Cooper's hands were already in the deep, warm water. When

my hip hit his, his hands splashed water across the counter, where some of my work files were sitting.

"Damn it," I cursed, grabbing the papers quickly, but they were already covered in big wet splotches. I spread them out on the opposite counter, peeling apart each of the sheets.

Cooper dried his hands and came over to help. "What's all this?" he asked. I looked up at him to see him eyeing the project projections I'd been working on before he'd arrived. He started reading them, skimming over the sheets quickly before I could take them back.

"Nothing, nothing. Just something that Nancy and I have been trying to put together."

His jaw ticked as his eyes moved over the pages. "This is the Jackson account, Emmanuelle. *My* Jackson account."

16

"C ooper, there's a perfectly good explanation for this," I began. Though the company had approached me, not the other way around, he was right. I should've told him instead of hiding it from him.

"Is this why you wanted me to take a leave from the CDO? You pushed me out because you didn't want me to hear about this?"

He slumped against the counter, the papers hanging at his sides. "I can't believe you're trying to bring this back after what happened to me last time."

To me. Typical. My feelings of nostalgia went away as quickly as they'd come.

"I understand that you're having some feelings about this."

"Double-crossed is a feeling, yes. Why wouldn't you tell me about this? Or at least ask me if it was okay to reopen the deal?"

I rolled my eyes. "Cooper, please stop being dramatic. You're on leave from the office, and you weren't exactly Mr. Present when you were there. I haven't been able to run a ton of stuff by you because you haven't been around. Besides, *I* didn't do anything to you. The Jacksons reached out to me about renegotiating, and I figured it was worth a shot. I wasn't trying to go behind your back or hide it from you. I just wanted to keep a lid on it until I knew what their interest was," I said honestly, continuing to separate the papers that were dripping wet. Thank God these were just printouts that I'd been scribbling on. Printing new ones would have to wait until I got back to the office.

"They're coming in this week," I offered, reaching out to pry the projection sheet from his fist.

Cooper's posture was loosening up, but he was still annoyed. His lips were pressed thin, and his brows were knitted together. "I just don't know what to say. I can't believe I didn't know about this."

"There isn't anything *to* say, Cooper. I'm taking advantage of an opportunity that I was presented with."

His blue eyes showed the hurt he was feeling. I didn't like that I'd made him feel badly, but I was also smart enough to realize that if the roles had been reversed . . .

"Cooper, you'd have done the same thing if given the chance," I told him, showing him a few of the dry sheets. "You know that it's true. If I'd had the same history with a company and been out for a few months, you'd look at it as an opportunity for the CDO and go for it. I would have understood, and now I'm asking you to do the same. Besides, this isn't about me. The town needs this business."

Cooper quietly flipped through the pages of the research that I'd saved from his compilation six years before, along with the updated sheets Nancy and I had put together.

"It wasn't our time then. You were still figuring out what direction to go in, and the council wasn't totally on board," I said. "And—"

"What I did was the problem, too. Just say it."

"I don't have to say it. We both know it had everything to do with the deal falling through."

"And in the end it blew up in our faces." He sighed, rubbing the back of his neck. "I get it. I'm still irked, but I see why you didn't tell me."

"I don't know if you know or not, but Mr. Jackson suffered a massive stroke a couple years ago. He's doing better now, but the company was thrown into a tailspin just after it happened. His children had to gain a controlling stake in the company to get away from, well, Haley. They're the ones who reached out."

He nodded. I didn't have to go into more detail, but it didn't feel right keeping this quiet now. If he lost the election and came back to the office, he'd have to know what we were dealing with. So I launched into my spiel.

"I'm redoing aspects of the first presentation, including how recent town developments make Hope Lake an even better fit for the business now than it was then. The CDO is stronger than ever, and with the support of the mayor's office, the support of the town council should follow suit. And I decided that if they say no again, even with all of the changes, I would close the chapter in this book. If it works, though, it'll be an amazing opportunity for Hope Lake."

"What made the family change their mind and come back?" he asked, holding the latest photo of their board. "They weren't exactly big fans last time."

"*Mr. Jackson* wasn't a fan of some things. I think it was because the idea of seeing the business he built from scratch being taken over by someone else—someone who had very different ideas from his—scared him. But since his children have taken over, they've made some bold moves in revamping the whole JOE brand. New president, new branding, new pitch—maybe we'll get lucky."

Wordlessly Cooper moved on to the updated metrics that I'd been putting together in whatever free time I had, which wasn't much. Between helping his election, working, and training Nancy to take over his job, it had mostly been done over a glass of wine at midnight.

He didn't say anything as he scanned the numbers. No questions, comments, or even a facial expression to help me glean what he was thinking. I couldn't take the silence anymore.

"Cooper, look at this from a mayoral perspective. Think about the optics for the office. With Kirby coming at you left and right, we need this. And if this works out, I promise I'll say you had a hand in it—after all, this was your idea first, and the voters should know that."

"Okay, I get it. You're right."

"What?"

"I said you're right. Don't gloat." He smirked. "You're on a roll. That's twice in one day."

"Twice in one day?" I asked, feeling a slight ripple through my veins.

As if sensing my unease, he stepped forward. A small spark ignited behind his blue eyes, and for a second, the old Cooper was back. The one he had apologized for earlier. "Twice in one day," he repeated.

"Good," I said, satisfied. "I'm glad."

He snorted, putting down the paper and scooping up his bag of leftovers. "You always have to have the last word."

I narrowed my eyes. "I do not."

"See what I mean?" he said, shaking his head.

"I don't know what you're talking about."

But I did.

"Everything doesn't have to be one-upmanship, you know. You can quit while you're ahead," he said. "I said you're right. I'm dropping it."

"Okay." I stepped out into the living area.

He followed, hot on my heels. "Fine."

"Stop it. *You're* doing it now," I snapped. Turning quickly, I ran into him.

He caught me by the arms, steadying me on my feet. "I don't know what you're talking about," he said in a falsetto, throwing my words back at me.

Cooper squeezed my elbow, and I became aware of how close we were standing. I could feel his breath, the heat from his hands through my shirt, and there was that tingle again. If he leaned down just a smidge . . .

The thought caught me off guard, and my breathing stuttered.

"This is ridiculous," I huffed, stepping back and trying to clear my head. "You enjoy baiting me."

"Me? Oh, please. You enjoy being tough on me, Emmanuelle. I swear you get off on it."

"I beg your pardon?" I lunged at him to slap his arm, but he sidestepped me, catching me in a sort of backward hug with his hands wrapped around mine. "Let me go!" My voice sounded weak in my ears. Not from fear but because deep down, I wasn't sure I wanted him to.

"Say please," he taunted.

"Get bent," I barked, shimmying to try to loosen his grasp.

"Apparently not," he whispered, his lips grazing my ear ever so slightly.

I halfheartedly tugged my arms from his grasp, but his hands wrapped around mine, keeping us close. "That promise of yours didn't last very long."

"Oh, I think we both have an idea of how long I can last, Emma."

"Jesus, Cooper, can't you curb the innuendo for a minute!"

Cooper sucked in a breath at the same time I did. In our precarious position, I noticed something. A very *hard* something pressed firmly against my backside. Upon realizing that I had felt it, too, he let me go, backing away quickly as if I'd burned him.

When I turned to face him, he wouldn't look at me. His chest was heaving, his fists clenched at his sides. He finally looked up, and I gasped. His eyes were intense. He licked his lips, and his gaze fell toward mine.

Just then there was a pounding at my front door. "Excuse me, Miss Peroni!"

"It's my neighbor," I whispered, nervously glancing toward the door. "I think she saw you come in earlier."

I opened the door. "I'm sorry about that, Mrs. MacGuire," I said, brushing my hair back from my face. "Did you need something?"

She harrumphed. "Yes, I need you two to stop arguing. I could hear you in the stairwell. You sound like an old married couple!"

She turned on her heel and marched away, leaving me stunned in the doorway and Cooper chuckling behind my door.

"That's accurate," he said, putting his hand over mine on the door.

I slid my hand out from beneath his, hating the way my skin felt electrified. "I beg to differ."

He leaned over, close enough that I could count the freckles on his nose. "You've got my balls in a vise. Feel better, Captain."

I watched him retreat, bouncing down the stairs without a care in the world. When the door closed behind him, I tugged at my hair, wondering when exactly I had lost control of my feelings for Cooper Endicott.

Silly Emma. You never had it.

A FEW DAYS LATER, I was brought face-to-face with another scandalous headline. No surprise, this one was outrageously more misleading than the ones that had come before.

ROGERS PROMISES MORE NEW JOBS
WITH CHAIN BUSINESSES

That beauty joined the likes of MAYOR PERONI'S UNPAID TAXES, ENDICOTT ANCESTOR'S STOLEN LAND, and my personal unfavorite from the day before, GOVERNOR BRIBING LOCALS FOR VOTES FOR SON.

In the article, Rogers explained why throwing in some competition for local businesses would improve the town's economy and satisfy what the people of Hope Lake had been asking for; but why do that if they didn't have to? We had pretty active town hall meetings where people came out and aired their grievances about things that needed improvement, so to speak. Hardly anyone mentioned that Hope Lake desperately needed a Chick-fil-A or a Best Buy. If you really wanted something from a big-box store, you just went to Barreton.

The article quoted Rogers as saying that he had secured a few chains to build on the town-owned land that was part of an area that for decades people had agreed not to touch. Why the hell was he willing to destroy beautiful forestry by plopping a Home Depot or a Walmart in the center of it? Besides, how was that even legal? Even if he became mayor, he couldn't unilaterally mandate such an action. It was as though the person writing the article had no idea how town government actually operated.

I texted Mrs. Mancini to see if she'd seen it, and she responded with a FaceTime call from her and her merry band of gossipmongers during their daily walk.

"Mrs. Mancini, you could have waited to call me until after your exercise," I said, holding the phone high enough so she could see my face and not just my chin.

She was huffing and puffing. I didn't know if it was from exertion or annoyance. "My dear, I'm assuming that you're calling because of that salacious piece in the paper this morning. It'll be over my dead body that we get a Mama Francine's or whatever the hell it's called in Hope Lake. No way, no how. Right, girls?" she shouted to the group behind her, who cheered in agreement.

"Good, make sure you tell everyone you know that you're fully against it. Big businesses are the last thing we need in Hope Lake. Not to mention destroying open land."

"You tell that honey of mine, Cooper, that he needs to get in front of a camera to address this. Especially with that beautiful girl he was showing around town this morning. I'll call the station in Barreton to come tomorrow afternoon."

I nodded and said good-bye.

Whitney was here?

"Good," I said to myself aloud. The louder I said it, the more convinced I'd be.

"Great, awesome. Super!" Apparently I really liked adjectives.

Whitney's being here must have meant that she was on board—the last piece of the campaign puzzle we needed had fallen into place. That was good news. So why did my stomach feel like it was being stabbed by tiny pirates?

I called Cooper next. Straight to voice mail. According to my pocket calendar, he was at a budgetary meeting with his campaign finance guy—aka Nick—meaning that they were at the diner having pie and coffee and pretending to talk about numbers. "Screw it," I said to the empty room. I needed to talk to him about Whitney face-to-face. Why I thought that was a good idea, I'll never know.

IT WAS THE LUNCHTIME RUSH at the 81 Café, so I was lucky to find a spot in the parking lot. Well, it wasn't really a spot. I squeezed directly behind both Nick's and Cooper's vehicles, knowing that they weren't going anywhere anytime soon.

I could see the two of them chatting in a booth near the window, their menus still open on the table. *Thank God.* My stomach growled loudly. I hadn't had time to eat before heading over.

When Lila, the longtime waitress, saw me walk in, she waved me over to where Cooper and Nick were sitting.

"Want your usual?" she called out between snapping her gum.

"Yeah, thanks. I'll be eating with them. Put my salad on Nick's bill," I joked, sliding into the booth across from the stunned-looking Cooper.

"Why are you here? Did I miss a meeting?" he asked nervously, pulling out his phone to check the calendar.

"Nice to see you, too, Cooper," I quipped, pulling the Cooper calendar from my purse. "I just thought I'd join you guys before you headed to the food pantry for your volunteering duties. P.S., Nick, I need your muscles to get some bags out of my car." My trunk was stuffed full of donations that the office had gathered and Cooper would be delivering that afternoon.

Cooper pouted. "What about my muscles?"

I raised an eyebrow. "I'm sorry, Cooper. Can your muscles help little ole me get the big heavy bags out of my car?"

"Okay, you two. Let's simmer down," Nick interjected before Cooper could respond.

"So how are the finances?" I asked, laughing to myself because there wasn't a stitch of paperwork on the table. Or a laptop, file folder, or really anything else that would have shown that they were discussing campaign donations.

Nick shifted uncomfortably. "We were uh, just, erm . . . talking about numbers."

"Oh, numbers. I like numbers," I teased, taking a sip of Nick's water.

"Aw, come on, now your lip gloss is on the straw," he groaned, pushing the glass back to me.

I took the napkin and wiped it off. "You're such a baby. Where's Henry?"

Cooper sat up straighter and took a pack of crackers from the basket on the table. "Audiologist."

As a kid, Henry had suffered some hearing loss in both ears that had caused him to need cochlear implants. Twice a year or so, he had to visit the closest specialist, who was in Barreton. Otherwise, I wasn't sure Henry would ever have left Hope Lake.

"After that," Nick continued, "he was going to shore up a few more details for the election day party at the house."

At the house. That meant Campbell Manor.

"I can't believe the election is already next month. Is everything set?" I asked.

Cooper shrugged as Lila brought our lunches over. Club sandwiches for both Nick and Cooper and a Cobb salad for me.

Nick bit into his sandwich with gusto while Cooper poked at his on his plate.

"Can I help with anything?" I asked. "I know the governor has people on it, but let me know in case there's something I can do."

"I guess we're good," Cooper said, looking to Nick, who took a massive bite of his sandwich and shrugged. "I honestly don't know. There's about a dozen people handling it. I'd say you're better off asking my mother. She's organizing the caterer and the photographer and things like that." The vein in his forehead started throbbing. Angry Cooper wasn't anyone I felt like dealing with, but my curiosity got the better of me.

I lowered my voice. "Is something going on? I get the impression that you're unhappy to see me. Was I interrupting something?" I hadn't meant to say the last part out loud, but since it was out there—I ran with it. "I can sit elsewhere if so."

Neither answered. They gave each other a look instead.

Grabbing my plate and glass, I began to slide out of the booth when Nick stopped me. "Don't be silly," he said quickly. "We were just man-chatting."

"And what exactly is that? Am I allowed to know, or are you breaking the ancient order of the man code by telling me?" I set the plate down and settled back against the vinyl seat. Tenting my fingers under my chin, I pretended to be riveted. "Is this where you discuss workout routines and sex positions? Because if that's the case, I'm definitely moving. Some things should remain sacred. I'll never be able to look at you again knowing what your kinks are."

Nick chuckled, hooking his arm around mine to keep me in the booth. Cooper wasn't making eye contact, instead staring down at his plate as if his turkey club were a beautiful piece of artwork that he couldn't take his eyes off of.

"I'll tell you whatever you want to know. I'm an open book," Nick joked, starting a rudimentary drawing on his napkin.

"Oh, my God. I can't unsee that! You ass." I laughed, grabbing the napkin from him and balling it up.

I tossed it next to Cooper. That's when I noticed that today's newspaper was folded up on top of his jacket.

Nick followed my line of sight. "Yeah, it's not great."

That explained Cooper's unusually foul mood. He seemed extra salty today.

Before I could tell him not to worry about it, we'd figure something out, his phone started ringing. "Excuse me," he said, sliding out of the booth with the phone up to his ear. "Hey, thanks for calling me back."

He disappeared outside, and I could see him pacing in the parking lot. He didn't look stressed now, though. Quite the opposite. Whoever he was talking to seemed to be defrosting his mood.

"What's up with him?" I asked, biting into a juicy piece of chicken. "It seems like more's bothering him than just the article."

"It's sort of a combo of all of it, I think. He hasn't really said much about the campaign other than quoting you about needing to change the narration."

"Narrative," I corrected, laughing when Nick flipped me off. "Hey, it's not my fault you only half-listen."

"This is exhausting. I don't know how any of you are doing it. I'm only in charge of the finances, and I'm ready to set it all on fire from the stress. I keep asking myself 'Am I keeping track of everything? Have I missed anything? Did I calculate something wrong?' I double- and triple-check my records so that everything is on the up-and-up. Meanwhile, he's running around trying to be a stand-up guy and getting shat on every time he turns around. And you're busting your ass to keep him in line. I mean, I know you expect this kind of shit with politics, but it's brutal. Why anyone wants to put themselves through this is beyond me."

Glancing around the restaurant, I wondered how many of the fifty or so people inside believed what yesterday's headline had claimed—that Cooper's mother was trying to bribe votes for her son. I hoped not many people believed something so obviously false, but the odds were that some of them would. Up to now, the paper had always been trustworthy. In and of itself, that was infuriating.

"We have to find out who's running wild at the paper. Get them to ease up on the slander. We're chasing our tails here trying to stay ahead of it all."

"Whitney thinks she knows who it is. Or at least who it *likely* is," Nick said around a bite of his sandwich.

My fork hovered in front of my mouth. "You've talked to Whitney? About this?"

He nodded, continuing to chew like it wasn't a big deal. I guess theoretically it wasn't. Nick and Henry had known her for as long as Cooper and I had. "She was just here. You missed her by two minutes. A real peach, that one," he said with an eye roll. "I swear, as often as she's been here, you've done a masterful job of avoiding her. I wish I could learn that trick."

"Wait, what?"

"Which part do I need to repeat? Whitney being here? I thought you knew that. She's been staying at Cooper's and working from there until she has to head back to Philly. Apparently her firm might relocate her to Barreton. She'd be so much closer," he said, a shudder rolling through him. "Anyway, she thinks the person trying to defame Cooper at the paper is an ex-girlfriend. Someone who knows what would hurt him the most. Anyone who knows him knows how much he loves it here and how badly he wants this."

"Turn the town against him using a resource they trust and hurt him that way," I added, seeing a clear picture. "It's brilliant." I hated that I hadn't thought of that.

You hate that she thought of it before you.

"Whit thinks so, too," he said, the nickname sticking in my craw. "He's been running all of this by her. Like a second opinion, I guess?" He hooked a finger outside to where Cooper was pacing the sidewalk with the phone pressed to his ear.

"That's probably her again. The calls are nonstop," Nick added, squeezing an obscene amount of ketchup onto his plate.

He looked irritated, which made me irrationally happy since I knew it was because of Whitney.

"That's a good theory," I admitted, but the more I thought about the paper, the more it didn't make sense. "But it can't be a girlfriend. Peter's got final approval over everything that gets printed. It has to go deeper."

"Good point. I wonder what it could be?"

"Can I ask you something else?"

He waved a french fry toward me to continue.

"Does Cooper not trust me? Is that why he's asking Whitney's opinion about all of this and not mine?" My voice sounded weak, and I hated myself a little bit for it.

"Nah, I don't think it's that. They were talking about other shit, and she asked about the paper. It happened one night after he first talked to her about this whole thing. Bee tee dubs, I still can't believe she's who he's brought out of the dugout for this."

"I don't understand your sportsball lingo. Explain."

He rolled his eyes. "It's a baseball term. I would have said stable or harem, but I figured that would have gotten me a fork to the hand or something."

I nodded. "You're right, it would have." It wouldn't have been the first time I'd slapped him with silverware for an assy remark. "So what does 'the dugout' have to do with Whitney?"

He sighed. Drama wasn't something Nick subscribed to. He was more of an "air out your business like a grown-up" type of guy than a gossiper. "It's just that Whitney caused so many damn problems in the past that I'm surprised he'd choose her for this. Well, lemme rewind. First off, I was shocked when your pops told him to get a lady friend. I figured if Enrico and the governor wanted Cooper to look respectable, they'd have him date someone like you."

I choked on my lemonade. "Excuse me? Are you high?"

"No, thank you very much. I'm serious. Henry agrees with me, too. If you're looking for the perfect pair to take on the world, it would have been you two."

Slack-jawed, I stared at him, trying to see his side of things. "We needed someone who had a well-known romantic history with him."

"I'm just saying, you two would have been an easy sell. As Henry said, 'It's been practically written on the stars.'"

"It's written *in*—you know what, never mind."

I would be speaking to Henry later.

"Listen, Fakespeare. I think you're both hanging around with my mother too much." This was starting to sound like her bizarre hope of me and Cooper ending up together.

"You know I love Sophia. Tell her that I'm here whenever she wants to leave your father for me."

I mock gagged. "You're disgusting."

"You love me."

"Like an STD," I whispered to Nick just as Cooper was coming back inside.

"Was that about today's article?" I asked Cooper as he slid back into the booth. He nodded. I sighed in exasperation. "My father is calling Peter again to try to sort out the articles. He's been avoiding him, which isn't a great sign. Mayor Dad says he hasn't seen him in months."

"Hey, is everything okay?" Nick asked, stealing one of Cooper's potato chips from his plate.

Cooper didn't touch his sandwich, instead poking at it with a pickle spear.

"Yeah, I'm good," he finally said, turning back to us and scrubbing a hand over his face. "Do I have time to run home?"

"Are you asking me for permission? Or talking to yourself?" I teased, but he wasn't laughing along with me.

"You *are* the captain," he bit out between his teeth, waving to someone who had just walked in.

"I suppose, but I'm not your keeper, Cooper," I snapped, uninterested in being his punching bag because of his bad mood.

"Sorry, sorry. I'm just . . . I don't know. Stressed. Aggravated. On an edge so thin, I feel like one misstep and I'm over a cliff," he said quietly.

"Care to tell me what's up?" I asked abruptly, causing both

Cooper and Nick to jump a little. "Are you annoyed because I included the trip to the food pantry today? I don't want to wear you down, but it's a great opportunity to show you being philanthropic. A way for people to see that you care about needy families even if they're not necessarily from Hope Lake."

"I'm following this schedule to a tee, and I know why it's needed, but it's just so much I feel deep-fried. Whit thinks it's too much, too. That I should pare some of it back."

I lowered my voice, not wanting to draw the attention of the crowd of people who had just entered and were milling about by our booth. "*You* asked *me* for help. I didn't go chasing you around to take on this headache. If Whitney has an opinion, she can come to me with it. I'm only here to help, and her going against the plan isn't helping."

Whitney was always like a little argumentative bee in his ear.

"I'm not trying to sound like an ass, but she's right. You don't explain anything to me, and it's frustrating. You tell me what to do in as few words as possible. For someone who normally likes to talk, it's pretty apparent that you don't want to converse with me."

"Oh, please! All I try and get you to do is talk and tell me what's wrong, and you're Mr. Subject Changer!" I exclaimed, picking up my fork. I felt Nick stiffen next to me.

Cooper threw his head back and roared with laughter. It was so loud and booming that half the restaurant turned and smiled. At least they thought we were having fun. "You do talk and talk and talk, but it's *at* me, not *to* me. I'm not a lapdog for you to train."

"Oh, so now I'm supposed to take advice from Whitney on how to talk to you? That's rich coming from her."

Cooper narrowed his eyes. "Jealous?"

I bit my tongue before I could say another word. How had this devolved so quickly?

But I couldn't help myself.

"Of Whitney?" I said hysterically. "As if."

Yes, was what I should have said. I'm sure it was written all over my face.

, ...ing a

o be. Fuck.

e voices in

l a fucking

even three

ething rash

think her

walk today

"Emma, no!" he snapped, crumpling the napkin and tossing it onto the plate. "I don't want her."

"Could've fooled me," I said, feeling the hurt and doubt creeping up.

"Hey, come on, guys. Don't make me separate you two," Nick interjected. "We're all friends here. Who wants dessert? Let's all have a piece of pie. Pie is safe. No one gets mad at pie. Apple pie for us all!" He looked to the waitress for help. She took one look at the table and turned around. *Smart move.*

"No pie. I'm not hungry." Which was true—if I ate anything right now, my rolling stomach would revolt.

"I'm good. We're all good, Nick." Cooper sighed, but nothing about his tone seemed genuine. He was just trying to change the subject.

"So what else is on the agenda today? Anything fun?" Nick asked desperately, trying to pull the conversation out of the gutter. "Where the hell is the waitress?"

"Can I get the check, actually?" Cooper asked, pulling his wallet out of his pocket. Without waiting for it to come, he threw too much money on the table.

I pushed the cash back at him. "I'll get my own lunch!" I slapped a twenty on the table. "Think long and hard about what you want here, Cooper. If you're exhausted, fed up, and stressed now, what's it going to be like when you're mayor?"

Sliding out of the booth, I threw my purse over my shoulder and turned to Nick. "Instead of *financial* numbers, you may want to explain to Cooper about *poll* numbers. Even with the bullshit headlines, they're reporting that if that election was today, he'd win in a landslide. I'm sure Whitney could have told him that, though. I certainly had nothing to do with it." Ignoring the stunned expressions on their faces, I headed out into the damp air.

17

Emma, you can't squeeze in another meeting today. It's literally not possible," Nancy said, coming into my office with yet another cup of coffee.

"You realize this isn't your job anymore, right?" I said, gesturing at the cup. "Come to think of it, it wasn't really your job before." Nevertheless, I took it gratefully. After the past couple days, I was a step away from having a caffeine drip hooked up.

Behind Nancy was her replacement, hot on her heels with a notebook and a beaming smile. Her name was Anne, she was about forty, and she was one of the happiest people I had ever met. As in, she was happy. *All. The. Time.* It took a bit of getting used to. Not that Nancy wasn't always chipper, but Anne's personality went above and beyond. She was a mom of twin four-year-old boys, and I think being out of the house with other adults was keeping her spirits high. She was positively ebullient.

"I'm happy to take another meeting. Working keeps my mind off of other things," I said lightly. Like Whitney being here. In my town. Or fighting with Cooper or planning stuff for Cooper or kissing Cooper.

Or the one that had popped into my head at three this morning: Whitney kissing Cooper.

Setting the cup down, I rubbed my eyes, trying to will some life into my face. I was exhausted from working endlessly on the Jackson project. The Jacksons' schedule was jam-packed and Monday was one of the only times they had free, so we had to make it work. No matter how crammed the prep time was. The words had been floating off the pages for the last hour. "I hate that word, you know."

Nancy laughed. "*Squeeze* or *meeting*?"

I picked up the cup. "Neither. I hate *literally*. It's such a throw-away word. One of those words that people put into sentences just to make them longer or to make something sound more dire than it is." I gulped the barely warm coffee and spat it back into the cup, disgusted. "Gross! What the hell is in this?"

"Nothing, unfortunately. I was going to spike it, but I thought it would backfire and make you more sleepy. Then I forgot to re-heat it since it came from the pot I made this morning—which is why it's cold. But I figured you could still use the caffeine."

"Where's the sugar?"

"We're out. It was Cooper's turn to bring in supplies right before he left. We never redid the list of who brings in what to account for him not being here anymore."

I ignored the pang I got thinking about him. Instead I focused on the bitterness in my mouth. "I'll still take it, but it's gross. Anyway, what about my meeting? Were you able to get my dad up here? What is this for again?" I started pacing around the room. If I didn't keep moving, I was going to crash and sleep for a month.

Nancy stopped me before I could finish my lap. "You realize you can see Mayor Dad anytime you want, right? It's part of the whole 'dad' thing. It's basically a rule."

"I know that. I just don't want it to look suspect, that's all. I want it on the books so when the Jackson deal goes through, people see that we busted our asses to get it done." I collapsed exhaustedly into my squishy seat.

I could hear Nancy and Anne murmuring beside me. Words like *She needs to get some rest*.

They weren't wrong. There just wasn't time. "I can hear you," I groaned.

Anne excused herself to make a few calls.

"You know I love you, but you're not as young as you used to be, you know," Nancy teased.

"I'm not old, lady," I shot back, lifting my heavy arm to slap her knee.

"Semantics. You're sleeping for, what, a few hours a night if you're lucky? Where's the *you* time? When was the last time you went out and got yourself laid?"

My eyes popped open. "Laid or *good* laid?"

She snorted derisively. "Either. Is there really a difference?"

"Of course," I said, thinking back to the last guy I'd dated. Mediocre was the kindest description I could have given it.

"That's so depressing. When was the last time you got laid? Either good *or* meh."

A throat cleared from the doorway. "This isn't the conversation I wanted to walk in on," my father muttered. "I had a five o'clock appointment with my daughter. I can come back when this topic is—" He paused, shuffling backward into the hallway. "Never. I never want to come back."

With his hands over his ears, he stammered, "L-Let's reschedule. I'll stop back in later or never. Nancy, would you mind heading down to my office instead?"

"Take five and close your eyes," she said, closing the door behind her.

After they left, I sat staring at the wall for a few minutes until Cooper knocked on the door. "Am I interrupting anything?"

It must have gotten chilly outside because his cheeks were pink and he was rubbing his hands together. The deep blue puffy vest he was wearing couldn't have provided much warmth. The effect was there, though. He looked less like a loaded Wall Street guy and more like a guy who'd just returned from a casual hike in the woods.

"Come on in. I'm not great company at the moment. A bit preoccupied," I admitted.

He closed the door behind him. "You ready for the Jacksons next week?" he asked, glancing down at my opening proposal for the meeting.

"Yep, want to read?" I asked, handing it to him.

"Present it," he suggested, handing the speech back to me. "Wow me."

"Are you sure?" We hadn't yet discussed what had happened at the diner. That was the MO with Cooper and me. We never discussed anything. Ever. It was part of the reason that we had gone on so many years being antagonistic to each other.

"Honestly, go for it. Consider it my penance for being a dick the other day."

"I wasn't exactly a peach, either," I admitted, feeling better already.

He shrugged and held up his fingers in a peace sign. We had a way to go, but it was better than being stuck on the side of the road.

"It's not weird if I do this speech for you?"

Shaking his head, he motioned for me to speak. "Go for it. I'm all ears," he said, moving to lean against the corner of the desk. "I'm here for moral support. Maybe I can give you a few pointers."

"Oh, yeah? Like what?"

Cooper pushed off from the desk and walked toward me. Closing the small distance between us, he stretched out his right arm behind my head.

The small clip that held all my hair back was pulled out slowly, the strands falling down my back and over his hand. "Better," he said, tucking the clip into his vest pocket. "You look more approachable now. Less intimidating."

He kept his eyes on mine while I fought for a witty comeback. It never came. "Thanks," I said lamely.

"Don't use the podium in the conference room. Walk the space with your shoulders back. Like this," he said, touching my shoulders gently to straighten my posture a bit. His hands lingered just a second too long before they slid down to my elbows, finishing with a small squeeze. Was that for good luck or a signal to continue with the speech? Or . . . did it mean something else?

"All right, let's see it," he said, clapping his hands together and interrupting my psychoanalyzing. "Forget it's me here, and keep going through to the end."

He watched carefully as I pulled my note cards out and took a deep breath. I ignored the fact that he was intently watching me and focused on my speech.

"When my father was first elected to office more than two decades ago," I began, "the town had just closed one of its last factories. The economy was crippled in a way that people hadn't seen in their lifetimes. The loss of jobs was a slow, depressing descent into the unknown for its eight thousand residents. People fled in droves because we didn't have any big businesses hiring, and there were no new businesses coming in to replace all of the factory businesses we'd lost—along with all of the jobs that had gone with them.

"Those hard times didn't deter my father or the town council. They had to focus on the positive. So after a bit of panic and a lot of work, they started making some changes. They looked to big cities for inspiration. What worked there could work in a small town, too. Now, the changes weren't immediate. Everything took time, but in a town named Hope Lake, people pull together. Your neighbors are your friends here."

Cooper sat across from me, a blank expression on his face. Nothing indicated how I was doing; and I wanted to do well. It was more than just proving to myself that I could do well with the Jacksons. I needed *him* to know that I could do it.

"One of the main points that never got lost from Hope Lake," I continued, "was the focus on enriching the town and making life better for its citizens. Immigrants first came here hoping for a better future, and a better future is what we hope to continue to deliver for years to come.

"In a town remembered for coal miners and steel factories, Hope Lake's council and leadership embraced wind power and clean energy. Companies pushing a green future were courted. Furloughed factory workers were trained to work on turbines, grid building, and solar installation. Eventually, empty factories morphed into apartments and turbines sprouted like cornstalks in once-empty fields. Years ago, Hope Lake was looked down upon as a small-town tourist trap. The poor man's Poconos. But instead of being put off by that description, we've embraced it, catering to the crowd looking for something different: quaint, cozy, family-oriented businesses that aren't absurdly expensive and out of reach. That draw people in who need an escape from their busy lives in the city. Hope Lake is their home away from home. And we hope it will become your home, too."

I carried on like that for a few more minutes. Finally, after my last word hung heavily in the air, Cooper stood. And to my relief, he looked impressed: a nugget I would carry with me proudly.

"What do you think?" I finally asked.

He cleared his throat. We weren't far apart, but it felt like there was a field of empty space between us. Maybe my taking over the Jackson deal really *was* bothering him more than he was willing to admit to me.

"Honestly," he said slowly, a grin spreading across his face, "if they don't like it, we don't want them here. But don't tell anyone I said that." He ran a hand through his hair, looking thoughtful. "I do think you need a couple more lines and one killer ending, though. Something about why Hope Lake is perfect for JOE— especially why we're better than the Poconos. That could seal the deal right there."

Nodding, I stacked my notes and tucked them into my back pants pocket. Cooper's eyes followed the movement until he realized I was watching him. I quickly turned away, embarrassed at catching him in the act.

"Good luck. I'll be waiting for an update."

18

The night before the pitch, I couldn't sleep. It wasn't nerves but an eagerness that kept my mind in a constant whir. It felt like it had in college just before a huge test. It went above and beyond just being amped up—I was tossing and turning, pacing and staring at the cracks in my ceiling for hours.

Finally I queued up a marathon of Bob Ross on Netflix. It usually took only one sweetly whispered phthalo blue for me to be snoring until morning. And thankfully, sometime around four, I crashed. Unfortunately, I did so curled up on the sofa and woke with a crick in my neck.

Even in the heat of the shower, I couldn't fight the chill that snaked down my spine as I thought about the presentation. *Everything is perfect,* I tried to convince myself. I knew everything was set and that there was no more prep I could do, but something still wasn't sitting quite right. There was a looming feeling that I couldn't quite shake. It was more than the presentation at stake—it was everything. So much good could come from this. Not just for the town but for the CDO, with Cooper as the next mayor.

The pressure was on me to deliver. And I was determined to do so.

"You're so excited," Nancy commented at the office, walking

alongside me as I paced a circle around the conference room. "You'll do fine—you just need to burn off some of this nervous energy. Think about the champagne afterward." She didn't say anything further, just remained a reassuring friend beside me. I needed it.

We'd painstakingly arranged and rearranged the room in an effort to make it inviting yet formal. Businesslike but friendly.

Historical photos from various areas of town had been pulled from other offices and departments and placed strategically along the Jacksons' route from the front door of Borough Building to the conference room. They were scenes of Hope Lake that told a story of our ever-improving town—a story that would hopefully continue with my speech and with the Jacksons' business.

"It's okay to be nervous, too. I'd be worried if you weren't," Nancy said.

"That's the call," I said unnecessarily as the phone in the hallway rang. Anne answered it, and upon hanging up, she shouted, "They're here!"

"It'll take them a couple minutes to get up here," I said to myself as I shook out my arms, rolled my neck, and prayed that my stomach would stop with the somersaults.

It felt like only ten seconds had gone, but just as I was about to pour myself a glass of water, I heard the elevator ding.

"Here goes everything." I smiled and walked into the hall to greet them.

"THEY SEEM TO BE in a good mood, right?" I whispered to Nancy as the Jackson family got themselves acclimated. We'd agreed to give them a few minutes to settle in before we started with the official presentation. Some of their team were helping themselves to coffee and snacks while we waited for the rest to file in. Anne was excitedly waiting by the doorway, keeping an eye out for anyone who looked lost.

"So far, so good," Nancy answered.

Scanning the room, I recognized only a handful of faces from our last meeting as the Jackson family took their places at the conference table. Mr. Jackson's two sons, Christopher and Matthew, were sitting front and center. His daughter, Maria, was toward the back with a notebook, ready to roll. All people who should have been present. But the woman at the head of the table was the last person I thought we would see.

"Haley Jackson?" Nancy hissed, and I nodded. Her phone began buzzing.

Something felt off. None of Mr. Jackson's children had addressed her in any way. In fact, they all had their chairs turned so their backs were to her. "I'll be right back," Nancy whispered, and with a glance at her screen, she slipped out the door into the hallway.

In updating my research on the family and the business, I had never considered that Haley would still be in the picture, let alone a deciding member of the business. That added another level of stress that I wasn't prepared for.

"We're ready when you are," the elder son, Christopher, said, smiling from his seat at the front of the conference table. I cleared my throat and wiped my palms, giving him a nervous smile. My eyes flicked to the door. Where was Nancy?

"Thank you all for coming," I began, happy that my voice wasn't wavering. "We're very excited to present this revised proposal to your company. I hope that you enjoyed the breakfast?" A few nods and grunts of approval came from the table.

"It was great!" Christopher said with a smile, relaxing back into his chair and clasping his hands in front of him. He looked at me expectantly—it was clear he wanted me to start.

I glanced toward the door again. Still no Nancy. I guess I would be running this show solo.

"Can we get started?" Haley asked nasally, tapping her long red nails against the table. "I'd like to be back on the plane and headed home to my husband sooner rather than later."

Taken aback, I looked at Christopher's daughter, who shot her stepmother a bone-chilling look. Haley couldn't be much older than me, which meant she was younger than his adult children. That had to make for some interesting holiday dinners.

"Emma, we're *all* eager to see what you put together," Christopher said smoothly, also giving his stepmother a look. "Whenever you're ready." With an encouraging smile he settled in, and I began.

TWENTY-FIVE MINUTES LATER, I was finished. I was exhausted but beaming. Somewhere toward the end of the presentation, Nancy had sneaked back in, practically gluing herself to the wall so as not to draw attention to herself. Looking around her, I'd hoped to see my father walking in. He was supposed to be there to show that the CDO had the full support of the mayor and council.

A sense of worry bloomed in my stomach when he never showed. Swallowing back the anxious feelings, I smiled at the group. "We'll give you the room to discuss any questions you might have and be back in about twenty minutes."

"Make it ten," Chris said confidently, before turning to his sister to confer with her.

Please let that be a good sign, I prayed as I walked into the hallway—just in time to run into my father and Cooper, both looking panic-stricken.

"How much time do you have?" my father asked, before leaning down and kissing my cheek.

"What happened? I thought you were coming in?"

"We need to talk," Cooper interrupted, taking my elbow to guide me toward my empty office, my father following close behind.

I pulled my arm from his grasp and scowled. "Why are you here? And why weren't you in there?" I added, looking to my father for answers. More than anything, I felt disappointed. I was gutted that whatever they were doing was more important than this.

"Emma, honey, hear him out," my father said calmly, trying to mediate the situation. "It's important you hear this from Cooper, before . . . you know what, just go ahead, Cooper."

Cooper paced, running a hand through his hair. "Have you seen Rogers's campaign Facebook page today?" he asked nervously.

I stepped toward the center of the room. "What the hell does that have to do with anything?"

He took out his phone, turning it toward me.

On the "Rogers for Mayor" campaign page was a shadowy photo taken near the site where we wanted the Jacksons to build: a beautiful expanse of land that was currently sitting vacant. It was the same site we'd proposed to them six years ago. In the photo, you could see a much younger Cooper standing with his arms around Haley Jackson. Pulling the phone from Cooper's hand, I swiped through the photos of Cooper and Mrs. Jackson.

I'd seen them before, of course. The first time around, they'd been splashed all over the *Journal*. But the new photo that followed was what was unexpected.

There, at the same site, was Cooper standing in his suit from yesterday's function with none other than Mrs. Haley Jackson.

"Tell me that this isn't—" I began, but paused when my hands started shaking so badly that I couldn't see the post clearly.

"You can't possibly be this stupid," I snapped, still unable to comprehend what I was seeing.

Cooper interrupted. "Emma, it's not what you think—"

"It doesn't matter what I think. Or what happened. Or what line of bull you're going to send my way. It matters what *they* think." I pointed to the wall between us and the Jacksons. "It matters what *they* think!" I shouted, motioning to the window toward the whole town.

I flipped the image to the main post again. It wasn't tawdry in any way, the two of them standing a foot or more apart, but what did it matter? The next screen cap was a text statement from Kirby Rogers:

> They tried to hide it, but we got the scoop. Mayoral candidate Cooper Endicott can be seen here doing his best to *seal the deal* with JOE founder and majority stakeholder's wife, Haley, nearly a decade ago and *again* last night. It's like the saying goes, a leopard doesn't change its spots. Wonder what the family will have to say about this? We here at Kirby's campaign headquarters have to think that Endicott's wanton and reckless behavior has put this lucrative project and dozens of jobs at risk, *again*. Is that the person you really want running this town? Elect Rogers for Mayor of Hope Lake: Respectable, Honorable, and Steadfast.

The color drained from my face. I was feeling it now along with a woozy, light-headed rush that was the result of all my blood moving south in a hurry. I looked down at my shaking hands to see their normally olive tone looking sallow. If I looked in a mirror, I wagered that I would see the same.

"Emmanuelle, it's not how it looks!" Cooper insisted, reaching a shaky hand out to take his phone back. "I'm not an idiot. I know you think that right now, but I need you to listen to me."

I gripped the phone tighter, turning to face away from him so I could look at the new photo again.

"Emma," my father said, touching my shoulder. I turned as he stepped toward me and took the phone away. He pushed it into Cooper's hand, and for the first time, I saw that he, too, was furious with him.

"You have to listen to me, Emma. You know I wouldn't do this to you," Cooper insisted as my father slipped out of the room to speak to Nancy, who was waiting in the hall.

"It's the old photo plus a new one, but it's not what you think. I swear to you, Emma, I wouldn't do that. Not now . . . not after . . . tell me you believe me. Say something," he pleaded, and when I looked up, he looked as nauseated as I felt. "Say you believe me."

"Why? Because this isn't something you'd do? Risk a project that we've spent months—wait, no, *years*—on just to get your dick wet?"

He reared back as if I'd slapped him. "That's all I am to you? Your opinon about me hasn't changed at all. I'm just that same guy without any redeeming qualities."

"You're saying this isn't a new photo of the two of you to-gether?" I shouted, pointing to the phone in his shaking hand. He looked like a cross between crushed and furious. I'm sure my expression was a mirror image.

"It is, but it's not what it looks like. Not that it matters—it's clear that nothing I do will make you see me differently."

I shrugged. "You haven't exactly proven to me that you're above all of this," I said, flailing my arms around. "I thought we were making progress." I wasn't sure myself which version of Cooper I was referring to: Cooper the candidate or Cooper the former friend of Emma.

All I knew was that in the pit of my stomach, an ache was growing that I wasn't sure would stop until it swallowed me whole. At the bottom of it was Cooper and this deal that was likely lost— yet again—thanks to him. I didn't know which was worse, the loss of the deal or the loss of my faith in Cooper, and I didn't have time to consider it because Nancy and my father appeared at the door looking distraught. "Emma, they're asking for you."

Numbly I rolled my shoulders back and turned to my father, ignoring Cooper entirely.

"This could have been incredible. All that hard work . . . wasted," I whispered defeatedly, and I walked out the door and into the conference room just in time to see the Jacksons pulling up the photos.

19

Over a pitcher of beer at Hope Lake Brewing Company, I explained my version of the shittiest day on record to Henry Mercer, the most levelheaded person I knew.

"He called me this morning, panicked," Henry was saying to me as I downed yet another beer. "You've got to know that nothing happened. They cropped the photo. Nick and I were there with him before dinner, when this was taken. Cooper and Haley said hello to each other, and that was it."

"Why were you there?" I asked with a hiccup. I didn't like the way Henry looked at me. It was that pitying sort of look people gave SPCA commercials. You wanted to help, but you just didn't know where to start.

"I think it was twofold," he began, sliding the beer away from me. "I think he was slaying his Jackson demons by revisiting the site, but more important, he was proud of you for going for it. He was going on about your vision and how it was better than anything he had ever come up with."

I looked up, surprised. "Really?"

"Emma, he's been talking about it for days. Since you told him about it, really. He's so proud of you. You've got to know he carries an incredible burden because he screwed it up the first go-around."

The beer gurgled in my stomach. This wasn't what I wanted to hear. I *needed* to, but it still hurt. My reaction had been over the top and cruel. Knowing that Cooper had been there only because of me made it that much worse.

I already knew that the photo had been cropped. My father had explained it after Cooper, and the Jacksons, had left. The photographer had told my father that it had deliberately been done to mirror the original, which he had also taken. "Cooper tried to explain himself, but I was so enraged I couldn't look at him, let alone hear anything he was saying."

"That's understandable. Don't beat yourself up too much. It's not like it's *not* in the realm of possibility for Cooper to do something so idiotic."

"Even so."

He patted my hand. "Even so nothing. You jumped to a logical conclusion. You can't be tarred and feathered for that."

That made me feel worse—after all Cooper had done to try to improve himself in my eyes, I had cast my old prejudices against him without a second thought. "I just can't believe what Kirby did to him."

Henry nodded. "I told Cooper to call you to warn you, but he didn't know what your reaction would be and didn't want to upset you before the meeting, so he decided to approach your dad before talking to you in person. He was understandably nervous about how you'd react." Henry pulled out his phone to show me a photo of Cooper looking distraught at what appeared to be his house. Then a copy of the original, uncropped photo that my father had gotten from the newspaper. I just couldn't bring myself to look at it again.

Sure enough, Cooper and Haley were at the forefront near the water, but instead of being alone, they were with Henry, who was standing just behind them, and Nick, who was looking down at his phone and not paying attention to anything. I shook my head.

"Don't kid yourself," I said. "He didn't care what *I* thought—I'm sure he was only nervous about the campaign. Cooper doesn't care about anything but himself—that much is as clear as this glass." I chugged the rest of my beer and held up the glass for Henry to see. "See? Clear. If he *did* care about what I thought, he wouldn't have been there. With her. Again."

Henry tipped his head to the side, leveling me with his sympathetic eyes. "You already know that's not true. Besides, she just showed up."

Taking Henry's unused beer glass to substitute for my empty one, I swallowed another sip of beer to clear the dry, scratchy feeling in my throat. Cooper being proud of me was an odd feeling to process.

"Say something, Ems. I know when you're chewing on something troubling," Henry said, taking my hand in his and looking at me with serious eyes.

Henry was one of those guys men wanted to try to arm wrestle and women just straight-up wanted, but he was content with being everyone's friend. He wasn't just tall, dark, and devilishly handsome; he also happened to be kind, wickedly smart, and the sort of human who just loved helping people. Like Nick, he had always been like a brother to me. Henry would forever be known as Henry, the Fiercely Loyal. It didn't matter what your relationship was with him—family, friend, student—if he believed you to be a good human, he'd do everything in his power to defend you.

I sighed. "Right now I just want to be mad. I'll be fine in the morning, but for now let me be drunk and drown in self-pity. I'm so disappointed. I'm allowed to be disappointed, right? I should have seen something coming. Had a contingency for every possible scenario."

Henry held up his hand. "Now, hold on a minute. You're not to blame for this at all. So there's no reason to be disappointed in yourself. Period."

"Logically I know that, but I'm still feeling like shit."

"Fair enough," he said, pouring me another beer. "Last one, missy. It's a school night."

An hour later, I was feeling both marginally better and worse.

"You're my favorite, Henry. I tolerate Nick, and I love Cooper, but you're my favoritest. Is that a word?" I mumbled, giving his chestnut hair and deep blue eyes a once-over as I tried to pour myself another glass, sloshing some beer over the glass in the process.

"Okay, that's enough for you, young lady." He gently took the pitcher from my hands and smiled—one of those heart-stopping, bright, sexy smirks that made most women in town fall-down stupid. "Emma, I love you, and when you sober up in the morning and remember what you just said, we'll have a good laugh together."

"Ugh, I can't drink anymore," I admitted, followed by a very unladylike hiccup.

Henry signaled the bartender for the check. She, like most of the women in the place, got a bit dreamy-eyed watching him as he smiled innocently at her. For someone so ridiculously intelligent, he had zero common sense when it came to his effect on women. *Zero.*

"You should have been the one to run for office," I said seriously, watching as she drooled over him. "It would have been so easy. Everyone in town loves you. You're a good listener. There aren't any manwhorey skeletons in your closet. You're just . . . *good.*"

"Though I thank you for that," Henry laughed, "I have enough going on. Besides, public office requires public speaking. Unless I can quote Shakespeare and deal only with teenagers, I don't think I would win. Cooper, on the other hand—"

"Has had every chance handed to him and still managed to shoot himself in the ass."

Cooper had called me repeatedly throughout the day, but I'd kept sending him to voice mail. After speaking with my father, I wasn't mad at him, but that didn't mean I wanted to talk. The last time I'd checked my phone, he had already left a dozen messages.

"Can I be honest?" Henry asked. I nodded. "I don't think it's going to be that bad. Cooper uploaded the undoctored photo to his campaign site, the news ran it, and it's been shared across Facebook, Twitter, Insta, and Snapchat. Every social media platform we have. Kirby was tagged every time someone accused him of being the culprit. We even got the *Journal* to agree to run the real photo to make sure we catch all the people who didn't see it on social media. Sure, some people will still be mad, but for the most part—"

"Ever the optimist, Henry Mercer."

"Honestly." Henry nodded. "Tell me again how the Jacksons ended your meeting today?"

"'Obviously this puts a negative spin on things, Emma,'" I said, mimicking Christopher's stern voice.

"Is there any hope to salvage it?" Henry asked, sliding the half-full pitcher farther away from me when I reached for it.

I was already on beer number six for the night. Well, not quite. Some had spilled on my shirt, while some was in the neighboring glasses of the other bar patrons because Henry had thought he was being slick by giving it away. With the fall semester in full swing, Henry was casually nursing his orange and cranberry juice cocktail like the good teacher that he was.

"Have they gone back to Seattle yet?" he asked, eyebrows raised, as I drained my glass.

I shrugged. "I called Christopher a few times, but it went straight to voice mail. I'm not holding my breath. It was a good deal, but if they think the press is only going to run the old scandal and hurt business, they may just say screw it. It's not worth the frustration or the time and money to change people's minds with ads. The new photo might help, but I'm not counting on it."

The family had stood and walked out of the room in a show of solidarity.

"Once my father explained everything to me, he emailed the family detailing what happened and included the original photo. They didn't respond, but it's possible they'll reach out. It might just be a saving-face thing right now." Even with the photo that had proven his innocence, seeing that first image must have felt like Cooper—and by extension, Hope Lake—had disrespected the Jacksons and their business all over again. That was a hard thing to come back from. I huffed in frustration.

"We're supposed to be helping his image. Making Cooper seem less . . . Cooperish. He's supposed to be wooing Whitney. Being the perfect political power couple." I signaled the bartender for another pitcher. "You know about that, right?"

He nodded. "How do you feel about that?"

"Want a shot?"

"I suppose that answers my question," he said, laughing.

"Oh, Henry. Always the peacekeeper." I sighed, standing to pat him on his lovely tousled head. "Where to now? This place is boring." I looked around at the pub. A handful of regulars were sitting at the bar, coming in after their softball game, stopping for a pint on the way home. Other than that, the place was empty.

"We're headed home. Where you're going to sleep this off," Henry told me, bending to pick up my purse. "Will you be walking or piggyback riding this evening?"

"Piggy, please. I don't know that I'll make it very far on foot," I said through a yawn. He slung my purse over his shoulder, confident enough to strut out of a bar with a hot pink Kate Spade on his arm.

He laughed. "My guess is that you'd give up on making it home and sleep it off under the table. It would be like that time you visited me at Penn State over spring break and fell asleep curled up underneath a bath towel."

"I haven't had vodka since." Hiking up my skirt, I jumped on his back. He didn't even flinch. Instead he reached into his pocket to pull out his tattered wallet and pay the bill. It was as if there weren't a person attached to him like Yoda.

"Onward, Skywalker!" I hollered, resting my head on his shoulder. Reaching back, he hooked his hands beneath my knees and walked swiftly out of the bar and into the unseasonably cool night, humming the *Star Wars* theme song. He'd parked at the end of the lot, and the rocking motion was doing me in.

"Thanks, Henry," I whispered as he deposited me into the passenger side of his ancient Jeep. And with that I drifted off to sleep.

"STOP SPINNING," I GROANED, rolling over in search of the cool part of my pillow. Forcing one eye open, I saw that it was morning, but it looked miserable outside.

Good, it matches how I feel.

Resolved to get up, I scrubbed my hands over my face. They came away sticky from day-old mascara, dried-up beer, and Lord knows what else. When I stretched, I heard a crinkle and looked down to find a note stuck to my shirt with a safety pin.

Emma,
Morning, Sunshine! Don't be stubborn, take the Advil I left
and drink the whole bottle of water. You're off work until
Wednesday. We saw Nancy last night when I was carrying
you up, and we both agreed you deserved a day off. She let
me in and helped me get you dressed in your PJs. Didn't peek,
I promise. :) For the record, you shouldn't sing the Golden
Girls theme song at the top of your lungs at midnight. Your
downstairs neighbor was fit to be tied. And you're not going to
be a crazy old spinster and live out your days with only your
three best friends for company. Nick, Cooper, and I are your
three best friends, and we wouldn't let that happen. Eat some
toast, drink lots of water and the Gatorade (it's in the fridge),
and call me in the afternoon when you come up for air.

XO Henry
(AKA Dorothy. Nick is clearly Rose and
obviously Cooper is Blanche. That, by default,
makes you Sophia. Your mother will be thrilled.)

I racked my brain for any clear recollection after leaving the bar. All I remembered was belting out the *Golden Girls* theme song a dozen times while Henry was carrying me from the Jeep into the building and up all five flights of stairs. I was sure he deserved to be sainted for whatever I'd put him through.

My stomach rolled. I shot off a quick text thanking him for taking good care of me and apologizing for the singing. His response was that he had turned off his implants.

Ignoring my lurching stomach, I swallowed the pills and took a big swig of water. With nothing on the horizon but sleep and television, I snuggled back under the covers, ready to drift off again and ignore the rest of my responsibilities.

By the time I swam up from sleep a second time, it was nearly two in the afternoon and I was starving: always a good sign post-bender. After a quick shower to scrub the dried makeup and beer off my face and the drool from my hair, I stumbled down the stairs and into daylight. It was overcast and a relatively mild day, but between the hangover and the queasiness, it might as well have been ninety degrees and sunny.

I pulled a hat down over my eyes and walked the short distance into town. There was no way I would have the coordination to ride my bike, and driving didn't seem like the best idea, either. I wasn't a big drinker, so a few beers usually did me in—never mind six. Add in the fact that I'd skipped dinner, and I was probably still partially hungover.

Near the post office, my phone pinged with a group message from Henry and Nick with an invite to meet them and a few of Nick's employees at China Garden for dinner whenever I was feeling up to it. It was followed by a message from Nick explaining that he had to eat at a certain time or he got hangry.

ME: Raincheck? I'm still feeling green. How's Wednesday? We can discuss my thoughts on the landscape reno for all the public spaces next summer?

NICKY POO: Do u ever not work?

HENRY NOT THE 8TH: She's always thinking, it's why she's the best at her job. Wednesday is great, Ems. We'll pick you up at 7 sharp.

NICKY POO: Pizza and beer 🍕 🍺 Wed. ur treat

FEW THINGS MADE ME HAPPIER than sitting on a park bench, people watching and gnawing on a soft pretzel. Especially when I was forced to seek out a bench because I was light-headed. *Thanks, hangover.* I felt lousy. Watching the town enjoying the fall weather made me feel marginally better.

Young, sporty couples zipped around the park paths with their sleek helmets and bells. You could always count on yoga in the park, no matter the weather. Today there were dozens of brightly colored mats covering the grass. The Hope Lake seniors' group walked around picking up imaginary litter so they could scope out the town and collect gossip, not trash. Now, that was a sight to see. If I ever needed information fast, I would just go to Mrs. Mancini and her league of extraordinary meddlers.

The usual crew was walking toward me now as I sat quietly under the gazebo the town had erected about a decade before. It was sort of an odd piece of architecture, one of those things that you thought you needed because you thought people would use it, but then it just sat there and collected dust. The only time it was really used was at Christmas, when it was filled with caroling children dressed like Charles Dickens characters.

And it was normally a peaceful spot to relax and hide in. It would have been the perfect hangover recovery spot if I hadn't had to listen to Mrs. Mancini and her crew banter about who was pregnant, who was moving home, and, yes, who Cooper Endicott was currently "seeing." Not exactly something I wanted to chat about in my half-dead state.

Before they saw me, I scooted down so that I was hidden behind the arborvitae that Nick's landscaping company had planted around the gazebo a few years back in an effort to make it more inviting. I'd never realized how perfect a fence they were until I needed them to hide behind to eavesdrop.

Mrs. Mancini, with her powder blue tracksuit and matching Nikes, commanded the small group like a general leading an army. Having the elder Dr. Bishop rolling along beside her on her hot pink motorized scooter made the entire spectacle a hoot.

"The wife was to blame," Mrs. Mancini was saying. "I heard that she came on to Cooper *again*. Practically threw herself at him while the two friends just stood there dumbfounded. You know him, he never could resist a pretty face. Even one as cosmetically altered as hers. It was like shooting ducks in a barrel." As she relayed the gossip to her posse, Mrs. Mancini fanned herself with a thick hand. To prove that the drama was almost *too* much, I guessed.

"You mean fish, Suzanne. Fish in a barrel," one of the other women piped up.

"I know what I said, and I said what I meant, Clara," Mrs. Mancini snapped, turning her back on her friend. The woman hated being corrected almost as much as she hated realizing she was wrong.

Someone cleared her throat. "Kirby's airheaded wife was at the dry cleaners this morning bragging how he was going to be a shoo-in now. What a nightmare Rogers will be to deal with if he's elected. He's so condescending."

"Rogers said he was cutting what little bit of funding the seniors' group has! We can't let that happen," the elder Dr. Bishop chimed in, earning echoes of agreement from the rest.

for. Not just the seniors.
ts and after-school pro-
ni added sharply.
 in chorus, and if they'd
ave clutched them.
or grants. And don't for-
that Barreton University
ng off each idea on her

for a few more minutes
Although I couldn't hear
ar Mrs. Mancini's voice
 Jackson nonsense was
nd he's got that gorgeous
 thought he was—you
 sense of stability."
asn't like it was a state
onquests like Boy Scout

er night at dinner—that
 is she so serious?" Dr.

An alarm sounded from someone's phone. "That's time. Ready, girls? Let's get in another half mile before poker," Mrs. Mancini instructed, and after a chorus of grunts and complaints, the group left in a single-file line of varying shades of rainbow-colored track-suits.

Fishing out my cell phone, I called in reinforcements.

"My darling," my father answered. I could imagine him sitting on his soft leather chair smiling as he stared out the stained-glass window. "What do you need? Are you feeling better? Nancy said you were under the weather and had to use a personal day."

"If by 'under the weather' you meant 'drank myself into a stu-por,' then, yes, I'm sick."

"I think that leaves you with only three hundred sixty-four days left." He laughed. He wasn't wrong; I never took days off. "I can send your mother over with some soup?"

"Are you still in the office?" I asked, slowly standing up. The world had mostly stopped spinning, but I still wasn't taking any chances.

"Yes, why? Have you heard anything from any of the Jacksons?"

"Dad, take a breath. I just need to talk," I panted, turning a corner and nearly running into a cyclist. "And no, nothing from them."

He sighed. "Things will work out how they're supposed to. And, kiddo, I know Cooper is sorry. You should probably talk to him."

I didn't need to talk to him. Sometimes you just needed to chat with your dad. "Can you leave a few minutes early? I'll wait outside your car."

On my way to Borough Building, I wondered if Whitney was still around or if she'd already gone to Barreton. There had been a handful of public appearances by the two of them together. Dinner, a movie, a couple hikes to show Cooper in touch with nature.

Was this a rekindling of their relationship and not just a

political ploy to get him elected? That was something that I was actively wondering about. Could I deal with Whitney in Hope Lake for the rest of time? I had avoided them for years after I found out they'd gotten together. What would I do if she actually moved here?

Thinking about it brought to mind something that I'd toyed with once before, after Cooper had come home from college and started working at the CDO. When things had blown up with Mary Nora, I'd considered doing something I never had before.

Leaving Hope Lake. Maybe it was time for me to consider it again.

20

That afternoon, the ride to my parents' house took significantly longer with my father driving. He prided himself on stopping to chat if he saw someone he knew. Or carrying out a recycling tub to the curb if he saw someone struggling. He drove just below the speed limit, waving at everyone he passed like a pageant participant. As a result, it took almost a half hour just to get to the edge of town. Ever the politician, my father.

"Dad, are you going to miss this? Waving to everyone wherever you go, being the mayor that people can always count on? Twenty-six years is a long time," I commented as he reentered the car after shooing some deer back into the woods. Driving up the side of the mountain, you never knew what animal you might encounter—and my father cared just as much about the safety of Hope Lake's animals as he did about its human citizens.

He thought about it as we drove up the winding road. The car windows were all cracked open to let in the crisp fall air. His usual sixties rock was playing softly on the radio, and his tie was tossed on the backseat of his Grand Cherokee.

My dad sang a line of the Beatles song "Blackbird" before glancing over. "I'll miss a lot of it. Not all of it, but a lot. The benefits of retirement outweigh the sadness of leaving, though."

I turned, pulling my leg up onto the seat to watch him drive. My father and I shared many of the same features and behaviors, including the inability to mask our feelings. If he was lying, I'd know it from the way his nose would twitch or if he swallowed just before he spoke. There weren't any of the normal tells now, though. He looked genuinely at peace.

Still, I was curious. "Like what? Tell me what's the hardest thing to say good-bye to."

"What will I miss the most? I'll miss seeing you every day." He glanced over with a smile. "I'll miss the energy of the building. Fixing problems, finding new projects to take to the council. Like you, I love coming up with new ideas to benefit the town. But I won't miss the headaches. The long days away from your mother; missing the opportunity to travel with her because I'm always at work or working from home. I'm not getting any younger, you know."

"Don't tell Mom that—she's older than you!"

"Only by a month, and trust me, I make sure she knows about it every year. It's a highlight of our marriage to still be able to tease her mercilessly about her age."

He got the faraway look on his face that he always had when he thought of my mother. My heart did a little flip. What was it like to be that much in love with someone?

An image of a smiling Cooper flashed in my head. I held it there for a brief moment before pushing the thought and the image to the back of my mind and firmly closing the door on them. Back to reality.

"Seriously, though, Dad. Why are you retiring? You're still youngish, you're healthy, and you have a lot left to give," I said.

He patted my hand and smiled sadly. "I do have a lot left to give, and I hope that I'm able to continue doing so long after I retire. But I want to be a bit selfish, too, and give what time I have left to your mother. You know that I barely remember my own mother. She died when I was so young, and Nonno Peroni died right after your mom and I got married. You never got to meet him. He would have loved you, by the way. He was a little older than I am now when he died.

"The past few years I've thought—what if I go early, too? I have so much left to do and see. I don't want to leave this party early, but if I keep working like I have been, I'm afraid that I might. So I want to use the time that I have left to do everything I haven't been able to do as mayor. I want to travel. See where my family is from and go on an adventure. Maybe we'll go hiking or skydiving or parasailing—it doesn't matter.

"What *does* matter is that I can't do that if I stay in this job. Too many people rely on me here, and I feel like if I continue wondering *what if,* I'm being unfair both to the town and to myself and your mom. I need someone I know loves Hope Lake as much as I do to follow me as the next mayor. Cooper is that person. No matter what stupid nonsense he gets himself involved in—and I know it's all stupid—we have to help him get the job that we both know is rightfully his."

We were quiet for a second before he popped in one more tidbit. "You know, I don't worry about you because you're stronger than I ever was. You're such an incredible woman, Em. I'm so proud of you." I could see he was getting misty-eyed.

I gave him a watery smile. "I love you, Dad," I whispered, rifling through my purse for a tissue.

"I love you, too, and I know things will work out. I have faith."

We were quiet as he turned onto the gravel drive leading up to the house. We were met by another family of deer. After he tooted the horn once, they scurried back into the woods and we continued rumbling up the drive. My dad gave my hand a squeeze.

"No matter what I've done as mayor, kiddo, you're my most crowning achievement. Never forget that."

WHEN WE FINALLY ARRIVED AT THE HOUSE, my mother was in the front garden, wrapping burlap around the shrubs in her favorite gardening outfit: shoes with heels so high that they sank into the muddy earth when she walked and her favorite zebra-print pants, which were currently covered in dirt. An interesting wardrobe choice, but "they had enough give" for her to be able to bend over. Her low-cut top wasn't what she called "church attire," because she had a fear of angel heads turning, but it was fine for gardening. No coat, because she hated them, but she did have a chic scarf tossed around her shoulders for "warmth."

"My darling," she cooed, pulling me into a crushing hug. "You look depressed."

Holding me out at arms' length, she examined my outfit with a critical eye. I knew I wasn't winning any fashion awards with yoga pants and a hoodie, but really, did it matter?

"Mother, I'm—" I began, but she smothered me into her ample chest again. "Moffah," I mumbled.

She patted my head and jiggled her boobs just enough that I couldn't help but laugh. It was like being repeatedly slapped in the face with raw chicken cutlets. "There, there now. Mamma made you some *special* soup to help you feel better."

My ears perked up, and I stepped away for a much-needed breath that wasn't laced with Chanel. "You made pastina?"

Nodding, she beamed at her job well done.

"Thanks, Mom." I hugged her and darted up the steps into the kitchen, then skidded to a stop.

The room smelled like she had been cooking all day. It reminded me of when I was a kid and she was expecting a crowd to come over. When my father had first run for mayor, they hadn't wanted to have the fancy dinners and schmoozy benefactor parties most politicians did. They wanted to be of the people and for the people, so my mother and her friends had hosted them at our house. You'd never have known that the events weren't catered by some huge company in Barreton.

Today it was a similar setup. It smelled like she was making sauce and meatballs, of course, but also pierogi with onions and butter. Those must have been for the church ladies' meeting to-morrow night. Her famous rum bundt cake was on a rack cooling in the center of the island.

It looked every bit like a well-loved home. Varying-size pots were washed and drying next to the sink. One was still simmering away on the stove. I wagered that that was my soup. I grabbed a bowl and spoon and served up a hearty dish of it as my parents walked in.

"Thanks for dinner," I said gratefully. The warm broth and soft pasta would improve my miserable mood, at least a little bit.

"Anytime, Em, you know that," Mom said. She pulled up a stool to sit beside me and gave me crackers for my soup. "You've got that look." She crossed her arms and stared at me for a mo-ment. "Something is up, and it's not just the Jacksons being fools."

I took another scoop, thinking that the more comfort food I ate, the more comfortable I would feel. Unfortunately, it didn't work that way.

"The Jacksons aren't being fools, though, that's what sucks," I admitted, dropping a cracker into my soup. "I would have done the same thing."

She sighed. "My girl. Always so levelheaded."

"That's one way to put it."

"Why can't Kirby do something monumentally stupid like em-bezzle money from his campaign or pick up a hooker?" I sighed. "Just one wrong move from him, and this would all go away."

I dropped my head into my hands, feeling the nausea from earlier bubbling up again. In an effort not to be tempted to look or comment, I had deleted Facebook and Twitter from my iPhone. The regular email alerts from the newspaper were sent immedi-ately to the deleted folder. My television hadn't been turned on since the incident.

"Emma, this doesn't have to be your problem anymore," Dad said, moving to stand next to my mother. With her crazy heels kicked off, she was the perfect height for him to rest his arm over her shoulders. "Social media is, of course, the worst, but we revealed the uncropped image to the public so quickly that it's actually not that bad. Maybe the deflection to Kirby is working. I would love it if this backfired on him." My mom nodded in agreement.

Dad lifted her hand and kissed the top of her knuckles. It was something he often did when he was feeling anxious. She was his anchor, the shoulder he leaned on, and vice versa. As often as I teased them about being lovey-dovey in front of me, it was a great benchmark to have for a relationship. If I had someone who looked at me half as lovingly as they looked at each other, I would be happy.

"Besides," Dad said, keeping his voice even, "Whitney is here. She seems to have a good head on her shoulders. And she obviously cares about Cooper."

Mom looked miffed. From day one, she had *not* liked Whitney. They had first met when my parents had been moving me into my freshman-year dorm, while Whitney's family had one of their staff there setting up her room for her. Instead of helping her get acclimated, her parents were dining with the president of the college. We had been diametrically different in every possible way, and even on that first day, it had shown. We'd had opposite takes on everything, from appearance to wealth to views on the world. She probably would have lived in the apartment the family had purchased for her, but it was a rule that freshmen had to live in the dorms if they weren't close enough to live at home.

"Sweetheart," my mother said gently. "You don't have to clean up for Cooper anymore. She's here now—so let her worry about him." She said it in that mom tone, the one that let you know that she knew what you were thinking but wouldn't dare say it because it would likely hurt you too much. Her eyes were swimming with sympathy, and I wanted desperately to change the subject.

"Em, it's one thing for you to help with the campaign, but this—this seems like it's going above and beyond."

Mom and Charlotte, the younger Dr. Bishop's daughter and

one of my very best female friends, were the only two who knew what had happened between me and Whitney all those years ago.

Knowing that they'd had sex in my dorm room after I had just confided in Whitney about my potential feelings for Cooper had felt like the greatest slap in the face I could have received. It was one that I had clearly never recovered from. Even all these years later, the nagging feeling in my gut resurfaced whenever I thought of them together.

"This is a project. A job. As I said before, I've never looked at this as helping *him*. It's for the benefit of the town. So that the rest of Hope Lake doesn't suffer."

I gathered up my bowl and spoon and set both into the farm-house sink.

When I faced my parents again, they were having a silent argument. Their eyes spoke volumes, even if they weren't saying anything.

"You're going to have to talk to him, Emma," my mother said slowly, taking my hand in hers. "Make him listen to you about things." She slid a glance toward my clueless father.

I nodded. "We're going to have to have a conversation. I'm going to have to eat some crow for flying off the handle the way I did, and maybe I'll bring up Whitney. No guarantees."

My father rapped his knuckles on the table. Two quick knocks against the sleek marble. "That's my girl. Backbone of steel."

If only he knew.

With a pair of awkward hugs, I made a quick escape. I was on the porch getting coated in a fine mist before I remembered that I had ridden here in my dad's car and I had no way to get home besides a chilly walk in the unexpected rain.

Just as I was about to turn around to ask for a ride, my mother was bouncing down the stairs, dangling keys. "I thought I could drive so we could talk? Unless you'd rather your dad take you back to town?"

Shaking my head, I walked silently to the car, chewing my lip anxiously. What she had to say must have been important. My mother *hated* driving. If Hope Lake had been big enough for more than one Uber or Lyft driver, she'd have been thrilled. But we had only the one, and he was a hot commodity with the senior circuit, so he was almost impossible to book. So in lieu of that convenience, she had my father drive her everywhere. Her barely used Subaru sat in their garage until an occasion like this presented itself.

It took a few moments for her to remember how the windshield wipers turned on and where the headlights were. A part of me wanted to shove her into the passenger seat so I could drive, but I figured she needed the practice. As if to prove my point, it took her ten minutes to back down the driveway with her herky-jerky brake work.

"When I come back, maybe I'll back it into the garage to make it easier," she suggested, smiling over at me.

I winced before I could catch myself. She saw it thanks to the bright dash lighting. "Okay," she huffed. "Maybe I'll just go for it."

Once we finally made it out of the driveway, she hovered just under the speed limit—but unlike my father, it was not so she could wave to constituents. Instead, it was out of the fear that we would probably die if she started speeding.

"I know this whole Cooper thing is hard, dear," she said. "But he's a good man." Her eyes never wavered from the road. I didn't know if that was to avoid looking at me or if she was genuinely worried about her driving, but either way when I tried to interrupt, she shushed me. "You'll have time to volley a counterargument in a moment, but for now let me finish."

She paused, shifting in her seat until she could see better over the wheel. "He *is* a good man," she repeated. "He may not always show it or even believe it himself, but he is. He's not lost, he's just taking his own sweet time figuring himself out. And you have to let him. You can't be the one to help Cooper find himself, because that's his job. And if you don't let him do it, you'll have put yourself through the wringer for nothing."

"What am I supposed to do?" I hated that I sounded unsure, but I was. I felt like a tornado spinning through a field. Confused and apprehensive weren't feelings that I was used to—certainly not ones that I projected in front of my mother. She'd raised me to be strong and independent and to make decisions with conviction. She'd bought me my first bra in fourth grade because I'd skipped the training phase and gone right into B cup. At sixteen, after she'd caught Jason Bell and me dry humping after a swim meet, she'd enrolled me in sex ed classes and had me volunteering at the church. She had taught me how to take care of myself and to be proud of who I was.

Basically, to take no shit.

But at what point should I say "Screw the big picture and have a little self-preservation"?

"You have to decide what's important to you. Your feelings about him, whatever they may be, and you don't need to tell me what they are. Or him winning. None of it is important if you're lost. You can't put him first if you're going to lose sight of yourself. His feelings are no more important than yours. You come first. Period. If you decide that this isn't something you can handle, you find another way around it. Make him clean up his act in another way."

I picked at fuzz on my shirt, unwilling to glance over at her. I didn't want to see the worry on her face. Hearing it in her voice was enough.

"But what if I back out and he loses?"

"Then he loses, Emma. His mistakes aren't your fault."

She was so matter-of-fact it was unnerving. My mother was always a flurry of bold emotion: anger, sorrow, and happiness were usually turned up to ten. This, her being so black and white, was hard to process. Especially when my stomach felt like churning waves crashing over spiky rocks.

She jerked the car to a stop in front of my building. The brief misty rain had ended just as we'd crossed over the old covered bridge into the town proper. The sidewalks were still wet, though,

nning in rainbow

er finger under my

She'd turned her

much as I'd done

e.

de from the cloth-

urvy with a side of

, were staggering.

21

A few days later I groaned aloud as I reached my landing. "Oh, look, another inflammatory article left conveniently on my doorstep. Surprise." Rogers's latest campaign plan was printed in bold across the front page. Apparently he wasn't interested in just slashing funding from my department, the seniors, *and* the children's programs, he was now also going after teachers. Because really, what else was left for him to strip from Hope Lake?

ROGERS TAKES AIM AT FAILING HOPE LAKE SCHOOLS, PROMISES SWEEPING CHANGES

Hope Lake had a pocket of three small schools that were in no way failing. In fact, they were thriving thanks to a couple afterschool programs that Mayor Dad had sought and received funding for with the help of the CDO. Our district had some issues, as all did, but the schools were generally very good. Cooper even had the idea of using the Hope Lake model to encourage the district to mirror it across all schools. State records proved it was working, so why not spread the ideas around? Apparently no one had read *that* in the paper. I jumped on my phone, pulling up the site. The comments section online was once again a pit of vicious remarks that made me wonder where the people were from. The anger they harbored was unlike anything I'd seen from a Hope Lake resident.

The only real bright side in Kirby's harried campaign strategy was that his focus was on literally everything. Instead of capitalizing on one aspect and developing a clear, concise agenda—as he should have—he was throwing a bunch of irons into the fire. The whole thing was disjointed—and frankly stupid on his campaign manager's part. Thankfully, with all the balls in the air, the fascination with the Mrs. Jackson fiasco had died down quickly. Still, we were reeling from its impact.

Each headline and lie of Kirby's chipped away at Cooper's likability and lead. There was just too much fodder against him. All the little digs had started adding up in people's minds. Even the people we'd thought were a lock for voting for him were beginning to distance themselves. We couldn't book him for certain events anymore. Speaking engagements were being canceled, yard signs were disappearing, and even the seniors' bingo afternoons had a new caller.

I shuffled into the apartment carrying everything as best I could, leaving the paper and the flowers I'd bought from the grocery store on the half-moon table next to the door.

Cooper and I hadn't spoken in what felt like forever, but it was really only a couple days. That had been my choice, and he had respected it. There was a suffocating amount of guilty feelings that I couldn't explain away, and I wasn't ready to confront them yet.

Everything campaign-related was now being handled via email or text or through intermediaries such as Mrs. Mancini or the elder Dr. Bishop. Even my father had taken to delivering messages. Removing myself from the campaign had been necessary for my own peace of mind.

"We have to talk, Emmanuelle," Cooper called through the door.

I whipped it open. "Em-ma. E-M-M-A."

"We can argue over your name and what I call you after you hear me out!" he barked, sliding into my apartment before I could close the door on him again.

"You've got a terrible habit of inviting yourself in when you're not welcome."

"We're friends, and this is your house. You're always welcome in my house, too. It is what friends do."

Friends. There we go with that word again.

"Cooper, why are you here?"

"Because I have a friend who is avoiding me. Because that friend whom I've known all my life can't get over that I made a mistake a decade ago. I'm here because that friend is clearly not interested in my apologies," he replied.

"You have nothing to apologize for, Cooper. And I'm not still mad about that. It's water under the bridge."

He stepped forward. "Then why are you avoiding me? I call, you just send a text response. I knock, and you pretend that you're not here. I stop by the office, and you're conveniently on the phone."

"I'm really busy. If we're done, I'll see you out so I can have my dinner and finish up my work," I said, uninterested in going around and around and twisting my confusing emotions up even more.

He quietly paced a small square in my living room, his jaw ticking in the way it did when he was annoyed. "What now? I said everything is fine. We're good. No hard feelings."

"I'm assuming by your attitude that you don't care that I am genuinely sorry for potentially fucking up this deal, even though you know it wasn't on purpose *and* it was completely out of my control."

Cooper's explanation had taken the edge off with the media circus, but people were still talking about it. Again, it didn't seem that facts mattered.

Is Cooper too immature? Can he handle the pressure?

"Are you finished?" I asked, turning to see him staring at a photo on the wall.

"No."

"I was being facetious. Honestly, I don't need to hear any more. I know you better than you think. I know that you've probably spent countless hours beating yourself up about everything. No apology was needed, but if it ends this song and dance, apology accepted."

"Thank God."

I opened my mouth a few times before shutting it. Why were things like emotions so easy for guys?

"I expected it to be harder to get you to leave."

He shrugged. "Oh, I'm not leaving. We're not done."

"Don't you think that this is problematic, Cooper? I'm all over the place with you. And you are with me. We're a ticking time bomb. With the friendship, the election, just life in general. I don't want to be mean, but I'm not sure any of this is healthy for either of us."

"What do you mean? We're friends. That's more important than anything else, Emma."

Emma.

"Let me have my feelings that you're you and I'm me and together we're not just oil and water but . . . well, whatever is worse than that," I rambled. I wasn't sure how much, if any, of what I was saying made sense, but at least I was being honest. Honest was messy, and this was definitely messy.

He ran a hand through his hair and sank into the buttery leather chair that was my favorite to curl up in when I wanted to get some serious work done. It had a way of comforting me; maybe it would do the same for him. He looked tired, his blue eyes dull; his skin, though still a bit tanned, didn't have that healthy glow. With his head in his hands, he looked genuinely defeated.

This went beyond the usual level of mistakes that he made and apologized for.

"I don't know how to explain it. I just needed you to believe in me."

"I do," I said.

"I feel like there's a but coming here."

"No buts. No ifs and/or eithers," I said, ignoring the weird burn that was happening in my chest. "We're still a wreck, though. You have to admit that."

He splayed his hands out wide on his legs. "That's not true. We just need to find our friendship glue again."

I sighed. "You're relentless. This is unhealthy. We bring out the worst in each other, I think."

He didn't disagree this time. "We weren't always like this."

That was a conversation for another time. I was already all over the place. I couldn't take much more.

"Cooper, do you really want to do this? This is a huge responsibility. Can you handle it? Tell me the truth."

He chuckled darkly. "The truth? The truth. I'm not used to telling the truth to myself, let alone someone who knows all my history."

"Who better to start with, then? Just try. It's just me and you, Cooper."

He tugged at his hair, making it even more mussed than it had been when he walked in. "I want this *so* badly," he began, looking blearily up at me. His eyes were even more bloodshot than I realized.

"I know that, Cooper. I never thought you'd run unless you really wanted to win."

"It's not just that. I really want *this*: to carry on your father's legacy, to keep making Hope Lake a better place. I want this so much that I can't stop screwing up on the way to winning. I can't seem to stop. Just when I make some headway, I trip. Then you fix it, and lo and behold, I manage to fuck it up again. I think I'm waiting for you to just give up so then I can, too. If you give up on me . . ." He paused, looking back down so his eyes were trained on the wine-colored rug at his feet.

"If I give up, then what?"

I didn't want to hear the answer, but I asked it anyway. I'd never seen him this torn up over something. It was unnerving, and I really did hate it. It brought up feelings that I'd once had for Cooper. A time when I'd thought we could have been more than just friends.

"When you give up, then I know that I really shouldn't have done it in the first place. That every naysayer was right. That I can't escape the shadow of the Campbell legacy or my reputation to make my own way."

I knew what he was feeling. Growing up in a family where you're constantly measured against a parent or, in this case, also an ancestor, is difficult. As if it weren't bad enough growing up and going through being a teenager, a young adult, and an actual adult. Having to live up to incredibly high standards that you're born into adds something that many people don't understand.

But *I did*. I could appreciate the pressure he was under. The need to find his own place and his own way. And as much as I hated to admit it, someone else we both knew also understood this. Whitney. Like me, she was in a position to help him. In a lot of ways, she was more important to this operation than I was—which was a hard pill to swallow. She was the face people saw and credited with saving him and the campaign. I swallowed the feeling of irritation that climbed into my throat when I pictured her on Cooper's arm. After all, that was how I'd wanted it: her front and center and me in the background.

"Cooper, listen to me." I sighed. "At the end of this, we're still whatever we were before. No matter how ugly or how pretty. We're Cooper and Emmanuelle. Whether you're mayor or back in the office driving me insane. We're still us."

"Emma," he said softly, and I swore my name broke as it left his lips. Whenever Cooper called me by my nickname—maybe because he did it so rarely—something sparked in me that I was always quick to dump a bucket of water on. It was another time, another life, and another memory I needed to forget.

"What?"

"Promise me that at the end of this, we'll still be what we were before."

I laughed. "Two people who make each other crazy?"

It was his turn to laugh, but his laugh held no mirth. It was resigned and tired, and I didn't like it. I wanted the old Cooper back. The one who pushed every button and enjoyed it.

"Emma," he said skeptically.

"I promise."

"Where do we go from here?"

"You go straight home. I'll talk to you later. There's something I have to do."

IT TOOK TWENTY MINUTES after Cooper left for me to get up the nerve to make the call. I hadn't spoken to Whitney in years. The last time I'd spoken to her had been nearly six years before at a UPenn alumni event, when, upon seeing her with Cooper as her plus-one, I had turned on my heel and walked the other way.

I'd brought Henry as my date because the guy I was seeing couldn't make it and I'd hated the thought of going alone.

Over the years, anytime Cooper or Whitney had needed a plus one, they'd brought each other. I hated that. Even though election day was getting closer, I still didn't really know what their relationship was, and I wouldn't ask because I feared the answer. I avoided them every chance I got and had been lucky enough not to run into her yet. But I knew that had to change.

I'd found her phone number on her law firm's website. I could have just asked Cooper for it, but frankly, I didn't want him knowing that I was contacting her.

My iPhone sat on my coffee table, with only one number left

to push before hitting the green call button. I just needed to leave a message to ask to meet her. I needed to see her and get it over with. Steeling my nerves was never my strong suit. My emotions were usually easy to read, plain as day on my face. My voice was the same: it would shake if I was angry or nervous; it got high-pitched if I was arguing.

Whitney was someone who drew out every emotion from me: hurt, betrayal, annoyance, and anger.

So. Much. Anger.

After another half hour of stalling and scribbling down some talking points, I called her firm, my heart jumping in my throat as it rang. "Sinclair, Saxonburg, and Frankweiler answering service, may I take a message?"

"Hello, I just need to leave a message for Whitney Andrews."

"Hold, please. She's still in the office."

"No, no, no. Just a mess— Shit."

She transferred me instead.

"Don't answer. Don't answer. Please don't—"

"Whitney Andrews." Her stern voice hadn't changed—it still rubbed me the wrong way.

I looked down at the sticky notes I'd written, trying to find the words, any words, to start this conversation. The words died in my throat.

"I can hear you breathing. I charge four hundred dollars an hour, so if you're not going to say anything, Emma . . ."

"Whitney." I sounded flat, annoyed. "How did you know it was me?"

"It's the Hope Lake area code, and it's not Cooper, his office, his parents' house, Henry, or Nick. Process of elimination meant it was you."

"This is why you get paid the big bucks."

"You're certainly right there."

"I'm going to assume you know why I'm calling?"

"If it's about recovering from Jackson scandal 2.0, I'm handling it. I have been and I'll continue to. We're going out to dinner this weekend, and we'll lay it on thick for the cameras as usual. Not to worry."

That was why I'd wanted to leave a message. I picked through the Post-its I'd covered with my talking points, trying to get the conversation back on track. I was supposed to be firm, take charge, and be to the point—not flustered.

"Handling it how? As his lawyer or his girlfriend?" I volleyed, not knowing which, if either, was an accurate description.

"Oh, Emma," she scoffed. "Your little fishing expedition is so cute. I'm *not* his lawyer, but you knew that. Look, I'll be back in town tomorrow after court."

"Want to meet for dinner, coffee, or—?" *Cage match? Bar fight?*

"Dinner is fine."

"I'll make arrangements."

"You do that."

"We can discuss."

"Cooper," she said by way of ending the conversation.

"Yes, Cooper. We have nothing else to talk about."

"That's for sure."

Before I could get another word in, she hung up.

"Bitch."

"WHAT TIME are we meeting Nick at HLBC?" I asked Henry, holding on to his arm for guidance. After the bout with conjunctivitis, I'd been warned by my eye doctor to take it easy with the contacts—plus, after the extralong days and nights, my eyes were constantly red, bloodshot, and strained. Unfortunately, the fact that I *never* wore my glasses meant that I constantly forgot them at home. Hence Henry the Seeing Eye dog.

We were off to celebrate the council's recent approval of HLBC's application for expansion. I wasn't asking questions, just counting it as a win.

"We're meeting him in about twenty minutes. We'll make it. Unless you want to stop home and grab your glasses?" Henry asked, looking at the line for ice cream at Viola's Sweet Shop. Whenever a smidge of warm weather hit—even if it was a sixty-degree day in October—she had a crowd.

"I'll be fine. If I go home, I won't want to leave. I can see enough not to become a road pizza—I just can't drive or see more than a few feet in front of me. Everything is a bit fuzzy." I started rummaging around in my tote for my wallet. "God, I'm in a mood."

After last night's conversation with Whitney, I was fit to be tied. That had probably added to my eye problems and stress headache, which had formed almost the second I'd hung up the phone with her. My head throbbed every time I thought about our upcoming meeting.

Last night I'd slept terribly, staying up half the night and still managing to be late for work. All day at the office, I'd been bitter, especially after Anne had brought me yet another newspaper with a scathing headline. That one had mocked the governor for coming to town to throw Cooper's election-night party. My mood had soured so badly that by the middle of the afternoon Nancy finally said she thought I needed to cut out early or she was going to call my mother.

She didn't need to threaten me twice.

"Your money is no good here," Henry said, pushing my cash away as I took it out of my wallet so I'd be ready to go once I ordered. "Even if you weren't miserable, you're not buying your own ice cream. My mother would have had my head if she'd known I let you pay."

I curtsied. "You're so chivalrous, kind sir."

"Don't take this the wrong way, but if anyone deserves free ice cream, it's you."

"Should we get Nick one for after dinner?" I asked, spying his favorite black raspberry, which was almost gone. "There won't be any if we come back here."

Henry laughed. "You want two ice creams today? I said *you* deserved ice cream—Nick can get his own."

"I'll pay you back—he'd be pissed if he heard we stopped for ice cream without telling him. When we get to HLBC, Nick'll throw it in the freezer. Although I'm pretty sure he's already got a gallon of this in his freezer. You know Viola has a soft spot for him. As soon as it's made, she calls her little Nicky so he can stop by to pick it up."

After we finally got to the head of the line, paid, and started eating, my stress headache nearly disappeared thanks to a healthy onset of brain freeze. By the time we reached HLBC, my ice cream cone was gone and Henry was throwing our papers into the recycling cans. Inside the restaurant, Nick was sitting, playing on his phone and snacking on what I could only assume was round one of his dinner feast. I had never seen a man who could eat as much as he did and still stay ridiculously fit.

"What's good?" I asked, sitting across from him at the small bistro table.

The shiny wood table was spattered with pasta sauce. "Did you actually get any into your mouth?" Henry asked, grabbing a napkin and tossing it to Nick.

Nick rolled his eyes, wiping his face before moving to some sort of deep-fried ball. He held it up to us. "These are so good. He's got a piece of mozzarella stuffed inside them, and he's got jalapeño ones, too. I could eat these all day for the rest of my life and be happy," he said, leaning back to unbutton his jeans.

"You're so classy," I joked, cutting one of the fried balls in half and seeing meat inside. "Are these meatballs?" Before he could answer, I popped it into my mouth.

"Holy shit, these are the best things I've ever eaten." I groaned, then automatically slapped my hand over my mouth. "Don't tell my mother!"

It was too late. Nick had recorded my reaction. "I'm sending this to her later," he teased, slipping the phone back into his pocket.

"You're such a shit. I'll never bring you her cooking again if you send that to her!" I threatened, but we both knew it wouldn't matter. If I stopped taking the guys food, she would just invite them over or send it to them instead. Between them and Cooper, she had all the extra kids she could ever want. And she kept all her kids well fed.

"You love me. Deep down, I know you do."

"It's very deep down. Believe me."

"Whatever, I'll take it," he said, sipping his beer.

The server made her way over to get our order, and against my better judgment, I ordered a beer to have with the guys. I was so tired that I knew one beer was likely going to put me to sleep, but still, HLBC's craft IPA was too good to pass up. "Tonight couldn't have come at a better time."

"Yeah, I heard things are really ramping up with the campaign. Need any more help?" Henry offered, pulling out his phone. "I'm not on detention detail for the next month, so if you guys need something, let me know."

"Same here!" Nick chimed in. "I'll be working the polls that day. And I mean P-O-L-L, not P-O-L-E, though I'm sure I could get a lot of votes for Cooper if this body was working the steel." He threw his head back and laughed at his own joke. "Get it? *Poll* and *pole*?"

"You realize you're saying this to an English teacher, right? I know what a homophone is," Henry said, rolling his eyes.

"I don't know what that means," Nick said seriously. "I just meant that *poll* and *pole* sound the same but are spelled differently."

"Yes, and they mean different things," Henry began but stopped. "You know what, never mind."

"I never want to have this discussion again." I laughed, tearing off a piece of bread from the basket.

Nick shrugged and continued to eat. "Are you going to have room for dinner after that?" I asked, but honestly, I knew the answer. *Yes, yes, he would.*

After we ordered dinner, we sat and I unloaded. Having a relationship like ours was a hard line to toe. We knew nearly everything about one another. For Nick and Henry, that included all the bullshit that went along with Cooper and me.

"What else is going on besides work, the campaign, and trying not to murder you-know-who?" Henry asked around a mouthful of pizza. "Anything exciting with your life?"

I thought about that for a minute. Was there anything exciting? Nothing that I could think of to share with them. Best friends or not, I wasn't about to let them know that I was contemplating driving two hours into New York or Philadelphia just to find someone for a one-night stand—because I couldn't possibly sleep with someone with no strings attached around here. Even if I went to the next county, people would still recognize me. I had been thinking about it for a while. The stress, the long hours, the exhaustion. Maybe if I just let off a little steam, I'd feel better. Rejuvenated.

"Maybe I need a date," I said as the waitress brought us our food.

They both smiled, and Nick rubbed his hands together. "Can we fix you up?"

"Not you," Henry said sharply. "It'll be like that time you tried fixing her up with the married guy." He expertly dodged the flying chicken wing that Nick launched in his direction.

"That was an *accident,* Henry," Nick said as Henry composed himself. "You're so judgmental. This is why you're single."

Henry shrugged. Single or not, he didn't care about his relationship status. He'd told me once he was like a sexual camel—he was okay to go without sex for a while. He had a totally different view about relationships than his friends did.

"I need someone normal," I stated, and bit down on pizza crust.

"Since when?" they both asked, and immediately punched each other in the arm. "Jinx!"

"My God, I'm dealing with twelve-year-olds."

"You love it," Henry said, and he was right. I did.

"Someone without baggage. Attractive, fit, and *not* married."

"You really just need to get laid," Nick said, sliding a basket of chicken wings my way as if the greasy goodness would help my situation.

"Seriously, Nick, is that all you think about?" the waitress chimed in as she walked over with another basket of wings.

"Yes," Nick, Henry, and I said in unison.

She tutted, depositing the basket on the empty space at the table. Cooper wasn't the only one in town with a colorful past.

"I need a distraction, so maybe you're right," I agreed once she left.

"Distraction from what? It seems to me like you need *less* stuff on your plate, not more, Emma," Henry said sagely. "Including one-night stands. Is Cooper bothering you? Or the campaign?"

"Whitney's coming to talk tomorrow," I explained, loving that they both froze with chicken wings in their hands, stunned. "I've managed to avoid her thus far. I think we're both trying to ignore that the other exists. Sound familiar?"

After a few seconds, they shook their heads and glanced at each other. "Say what, now?" Nick asked, pulling his chair closer. Henry did the same, and they clapped their hands on my shoulders, leaning in and creating a quiet zone walled off from the rest of the restaurant.

"There better not be wing sauce on my shirt, and you heard me," I whispered, feeling the annoyance bubbling up again.

"Whose brilliant idea was this?" Nick asked before draining the rest of his beer. "Not yours, I'm assuming. Why are you talking to her? Didn't that end . . . *badly* last time?"

"I called her, so I guess I invited the riot."

"You got balls, Ems."

Henry tapped his ear, pretending to adjust the hearing aid wire that disappeared inside. "I must have misheard. Whitney is coming to talk to *you* tomorrow? And you invited her to. On *purpose?*" He had that thoughtful look in his eyes. The one he got when he was thinking too hard.

Nick whistled, leaning back in his chair. "Balls of steel."

"Emma, why?" Henry asked. Pushing his seat back, he wiped his hands and took another sip of his beer.

"It's time to bury the hatchet."

"Let's not aim for her back, though, okay?" Nick offered, trying to come off as funny. "Why does she hate you so much, anyway?"

I swallowed. That was the question of the decade.

"No idea," I said. At my words, Henry set the mug down and tipped his head to one side. They didn't know the truth about what had happened between Whitney and me. At least, I'd never told them. But I'm sure it wasn't hard to figure out what our issues were.

"Do you want us to come with you? As a sign of solidarity?" Henry offered.

"Or two people to be witnesses that it was self-defense if you kill her with your pinky?" Nick joked.

"I'm good, but thanks."

Smiling, I took another piece of pizza.

"Offer stands," Henry said. "How are you going to do this?" He took my hand in his. He didn't care that it was greasy from the pizza or that my nails were chewed down to the quick.

Easy question, impossible to answer. "Eh, it'll be fine," I lied. Judging by his face, my answer was unconvincing. "I just want to make sure we're on the same page, and to do that I have to deal with her face-to-face at some point. It's not like we'll be in communication forever. It's just until this damn election is over."

I hoped so, anyway. The prospect of Whitney staying perma-nently was something that I'd definitely considered. I never had known what was going on between them, but I assumed it had never gone anywhere because of his lack of commitment. And to be honest, I'd always avoided any conversation about Whitney.

But the fact that they'd stayed in touch this whole time meant that there must have been *something* meaningful between them. And that *something* always had the chance of rekindling.

"You're a better person than I am," Nick said, interjecting into my thoughts. "No way would I be able to deal with someone I had that sort of history with." He waved the server over for another beer. "That would be like me working on a huge project with Penny's husband."

Penelope Manning was Nick's ex-girlfriend and possibly the love of his life. He rarely mentioned her anymore, so for him to bring her up now, it must have been serious.

"Nick, the difference is that you and Penny were *together* when she, you know—" I paused because I hated bringing up Penny cheating on him with her future husband. "That was different from me and Cooper. We weren't a couple when he hooked up with Whitney. We weren't anything but friends."

They didn't think I'd caught it, but I had—the subtle glance between Nick and Henry. I ignored it and continued. "Let's focus on getting me a date. How about that guy?" I pointed to the good-looking guy I'd noticed the second he walked into the bar.

The place was getting crowded, making it hard to see him, but from my vantage point he looked good in a dark pair of jeans and a fitted cream-colored sweater that stretched across his broad back. "Well dressed, I like it," I mumbled.

I squinted my eyes. Damn my lack of vision. The handful of guys surrounding him at the bar also made it difficult to see him. I could tell that he was talking to the waitress, and he kept his head down, likely looking at the menu. "Looks like a take-out order," I said, craning my neck over the crowd.

"I think you should go talk to him," Nick suggested, elbowing Henry, who chimed in with an enthusiastic nod.

Nick stretched his arms up and laughed. "He's probably your type. Look at him. Ivy League."

I slid a look at Nick. "How can you possibly know that from

here? Besides, looks aren't half as important as personality. He could be an egomaniac or married."

"I find it interesting that you lump those two together," Henry said with a laugh. "I agree with Nick, though. He's totally your type."

"You two are like the twins from *The Shining*. Creepy yet perceptive." I tossed the napkin down on the table and stood. "You know what? Screw it, why not. What's the worst that can happen?"

Brushing off my pants, I took a second to make sure my white blouse was still tucked beneath my wide black leather belt before pulling my hair from the ponytail I'd worn all day. Normally I wasn't someone who put much effort into talking to a stranger. Ha. I wasn't someone who talked to a stranger, period. But I decided to embrace the sexy walk that many women had mastered and go introduce myself to the guy. What did I have to lose?

Maybe it was the beer emboldening me or Nick and Henry's encouragement, but I started over to talk to Mr. Sexy Stranger. "Go get 'em, Emma!" Nick snickered. I ignored him. I was on a mission.

As I wove my way between the people at the bar, the closer I got to the guy, the more intrigued I became. I noticed that his hat had the UPenn logo on it. It was faded and tattered, but it was definitely it. So he *was* Ivy League.

"Hey, there," I said, forced to talk to the man's back because he was so squeezed in between two other people at the bar. "I'm Emma. I was just wondering if I could buy you a drink?" Not my best line, but did I even *have* lines?

Not really, but I was going for it.

His posture stiffened slightly. "They've got a great local beer here," I continued, not knowing if he could even hear me over the noise.

It wasn't until I tapped him to get his attention that I realized my embarrassing mistake.

His back muscles seized up under my touch. It was as if my

hand were electrified—I couldn't move it from the softness of his sweater.

EMMA THOUGHT: Make a LASIK eye appointment *stat*.

As he turned, I tried to find an escape route, but it was too late. I had nowhere to go but forward, because of course, at that moment, more patrons crushed toward the bar to get another round.

His hand reached out to touch my elbow, pulling me toward him. It was my turn to stiffen. He leaned down to whisper in my ear, "You want to buy me a beer, do you?"

I would never live this down.

"Hey, Cooper."

I didn't say another word—instead I shoved my way through the crowd, ignoring the loud complaints from everyone I pushed through. When I arrived back at the table, red-faced, heart thundering, and keenly aware that Cooper was hot on my heels, I punched Nick in the arm. At least, I *thought* it was his arm. I would never be able to trust my vision again.

"You ass!" I sneered under my breath. "You *knew* I couldn't tell that it was him. I'll never forgive you!"

He snickered, elbowing Henry, who at least had the appearance of being remorseful for sending me to the wolves.

"Look who I ran into at the bar," I said through gritted teeth, refusing to look over my shoulder at Cooper. Why was he standing so close? He had to know it was an accident—I wasn't actually attracted to him. If he had been a stranger and my eyes had been fully functioning, I'm sure I would have stopped my attempt to pick him up.

I turned slightly to glare at Cooper, mindful of the fact that he was standing directly behind me. My body felt like a live wire, knowing he was just within reach. And my ears were hot. What an odd part of my body to feel warm. In fact . . . my whole body was starting to feel hot. "Why is it so damn warm in here?" I asked, fanning myself.

"It's not," Cooper said, leaning down again. His lips brushed the shell of my now possibly on-fire ear and I jumped, bumping into our table and sloshing beer over the mugs. I had to get out of there. I was mortified and hot and bothered, and a myriad of other feelings were climbing up my throat and choking me from the inside out.

I slapped my hand down on my leg and laughed. "I can't believe I forgot about this thing I have to do. So, uh, I gotta go."

This. Thing.

I held a master's degree, for pity's sake, and I'd actually said "this thing" as if I couldn't think of something a thousand times more believable.

"Oh, really?" Nick chimed in, and I could tell he was fighting back a smile. "I thought you wanted to chat with the bar hottie? Isn't that what you said? I'd like to— Henry, what was it?"

EMMA THOUGHT: Kick Nick's ass after LASIK.

"I don't remember, Nicholas. I think Emma was just confused." Henry stood, coming around the table to give me a hug. "It's not a big deal, don't leave," he whispered, giving me a second squeeze.

I couldn't explain to them how embarrassed I was or how genuinely perplexed I was at how I was feeling. Cooper had . . . turned me on? I needed to leave. Now.

"I've got stuff to take care of. I'll see you guys later. Cooper, you can have my seat."

Without turning around again, I made my way to the front door.

22

UNKNOWN NUMBER: When and where
are you meeting me?

The text came through just as I was biting down on my salad. I knew I had to eat before meeting her. Plus, I didn't trust myself with silverware around her. I missed the lettuce and hit my tongue instead. The phone was sitting next to my plate, staring up at me like a land mine. I took a chapter out of Nick's playbook and responded.

ME: New phone, who dis?

Juvenile? Yes, but I didn't care. It was something to throw her off her game. I needed to have the upper hand with Whitney. If I gave an inch, she would walk all over me. Plus, *she* was meeting *me*. This is my town, honey.

UNKNOWN NUMBER: Cute. I charge by
the hour.

"I've heard," I said to my empty office. It was nearly five o'clock and the whole building was deserted, most headed over to the high school to watch the school's theater group, the Primary

Players, performing *Les Misérables*. I was torn over where to meet with her. We could have met anywhere. But everywhere seemed to have disadvantages.

Here at the office?

No witnesses, though maybe that's a good thing.

One of the pubs?

Beer and hard liquor didn't seem like the wisest of moves.

Notte's?

I paused on that one. *Might be good to be in a place that means something to me*, I thought. A place I'd had a hand in creating would give me a sense of control. Plus I could lord its success over her as proof of how good Cooper and I were together.

How well we *worked together*.

> **ME:** You can meet me at 6PM / Bella Notte. It's by the river.

"Don't fall in" was what I wanted to end with, but I kept it civil. For now, at least. Checking my makeup, I added a little more concealer under my eyes to try to cover the violet shadows that seemed as dark as an eggplant under the harsh office lighting.

After getting home from the pub the other night, which had taken a lot of effort on my part since I couldn't see anything, I worked for a bit, updating Cooper's campaign Facebook page with photos of the setup for the upcoming election-night party. People loved seeing the inside of Campbell Manor, and judging by the number of "Wow!" reactions to the posts, it was a smart move. It wasn't just the photos of the interior that generated a heavy social media response. The highest number of post engagements and impressions were thanks to a candid shot of Cooper and Whitney together. Her head was resting on his shoulder, and he was placing a light kiss on her forehead.

They looked happy, content, and very much a couple.

That was what I'd wanted to happen. What should have made things easier, and yet . . . I thought about what had happened with him at the bar.

Shaking my head, I rubbed the center of my chest to rid it of the odd ache that was blooming there. *I must be coming down with something.* My brain was fuzzy, too. I just wasn't feeling myself.

The next few weeks were going to be intense with a bunch of last-minute events, all of which would lead up to the party on election night.

Cooper—I hoped, at least—wouldn't be able to screw things up in the next couple weeks.

If he did, I would kill him myself.

I rode my bike slowly out to Notte's, wanting to enjoy the last of the good fall weather. The last time I'd taken my bike here hadn't exactly gone as planned, and in a lot of ways, I credited that night with the current path I was on.

Pulling into the parking lot at one minute before six, I wasn't surprised to see that Whitney's car wasn't there yet. I had been going to try to be fashionably late, but I wasn't wired that way. It would have made me crazy.

I went inside after leaving my bike at the side of the restaurant. There was wine inside, and wine was needed.

I ordered a glass of Valpolicella and then sat and waited, wine in shaky hand. This time I was prepared for the wait, and I opened the book I'd brought with me to pass the time. When Whitney arrived, I wanted to seem aloof—like I was enjoying my time sitting alone. Again I hoped to have the upper hand.

Silly Emma.

At 6:29, Whitney Andrews breezed into the building, turning heads and dropping jaws. She strutted in with sky-high black Louboutin heels, an indecently tight gray pencil skirt that my mother would have loved, and a stunning pewter-colored bell-sleeved sweater that looked like it was sewn to her shapely figure.

Before she even sat down, Whitney called to the server who was standing at the bar to bring her a double gin and tonic.

"Emma, you look *well*," she said by way of a greeting, looking down her patrician nose at me. Her icy blond hair was pulled back in a low chignon, and she wore delicate pearl earrings.

"Are you sure you want to drink something that strong? Aren't you driving home?" I asked, thinking how wrecked I'd be if I had that much alcohol in my system.

"Aw, concerned for my well-being?" she mocked.

"Not especially."

Whitney tossed her head back and barked out a laugh. She leaned an elbow casually on the table and swirled the red plastic stirrer in her glass with her other hand. "Sharp-tongued Emma is out tonight. I wondered which of your personalities would make an appearance."

"Funny, I just assumed bitchy Whitney would be showing up."

"Touché," she huffed as the waitress set down the glass. She raised it to her nude-colored lips.

Emma 1, Whitney 0

"Have you seen Cooper?" I asked, setting my phone to vibrate. I might have wanted to hit her with it, but I wasn't rude enough to risk having it ring during our chat.

"That's why I was late." She winked, smirking when my lip twitched.

Ignoring the implication, I kept grinning, even though my stomach was in a knot. So I figured I'd get straight to why I'd wanted to meet her. "I would like to discuss the party at the Manor. With the election being only two weeks away, I feel like we still have some headway to make and not a lot of time to score points with the most influential voters."

"And?" she asked, clearly bored by my concerns.

"You realize how important your role is, right?"

"Of course I do," she said, sounding offended. "I've been here for weeks, laying the groundwork all over town." With another wink, she took a sip of her drink.

"Is there any way to be here more consistently? You know, present a unified front? Right now it still looks a bit casual. I know you attend events with him, but it's not enough." I hated the wobble in my voice. "The governor knows you're coming to the party and will have a photo taken with you, Cooper, and Mr. Endicott at the event."

"How *is* Sebastian?" she asked dramatically, resting her hand over her chest. "Good news as far as Cooper aging gracefully goes."

"Can we focus?" I snapped, taking the small calendar from my purse.

"On what exactly?" she volleyed, draining her glass and motioning to the nearby waitress for another. "The miserable job you've done? I'm not surprised, of course, but I thought even *you* could have handled this. Cooper seems to think you're capable. Why, I don't know. It's clear that you're in over your head, Emma."

I hated the way she said my name. It was as if I were gum on her shoe sole or an unruly toddler. It made my skin crawl.

Her phone buzzed with a text. Grabbing it, she smiled coolly as she scanned the screen. "It's Cooper. Should I tell him you said hello? He wants to know if I'm behaving. I'll just respond that I am *for now*—you and I both know I won't be later."

Emma 1, Whitney 10

My scoring system sucked, and my glass was empty. I wanted to get the bottle and a long straw and get the hell through dinner. Screw dinner, I just wanted to get the hell away from her.

"What else do you need from me?" she asked, bored. "I have a conference call with our LA office in thirty."

"Let me get this straight. You're late, you come in only wanting to argue. Why'd you even bother making an appearance at all?"

Whitney rolled her eyes. "Emma, really? I was curious. I had to see for myself how backed up you were with everything."

My irritation bubbled over. Unfortunately, it was in the form of what I was sure was a bright red, blotchy face. I steeled my nerves. Leaning over the table, I sent what I hoped was a home-run dig at Whitney. *Look at me and my sportsball term!*

"Oh, I've heard you *handle* Cooper. It sounded quick and unenthusiastic from where I was sitting."

"Tsk, tsk, Emma. All these years later and still so easy to bait," she said with a witchy cackle.

"What's that supposed to mean?" I asked, shifting in my seat. My bravado was wearing off.

"You're still in the dark, I see." She mock pouted. "I thought by now you'd have come to terms with it, but I guess not. Sad, really."

It was my turn to roll my eyes. "Enough with your word salad, Whitney, just spit it out."

It probably wasn't the right time or the place for this to happen, but Whitney was like the bait at the end of a giant hook and I was the poor, naive fish who took a bite.

She must have been waiting for me to acquiesce because she launched a verbal attack that sounded so rehearsed, it was as if she'd waited all these years to drop the truth bomb on me.

"You've got feelings for Cooper," she said, straight-faced. "If I had to guess, you've always had them and just denied, denied, denied it. I saw it day one in the dorms when he helped carry your stuff upstairs. You even told me in college that you were thinking that maybe this was a good time to explore the option with him since you two were finally away from home, all alone, without the other two barnacles attached to your hips. Maybe you could try out romance without the eyes of your sleepy little town watching. I remember it like it was yesterday. I still see it now how many years later." Hearing her bring that up made my blood boil hotter.

"Let's say you're right. What kind of woman does that make you?"

Her eyes narrowed. "It makes me willing to take what I want. Unapologetically and repeatedly."

I chuckled, but the laugh held no joy. "That's just a nicer way of saying you're a bitch. And you're a crazy bitch, because the only feeling I have for Cooper is contempt."

She ignored me. "Who knows why, but you're choosing to ignore your feelings or maybe you just won't let yourself believe them. Either way, I still feel so badly for you. I always have. It's pathetic, really. Unrequited love has got to be an awful feeling. Especially at our age."

I sputtered, hearing the words coming at me. "I'm not—" I couldn't say the rest. "I don't have . . . I'm not . . . you're insane."

She stood, smoothing her skirt and scooping her Prada bag over her bent arm. "Whatever you say, dear. If it helps you sleep at night, all alone in your big bed, keep denying it. As far as Cooper goes, I'll take *good* care of him. You worry about your little campaign, and I'll handle him how I always have. People in this town won't know what hit them when we show up on the scene like JFK and Jackie. Maybe I could be Marilyn instead. Far more interesting, don't you think?" She drained her glass. "We've laid the bread crumbs out the past few weeks—he'll have this in the bag. I don't take on a client unless I know that I'm going to win. If you need anything more from me—anything that comes up on your little *agenda*—text me the details. Next time you call an in-person meeting, I'll charge you what I charge everyone else."

She breezed out of the restaurant much the same way as she'd walked in. People turned to watch her walk out while I sat with my jaw sitting on the table. It wasn't her dramatic exit that had shocked me—that was typical Whitney—but what she had accused me of. I crossed my arms over my chest.

I did *not* have romantic feelings for Cooper. No matter what Whitney Andrews thought.

I GOT AS FAR AS NOTTE'S PARKING LOT before I realized that not only hadn't I paid the bill but I'd left my purse, phone, book, and keys sitting on a chair. I had been that thrown by my conversation with

Whitney. But I didn't have time to analyze my reaction to what she'd said. We had a campaign meeting at eight tonight at Dr. Bishop's house, and I had to see Cooper.

Shooting off a quick text, I asked him to meet me a bit early at Dr. Bishop's. We'd be able to talk in her parlor without worrying about anyone overhearing us. *My* confirming what I already knew: that I didn't have feelings for Cooper. A quick conversation. The more I thought about it, the more I felt confident in my thoughts. Whitney was just trying to goad me, and she'd just so happened to find a weak spot in my armor.

It isn't so much what she said that has me rankled, I thought. *It's what she implied.*

I haven't burned that friendship bridge, I thought defensively. *She* had by screwing the guy I'd thought I might like. *Might* being the operative word.

A word sandwich meant nothing if there wasn't any beef between the buns, as Nick would sometimes say. "Great, now I'm applying Nick's quotes to my life. It is the end of days," I said to my bike.

After heading back to collect my things and pay, I biked slowly toward Dr. Bishop's house, figuring out along the way what exactly I was going to say when Cooper asked why I needed an early meeting. *Although,* I thought as I pedaled down Main Street, *I don't necessarily have to say anything.* I could just stand there, take one look at him, and realize that there wasn't any truth to her comments. I'd been alone with Cooper a hundred times over the years and nothing had ever sparked to life.

Then what happened at the bar? a small voice asked me.

Nothing! another voice chimed in. *Nothing happened at the bar. I thought I saw an attractive albeit blurry guy, and I made a move. It doesn't matter that it turned out to be Cooper.* I continued arguing with myself during the short ride over.

When I finally turned onto Dr. Bishop and Mrs. Mancini's street, I pulled over. Dr. Bishop's driveway was already filled with cars, some of them spilling out onto the street or in Mrs. Mancini's driveway. Ugh, why was everyone here so early? Of all days!

I pulled off the road, tucking my bike into a patch of trees so that I could watch the people milling about on the porch before going inside. Cooper's car wasn't there yet. So much for our getting to talk.

As if my front tire were going to answer me, I continued arguing with myself. "Cooper *is* an attractive guy," I said out loud. "I'd be blind not to notice and lying if I said he wasn't." There, see, I was feeling better about this already. I just needed to talk it out.

"There's a difference between finding someone attractive and being attracted to him," I said confidently. "Hell, you can even argue that there's a third difference, that being whether or not you'd ever act on feeling attracted to someone or finding someone attractive."

While I was ranting to myself, Cooper's SUV pulled in front of the Bishop house. He slid from the seat and looked across the street to where my bike was hidden among the trees. To confirm my very scientific findings I repeated, "Cooper *is* attractive. I'm not attracted to him, and even if that were the case, which it's totally not, I'd never act on it, because, reasons."

I smacked my lips together because out of nowhere my mouth felt dry and itchy. *It's because I'm sitting here like a crazy person talking to myself about being attracted to someone.*

A liar's mouth always itches when he's talking. Another Nick-ism.

"Oh, please. It's not because I'm lying," I said, laughing to myself. Or was I laughing *at* myself? At that point, I didn't know or care. "I'm not lying."

This campaign really *was* wearing on my last nerve. I made a mental note to take several personal days after it was all over.

Rant over, my attention was drawn to Cooper. He had jogged over to Mrs. Mancini's property to help her across the grass once she got out of her car. His arm was slung around her shoulders, and she was laughing at something he was saying. As they walked, I watched him look around the area. Was he looking for me since we were supposed to talk?

Yet again, Cooper was dressed casually. It made me happy that he was continuing to take my advice and look more approachable. The jeans he was wearing looked similar to what he'd had on at the bar the night before—dark and tailored—but there wasn't a snug sweater to appreciate. Instead he wore an untucked flannel shirt and boots.

Just as I was about to walk toward the house, Whitney's car rolled up. She parked haphazardly in the driveway, half-hanging onto the road. Not that it mattered, since this road had only two homes and it was a dead end. Looked like those two double gin and tonics *had* been a bad idea.

As she got out of the car, I noticed she'd changed her clothes since dinner. Now she was wearing a pair of superskinny black jeans, paired with the heels and a cropped black leather jacket. She looked more relaxed than earlier, with her long hair released from the bun and swinging freely against her back.

She must have changed at his house. No wonder she looks relaxed.

I guessed he was having her formally meet the group tonight. Henry and Nick knew her, of course, but the rest would be getting their first introduction. *Lucky them.*

She marched up to Cooper, who had safely delivered Mrs. Mancini to the front porch, and she slid her arm around his waist, resting her head briefly on his shoulder as he leaned down to kiss the top of her head. It looked like the frigid bitch exterior from earlier had melted. Cooper turned to Mrs. Mancini just as Whitney stretched her hand out. *Mrs. Mancini isn't a hand shaker,* I thought smugly. She thought it was impersonal. So imagine my surprise when Whitney was enveloped in a crushing hug that practically lifted her from her heels.

Cooper looked around the yard again as Mrs. Mancini let Whitney go, and then, with me nowhere in sight, he turned back to Whitney and smiled. It lasted only a second because Mrs. Mancini pulled her toward the house, but I caught Whitney smiling back.

They looked happy. *She* was happy when she looked at him.

He pulled out his phone. The rectangular screen illuminated his face, and I could see his frown. *I wonder.*

Grabbing my own phone from my pocket, I tapped out a quick message.

> **ME:** I'm not coming

> **JACKASS:** What? Why? We need you here to run the show

We. Not *I.*

I pretended that the difference didn't bother me. I ignored the itch on the inside of my cheek.

> **ME:** I'm sending along the talking points to Nick and Henry. They'll manage the crowd. You're almost to the finish line, Cooper. You've got this.

> **JACKASS:** Is it because of Whitney? She said you guys argued. Don't listen to anything she says to you. She just likes to rile you up. You know that.

I started typing something a few times before I just stopped. The dots would blink on his side, and I didn't want him to know that in truth, I didn't know what to say. I shouldn't have let her rock me. Someone who didn't really know me *or* my feelings for Cooper. *About* Cooper, I mentally corrected, but it didn't matter. That

23

n the time that had passed since the event at Dr. Bishop's house, I had actively avoided Cooper. He'd call; I'd beg off, saying I'd return it later and then not. He'd text; I'd ignore it or pretend that I was driving with Do Not Disturb on.

Ignoring him was putting me under a great deal of stress. Again. This was beginning to become a habit when something I didn't like happened. It was how I'd handled the whole Whitney and Cooper situation the first time: I'd avoided it. I knew I couldn't keep up with the act much longer, but I intended to do so for as long as possible. So much for handling it head-on.

Before I could face him—and Whitney's still unsettling accusation—I had another problem to deal with: I'd agreed to take my mother shopping for the election party.

"How are things going?" she asked as I drove us to Barreton.

Maybe this won't be so bad after all.

I smiled. "The numbers are good but not great. What if there's a fire that needs to be put out? Things are improving, but I'm still worried. A fast pitch can come out of left field." *Sportsball lingo is my favorite.* Another Nick-ism.

My mother looked confused but shrugged. "Then someone

onalized. "So many of us

said I hadn't considered
he Cooper-and-Whitney

alized that we would be
hadn't intentionally been
ng the other entrance to
is was easier than waiting

as I rolled to a halt at the
't look. I refused to look.
d the time that had pas
I had as crush myse

time.

street, in an unassuming
up in, his house was a
shutters and a stamp-size
again. This was begini
ner and Cooper
tountry li

ay, the front door of his
BMW.
side his house.
er at the door, or did she
he lean down to give her
up to kiss him?
reach up on her tippy toes
bus are three separ

p myself.
Ma be the d
t Find Cooper Attractive
e road that crashed into I
worried Won part-hea
say, I know ha

ching my arm.
bing at the spot where it

Then I heard it. The beeping horn behind me. I didn't even realize that I had stopped in front of his house and was staring inside his front door like a crazy person. To the right of the front door was a pair of windows that I knew led into his living room, with the curtains drawn. From where I was, I could see his hand resting on the curtain to pull it open.

I gunned it, blowing through the stop sign that I'd probably spent a solid two minutes at while I was glaring into Cooper's house.

Thankfully, I didn't cause an accident.

I did, however, get pulled over.

After getting my traffic ticket from Chief Birdy, I made a mental note to pay closer attention to where my mind was wandering.

The rest of the way to Barreton, my mother was surprisingly quiet. I could always tell when she was biting her tongue, which wasn't often. She was usually the first to tell you what she thought, consequences be damned.

"Just say it," I blurted out as we pulled into the mall parking lot.

"Remember when we talked the other night about Cooper and your feelings about Whitney being the one to help him?"

It was my turn to sigh as I parked. "Yes?"

We got out of the car and walked quickly into the mall. The weather app said that it might snow today. Judging by the glaring white sky, it would be happening soon.

"I spoke to Clare earlier."

No surprise there. They spoke all the time. They'd been friends all their lives, and even though she was the governor, Clare spoke to her hometown friends often.

"And?" I asked, wondering why there was a dramatic pause in this story.

"We spoke as mothers. Not as Governor Campbell and the mayor's wife. She's concerned about her son. Much as I'm concerned about you. This whole thing . . ."

"I'm afraid I don't understand," I interrupted as we walked into the department store, because I did know what was going to come next.

"Emma," she began, but I held up my hand.

"Mother, I love you, but sometimes you needle and needle me until I want to snap."

"We just don't understand why you and Cooper never—"

I rubbed my chest, feeling a familiar ache well up. The cold sensation that always seeped through me when I thought about the unanswered *why*.

"Listen." I took a deep breath. It was now or never. "I'll say this once, and I should have probably brought it up ages earlier, but I don't like to talk about it. Basically, at one point, I probably was in love with Cooper." I paused when her hand flew up to her mouth.

"Stay with me, Mother. At least the teenage version of what love is. The overwhelming feelings, the sleepless nights, the walking past his house a hundred times. It was so much worse for me because we were friends. The four of us were a unit, and I was hoping that Cooper and I—"

"And did you?" she asked tentatively, reading into what I was trying to say.

I swallowed, closing my eyes behind my sunglasses. Tears welled up, but I blinked them away. "Once, but not in the way you're thinking, calm down. It was the Christmas before we graduated high school."

It was clear by the widening of her eyes that she knew what I meant. *When* I meant. "Your last party at the Manor?" she asked tentatively.

"Yep. It was the first time I witnessed Cooper the Casanova. I'd thought maybe we could be more, starting with that night. But I was wrong. I would unfortunately make that mistake again."

"With Whitney?"

I nodded, again getting that flashback of her looking up at

me when I opened the dorm room door. She had smiled before tapping him on the shoulder. She'd wanted to have him look at me standing brokenhearted in the doorway. "Let's just say Whitney was the proverbial last nail in the particular coffin of any potential romance between me and Cooper."

My mother looked upset. Not at what I had revealed but at her role in making me relive it. "I'm so sorry, Emma," she finally said after gathering herself together. "I understand now. I wish, I guess—I wish I'd known sooner so that I didn't keep pushing the issue. I just always thought—"

"Trust me, I thought so, too. I just learned to ignore it and realize it for what it was: a childhood crush that had no steam in making it into adulthood."

"So you don't have those feelings for him anymore?"

That's the million-dollar question.

I shook my head. "There just isn't a Cooper-and-Emma happily ever after, Mom."

She pulled me in for a hug. "As long as there is an Emma's Whatever Makes Her Happy Ever After, that's all I care about. But no more meatballs for Cooper."

"Ma, you can't withhold the meatballs. It was a long time ago. Besides, that's just cruel."

"Fine. I'll just make them smaller." She linked her arm in mine, and we walked over toward the dresses.

"Are you sure you're fine?" she asked.

"I'm fine. We're fine. There isn't anything for anyone to worry themselves over as far as Cooper and I are concerned. I just want to get through this party and the election and be done with it. Then maybe I can move on with my life, too."

She didn't look convinced. "Don't frown like that, Mother," I said, "or you'll deepen your wrinkles."

Her finger flew to her forehead. "Don't tease me like that, Emmanuelle," she mock threatened. Lifting her hand, she cupped my cheek. "You're worrying me."

"I'm fine. I know what I'm doing."

She tapped my temple. "This is fine. I never worry about that."

Then she lowered her hand to my heart.

"I'm worried about this."

TWO DRESS BAGS were hanging in the backseat of my car when we drove home. My mother, surprisingly, had picked out a semitasteful one for herself. There was, of course, a questionable amount of cleavage, but I couldn't expect a miracle. I even listened—well, partially listened—to her advice and chose a simple off-the-shoulder lace dress that she'd suggested (although I went with the tea-length version instead of the one that barely came to midthigh). It wasn't what I normally would have chosen, but I had to admit, the deep wine color looked gorgeous with my complexion. It had a swishy, flouncy skirt that danced around my knees and gave it a flirty, feminine look that I loved.

As I was dropping my mother off at her house, my phone pinged with a text from Cooper. My stomach did a little flip. Had he caught me staring into his house earlier?

Maybe, but if so, why wait to confront me about it?

I waited until my mother closed the front door before I opened the notification.

JACKASS: Need to talk. Have a second?

ME: In Barreton shopping with my mom. Gotta be off my phone. Email and I'll respond later?

A little white lie never hurt anyone. I was both mentally and emotionally exhausted after shopping with my meddling but well-meaning mother. I just wanted to draw a bath, have a glass of wine, and crawl into bed early. It was going to be a long night at the party on Tuesday, and I needed to get some rest now.

JACKASS: You're back already. I saw you driving up the mountain. It'll be quick and my house is on the way to your apartment.

Does he have cameras everywhere in town?

JACKASS: She isn't here if that's why you're stalling.

ME: Who?

JACKASS: You know who.

ME: Voldemort?

JACKASS: Let's try this again, smart-ass. Whitney isn't here. If that's why you're stalling . . .

ME: It's not.

It is.

JACKASS: Front door is open

I took the longest way to his house that I could. It involved a trip that had me circling the block twice and parking halfway down the street so that anyone who recognized my car wouldn't know where I was headed.

Even though Cooper had said the door was unlocked, I still knocked as I pushed it open.

"Cooper?" I called out, standing awkwardly in his foyer.

"In the kitchen!"

"Okay, I'll wait by the door, then."

I'd been there before, but not in the past two years or so. Not much had changed since the last time I'd been invited over. He'd extended the invite often, but I'd always found a reason to bail. Game night, football night, birthday celebrations for one of the guys—if a party wasn't in town, it was here.

"Come on back, I'm in the middle of making dinner."

"Oh, I can come back later. No worries," I shouted, backing up against the front door. "Just . . . call me when you're done, and I'll come back later."

"Don't be ridiculous. You're already here!" he called.

"Shit," I muttered, kicking off my shoes and padding across the rustic hardwood floors that ran throughout the house.

Cooper's house was homey, not a bachelor pad by any stretch of the imagination. He took pride in it. It felt like him, with warm-colored walls and antiques strewed about over old-world-style furniture.

A white swing door hung between the dining room and kitchen. I took a deep, calming breath before I pushed it open, revealing Cooper dressed in a quirky plaid waist apron and low-slung jeans. His tattered gray T-shirt said DREXEL CREW and had the dragon mascot in the center. It had seen better days, but it looked just as good on him as a thousand-dollar suit.

"It's hot," I blurted out, and immediately closed my eyes to pray for the ground to swallow me whole. "In here."

What was wrong with me? This was Cooper. Nothing had changed. This whole notion of attraction was ridiculous.

Except that my heart was pounding, my breasts felt heavy, and my mouth felt dry. Whitney's words came racing back.

When he looked over at me and smiled, I had to lean against the counter.

"Hey, how was shopping?" It was a simple question. One that I couldn't find the words to answer.

"Good. Fine. Super. Dress," I rambled, feeling clammy and feverish. *This is all in your head.*

But it wasn't just my brain shorting out. My stomach was gurgling like a swirling drain, my heart was stuttering, and as for the rest of me, I was keenly aware that he was affecting my southern hemisphere.

It's like you've never had a conversation with a man before.

This isn't a man. This is Cooper.

Who is a man.

EMMA THOUGHT: Stop overanalyzing.

"So what's up?" I asked, looking around the kitchen. Nice rug. Cute blinds. Modern tools. I catalogued everything, refusing to look at Cooper. Or Cooper's jeans. Or how Cooper looked in his jeans.

"You're probably wondering why I asked you to come over."

I rocked back on my heels. "I figured to talk shop?"

"Something like that," he said casually, fiddling with whatever was on the stove. "You asked to meet me the other night at Dr. Bishop's before everyone else came, but then you didn't show."

"I had a thing."

"Always a thing with you lately. Curious." A heavy silence hung in the air between us. I knew he should lead the conversation since he was the one who had invited me over, but I couldn't take the tension for much longer.

"We have to talk," I sputtered, sinking down on the counter stool. Four words that translated into *I am so fucked.*

He laughed. "I know. That's why I asked you to come over."

Clearing my throat, I inhaled and had to swallow a moan. How I hadn't noticed before was beyond me: the kitchen smelled incredible. I needed to get this over with, or I might faint from a combination of nerves and hunger. "I'd like to go first."

"Okay. Sounds serious. Do we need wine?" he asked, and I heard the glasses clinking as he reached into the cupboard to grab some.

"Yes! I mean, sure," I corrected after his teasing laughter. Squeezing my eyes closed again, I counted to twenty.

Slowly I opened them, squinting as they readjusted to the bright kitchen lighting. He had poured two glasses and was sliding one over to me.

"Thanks."

"If I remember correctly, you liked this one."

I took a long sip, glancing at the label of the wine bottle on the counter. I *did* like this one. A lot. I had two bottles of it in my apartment right now, as a matter of fact.

"Maybe you should go first. You said we had to talk?" I asked quickly, losing my nerve. Whitney's words circling around in my brain had caused it to short out. After taking a large swig of wine, I felt myself relax. *Slightly.* "Is it about the numbers? Because it's looking really good. I don't want to sound confident, but—"

"No, no, *be* confident. It'll be close, but I have a good feeling. We'll talk after dinner." Cooper smiled, and the flutter in my belly turned into a tidal wave.

"Did you eat?" he asked, stirring something on the stove. "This is nearly done. Just a few more minutes."

"Smells good." It did, and my stomach noticed, too, choosing that second to rumble loudly. He laughed.

"You're distracting me." I crossed my arms over my chest. "I didn't mean to invite myself over for dinner. I had an agenda."

"You always do." Cooper chuckled, coming around the island with two bowls and silverware. "Mind setting up?"

Nodding, I took the place settings and set the table near the window that overlooked his backyard. How was this going so off course? *Focus.*

"Cooper, I'm sure you're busy. I am, too, so I don't have to stay for dinner. We can just get this over with and I—"

"Always in a hurry, Emmanuelle. How about this? Tell me about your day. I miss the office, you know. Any gossip?"

"You sound like Mrs. Mancini," I said with a laugh. The nervousness of being there alone was starting to melt away. Could we do this? Be friends again?

Thinking about what I could tell him, I remembered my earlier conversation with Anne and Nancy just before I had left the day before. "Anne is pregnant again. She's losing her mind because she thinks it's another set of twins."

His eyes went wide. "That's a lot of twins."

"Very astute. You're taking math lessons from Nick, I guess."

I sat, pulling up a stool at the counter while he tinkered at the stove. A sprinkle of salt, a pat of butter, a stir and a ladle of something from the other pot into the deep pan he was working over. "I got an interesting email today," I said casually.

"Oh, yeah?" he said, dropping in a dash of parsley. "From?"

"Christopher Jackson."

He tensed, and his hand stopped stirring for the briefest of seconds, white-knuckling the spoon. "How's he doing?"

"He's good. Want to read it?"

He exhaled deeply, a long, cleansing *whoosh*. "I do, but I don't. I really don't think I can take more bad news today."

I chuckled. "I can appreciate that. What if I said it was good news?"

He lowered the gas and turned to face me, a wicked smirk on his lips. "There's a good chance I would strip naked and run down Main Street."

I looked at him in disbelief as I fought to ignore the way that made my heart speed up.

"That escalated quickly. While I'm sure many people would pay good money to see that, I think we need to keep you clothed until election day."

"Wait, I mentioned getting naked and you're not going to yell at me? Hold on, let me write this down."

"I'm going to leave if you keep this up. This has already gotten off track."

"Noted. So? Jackson?"

He had a hopeful look in his eye. It made him look so young. Like the Cooper of old, the one I remembered before our friend-

ing the facility to Hope
l that even with some of
them."

lief, sounding both proud
the underlying wobble of
incredible. You're amaz-
told Enrico that if anyone
you."

hole office. It's outstand-
e."

your voice, you're holding

s hair. "If I lose, I'm back
ing out so that I'm not ac-
and that presents a whole

iations with their team, I

vorrying the inside of his

noment so I could focus
s on me. What that was
y, "that the only way the
:ood that you would play
cer at the office or as the
-go."

risk that? What if they

"You were the reason we
It was only right, Coo-
I just ran with it." I felt
king down at me. Clear-

ing my throat, I added, "You'd have done the same. You made one mistake six years ago, and you're an incredible asset to the team. The Jacksons agree that they have to do what's best for business here, and Hope Lake—*and* your involvement—are what's best for business. Consider it forgotten."

He nodded, turning back to the stove. "Emma, that's incredible. I—thank you for that," he said, his voice softer as he brought over the deep pan with a ladle.

Emma. For a simple four-letter word, it was wreaking havoc on my insides.

"What's for—?" I began, but once I took a deeper inhale, I stopped in my tracks. Peering over the bowl, I gasped. "You made risotto?"

The tips of his ears were red when I looked at him. "Yep." He sounded like Henry for a second there. Bashful and unsure. "I was in the mood for it, and I knew you liked it. So, surprise."

I chewed on my lip and thought of something witty to say. Even something sarcastic at this point would have been better than what I was doing, which was sitting and blinking at Cooper.

And smiling.

"Hold on. You made this assuming I would be here for dinner?"

"Maybe," he said, adding a shrug. Placing the pan back onto the stove, he joined me at the table.

There was that dry-mouth feeling again. I gulped more of the wine, straightening up on the seat. Cooper took that as a cue to serve up the thick, creamy risotto. In it were plump shrimp and diced asparagus.

"Where did you learn how to make this?"

"Your mom taught me," he said bashfully. Pouring himself another glass of wine after both bowls were filled, he took a sip while I processed that information.

"She *what*?"

He nodded. "The three of us go over to your parents' house

once every few months, and she teaches us our favorite recipes. Nick had meatballs and vodka sauce, Henry wanted her lasagna, and I asked for risotto and some desserts."

My mother had kept a secret from me? That she was teaching my friends to cook without my knowing about it? I was both proud and annoyed at the same time.

"I had no idea," I said, sipping my own glass of wine now. I enjoyed the warming of it versus the sheer fire from earlier. I would have to slow down, or I'd be in trouble.

"If I say this is delicious and it gets back to my mother, I will kill you and no one will find your body."

"I believe you. It's why you don't have a knife." He winked.

He winked.

He winked? Cooper winks at you only if he wants to get into your pants.

EMMA REMINDER: Cooper winks at everyone. Probably even animals. It means nothing.

In the back of my mind, I was minutely aware of a shift happening. I couldn't tell what it was or why it was happening. I just knew that something was dancing around trying to make me acknowledge it.

You're supposed to be talking to him.

Proving that this is all in your head.

There isn't any substance to Whitney's assumption.

There are no feelings here.

The feelings I was experiencing now were more than just the wine talking. More than being lonely for male company and being in close proximity to a man who exuded unabashed sexuality. My skin felt hot, too tight, and it wasn't dainty little butterflies fluttering around my stomach—these were more like dangerously horny, stripteasing dragonflies that were willing to throw caution to the wind.

Instead of broaching the subject, I shoved a forkful of risotto into my mouth.

I then proceeded to moan. It was loud and deep, and it didn't sound like it involved food. "That's so good."

Cooper's fork clattered to the table, spraying rice across it. A shrimp plopped to the floor. I couldn't look at him. Nothing good would happen if I looked up.

"Emma," he said, drumming his fingers on the table. "Say something. What did you want to talk to me about the other night at Dr. Bishop's?"

I pursed my lips, pulling the bottom one in under my top teeth. "Whitney said some things that got me thinking."

He blew out a long breath. "She said the two of you talked, but she wouldn't tell me what it was about. You're upset. I can fix this. Tell me how to fix this."

If only it were that easy. "This is different from the campaign. I can't tell you how to fix it because it's not you who has to fix anything, Cooper. I have to—well, I have to think about how much truth there is to what she said."

Not looking at him was getting to me. I wanted to see his face. To confirm my suspicions that he would be looking at me like he always did when I made eye contact. That I wouldn't see something that hadn't been there before.

When I looked up, he had his fingers on his temples, rubbing in circles.

"If I can't fix it, where does that leave us?" he asked, motioning between us. He was looking over at me with those big eyes, and the tidal wave of emotions escalated into a typhoon.

Where does that leave us? There was another million-dollar question.

"I don't know," I mumbled.

"Emma." His voice broke just a bit at the end of my name.

"She thinks that I have feelings for you," I blurted out. Well, that dam was open. No point in stopping the flood now. "Unresolved ones. From, like, way back. Way, way back. Back in the day. Feelings that aren't hateful, murderous, or violent. You know, *those* kind."

I grabbed for my wineglass at the same time Cooper reached for his. Simultaneously we raised them to our mouths.

Over tipped-back glasses, our eyes met, held, and flickered down at each other's mouths at the same time.

It was a game of wills, neither of us breaking the staring contest. Or the chugging contest, as it were, because we each polished off the wine in a few pulls.

"More wine?" he gasped, bolting up from his seat with our glasses in hand to fill them with the bottle on the island.

The wine was working through me like liquid fire. I felt it everywhere from my lips to my swollen breasts to the tips of my toes. "I really shouldn't," I said, shoving another forkful of rice into my mouth.

When I looked up, Cooper's eyes were on my lips again. My tongue darted out to lick across them, and I watched as his eyes followed my tongue from one side of my bottom lip to the other before it disappeared back into my mouth.

"On second thought, wine sounds good. Great, even. Let's eat at the counter. Standing. Standing is good for digestion." *What the fuck is wrong with you?*

I stood and carried the bowls and flatware to the island. Once I joined him at the counter with our glasses, I felt thirstier than ever. I grabbed my glass and drained it. He did the same. I reached for the bottle to refill at the same time as Cooper did. His hand covered mine.

It was hot and sweaty, and I wondered at that moment what his hand would feel like sliding against my skin. I swallowed, mindful of the fact that it wasn't just an abstract thought now. There wasn't a *what if I* in my mind. I had just had a full-blown sexual thought about Cooper, and I was 92 percent sure he was having the same idea.

I glanced down at the marble top between us while he poured out the bottle into our glasses. Two plates, silverware, a bowl, and a nearly empty bottle of wine separated us.

A hundred scenarios presented themselves to me, all clear as a bell.

Swipe your arm across the dishes, send them clattering to the floor, and launch yourself at him.

Lean over the table like in Sixteen Candles *and give him a sweet kiss.*

This is Cooper. Be yourself.

I drank what was left in my glass and set it aside. "Do you trust me?" I asked, looking up at him with what I hoped was a genuinely thoughtful expression.

He answered without hesitation. "Of course." Two simple words sent a different rush of emotion through me. One that I couldn't focus on in that moment. *Later.*

I walked around the island to his side, grateful that my legs didn't wobble.

Cooper, following my lead, moved to stand in front of me, mirroring my position.

We stared at each other for a few seconds before I took a step forward. Then another. Cooper backed up with each step forward that I took. I kept going until his butt hit the edge of the island. He couldn't back up any farther, and I wasn't sure if I could back away now even if I wanted to.

"Emma?" He gulped, and I watched his chest rise and fall beneath his thin shirt.

"This is a test. A scientific experiment that will help me prove a point."

He let out a shuddery breath. "What point? The feelings point?"

Was I even breathing? I felt light-headed and drunk, but I wasn't drunk. It wasn't the wine, it wasn't the warmth of the kitchen, it was this moment. *The test.*

"Is this okay?" I asked, closing what little distance there was between us. His hands came up on either side of my hips as I pinned him between me and the island.

"What are you doing?" he breathed as I slid my hands around his waist to pull him imperceptibly closer.

"Are you talking to me or yourself?" I whispered, running my nose along the column of his throat. I waited to feel uncomfortable. Awkward and strange.

This was Cooper.

I was willfully trying to seduce Cooper.

And I didn't hate it.

Quite the opposite, in fact, my brain screamed. I was enjoying this. There was a wanton surge of power running across my skin like a current, and I wanted to chase it. Follow the electricity to see how much energy we could produce.

My fingers curled the sides of his shirt up until I could feel his skin, warm beneath my touch. His body was on fire, and I wondered if it was even close to how hot I felt inside. My bones felt like cinder. Every part of me was burning up, and I loved and hated it equally.

"Just once," I begged, brushing my lips across his for a second. This time it was intentional. There were no accidents to blame. I wanted to see if these feelings were real. The kiss was so light, so fast, and so unexpected, I wasn't sure I'd even felt his lips. Until I did it again and his lips captured mine before they could skirt away.

"Once *more,*" he murmured, and the blood was now rushing so loudly in my ears I wasn't sure if I heard it.

Nothing was right, yet everything was. It was all too much. Too loud was the sound of my thumping heart. Too tight were the clothes on my body, which were keeping me from feeling his skin on mine. Too slick were his hands when they reached up to wrap around my hair. His hands twisted the strands and tugged, stretching my neck back so his lips could dance from my mouth to my throat to the fabric over my breasts.

"Emma," he whispered against my chest before he gently pulled my shirt down and kissed just between my breasts. He scooped me up easily, spun us around, and set me down gently on the island.

My hands were clutching his shirt, squeezing the fabric between my fingers. His lips were everywhere and somehow not in enough places. I wanted them on me and only on me. Who needed to breathe?

This wasn't just kissing. It was learning. We were well beyond the experiment—this was each of us figuring out what would drive the other one wild.

EMMA THOUGHT: Well, it seems like everything does.

My nails swiped down his back, earning a luscious groan from him. His fingers bit into my hips, and with each squeeze my chest swelled, begging for his lips to cover every square inch of me.

Urging me to lie back, he splayed his large hand across my chest, sliding down until he reached the button of my pants. Flicking it open, he helped me unzip and shimmy out of them before tossing them somewhere behind him. My shirt followed, but this time when he sent it sailing across the room, it landed with a wet plop in the sink. "Sorry," he mumbled before kissing across my rib cage.

Cooper's hands didn't stop moving. It was like they were memorizing each curve, each dip and inch of me. I couldn't seem to have mine land on any one part of him. He moved quickly, expertly, and like a man who wanted to do this as much as I did. That was a scary thought that I quickly banished into the box along with the other feelings that I was ignoring. There was enough to focus on right here.

The clock in the hall chimed loudly, trying to break through the cloud that my head was in. I shook away the cobwebs, sliding away from where his mouth was just about to come down upon mine again. Where I would have let it ravish me as I knew it would.

"What the fuck are we doing?" he panted, smoothing my hair back.

Seeing myself in the window, I looked wild. My black hair was everywhere, knotted from his hands being in it. Sticky from sweat and stuck to the side of my face. My hands were clawing at his chest, pulling his shirt over his head. My bare legs were wrapped around his waist, and he was staring down at me like he was about to eat me alive.

"Jesus Christ, Cooper," I said, taking in his appearance. He, too, was twisted up. His jeans and boxers were down around his ankles—I guess my hands *had* found somewhere to land after all. My panties were pushed aside, and he was ready. *So very ready.*

I pulled his mouth to mine again, sealing our lips together before I could mutter another word or question another thing except mumbling, *Condom.*

This was not how this was supposed to go. But I wanted it more than the next breath.

Cooper paused briefly to scavenge through his pocket for his wallet. Pulling out a condom, he searched my eyes once more.

Not trusting my voice, I could only nod.

With one slow shift of his hips, he was seated deep inside me. The sounds we made echoed through the kitchen.

There were words, but they died in my throat. They were passionate and poignant, and there was no way I was coherent enough to deliver them. Cooper was less interested in conversation and more interested in how much of my skin his lips could kiss. I lost track of the course he was taking as he dragged his wet lips across my body.

"Cooper," I chanted, trying to remind myself who it was driving me to release, because in that moment, I could barely believe it was the man in front of me.

A few times he tried whispering my name. It never came out fully. "Em, Ems, fuck, Ems," he swore as he came, shuddering over me.

He continued to rain kisses down my throat, across my chest, and then he pulled away briefly to stand to full height. His chest rose and fell as he tried to calm down. A shudder skipped through him every few seconds.

As for me, I wasn't sure I would be able to be calm again.

The plan had backfired magnificently. The test was supposed to prove that there was nothing there. That there wasn't a fire between us. That the hate was hate and nothing more.

I couldn't have been more wrong.

I had never admitted to myself that this was what I had always wanted, yet here we were, and I had no idea how to process this.

What the hell were we going to do now?

Cooper seemed totally oblivious to my distress. Taking my hands, he wrapped them around his body, holding me in a tight embrace. I stared out the window behind him, his reflection mirrored back at me. His naked back with my arms wrapped around him.

I wanted to keep that image in my head forever.

The realization that this meant something to me—that yes, try as I might to deny them, I *did* have feelings for Cooper—was starting to dawn on me, and my body froze.

As if sensing it, Cooper pulled away and brought my hand up to his lips to kiss my knuckles.

And I felt the rest of the shift. The new shift. The even more confusing shift.

Sweet Cooper wasn't what I'd expected from this, and it left me even more shaken than before the experiment. It seemed that he sensed the mood shift just as I did.

I tensed, now fully aware of our precarious positions and lack of clothing. Brick by brick, my walls were going up.

"No, no. You're not—" he began, but I slid down from the island.

My clothes were everywhere. My soaking wet shirt lay in a lump in the sink, my pants were behind him.

"I have to go. I'm sorry. I didn't think this would happen," I lied, pulling back and looking for a way to escape.

He looked hurt and confused, and I hated myself for being

the cause of it. "I'm so sorry," I said. "Tell Whitney—" I paused, thinking of everything I had ever accused her of being. I was that and worse. "Tell her I'm sorry. I didn't do this to get back at her."

"Stop fucking apologizing, Emma!" he shouted, spinning around and kicking over the stool. "Why are you apologizing? I wanted this just as much as you did."

"You're right. I know. I just thought it would have been different. I didn't think it would feel . . ."

"What? Tell me."

I pulled on my pants, searching around for my purse. My keys. My dignity? My shirt was a lost cause, so I grabbed Cooper's, slipping it over my head.

"Emma, don't go. We have to talk about this. This was— I have to talk to you about some things. Don't leave us like this," he started, but I held up my hand.

"Cooper, I'm sorry. I'm so very sorry, I didn't mean for this to happen. I didn't think she was right. This is— I did this to prove a point, and it backfired. Whatever this was. I'm sorry I let it get this far."

"What do you mean, she was right? What are you playing at? This has nothing to do with Whitney!" he roared, stomping toward me, looking frenzied.

I shook my head. "It has everything to do with her, Cooper. I— Holy Christ, I'm so sorry," I whispered, and ran outside.

I didn't even remember walking down the street. Or getting into my car. Or starting it. Or backing out of the driveway. Or driving away in a fog. All I knew was that I couldn't look up at his house because I knew he was there. Standing in the doorway, his shadow beckoning me to come back.

To finish what I'd started.

But I couldn't. The last thing Cooper and this campaign needed was another scandal.

And certainly not one that was my fault.

24

The following morning, my lips were still swollen. My heart was somewhere near my toes, and my eyes were glassy from being overtired. I couldn't sleep. I wanted to call Cooper to ask him what he was thinking. To text him and say again that I was sorry for acting on the feelings that I didn't understand. And for running out on him.

The other part of me wanted to tell him to come over for round two. I wanted more, and so did he.

That would be dangerous.

So instead I hid my phone in another room and tried to get some sleep.

When I exited my building a few hours later, I pulled up to a quick stop.

There were people shouting, a camera was in my face snapping away, a videographer was getting ready to roll, and right behind them all stood Kirby Rogers with a smug grin on his long, haggard face.

"Emmanuelle, are you involved with Cooper Endicott? Is that how you are securing a victory for him?" one man shouted, shoving a mic in my face.

"Emma, are you and Cooper involved? Is that why your father is rigging the election for him?"

"What does Mayor Peroni have to say about this? Doesn't this seem like a conflict of interest for him?"

"Emma! Emma! Emma!"

The shouts got louder, and no matter which way I turned, there was another person closing in. There was nowhere to run. I could see Cooper darting out of Borough Building and heading my way, my father hot on his heels.

My brain was working overtime, trying desperately to make sense of it all, when a woman managed to knock the wind right out of me.

She held up her phone and showed me a few time-stamped photos from the night before in front of Cooper's house, followed by a video clip of me running toward my car looking very disheveled. I looked confused, shocked, and another emotion that I wasn't willing to admit to myself. Not now, not ever. My shoes were in my hand, my pants were clearly unbuttoned at the top, and my hair—well, it didn't take a genius to figure out what we'd been doing.

"Emma, what can you tell us about your affair with Cooper? What about Cooper's girlfriend? How can we trust that either one of you is running a clean campaign when you haven't been honest with the voters?"

Kirby must have been watching us even more than I had realized. How could I have been so stupid not to think that someone from his team might be waiting outside Cooper's house for the perfect opportunity to take him down when he was at his most vulnerable? I had to give Kirby credit, but I wasn't about to let him take Cooper down this way.

Rolling my shoulders back, I shooed away my deer-in-the-headlights look and composed myself. I channeled every bit of confidence I possibly could.

"Ladies and gentlemen," I said loudly, thankful my voice didn't crack. "You've saved me the time from organizing everyone for our announcement. Yes, Cooper and I were working very late last night on the campaign. In fact, I've been his campaign manager for a

few months now. We agreed to keep my involvement on the back
burner so as not to draw attention away from the issues. Hope Lake
is Cooper's main priority, which extends to securing the election.
My involvement would have clouded that if it had been disclosed
to the public. Clearly, by your reactions to what was a simple campaign meeting, we were right in keeping it to ourselves. Just because
my father is the current mayor does not mean I cannot support a
candidate I believe in. This campaign has been a nonstop, fast-
paced ride, especially with the media circus in tow, but Cooper
has certainly handled it all with grace. I think it's a testament to
his youth and stamina. It's been like this for weeks: finalizing plans,
organizing data, and continuing to discuss the issues, and all at the
expense of his personal life, which he has tried to keep private."

"But, Emma, are you really telling us that nothing is going on
between you two?" the woman with the photos shouted, giving
me her best *oh, please* look.

I waved a hand, feigning nonchalance. I was smiling on the
outside and dying a little on the inside. I knew Cooper was hearing all of this, but what else could I say? They were going to
piggyback this onto the Mrs. Jackson scandal and rehash it all in
the press. There would be no coming back from it. And with the
election just days away, we couldn't risk any scandals. Not now.

"Oh, there's a ton going on between us." I grinned, my smile
so big it was beginning to hurt. "I think we've probably started
looking alike since we've spent so much time together—people
must think we're related!"

Buzzwords to throw them off the scent.

"We've been friends for nearly twenty-five years. Plus, don't
forget that we've been working together in the CDO since he
came back home to Hope Lake after college."

Make them remember that he's lived here all his life.

"You don't offer to run a campaign for someone unless you're
fully convinced he is the best possible choice for public office. I
think I have some experience with that."

Relate it back to your father, whom everyone adores.

"Not to mention the fact that Cooper is dating Whitney, who happened to be my college roommate and an old friend. How's that for a coincidence? Small-town romances are a favorite of mine. They reconnected once the campaign began, and it looks like a great storybook ending is coming for all involved." I made it through the last bit without throwing up on a crowd of reporters. That would have made the front page for sure.

The crowd began chatting among themselves. Kirby was starting to look nervous, the smug satisfaction on his face melting away. From what little I could gauge, it seemed like a positive shift, but I needed to lay it on thicker.

"The main thing that we want you to come away with today," I continued, "is that while the *other* candidate has no qualms about invading someone's privacy and wreaking havoc with fabrications and unfounded rumors, we've kept this election clean. We're working hard to prove that if you have no message, no plan, and no action other than smearing the other candidate, you're not the right man for this job. We hope to see all of you at the event this weekend, where we'll be unveiling more of Cooper's incredible new initiatives for Hope Lake.

"Now, if you'll excuse me: I have to get to work serving the people of this great town."

Without turning, I marched across the street. When I got to Cooper, who looked bewildered but was still grinning broadly because hello, cameras, I slapped him on the back jokingly and we walked into the building, the clicks of the cameras at our backs fading away to silence.

"WHAT THE HELL was that all about?" Cooper exploded the second the door to my office closed. We'd managed to remain silent the entire ride in the elevator to avoid prying ears. "What were you thinking?"

I was pacing, trying to formulate some kind of response. Instead of bull, I went with the truth.

"I wasn't thinking about anything other than protecting you. Protecting this campaign. I'm sorry that I blurted all that out, but in case you didn't notice, the whole thing just fucking blew up in our faces. I didn't have time to plan!"

"Everything isn't about planning, Emma! You could have just said, fuck, I don't know. Something other than Whitney Andrews is my girlfriend."

"The poll numbers would have plummeted, Cooper. Again. The whole reason we brought Whitney into this in the first place would have fallen apart. If you had another scandal involving a woman, or in this case two, could you imagine what they would think?"

I threw a stapler against the wall. It smashed through, leaving a hole in the Sheetrock.

"What, are you psychic now? You can't predict what people will think, Emma!"

"We both know what would have happened. Don't deny it, I can see it in your eyes. You know I'm right."

He spun around angrily. "After what happened last night, I thought things would have played out differently. In fact, I told Whitney everything and to go back home."

My hand rested over my heart. It was thundering so loudly that he could have heard it. "You told her what, exactly? Cooper, you didn't." I couldn't say the words *we had sex* out loud. I was barely saying it in my head.

"Of course I told her. She's my friend."

He paced my office as he pulled out his phone, presumably to call Whitney. He hit a few buttons and held the phone up to his ear, his jaw ticking the whole time. "Voice mail," he muttered. "Hey, it's me, call me as soon as you can. Something's happened . . . We got bombarded and— Fuck, just call me back."

I had never seen Cooper so disoriented. He was like a caged

animal, prowling in a pen and waiting to escape and attack the first creature in his path. Unfortunately, that creature was me.

"Cooper, I'm sorry, but why did you tell her about—"

"I've listened to *everything* you've told me to do. I've changed my hair, my clothes, the way I speak, how I walk. Do you know how much that hurts? Still? After all this time working so closely together? To know that there still isn't anything about me that you think is worthy of this goddamn race? I thought after everything . . . You're one of my oldest friends, and it's like you've never liked me at all."

I reared back. "What did you say?"

"You heard me," he scoffed, walking to the window to stare out at the town below. The crowd must have still been there because I could hear their voices floating up from below.

"Cooper, my feelings for you aren't relevant here. I have always believed you were the best person for this job. That's why I agreed to help. Nothing else mattered but you defeating Kirby. I did all this for you, but I lost sight of that somehow . . ."

"What you're saying is that you only agreed to run the campaign because you knew if I won, you would get whatever you wanted in the CDO. Me running benefited you as much as it did me. Don't pretend to be all valiant and noble—we're the same person, Emmanuelle. We both wanted the same damn thing. I was just honest about it."

"What do you want me to say? That you're right? That I did want you to win so that I would keep my job? Or that Hope Lake wouldn't fall into a pit thanks to that idiot? I won't apologize for that. We both know that. I was honest about it from the start."

He chuckled, but it wasn't a friendly chuckle. It was sarcastic, snide, and it matched the wicked grin that twisted his mouth. I noticed the shift immediately. He turned, and although his eyes were still cold and angry, they now held a fire behind them that scorched my soul.

"When you fucked me last night and then basically ran out

as soon as it was over, were you thinking of the campaign then, too?" he asked coldly, moving closer so that I was forced to back up against the wall. "Let's see how fucking *pathetic* we can all make Cooper look? Was that what it was?"

"That wasn't it, and you know it."

He moved another step closer. "*I* don't know anything. You don't tell me anything. I just have to guess. All the time, because Emma keeps everything inside."

I looked down, swallowing the feelings that were once again racing through my veins.

"Why is everything so off course?" I asked in a small voice. "I made a *mistake. We* made a mistake. It doesn't have to ruin anything."

How can we go back to the way it was before? I wanted to ask. The words were on the tip of my tongue, when his phone started buzzing, breaking the bubble we found ourselves in. He ignored it, but the moment passed. Fucking Whitney.

"We can't change what happened," I said out loud, answering my own question and trying to get us back on track. We could never go back to how it was before; in fact, Cooper on some level had always done this to me. It was never a simple response when it came to my feelings for him. He ignited every emotion in me, from love to hate.

He reached up, softly cupping my jaw with one hand while his other roughly curled around my hip, his nails biting into the skin beneath my skirt. It was as if he were warring with himself whether he wanted to remain angry or be gentle.

"Do it," I breathed, moving my lips against the finger that was near my mouth. My tongue darted out to lick it, and my stomach dipped when I saw his eyes flicker down.

"Oh, now you want this? You're pushing me on Whitney one minute and tempting me the next?" he demanded as he wet his lips, his eyes still on my mouth.

I reached up and pulled him down to me, slanting my lips under his for the briefest of seconds before he stepped back, panting hard.

"Make up your mind. Either I'm good enough for you or I'm not."

"It's not that simple."

He leaned forward and ran his nose along my cheek, up to my ear. Then he kissed me.

We were spiraling out of control like we had last night.

"Wait," I said, pulling away. "Cooper, we can't."

Before I could second-guess myself, I pushed him away. "I'm sorry, Cooper."

He leaned against the door, breathing heavily. "You have to work through whatever it is you're afraid of feeling. Slapping me, kissing me, fucking me, running away from me—whatever it is you do won't change the fact that there is something here that you're unwilling to accept. I accept it. I feel it, and I know you do, too, yet you're pushing me away. Trying to keep me in that safe space where you can control everything. You being my campaign manager—this was never just about the campaign for me. You had your reasons to be sure I won. Well, I had my own, and it wasn't just for Hope Lake." He took a deep breath while I held mine. "You weren't just a part of that. You were a part of every-thing. I'll walk out that door today and tell the first voter on the street that we're together and fuck the rest of it. If I lose the elec-tion because of that, then so be it. I accept that."

"You can't do that, and you know I can't let you, Cooper. I care about you too much to let you throw this all away."

"I'm not throwing it away if I'm gaining you. Why can't you let yourself see that?"

"Cooper, this is too much. I can't process all of this right now on top of everything else that's happening. I'm sorry."

With the lightest of brushes, I kissed his cheek, refusing to look at him.

He slipped from the office without saying a word.

Minutes passed with my standing against the door, hoping for him to come back in. To tell me to stop being a stubborn ass. But I knew I couldn't go after him. Not when I was this confused.

I went to the window to see the news channel and newspaper crews finally dispersing. Next to Cooper's Rover was the same black BMW that I'd seen parked in his driveway lately, except this time, the driver was just exiting it.

Even from four floors up, I could see Whitney looking livid. She leaned forward to kiss Cooper on the cheek, giving him a one-armed hug in greeting. Cooper looked nervous to see her, but I could see his anger, too, as he gestured up toward the building—presumably toward me. He must have been explaining what had transpired because she glanced up, searching the windows until she found mine. We made eye contact. She shot me a withering glare.

For once, I thought as they walked away, *Whitney isn't the bad guy here.*

I am.

I HOLED UP IN MY OFFICE and waited, ignoring the multiple calls from my parents and Nancy—even Dr. Bishop and Mrs. Mancini tried to get through. Everyone reached out except the one person I still hoped to hear from, and I wasn't about to call him. There was a fear choking me from the inside out that wouldn't let me.

What the hell was I going to do? There wasn't a book to read or advice to find online. I couldn't wrap my head around any of it—that I had slept with Cooper. He had been tender and sweet, and I had been a wild animal.

And most of all, he was willing to put it all out on the line. He was just waiting for me to let him.

It wasn't just what had happened between us that had me torn up inside. It was remembering his face as I had run out the door. It was thinking about what would happen to our dynamic with Henry and Nick. The four of us had had the same routine for so long, and now I would be responsible for the deterioration of it. Was it worth it?

Yes, I thought. No hesitation.

Sometime after eight, after a long day of distracting myself with work, I walked across the street to my apartment, climbing the stairs quietly so Nancy wouldn't hear me and come out. I wasn't in the mood to talk to anyone. Once safely inside, I scoured the internet, reading and hiding vicious comments. It wasn't possible to keep up with them. Thankfully, they weren't about Cooper. Or Whitney.

They'd found a new, easy target.

Me.

Mayor's daughter using friendships to get ahead.

Emma is the poor man's Whitney. Have you seen that fox?

Nepotism is alive and well in Hope Lake. Flunky daughter getting job and bilking taxpayers.

Since my night with Cooper had become public knowledge, I'd found out firsthand that people loved chasing the shiny new thing: the new piece of gossip, the latest political scandal. The Jacksons were all but forgotten now that they'd moved on to me. *Eventually,* I told myself, *they'll move on from this, too.*

For now, though, I was their target—and that was fine, I rationalized. If the target was on my back, that meant that maybe Cooper would be safe until election day.

After I took a much-needed shower, the timer on my stove dinged. Just as I was taking out the pizza I'd put in to reheat (carbs, as always, solved all my problems), my doorbell rang.

Quietly I padded over the cold floor to look through the peephole. If it wasn't someone I wanted to see, I thought, I'd just tiptoe away. No one needed to know I was home.

"You're as quiet as a rhino in heels. Open the door, Emma," Whitney's voice pierced through the door, and she rang my doorbell two more times for good measure.

I whipped the door open. "What?" I snapped.

She pushed her way in much like Cooper had when I was goopy-eyed and avocado-masked. She looked so out of place in my apartment. She was in a black wrap dress and knee-high boots with spiky silver heels. "Don't you *what* me. You did this, honey, not me. Now I'm stuck cleaning up *two* messes, and for what? This stupid goddamn town. You're both idiots!" She flung her arms into the air in exasperation.

"You agreed to help him, so do it. I'll worry about myself. Keep the focus on him."

"Christ, you're such a martyr. I can't stand it. You haven't changed at all, and neither has he. When it comes to you, he's so goddamn blind it makes me insane." She was practically frothing at the mouth, she was so angry. In that moment, I felt sorry for anyone who went against Whitney in court.

"What do you mean, when it comes to me he's blind?" I asked, pulling her toward me by one arm. "I don't know what you're talking about!"

"You're so naive, Emma. He's had you on a pedestal since day one. You just never saw it. But even though he worshipped you, I saw you for what you really were: an opportunist. Someone who would step on his throat just to get ahead."

"That's so untrue and unfair. I would never!"

She howled with laughter. "Oh, no? You'd never put something you wanted ahead of him? Do I need to spell it out for you? You've been using him this whole time to get ahead in your own career. The Jackson deal, the campaign itself, even you fucking him was about you putting you first. Hey, I'm not suggesting it's not genius. I'm just saying don't act all matronly and prudish when you're literally fucking him to try to prove that I was wrong."

"You're unbelievable!" I shouted, trying to find a snappy retort. "Why the hell is everything about you all the time? News flash, Whitney. I wasn't with him to get back at you. Did I want to prove you wrong? Of course. Did you put the thought in my head that I was ignoring my feelings about him? Yes, I'll give you *all* the credit for that. But it ends there. Getting back at you didn't even factor into the decision I made last night."

"But it *is* about me. Remember? This convoluted plan involves me *intimately*. I'm sure that's hard for you to hear after your little tryst, but that's the way it is."

"This lawyer talk is getting old. Just say what it is you're trying to say and get the hell out of my apartment."

She folded her hands behind her back and started circling me. I imagined her in a courtroom, addressing a jury. She would have been brilliant if it hadn't been so irritating. "I have a job for you both: don't screw anything up while I'm gone. That includes each other. Hands off. I'm in charge of protecting him. From himself and certainly from you."

"Who the fuck do you think you are, Whitney? And where the hell are you going?" I snapped, balling my fists.

She looked down at them and laughed. "I'm the bitch that's saving your ass. So keep your little fists to yourself."

Whitney pulled out her phone, huffing after she glanced at the screen. "I've got a case I'm trying tomorrow in Barreton, so I have to leave Hope Lake for a few hours. I'll be back tomorrow night."

"You can't leave now," I said, my voice coming out almost as a whine. *Who am I, and what am I saying? Leave, bitch. Don't let the door hit ya.* But that wasn't right, and I knew it. We needed her here now more than ever. She was the only one who could fix this.

"What will people think if you leave town so close to this happening? The whole thing will blow up in our faces."

Shaking her head, she leveled me with a brutal look. "No, Emma. It'll blow up in *Cooper's* face. Not yours. Listen, you've done as much as you could for Cooper. Let me handle the rest. We've got this now. I have it all figured out. Your job is to stay the hell away from him."

AFTER SHE LEFT, I sank onto my couch and clutched a pillow to my face until I fell asleep. I wasn't sure how long I slept, but a knock at the door jolted me awake. When I blinked and snapped myself out of it, I stumbled to the door, half-expecting to find Whitney there ready to yell at me. Again.

But instead of Whitney, it was Cooper who stood in the door frame. Wordlessly he closed the door, followed me inside, and pulled a chair close to sit across from where I sat back down.

"Go away," I said, pulling my legs underneath myself.

"I will, but you're going to listen to me first," he said, taking my hands in his.

He cradled them, rubbing his thumbs over my knuckles. It made me so tired—I just wanted to curl up and sleep for a week. I really wanted him to be next to me when I did it.

Stay the hell away from him.

"Cooper, I'm really sorry about everything, but I think you should leave. Someone could see—"

"I don't care who sees me here. I need you to tell me what happened the other night. No bullshit, no one else is here. This is just two people who know a lot of the other's shit, and we need to talk it out."

Pulling my hands away, I scrubbed them over my face, willing some life into my skin. Everything felt exhausted. "Whitney was right."

"And you're admitting this now?" he asked, his voice shaking. Like the other night, I couldn't look at him for fear of what I would see.

I shook my head. "I still don't know what those feelings are. If they're even real or just some seed planted by Whitney to cause doubt."

Looking down, he let his head fall into his hands. "So you don't have feelings for me?"

I smiled, laughing to myself at the absurdity of it all. "Cooper, I have *so* many feelings for you. About you. With you. That's the problem." I shook my head. "What I'm saying is, I don't actually know what I'm saying. I need to think, to process what the hell is happening in my brain, because right now I'm being pulled in a hundred different directions and it's making me crazy.

"Here's what I do know: I don't want to ruin our friendship or hateship or whatever the hell our relationship is. I need you to know that. You're one of the most important people in my life, and I don't want to risk losing you."

He nodded, scooting forward on the chair. "I agree, but know this: I can't stop thinking about what happened. About why it happened and where we go from here. And if you asked me to, I would do everything from the other night again. And again, until you told me to stop. I'm wagering that both of us wouldn't want me to stop."

"Cooper," I began, but he lifted a single finger to my lips.

"Years ago, back in high school, do you remember my New Year's party?"

I nodded, having a crystal-clear picture of that night. It was the first year his parents had let us stay and socialize with the adults instead of being relegated to the game room.

"That was the first time I saw you in a tuxedo," I said, remembering how struck I had been by how handsome he looked.

"I had my first glass of champagne that night, and all I wanted to do was kiss you," he said, his eyes trained on the floor. "I thought about it for weeks. It scared the hell out of me. You had just gotten your braces, and you were nervous about them. You wouldn't smile so no one would see them, and I hated not seeing you happy. You said you wouldn't kiss anyone until they were off. Something shifted when you said that. I couldn't stop thinking about kissing you. I talked to Henry about it and made him promise not to tell you what I was thinking. The day of the party, my mother said she was going to take the last of the Christmas mistletoe down, but I begged her to leave just one up. The one in her office. It was away from everything else. It would have given us a chance to talk. For me to find out if you thought about it, too. I just had to get you in there."

My mouth fell open. "I—I didn't know any of that," I said, smiling at the memory of Cooper awkward and unsure as a teenager.

"You finally got me alone in there." I gave him a sad smile. "I was so nervous that I bit down on your lip and drew blood. I swore I never wanted to kiss anyone else after that. Except you. But—" I added, thinking back to what had happened just after midnight. After we had left the safety of the room, the ball had dropped, and I had watched Cooper laughing as he walked away with another girl. She had pulled him down for a kiss near the fireplace just as the clock struck midnight.

"That was the first time I hated you."

"I screwed up. I didn't know what she wanted to talk to me about. I was stupid and young and that's no excuse, but I panicked when she kissed me. I felt an awful lot in that one moment that we were together, and then I wrecked it. You never looked at me the same way after that."

He was right. The hopefulness of young love had been gone. "I went from having a crush to being crushed, and I said in that moment that I wouldn't be hurt by you again. And then . . ."

"Whitney," we both muttered, him sounding resigned and me sounding irate.

"I had thought that maybe with us being in college, we could have a clean slate. Start over or try again," I said, thinking of my eighteen-year-old self. "But the day I walked in on you two, it was like that night all over again. I never understood why you two were together. It just didn't make sense to me."

"I could keep saying that I'm stupid, but I think you know that by now," he said. "This sounds bad, but I dated her to get you to pay attention. She pursued me, and it worked out because you two were roommates. We were always friends first, and she knew how I felt about you, but I thought that making you jealous would give me a way in; maybe make you talk to me about *us*. It was probably one of the dumbest decisions I ever made. As you and I both know, it completely backfired. Then we stopped talking altogether, and I knew no matter what I said, nothing would change how you felt about me."

"Maybe so, but I played a part, too. I isolated myself instead of hearing you out or trying to heal our friendship. I blamed you guys for icing me out, but really I was just trying to remove myself so I wouldn't get hurt. Again."

Cooper reached out for the hand that rested on my knee. He pulled away just as his fingertips grazed my skin. He sighed. "There's so much history between us, Emma. I want to know how we continue on after this. We can't go back to how things were. We tried that once, and look where we ended up. We can't just be friends. We need to know what's next. And I want to try. With you. I've been waiting for a chance to try, hoping that it might come."

I thought about it, but I couldn't focus on what I had to. Not with him there in front of me looking hopeful.

"I need some time to think," I finally said. "A lot's happened in the past twenty-four hours."

"How much do you need?" he asked.

There wasn't anything left but election day and then the party. We were at the final stage of the race, and Whitney was right—I couldn't get involved now. That would compromise the campaign, and that was one thing I wouldn't risk.

"Until the party."

He nodded. "I'll be waiting."

"WE HAVE TO HAVE a 'Come to Jesus,'" I explained, smothering a laugh at Henry's bewildered expression.

"So are we walking to a church?" he teased, taking my arm to link it through his.

We walked like that for a few blocks. As if he'd sensed that I needed a friend, he'd shown up at my door offering a nonjudging ear the day after the visits from Whitney and Cooper.

"I don't think I want to be on the same block as the church when I tell you what's going on," I admitted, resting my head on his shoulder.

"It can't be worse than the time you stole that car."

I chuckled. "Commandeered, and it *so* is worse than that."

When I had been twelve and Henry, Nick, and Cooper all almost thirteen, we had *borrowed* Cooper's dad's car to see if we could drive it.

It started off just seeing if we could start it. We could.

Then we had ended up getting pulled over by a state trooper and had all been grounded for a few months. In fact, I was pretty sure that we would still be grounded if it hadn't been for Cooper's smooth talking with our parents. Even then he was great with politics and schmoozing.

Henry and I turned onto Bedelia Lane, my favorite street in the whole town. It was where some of the oldest homes in Hope Lake were located. Beautifully maintained colonials lined the street on both sides. Hearty old paperbark maple trees graced the lawn in front of nearly every house. In the spring, buds would pop out and the thin branches would be full of light pink flowers. In the fall, the deep red and orange leaves made the street look like it was on fire.

Cooper's parents' house was at the very end of the long, winding street. With Clare and Sebastian living in the governor's mansion in Harrisburg, it was almost always empty, save for a few staff who kept it going for when they returned a few times a year.

As kids, we'd marveled at the sheer size of the stunning old colonial, which had been in his family for generations. It looked more like a compound than a house for three people. Sitting on top of a small hill was a three-story main house with stark white siding and smoky black shutters. A side building, which had once been a carriage house, served as their ballroom for local functions when the governor was in town.

The driveway and garages were now packed with white vans

with party logos on the doors; servers in black-and-white uniforms milled about the property, finishing up all the details for the party. The Campbells were famous for their parties. On New Year's Eve—just like the night that Cooper and I had had our first romantic "incident"—everyone got dressed up, including the kids, who ran wild outside and petered out before midnight. Food and drinks overflowed, and people walked home carrying sleeping children, all excited for next year. There was still a party every year, but it had lost some of the magic from when I was younger.

"Hey, where'd you go?" Henry asked, waving his hand in front of my face. "You went blank there for a second."

"Oh, sorry. Lost in thought."

The house and its memories always twisted me up inside. I had stopped attending parties there when I was seventeen, either begging off from going on the grounds of having too much homework or leaving the town to head into New York City to celebrate with old friends. My last party there had been the first time I had witnessed Cooper's unabashed love of women.

Staring up at the house, I wondered if eventually, someday, Cooper would live there.

I bit the bullet and asked Henry what he knew. "Have you talked to Cooper lately?"

He sighed, patting my hand. "I have, and don't ask me what it was about because I can't tell you. I promised."

"Give me something, Henry."

With a deep breath, he came to a stop. Taking my shoulders in his big hands, he said, "He wouldn't tell me what happened between you, but I know something did. Neither one of you is being honest with yourselves, and I'm afraid that it's going to ruin your friendship."

"It already has, I think," I agreed, looking up at Henry. His deep blue eyes looked concerned. "There's something brewing in my gut, and I'm ignoring it. I can't think about it now, and maybe

I never will. Whitney's here now, and she'll get him back on track. That's the focus."

Henry said, quite plainly, "You're a fool and full of it. Cooper, whom I love almost as much as you, is a goddamn idiot, and I could and should kick both your asses for doing this to each other. If you two got your heads out of your collective asses, you would make the perfect pair."

"I'm not sure that'll ever be the case, my friend," I said, linking my arm back in his. I ignored the flare of hope that sprouted at the thought. I remembered Cooper's words from dinner with my parents months before. *Are you interested?* That had been his way of trying. With me.

"You can't know unless you try, Ems."

Oh, we tried, all right.

"Let's say something happened. Then it didn't work. Where would that leave us? Not just Cooper and me but the four of us? The work we do together would be in jeopardy if feelings were hurt." *If my feelings were hurt.*

"You're being selfishly insane here. You realize that, right?"

"I've heard something similar to that recently. You're not the first person to call me crazy when it comes to Cooper Endicott." I groaned, hating that Whitney had been right not once but twice.

I loved that he was worried, but it also made me question just how bad this all would be. If Henry, the king of selfless decisions, was questioning my sanity . . . it would likely be worse than I imagined.

almost forgot to vote.

Okay, that was not exactly true. I sat in my car watching my polling station, waiting for Cooper to leave so I could go inside. It was the last polling location on his list. I knew that because I'd made the rotation and emailed it to him.

He called me, texted me, and even sent me an email, but I couldn't focus on anything but this. It hurt too much to think about.

Us.

Two little letters that certainly caused me a lot of pain.

Maybe he'd thought he'd catch me at this stop and force me to talk to him face-to-face, but I wasn't about to risk it. He was superstitious and stayed the same amount of time at every polling spot to schmooze the voters.

It was smart; he was smart. I hoped he'd secured a victory because of it.

Along with our small group of campaign strategists, there were high school students helping at the voting locations today. I had met with them and their parents over the past few days to coordinate the volunteer efforts. It brought me great joy knowing that they were there because he'd engaged them at the school.

Meeting with them made my days without speaking to Cooper a bit brighter. At least it gave me something to focus on.

Who knew, maybe one of these kids would be mayor someday.

As I saw Cooper exit, he took one last look around before ducking into his car. Nick was driving and pulled away from the curb. He'd drop Cooper off at home to change for tonight. Either way, there would be a party at the Manor tonight. Whether it would be a celebration or a sad state of affairs was anyone's guess.

Before I knew it, I was in the polling booth. My hand shook as I pushed the buttons to vote for him. I had felt the eyes of the polling workers on me as I entered the building. They were mainly elderly folks who loved politics, volunteering, or the free doughnuts and coffee they got throughout the day to mix in with their gossip session.

Nancy came in just as I pushed the SUBMIT VOTE button. After checking in, she waited for me to come from around the terminal.

"All set?" she asked, squeezing my hand. "You look beautiful, by the way."

I smiled, looking down at my dress. It was the one I had bought with my mother the day that Cooper and I— I stopped, feeling a flush creep across my exposed shoulders and face. Maybe that's why I'd worn it to vote. I had scheduled myself down to the minute, checking in with volunteers while finishing up administrative tasks that had been piling up at the office, which had left me no time to go home to change before the party. Besides, I'd known that if I went home, I'd never leave.

"Thanks, Nance. You're coming tonight, right?"

"Wouldn't miss it," she said, stepping over to the open terminal. We were two of the last people there.

Nancy thanked the man setting up her voting terminal. "Hey, I've got to vote first, and then I'll be over. Don't do anything exciting before I get there, okay?"

"No promises," I said, smiling to myself as I walked out to my car.

ON THE WAY OVER to Campbell Manor, I still hadn't thought about what, if anything, I would say to Cooper when I finally saw him.

I pulled onto Love Lane, an aptly named street because so many young couples went there to make questionable decisions in its surrounding dense woods. Generations of lovers had carved their initials into the trees over the years, and spending a night there with a special someone was a rite of passage for young people. Myself included.

It also had the perfect view of the Campbell Manor backyard—not that the word *backyard* was especially accurate. It was several acres of land that stretched out to the woods behind the house. Now, with the huge line of cars going up to the Manor, it was barely visible. There were a dozen or more cars waiting in front of me for the valet to get through them all.

Staring up at the house as I waited in the traffic, I thought back to all of the times Cooper and I had been there together and wasted time by not being *together*.

But then I remembered Cooper's words: "I was stupid and young." Not for anything, but I hadn't exactly been a pillar of maturity, either. I still didn't know exactly what I was going to do about him. About us.

My phone lay silent in my purse. There wasn't a message from anyone, not even Whitney gloating that things were looking good. Turnout in every ward was high. People were positive and engaged, and for that I was grateful. My job was over.

Tapping my fingers against the steering wheel, I thought about how easy it would have been just to turn around and drive away. To avoid seeing Cooper. To avoid seeing Cooper and Whitney

for me, and it wouldn't be fair to him to ruin what was potentially a huge night for him because I was unable to deal with my feelings for him.

The traffic at a standstill, I sent him a text.

> **ME:** Don't answer this. Enjoy
> your night. I just wanted to
> tell you that no matter what,
> Cooper, I'm proud of you and
> there is a lot of me that's always
> been in love with you.

JACKASS: [read at 6:47PM]

. . .

Those bouncing dots were easily the most annoying thing he could have done. Yet I couldn't help but laugh.

I pulled up his campaign page on Facebook. Front and center was a photo that had just been posted by Nick.

Two minutes ago.

It was Cooper and Whitney standing in front of the Campbells' massive parlor fireplace. It took up most of one wall, and the mantel was filled with photos of the Campbell family. His arm was linked with Whitney's, and they were beaming at the camera. The caption read:

> *Mayoral Candidate Cooper Campbell-Endicott*
> *and Whitney Jocelyn Andrews, Esq., waiting on the*
> *results at his election party.*

Below the photo were the reactions. A handful of shares were already registered, so I followed the first link, which led to the newspaper's home page.

The same caption was included with the photo, along with some juicy gossip as clickbait:

If the rumors are to be believed, we may be witnessing
a proposal tonight, too. Whitney Campbell-Endicott
has a nice ring to it, if you ask us.

At least it isn't negative press, I reasoned, feeling an overwhelming urge to get the hell out of Dodge.

A horn tooted behind me. I jumped, tossed my phone onto the seat, and moved up. I had been so lost in the photo that it was nearly my turn for the valet. No turning back now.

Inside, the house looked exactly as I remembered it. There was a coatroom just off the foyer, where I left my purse and coat. It was crowded, but not nearly as many people were there as I'd thought would be. *It's still early,* I told myself. *The polls aren't closed yet. Once that happens, people will be pouring in waiting for the results.*

There were cameras snapping candid shots of guests and someone walking around with a video camera documenting the comments by partygoers, and waiters walking around with hors d'oeuvres. Then the oddest realization hit me: I was being ignored, and it was glorious.

I could have been topless with VOTE FOR COOPER stickers on my nipples, and I don't think anyone would have paid me any mind.

It wasn't until the governor and Mr. Endicott waved hello that one of the reporters covering the party came over to ask for a photo. "Where's Cooper?" he called out, looking around the room for the guest of honor.

Governor Campbell tried working her way over to me, but the cameras were now blocking her path. She smiled politely, waiting for someone to move so she could join me. As it was, I was standing in the center of an antique rug all alone.

When she finally made it to me, she pulled me into a warm embrace, followed by Cooper's father, Sebastian. "Emma, darling, you look gorgeous," she said, mindful of the ears that were listening intently to our conversation.

"Thank you, Governor. So do you. I love this color blue on you," I said, playing right along with it, giving the press nothing but polite chitchat.

Clare Campbell looked nothing like her son save for the bright, slightly uneven smile they shared. Cooper was all his father from build to complexion to hair color. "I saw your parents earlier," the governor said. "I'm so glad they're here. I've missed them."

I smiled. "I know, they've missed you both, too. Perhaps now that Dad will have some free time, he'll be able to visit you more often," I suggested, knowing that it was something they'd already discussed and that the press already knew about.

Emma 1, media vultures 0.

The reporters looked bored, which meant I'd done my job. I was determined to keep things boring and scandal-free from here on out; at least until Cooper was elected.

Speaking of Cooper, I knew the moment he entered the sitting room. The hairs on the back of my neck stood on end, and my breathing quickened. It was as if my body knew he was nearby before I actually saw him. I gulped. Moment of truth.

"Cooper, how about a photo with your friend and her parents? Emma, where's your parents? Let's get everyone in this!" the photographer cheered.

Cooper's hand touched the small of my back, and it took everything in me not to jump a foot into the air. "Emma," he whispered, his fingers dancing along my waist. I was dangerously close to launching myself at him in front of a half-dozen cameras.

No one would be bored then.

Turning, I schooled my features in preparation to see Cooper in a tuxedo. Thinking about it and seeing it were miles apart. My heart fluttered at the sight of him. "Emma, you look lovely," he said, leaning down to kiss my cheek. "As always," he added smoothly.

I could hear the clicks of the cameras already starting. In the back of my mind, I knew that I should back away, smile gratefully, and move on, but I couldn't. I simply stared up at him, smiling and wondering just how much over my head I was in all of this.

Mindful of the cameras, the mics, and the way all of the journalists were leaning in for the scoop, Cooper joked, "Hope you remembered to vote."

My hand flew dramatically to my chest. "Oh, was that today? I'm sorry, I had a *thing*."

Cooper bellowed with laughter, tipping his head back. The reporters laughed along with him. "Yes, there was a *thing* today," he said. "Pretty important thing, too. Hope you made the right decision."

"Oh, I think I did," I said, smiling. I wanted to hug him. To send a small signal that would say, *I'm with you, no matter what,* but there were cameras trained on our faces, snapping away. They'd catch it, and although the voting had been finished as of a few moments before, I wasn't risking it.

There would be plenty of time for it later. For us later.

My parents hustled over, breaking the staring contest we were engaged in. "Emma, dear, you look wonderful," my father said, pushing his way in between myself and Cooper.

"Come, come, let's get this photo!" the photographer encouraged us, and instructed us where to stand. Cooper and my father moved to the center, with my mother behind my dad and the governor and Cooper's dad behind Cooper. That left me the odd man out.

"I really don't have to be in this," I insisted, backing toward the piano. I bumped into the player, sending discordant notes through the party. "Sorry, sorry."

"Of course you need to be in here, Emma," Clare insisted,

"You stay right here, dear," Clare said, taking my hand in hers to keep me rooted to the spot. "Whitney can stand on his other side."

Oh. My. God. How the hell was this going to look? How would anyone explain this one to the readership? Cooper had not one but *two* women on his arm? Thankfully, no one knew the history of the parties involved, and it would just look like two old friends, their parents, and his girlfriend stopped for a politically charged photo.

"Emma," Whitney said, gliding over to stand next to Cooper. Her dress had looked black in the photo I'd seen earlier, but up close I could tell it was actually a stunning navy silk dress that hugged every curve. No matter the color, it left nothing to the imagination. Her hair was sleek and wavy with a beaded clip holding up one side. She looked like she had stepped out of a catalog that catered to the rich and powerful.

Whitney placed herself directly between my father and Cooper, her arms around their waists, positioning her front and center. If ever there were a political power couple pose, that was it. I stood as far away from them as I could without it being glaringly obvious that I didn't want to be anywhere near them.

"Look this way, folks," the photographer said, and I forced myself to smile. Just then about a dozen other journalists caught on to the fact that they were missing a prime photography opportunity, so they latched onto us. Luckily, their shouting and the blinding camera flashes were a distraction from what was probably one of the most awkward experiences of my life.

"Okay, how about one now with just Cooper and his parents? Then Emma, the mayor, and your mom? Any other combos?" someone shouted, and one of the assistants started setting us up. We were positioned like mannequins: Arms here. Head tilted this way. Smile bigger. Smile smaller. Deep breath and exhale. More teeth. "Okay!"

"If it's all right, I'd like you to take one of Cooper and Emma, please," Clare said to one of the photographers. "After all, she played such a major role in the entire thing."

Before I could resist, Cooper spun around, turning his back to Whitney, who pouted for a second before plastering on her fake, bright smile.

"Relax, Emma," he whispered as he pulled me in to his side. His arm slid behind me, resting just above my backside. His fingers curled around the fabric above my hip—wrinkling it, I was sure, judging by how tightly he was gripping it. As if he were anchoring me to his side. The camera frenzy erupted again. I smiled, followed the shouting photographers' directions, and desperately tried not to reach over and place my hand over his chest like Whitney had. The moment was only made more ironic when I heard "Emma, lean in to Cooper a bit. Great!"

EMMA THOUGHT: The Fates are HILARIOUS.

When the photos were done, Cooper was pulled to the side by one of the local state representatives who were likely there thanks to the governor's invitation, and I was able to escape from the media frenzy to join the governor and my parents for some much-needed alcohol.

"This is a lovely party, isn't it?" Clare said, handing me a glass of champagne. "Makes me miss how we used to have them all the time. I remember the last time you were here—you had a similar look on your face then, too. Both of which I attribute to my son."

I smiled, embarrassed a little at how transparent I had been and apparently still was. "It is a beautiful party. Your staff did an incredible job." I feigned ignorance of her other comment. "I just hope we're able to celebrate tonight."

"Oh, I think we will. I have a feeling we'll be celebrating a *few* things tonight," Clare said, smiling into her champagne glass.

The cameras were now following Cooper and Whitney around the party, snapping every shot they could. They'd lob out a question about an engagement, and Whitney would beam at Cooper. The crews were eating it up. Cooper looked like a deer in headlights to me, but to everyone else, he probably appeared normal. I just knew him well enough to know that he was getting to the end of a very short rope.

Whitney, to her credit, didn't falter once with the questions thrown at her. The Hope Lake and state journalists were like the damn paparazzi in New York City, what with the number of questions and cameras they were throwing into their faces.

Whereas I could barely handle a few posed photographs, Whitney seemed to feed off the attention. Maybe because she was used to fielding questions in court, but whatever the reason, she was a pro.

"Whitney, if Cooper wins, will you move to Hope Lake immediately?"

"I have a huge clientele in Barreton that I need to figure out first."

"Whitney, are the rumors true? Are you and Cooper tying the knot?"

"You'll have to ask him that, but I hear spring in Hope Lake is a beautiful time for a wedding."

"They're perfect for each other," I murmured to the governor, who was watching me watching them.

The thought rankled me. No matter what I felt for Cooper, they were undeniably a solid pair. Whitney was obviously smitten with him, and no matter what Cooper felt for me, he must have had *some* feelings for her. They had a history, after all.

The governor touched my arm, patting it gently. "You of all people should know that appearances can be deceiving, Emma," she said simply, and gave me a one-armed hug.

I SPENT THE NEXT HOUR avoiding Cooper and Whitney in person but following them on social media. It was a bit creepy, but it was still better than the alternative: watching them play it up for the cameras live and in person. The cameras tailed them around the party, and I headed in the opposite direction whenever I saw them coming my way. Still, though, I made sure to stay updated on my phone. New pictures of them appeared every few seconds, with lots of likes and comments about the upcoming "proposal." *Gag me.*

Still, though, not everything was about Hope Lake's new power couple. There were comments about the election, too, with fans of Cooper's speculating whether he had enough votes to win and fans of Kirby's speculating whether he had enough scandals to lose. At one point, Henry livestreamed a short Q and A with Cooper, asking him questions that actually focused on what his platform was. There was no mention of any scandal or lowbrow remarks about his personal life: just facts. That gave Cooper the opportunity to set the record straight on quite a few of the underhanded headlines the paper had run and clear the air of any misunderstandings before the final vote was counted.

It was all I could do to stop myself from scrolling through the live feed that was updating with the polling results. With the polls closed for just under an hour, we'd start getting percentages in, and I needed to keep up to the minute with the results. My phone was nearly dead—who knew that stalking Cooper and Whitney could drain so much battery?—so I needed to find a plan B: the local news.

As unreliable as the papers had been, Hope Lake broadcasting was still a source I trusted. Every year the TV station held its own election party, tallying the poll results live. The closest television, I knew from years of visiting Campbell Manor, was in Clare's office. As I headed there, I fought to keep my nerves at bay.

What would happen if Cooper lost?

What would happen if Cooper won?

What would happen to *us*?

As I headed to her office, I saw Cooper and Whitney standing in front of its door, deep in conversation. I couldn't hear them, and judging by the looks of it, I didn't know if I wanted to. She was pacing in the small area, waving her arms around. She looked angry as she circled the space around him. Cooper had his arms crossed over his chest, and one foot was tapping the hardwood.

Judging by the look on his face, he would welcome a distraction. "Excuse me," I said loudly, standing off to the side so one or both of them would move to free up my path. "It's almost time."

"Already?" Cooper said, glancing nervously at his watch.

Giving him a small, encouraging smile, I ignored Whitney entirely. "Cooper, it looks good. I've been watching the results all night."

"So have I," he said, smiling and pulling out his phone. On it, the chyron was scrolling through.

Whitney slid me her usual annoyed look. "Good, we've got a long day tomorrow." She pulled Cooper in to her side and started rubbing his back. It seemed odd until I realized the crush of reporters behind me snapping away.

"Cooper," his mother called over them, waving her hand for him to join her. "We have a TV set up in the sitting room."

The ticker was not yet streaming on-screen, and I waited nervously for it to appear. For now I kept my eyes trained on the reporter, who was discussing the mood at the polls. "Clearly Hope Lake is excited for a change because they turned out for the polls. We are reporting a record number of voters in this mayoral election."

Cooper's face paled. My heart leapt into my throat.

A change. That sounded suspiciously like a Rogers phrase.

Does he mean a change in that they want a new direction for the town? They're tired of my father and embracing Rogers as the change? I wondered frantically.

Or is it that clearly Hope Lake is "excited for a change," meaning that people like the direction my father's taken the town in and they're ready for Cooper to take it farther?

EMMA THOUGHT: Now is not the time to overanalyze.

The TV cut to Kirby's campaign party just as Cooper's cell phone blared loudly.

His hand shook a bit as he pulled it from his pocket. Looking to his parents, he smiled nervously. "This is it," he said before turning his eyes to me with the slightest wink.

Rogers appeared on-screen taking a call himself before they cut away quickly to a commercial. *Son of a bitch.*

"Thank you, I can't thank you enough," Cooper finished, turning to the crowd of anxious guests.

"Well?" my father said, glancing nervously from the very quiet Cooper to a commercial selling furniture during an election day sale. "Cooper, who was it?"

"That was the election office."

"And?" nearly everyone asked simultaneously. He was about to speak when the news reporter appeared on the screen again.

Along with the ticker across the bottom:

**HOPE LAKE—MAYORAL RACE—RESULTS . . . ENDICOTT—
WINNER WITH 92% OF THE WARDS REPORTING**

The room went silent.

"Well, *that* was awfully anticlimactic," Cooper deadpanned, and the room exploded. Cooper was immediately pulled into a hug by his parents. His mother was smiling, her eyes filling with tears. Cooper's dad, the usually stoic attorney, was slapping him on the back and kissing his cheek.

"I'm so proud of you," his father said before kissing Clare. She kissed Cooper. It was a big Campbell-Endicott lovefest.

One by one, people pushed and shoved their way to Cooper. They got to him so fast that fighting through the crowd to congratulate him proved to be nearly impossible. I would inch up only to be sidestepped. My father pulled Cooper into a hug just as I touched his sleeve. Henry and Nick clapped him on the back as I reached for his hand. It seemed that my congratulating him was going to be an unattainable goal.

Over the course of the next hour, we exchanged stolen glances.

There were times when I thought we were going to be able to sneak off and talk, but Whitney was always around.

And even if she hadn't been, cameras were. The timing just wasn't right, and there was a very large part of me that needed it to be. He was my guy. And I really wanted my guy all to myself.

But that was impossible, and I knew I was being selfish. He was enveloped in dozens of hugs. Questions were volleyed at him by family, supporters, and reporters. Whenever Whitney was with him, I could hear her answering for him, not with him.

"We are so happy. This is just what we wanted. I couldn't be prouder of the campaign we ran."

I wanted to show her who the *we* was. Damn cameras.

Would it be so bad? The election is over . . . they can't take back his win if they find out I'm *the one he really wants to be with, right?*

At one point I heard my name, but it wasn't from whom I hoped. Governor Campbell was taking my hand and trying to get a journalist's attention. "You know," she said to a bored-looking cameraman who hadn't been able to get to the golden couple fast enough, "Emma was—" But it fell on deaf ears.

Whitney had just kissed Cooper lightly on the lips, igniting another round of photos and questions.

Slowly I slid my hand out of Clare's. There was that rushing through my ears that made me light-headed; but it wasn't the good kind.

Even though I knew that the kiss didn't mean anything— that they were like actors putting on a show—there was still a seed of doubt that was growing bigger and bigger the longer their lips stayed connected. Clare reached out to me, but I took a step back. Then another. Cooper glanced up just as I was nearly at the threshold of the room. His eyes went wide with worry.

Cooper pulled his mouth from Whitney's, but just as he stepped toward me, another reporter came at him, this one from the national news. Two more followed—the same ones that had been at the very first photo shoot with Rogers. They must have been in town waiting either way.

The line of reporters was a half-dozen deep. With Whitney still at Cooper's side, I took it as my cue to leave. There would be time for us to talk. There had to be. But for now I didn't need to see any more of it. What was playing on repeat in my head was enough.

With one more not-so-polite shove, I made it out of the sitting room and into the blissfully empty hallway. I could have hidden out there or in Clare's office until the party dwindled down, but I knew that wouldn't be until well after midnight.

And I was mentally exhausted.

"Emma!" I heard a voice call out just as I made it to the coat check room.

Cooper. My heart leapt a little bit; then I turned around and saw Whitney was on his heels.

So much for our getting time to talk.

"Congratulations," I said a little stiffly. Then, mindful of the handful of reporters at his back, "I'm so proud of you."

I was proud of *myself* for getting that out without my shaky voice giving away what I was feeling. Cooper looked confused, hurt, and annoyed. "Why are you leaving already? I don't understand—" he began, but then, as I flicked my chin toward the crew, he shifted. Political Cooper was back, and they were getting a front-row seat for it.

"Thank you for everything," he said to me formally. "I couldn't have done this without you."

Whitney took it as her cue to stand beside him, showing them off as a power couple thanking his campaign manager. "Ladies and gentlemen," she started, directing them toward me with a flick of her wrist. "Emma here was a key component of Cooper's campaign. I think she deserves a round of applause."

The reporters started hurling questions at me, but they sounded like white noise, an annoying whir keeping me from talking to him.

Whitney jumped at the chance to keep the focus on herself by answering the shouts from the reporters.

"Want a little scoop, guys?" Whitney asked. She was in her element. I bet she was formidable in the courtroom. "Ask Kirby's wife about the anonymous content that the *Journal* has been running, unchecked."

"What?" I gasped, trying to hear whatever else she was saying. Over the shouts from the press, I caught an occasional word: "wife, lies, published, nonsense."

Cooper must have seen my frustration and confusion, because he offered to fill in the blanks. He bent down and whispered in my ear, "Kirby's wife was blackmailing Peter, the editor at the *Journal*. She found out about him having an affair with a woman in Barreton—and she was using it to get him to print whatever she wanted about me."

"And Whitney found this out?"

He nodded. "I still don't know how, and frankly, I'm not sure I want to," he said, rubbing his hand on the back of his neck.

"I'll have to ask her." I started moving toward Whitney, but he grabbed my arm, preventing me from leaving his side.

"I'd rather talk to you about *another thing*," he whispered, his index finger lightly touching my hand.

I wanted to take it. To hold on to him and pull him into the office.

"We can slip out," he whispered, ignoring the *harrumph* that came from Whitney, who was clearly eavesdropping and far more adept at multitasking than I gave her credit for.

"You've got to stay, enjoy the party," I whispered.

"What about everything else?"

"There'll be time for that eventually, but now isn't the time. Come over tomorrow, when everything has calmed down. Hopefully you won't be too busy to squeeze in a conversation with an old friend, Mr. Mayor."

26

Within twenty minutes of leaving the party, I was holed up in my apartment in my fuzzy slippers and matching robe, sitting on my couch.

Popping open a bottle of my favorite wine, I settled in with a bowl of popcorn and some cheesy action flick on the local channel. The live ticker across the bottom of the screen kept repeating, showing exactly what I wanted to see:

HOPE LAKE MAYOR—ENDICOTT DECLARED WINNER

Someone had updated Cooper's campaign Facebook page. And Kirby's. His was less about his loss and more about how sorry Hope Lake would be for voting for Cooper. Clearly, he wasn't well versed on what it meant to be a gracious loser.

I didn't want to look, but I couldn't stop myself. The photos from Cooper's party were filled with images of him with Whitney. Some with his parents, some with mine. I enjoyed the one where my mother was giving Whitney a side-eye that could have stopped traffic.

Around midnight, someone started a Facebook livestream showing that the crowd was still going strong. They were dancing, and I could see that Cooper had loosened up and his tie now hung carelessly around his neck. Unable to torture myself by watching the livestream any longer, I decided to focus on the movie I'd settled on. But that didn't last long.

It could have been the weeks of overworking and sleepless nights that had finally gotten to me, or maybe it was my brain's way of forcing a little self-preservation on me. Either way, before I realized it, I was asleep on my couch, curled up under a Drexel blanket that I hadn't realized I had.

SOMETIME AROUND TWO, I woke to a slight tapping on my door. At some point, I'd rolled onto the remote control and sent the volume up about ten notches, but I had been so exhausted it hadn't even woken me up. The tapping continued before I turned off the news; then it stopped.

Then it started again.

There was no way I was going back to sleep now.

"Coming," I mumbled, knowing it was probably Mrs. MacGuire looking to yell at me for something. The volume most likely.

I opened the door, an apology ready on my lips. "Mrs.— Oh!"

"That's a new name. I'm used to 'Jackass.' 'Mrs. Oh' has a nice ring to it, though."

"Cooper, sorry. I expected it to be Mrs. MacGuire."

"I can see why I would be a disappointment, then. Sparkling conversation versus, well, me."

I laughed in spite of myself. "Cooper, what are you doing here?"

In the years to come, I'd replay this conversation over in my mind and wonder why I hadn't immediately kissed him. Or pulled him in for a hug. Or even just said, "I love you, thank you for coming here and knowing this is exactly what I needed."

He smiled and looked down at his shoes. His jaw ticked while he tried to come up with an answer. "I stayed for long enough. I answered dozens of questions. I had a few glasses of champagne. It was all wonderful, but . . ."

"But what?" I asked, holding my breath, waiting.

"You weren't there."

Looking up, I saw that his eyes were tired but still so happy. "I just wanted to tell you," he said slowly, "how much I appreciate everything that you've done for me. I, well— I couldn't have done this without you, Emmanuelle."

"Are you kidding me? You came all this way just to thank me?" I said in amazement, stepping inside so he could follow me. "Don't get me wrong, I'm grateful, but—"

His lips cut me off. Warm, firm, and just slightly tinged with champagne. His arms encircled me, holding me tight to him. "Stop talking," he murmured against my lips, nipping at the bottom one with his teeth.

"What—what was that?" I began, but he kissed me again, cutting me off.

"Please stop talking," he said, laughing and pulling me in for another hug.

Like a barnacle, I clung to him. Grateful that he was here and happy. There was so much to discuss, but for now this was good. This was *very* good.

We'd be good.

We sank back into the couch cushions, and he tucked me into his side. "This was the best night, but I couldn't stop thinking about you not being with me."

"Where's Whitney?"

"God, you know how to ruin a moment for a guy, don't you, Peroni?" he said, kissing the top of my head.

"I'm just wondering."

"I'm guessing on her way back to Barreton. I called a car service for her and told her to leave. She knows we'll only ever be friends. She knew that from the beginning."

Breaking eye contact, I paused, trying to look curious, not

gleeful. In an odd way, I had to thank Whitney. Later though—much, much later.

"Cooper, why did you tell her to leave?"

"I can't believe you even asked that," he said with a small laugh. "I told her that *we* had to discuss our future."

"*Our* future?" I asked as he slid his hand over mine. They were both sitting atop a tiny elephant on my pajama pants.

"Yes. Mine, yours, Hope Lake's."

"Ours?" I asked, squeezing his hand once. Then again to make sure it was there.

"I came here because I couldn't stand answering one more question without you there with me. I tried socializing, I tried going through the motions, but I was distracted. I needed you there as my anchor. You've always been that for me. The anchor that's kept me in Hope Lake."

"I'm never at a loss for words," I admitted, smiling up at him. "But I am now. Who would have thought that this"—I paused, waving a hand between us—"would happen."

He shrugged. "*I* knew. I'm very smart and intuitive, you know. It took us a while to get here, but no one ever said the path to happiness was a smooth one."

"Listen to you being all poetic," I teased. "We're a thing? An Emma-and-Cooper thing?"

"I think it would be a Cooper-and-Emma thing because, you know, the alphabet and I'm the mayor, so—" he said, twirling a piece of my hair around his fingers.

"We'll add it to the list of talking points. I'll schedule a meeting," I said, laughing when he tickled my ribs.

"You can be on top for now, but we'll take turns," he whispered, his eyes darkening at the suggestion.

"Cooper," I began, peppering kisses across his cheeks before planting one solidly on his mouth. "I feel like we're not talking politics anymore."

He shook his head and pulled me onto his lap.

"We've got a lot of work to do, Mr. Mayor."

"Oh, yeah? What kind of work?"

"*Work* work and *us* work," I said, unbuttoning his shirt and sliding my hands beneath it. "There has to be a new normal for us. None of this at the office." I leaned forward, placing a kiss over his heart. "And you've got to start answering your texts instead of leaving me hanging."

He laughed, a full-blown guffaw with his head thrown back. "That was on purpose. I didn't want to tell you that I loved you via text message. That's not very romantic."

I sucked in a breath. Giddiness coursed through me as I stared down at him.

"You love me?"

He nodded, pulling my shirt over my head. "I do. More than I ever thought I could love anyone."

Pulling me close, he cupped my butt and winked. "I've always wanted to do that."

Laughing, I wiggled around, earning a groan. "I have a few ideas," I said, lowering my lips to his for a kiss.

"You and your ideas. Tell me?"

"How about I show you?" I asked, pulling him up from the couch and leading us toward my bedroom. "By the way, congrats, Mr. Mayor."

With his lips sliding down my neck and shoulder, he whispered, "I really like the sound of that."

EPILOGUE

know you don't want to, but I need you to stand up there with me," Cooper said, pulling me in for a kiss.

Shaking my head, I sighed. "Cooper, I can't. It's not right."

There were people in the elevator watching us, but he didn't care. So much for our not being obvious at work. Or at the store or in town or anywhere, really. He didn't care who saw us together. Walking down the street, holding hands, kissing—nothing was off the table as far as Cooper was concerned.

Well, almost nothing.

I was still determined to keep him scandal-free.

Instead of letting me pull away, he tucked me into his side and planted a kiss on top of my head. We fit together just right.

It still made me antsy, even two months later, to be so affectionate in public. But Cooper didn't care. If anything, he seemed to get enjoyment out of it.

The calming part for me was how people reacted to it. I got a lot of "Finally" and "It's about time" comments. Apparently, everyone from Mrs. Mancini to Dr. Bishop had had an opinion about Cooper and my getting together.

No one had ever thought to share it with me.

After the election, there were questions about Whitney and

why she had disappeared so suddenly from Hope Lake. Why Cooper and I had gotten together so soon after their "breakup." Whitney simply told anyone who asked that she and Cooper had tried to make things work between them but as much as they cared about each other, it just wasn't meant to be. And she knew he'd always been hung up on me. She'd known that was true years ago. She'd stepped aside to let us be together.

Ever the selfless one.

Cooper and I didn't go public right away. In fact, for weeks, we were very, very private. Any and all time we could spend away from the public and prying eyes, we did. It was only after a few weeks that we found out that people didn't care. Well, except for our family and friends.

"When exactly did this happen?" my mother had asked when we first told her, hugging Cooper in between pointing an accusatory finger at me for not telling her immediately. My dad had simply smiled.

"When are you getting married?" Cooper's mother had asked, berating us for not telling her first because if we were getting married soon, her schedule would have to be planned around it.

"Can I be the best man?" Nick and Henry had said together before getting into a war of words over who was more qualified.

Mercifully, the rest of the town—Mrs. Mancini and her crew aside—pretty much left us alone. They were happy for us, sure, but it wasn't nearly as interesting a topic as the Jackson project. That was what had the town excited. The ground and the lake were frozen, so the company hadn't broken ground yet, but the construction plans were under way and its Facebook page was updated weekly. The town—and the tourists who came every summer—couldn't wait for Hope Lake's newest attraction.

But today was something that *I* was excited for. We were on the way to swear Cooper in as Hope Lake's newest and youngest-ever mayor. So we wanted a few minutes just between us. Something without all the cameras or our families with their moony-eyed expectations. My mother already had a list of names going for her possible future grandchildren.

All of it was a bit much, but we were taking it in stride. One of the things I'd promised myself—and Cooper—was that I wasn't going to overanalyze everything from here on out. We'd just continue on with our lives as they were before. Except with less arguing.

EMMA THOUGHT: Well, for the most part.

When we did argue—which was surprisingly rare, given our history—we found that tumbling into bed was the best remedy for it. That was one of the perks of finally realizing that we could channel our tension into more . . . fun activities. Too bad we hadn't thought of it sooner.

"What time is everyone getting here? We seem to be more than a little bit early," I said as we exited the elevator and headed into the empty courtroom.

"I'm surprised our mothers aren't here yet," he said, standing off to one side. "They think we're here to surprise-wedding them."

I choked, sputtering questions at him rapid-fire. "Surprise-wedding them? What? What do you mean? Why would they think that? Who told them that? Cooper Endicott, this is not a joke. My mother will show up in a dress if she thinks we're getting married! A not-suitable-for-a-wedding dress because I wasn't there to help her pick it out."

He took my hands in his. "Calm down, calm down, I'm kidding. Though this gave me a great deal of insight into how everyone, including you, will deal with it when I do propose."

That statement sent a feverish bloom over my skin. "When?" I gulped.

"*When*," he said matter-of-factly, dropping a kiss on each of my knuckles and paying special attention to the knuckle on the third finger on my left hand.

I could feel the heat rise to my cheeks, flushing my face in the best possible way. "Well, what if I wanted to propose to you? Not now, of course. It's only been a couple months—"

Cooper laughed. "You *are* very busy."

"Right?" I asked, tapping my fingers across the desk.

"In that case," he said, patting his coat pocket. My eyes widened.

"Emma."

He reached into his jacket and fumbled around. Just as he nearly pulled out whatever was inside, our families burst through the double doors of the courtroom and he pulled his hand away, empty.

I turned on my heel, glaring at the group. Cooper's parents, Henry, Nick, and my parents all stopped abruptly. "Go back out there, count to two hundred, and then come back in."

"Dude, that's all it tak—" Nick began, but Henry punched him in the arm.

"Not the time, man," he said, earning a few laughs from our parents.

"It's okay," Cooper said, putting his arm around me briefly. Kissing my lips gently, he turned to his father to shake his hand. Thanking him, my father, and his best friends for coming to the swearing-in, he then turned to me just as the judge was walking into the courtroom.

"What did we interrupt?" my mother asked expectantly. She was practically vibrating.

"Oh, nothing. I was just about to ask Emma—"

"Yes?" Clare interrupted breathlessly, earning a laugh from her husband. "What were you going to ask her?"

Cooper reached inside his jacket pocket again, his hand searching inside for something. "Oh, here it is. I was just going to ask her—"

I held my breath. My hands were sweating, my heart was racing, and my stomach was churning so much that I was grateful that I hadn't had time to eat breakfast before we left Cooper's house. Well, that was mostly because we decided that a quick shower followed by not-so-quick sex was more important than eggs.

"Yes?" I asked, heart in my throat.

"—if she'd read my speech. You know, make sure it's grammatically correct and all."

My mouth fell open. To be fair, everyone else's did, too. Especially once he pulled out the folded sheet of paper.

Not a ring box.

He held it up between two fingers and smiled. "What did you think I was going to ask her?" He looked pointedly at his mother, then at mine, then at me. "Emma?"

Shaking my head, I laughed awkwardly. I wasn't actually upset, just . . . okay, I guess I *was* a little upset. I hadn't thought about any of this until he had mentioned it, and now I was missing something I hadn't even thought I wanted.

"Sure," I said, "I'll go over it quickly while we wait for the photographer to get here." I held out my hand.

He held on to the paper tightly for just a second. "Are you sure you have time in your schedule? I mean—" he teased, finally handing it over.

I rummaged in my purse for a pen. One thing I had noticed in my years of working with Cooper was that he'd never met a comma he didn't misuse. If I hadn't proofed his speeches and reports, everything would have sounded like William Shatner giving a monologue, pausing at every other word.

I took a seat where defendants normally sat, ignoring the *harrumph* of the judge and leaving the group behind me chatting away. I didn't realize that they had gotten eerily quiet until I began clicking and unclicking the pen. Opening the paper, I glanced over when I saw Henry moving toward me, his iPhone raised and recording.

"What?" I asked, turning to him. Behind him were Nick and all of our parents, the judge, Mrs. Mancini, and a few other people from town. I hadn't noticed them come in. This was supposed to be a closed swearing-in, and the public was supposed to stay outside until Cooper came out for his speech. What was going on?

I looked for Cooper, who was kneeling next to my chair. "Ah, you haven't read it yet. I may have been a bit premature with all the bended-knee stuff," he said, running a nervous hand through his hair.

"Cooper?" I asked, my voice quaking. "What are—"

"Read it," he said, motioning to the paper in my trembling hand.

I didn't have to look. Seeing the nervousness on his face and the happiness on the faces of everyone behind him, I knew what it would say. Sliding my eyes across the page, I couldn't even finish reading the first sentence before my vision was blurred by happy tears.

Across the top of the page was the town seal. It was on Cooper's new letterhead.

TOWN OF HOPE LAKE
OFFICE OF COOPER CAMPBELL-ENDICOTT, MAYOR

Scribbled beneath it in Cooper's messy handwriting was the best thing I could have ever read.

My Emma,
I'm writing this in the mayor's office. At the mayor's desk.
Just before I sat in the chair, I crawled underneath the desk.
Beneath the desk, colored into the wood, is still a crayon
drawing of you and me together.
    It's always been us.
    It's because of you that I have this office, so I thought it
only right that on my very first day as mayor I use my very first
piece of letterhead to ask you the very first question of my time
as the mayor of the town we both love.
    Will You Marry Me?
    PS: Please say yes.

                              Yours Always,
                              Cooper

I vaulted myself off the chair and into Cooper's waiting arms, knocking us both to the ground in the process.

"So much for not loving public displays of affection," I mumbled, kissing him with everything I had. The crowd surrounding us cheered and clapped. Even the judge, who was one of the most stoic people in Hope Lake, was smiling.

"So what are you saying?" he asked between kisses, laughing when I pulled away to accept the ring he was holding. In all my excitement, I hadn't answered. I'd just dived headfirst without thinking. Or overthinking . . .

I smiled. This was one thing I would never have to think twice about.

"I vote yes, Mr. Mayor."

ACKNOWLEDGMENTS

I'm not the best at writing acknowledgments. I'm not sure that anyone is reading this, but, if you are, hi! Thanks for buying *On the Corner of Love and Hate*. If you borrowed it from your library, you are kick-ass, because libraries are SO important. Thank you for supporting them!

Still, it's a bit of a rite (write) of passage for someone, especially a newbie author, to write one.

With the world in its current chaotic and scary state, I wanted to write a character who believed in goodness and love. And who embraced the need for civil engagement. I'm a firm believer in voting. It's risky writing a semipolitical book but, overall, I wanted Emma to have a voice.

Her story was one that I wanted to tell. I hope you enjoyed it. Please vote.

So many people go into making a book. I'm so afraid I will miss someone, so if I do, please don't get mad.

To the fine folks at Gallery. You're the best—truly, I mean that. You're encouraging, wise, and vigilant, and you all love *love*. I'm so grateful to Lauren McKenna, Molly Gregory, and Jen Bergstrom for the support.

Keep reading for a sneak peek at the next
novel in the Hopeless Romantic series

MEET ME ON
LOVE
LANE

Available from Gallery Books in December 2019

1

The bus rolled to a stop. A blinking yellow light hung over a pair of rickety train tracks. They looked defunct with the chipped white safety bars remaining at attention on the rusted metal poles. Squinting through the darkness, I spied a large green sign next to the light. It swung back and forth in the May breeze.

HOPE LAKE
25 miles

The sign was barely legible in the dense fog. That's what happened in valleys like this—the fog would blanket the town until the sun burned it away. *Everything settles in Hope Lake. The weather, the people.* My mother's voice echoed in my head. *Remember that, Charlotte. Don't go back—it sucks people in.*

I remembered her words wearily, rolling out my neck. Every inch of me was stiff, cramped from the fabric seat and the stale bus air. It didn't help that I was wedged against the window thanks to the mountain-sized guy in the seat next to mine. His long legs were stretched out into the darkened aisle, perfectly positioned for tripping an unsuspecting person on their way to the onboard restroom. He was snoring away, oblivious to the fact that he kept half the bus awake with the sound. It only added to my sour mood.

The ride should have been only a couple bumpy hours by bus to my destination, a sleepy Pennsylvania town in the middle of nowhere. But with weekend traffic, road work, and a dozen drop-off stops that I didn't realize were a part of the route when I bought the one-way ticket, it had taken almost five and a half hours and it still wasn't over.

"I'll never complain about the subway again," I groaned, shifting side to side in an effort to jar the lumbering snorer, and my rear end, awake.

The bus rumbled along in the darkness, eating up the last five miles slowly. The snorer jolted awake when the driver sounded the booming horn as we finally pulled into the tiny bus station in a town called Mount Hazel. I wasn't back yet, but this was as close as I could swing relying on public transportation this late at night.

I descended the bus stairs, my purse and carry-on bag slung over my shoulder, and looked around. Everything seemed nice enough, at least in the transition between night and the wee morning hours. A small, clean bus shelter sat near the street, free of graffiti. The rental car place behind it looked freshly painted and well-kept. The only noticeable problem was that it was closed. Wasn't everything open twenty-four hours like it was in New York? As the last passenger disembarked from the bus and got into an awaiting car, I realized I didn't have many options to get me those last couple miles into Hope Lake.

"Ma'am, are you expecting a ride?" the kindly bus driver asked, scratching his well-past-five-o'clock shadow with his meaty hand. "I can wait a bit so you're not alone with, uh, everything."

He peered around me to the semi-pitiful stack of suitcases that I had begged and borrowed from people with the promise of returning them as soon as I could. The ragtag bunch contained most of my worldly possessions. He had removed them from the built-in bus storage and neatly propped them against the side of the small, darkened depot.

It may not have seemed like a lot when my roommate Parker and I were packing up the necessities, but now, seeing it in two piles with no way of getting it to where I was going, it appeared mountainous.

I smiled. "I did have a rental car, but clearly that's not happening." I waved back to the closed Enterprise booth. "I didn't realize they weren't open twenty-four hours, like they are at home."

"No, ma'am, not here. Most stuff closes about five or six in the evening."

"It wouldn't have mattered. Sign said they closed hours ago," I admitted, sheepishly checking my watch. It was just after four in the morning.

He looked at me disbelievingly. "So no one is coming? Are you from Mount Hazel?"

I shook my head wearily. "I'm headed to Hope Lake."

Realization dawned on him. "Is there someone I can call for you? I don't want to leave you here by yourself."

He yawned, and a nugget of guilt wedged itself in my stomach. This guy didn't have it any easier than I did with the traffic and delays. He was just as tired, or more. "I'll figure it out. Thanks, though."

The driver looked uncertain. I didn't know if there was some unwritten code that would prevent him from leaving a passenger alone. "If you're sure," he said finally, looking around the empty lot. The side with the rental cars was filled. I wondered which would have been mine.

"I'm just going to sit tight until the Enterprise people come," I said, glancing at the hours posted on the glass door. "They should open at eight o'clock, so not too bad."

The only thing surrounding me was the sound of crickets, a couple of hooting owls, and a suspicious-looking three-legged cat with a mohawk that was wandering around the parking lot.

"Maybe you could just call someone for a ride?" he suggested, seemingly unconvinced with my willingness to just sit under the streetlight. "Those fancy app drivers are finally around here."

"Really, I'm okay," I insisted, not wanting to add anything else to my nearly-maxed-out credit card. The rental car was prepaid without a refund. "I have a book right here," I said, pulling out a tattered print copy of *The Alchemist* that I'd borrowed from the Brooklyn Public Library. A hefty charge would be waiting for me by the time I got to return it. "I'll be fine. Promise."

Nodding, he reluctantly walked to the far end of the lot. His black pickup truck sat under a flickering lamppost that was teeming with some sort of large moth.

I gave him the most reassuring smile I could manage when he tooted the horn and pulled out onto the quiet, deserted road. I didn't falter in my decision to sit it out—until I heard the damn owl hooting again.

The outdoors and I were not copacetic. It was warm and sticky, and it wasn't even summer yet. My skin tingled as I thought about the insects. I wasn't a Girl Scout. I needed A/C and a glass of wine. *Can I make it back to New York before the end of August?*

Clearly, I didn't think this plan through.

I swallowed thickly. *Do I even* have *a plan?*

Sort of!

I pulled out my phone and dialed Parker. She'd be up now, readying for work.

"Shouldn't you be asleep?" she mumbled through a yawn.

"Are you working?" I sunk down onto one of the suitcases.

"Yep, just slid two cakes into the oven. On track for a banner day."

Parker owned a boutique pastry shop called Delicious and Vicious. They sold traditionally flavored cakes with not-so-traditional messages and theming to go along with them. Her business had boomed a couple months back after being featured on the Food Network.

"I need you to keep me company for the next couple hours," I explained, curling my legs under me. "A plan would have been smart."

"No shit."

"Shut up. I just meant that the car rental place is closed."

She sighed into the phone. "Get an Uber, Charlotte. Or better, call your dad." She punctuated each word with a short pause. It was an argument we'd had for the past few days. I didn't want to let him, or anyone else in Hope Lake, know that I was coming.

"Obviously, you're going to have to see him, and explain things, eventually. You know, like when you show up on his doorstep and say, 'Oh hey, Dad, I'm home.'"

I interrupted. "Here."

"What?"

"I'm *here*, not home. Home is where you are. *Here* is not home. This is a bump in the road. A sad little pit stop in my life. Nothing more, and certainly *not* home."

She huffed. "One thing is for certain."

"What?"

"You're not going to be writing the Hope Lake tourist advertisements," she barked, laughing as she repeated, "Sad little pit stop."

"I'm serious. I can't let this . . . *whatever* . . . distract me and make me lose focus of the end goal. Getting back to New York . . ." I paused, feeling a sense of unease wash over me. "To civilization," I finished.

"Whatever it is—a pit stop, a roadblock, or the start of something new—you can't just sit on the side of a highway alone in the middle of the night. It's like a Stephen King novel. Or better yet, an M. Night Shyamalan movie. He's from Pennsylvania, right? I'd be worried sick."

"You're enjoying my imminent demise a little too much, thanks," I lamented. "Wait a minute, the *start of something new*? You're either living in a Hallmark Channel movie or *High School Musical*, Parks."

She sighed, no doubt dreaming about Zac Efron. "Whatever, send me your exact location so if you go missing, I can have a lead to give to the hot country detective who'll want to question me about your disappearance."

"This isn't the country, *exactly*," I corrected. "It's just not the city." I put the phone on speaker so I could share my location with her via iMessage.

"Brilliant explanation, Sherlock. You know that anything outside of New York is the country to me. Okay, I'm sending you an Uber now. You're limited out there in the sticks on what type of vehicle will come pick you up, so hopefully whatever comes fits all your crap."

I sighed. "You don't have to do that, Parker. That's not why I called you."

There was a long pause. I could hear pots and pans clinking and clanking in her tiny kitchen. "I know it's not." I hated the thought of my recently not-so-broke friend sending her super-broke friend a charity Uber.

Then, something howled. It was coming from the thick wooded area next to me. *Were those eyes in the darkness?*

Okay, maybe I didn't hate the charity Uber that much. I wasn't going to last five minutes out here. This didn't exactly bode well for me being stuck in Hope Lake for the foreseeable future.

"I'll pay you back," I insisted, knowing that it would be a bit before I could. Things were *tight*. It helped that I was saving on not having to rent a place when I got there.

Parker grumbled. "Unnecessary. This is me helping you after you helped me manage everything after the coverage from the Food Network. Now, if you just took the job I offered you, you would still be here with me, in New York, instead of leaving me here all alone." She sighed longingly. "I have to let my idiot brother's idiot friend move in."

Even with all the press, she had thankfully stayed the same witty, generous best friend that I had had for the past fifteen years. Even if it meant offering her untalented-in-the-kitchen best friend a job.

"I'm sorry about that, but we both know me working as your assistant would have been disastrous. I burned water and destroyed your favorite caramel pot. With my luck, my first day on the job would be me burning down the entire place instead of a small stove fire. No, thanks."

Parker laughed just as a car drove past. *Not the Uber.* "I didn't think it was possible to be that bad at boiling, but, surprise, it was. I'm sure the fire department is still telling that story."

I pinched my face up, not that she could see me. "In my defense, I forgot about the stove because my phone rang and I got tied up."

"Fair enough, I know that was the last phone call you were hoping to get," she said kindly, having been there to witness my pathetic mood after I got the bad news.

The caller was the head of HR at the Brooklyn Botanical Garden. After almost three months of trying to find something new, it was the last job prospect I'd had before I officially gave up the search in New York. Sure, I could have gotten a job almost anywhere else, but I wanted a job in *my* field. Wasn't that why I was still paying off my student loans? The position at the BBG wasn't exactly what I had hoped for, but it was close enough and I would have been happy. Plus, there was the hope that the change of scenery would have been a good move for me. Getting out of the flower shop and into more of a business role with more responsibilities and a chance to move up would have been worth it.

It was just after they courtesy-called to say they went with another candidate with more community engagement experience that I decided to head back to Hope Lake with my tail between my legs. There were options, of course.

Sure, I could have found a way to stay—cater-waitering, something soul-sucking in Times Square, tour guide on the Grey Line tourist buses—but how long would that have lasted before the boredom crept in? I was in debt, desperate, and after a Come to Jesus conversation with Parker about my options, Hope Lake seemed like the best, well, *hope* to get my life back on track.

Plus, I figured that if I ducked out of the city for a couple months, the gossip that my former boss Gabrielle had started about me would die down and I wouldn't be shunned in the floral world any longer.

"Hey, not to beat a dead horse, but has there been any more Gabby gossip floating around?"

Parker sucked in a breath. "Do you want me to be honest?"

My stomach dropped. I thought it would get better if I left. "No, but yes," I responded, nibbling away at my thumbnail.

"She said you were trying to steal clients from her, and that some of the accounting was *off.* Which we know is a lie, but it's made people not want to hire you because they think you're shady. I'm really sorry, Charlotte. It's my fault that she's going after you."

The worry latched onto my heart and squeezed. If this kept up, August wouldn't be enough time for the damage to fade away.

"No, it's not. She was always looking for a reason to give me the boot. The cupcake incident just added to it."

"Still, I'm sorry. I should have done my due diligence with that order. I knew they were for her, but it was just so busy that day I let the assistants handle that one and never checked what the message was."

Parker's bakery had made a cupcake delivery to Gabby that was . . . poorly timed and not well received thanks to the order her husband—ex-husband—placed and had Parker's shop deliver.

"It's not your fault that her husband was cheating."

"With her sister."

"Still, where he dips his nib isn't your fault. Or mine, for that matter."

"No, it's not, but if it wasn't for *his* message on *my* signature banana foster cupcakes, she wouldn't have taken it out on you."

I snorted. "Maybe not, but it is what it is. I can't keep losing sleep over it. Besides, I'm here now, and maybe she'll find someone new to torture."

"You're so positive! This trip is working already."

I tried to focus on that sentiment. "It'll be good for me to help my dad with Gigi. She's getting older, and although he won't admit it, I know he could use the help. And let's be honest, I've been a pretty lousy granddaughter when it comes to visiting her."

As in not coming back to visit in—checks watch—twenty-one years . . .

"Yeah, but they loved coming to visit you in between all of your dad's incredible service trips. It's not like you haven't seen them often," she insisted, knowing how much I loved having both my dad and Gigi come to visit me in New York. "Remember how much fun Gigi has here?"

I nodded into the darkness. The rumble of an engine drew my attention. "I think the Uber is here."

Sure enough, a large diesel-engine truck pulled into the lot, headlights streaming across the cracked pavement. The driver was shrouded in the darkness of the vehicle. He didn't look like he was going to come out and help me with my bags. *What a gentleman.*

"Don't hang up. Keep me in your pocket until you're delivered to your dad's doorstep!" Parker insisted.

"It's like I'm a pizza," I said, laughing. I stood, slipping the phone into my shorts pocket.

Pulling the first suitcase up, I tipped my chin toward the truck bed. "Can I put everything back there?" I shouted through the partially open window.

As I asked, he picked up his cell phone. The brightness of the screen highlighted his face. Thankfully, he didn't look like a serial killer.

Neither did Ted Bundy.

Waving me back, he started yelling into his cell.

"Great, this will be a fine addition to the trip from hell," I mumbled. Then the first raindrop plopped onto my forehead.

I hurried as best I could with flip-flops on, running back and forth to lug the suitcases, considering some didn't have working wheels. The truck bed was thankfully empty, and had one of those covers over the top in case of rain.

Just my luck, by the time I slid the last suitcase inside, the skies opened up. At least my things didn't get soaked.